John Hookham Frere, Bartle Frere, William E. frere

The Works of the Right Honourable John Hookham Frere

in verse and prose

John Hookham Frere, Bartle Frere, William E. frere

The Works of the Right Honourable John Hookham Frere
in verse and prose

ISBN/EAN: 9783337194727

Printed in Europe, USA, Canada, Australia, Japan

Cover: Foto ©Raphael Reischuk / pixelio.de

More available books at **www.hansebooks.com**

THE WORKS

OF THE RIGHT HONOURABLE

JOHN HOOKHAM FRERE

IN VERSE AND PROSE

VOLUME I

MEMOIR BY THE RIGHT HON. SIR BARTLE FRERE

Second Edition Revised with Additions

NEW YORK

A. DENHAM AND CO.

LONDON BASIL MONTAGU PICKERING

MDCCC LXXIV

EDITORS' PREFACE.

N 1867, Mr. Pickering had prepared for republication all of Mr. Hookham Frere's literary remains which he could collect. Some of the works were in type when he applied to the author's family for their aid in making the collection as complete as possible, and also in correcting a biographical sketch which had already been printed.

It then appeared that, besides the works accessible to Mr. Pickering, there were others of considerable length and importance which had never been printed or published.

Mr. Pickering thereupon placed the whole of the materials he had collected at the disposal of Mr. Frere, of Roydon Hall, Norfolk, Mr. Hookham Frere's heir, and the present head of the family.

At his request, and on his behalf, two of his brothers, who had just then returned from India, undertook to do their best towards carrying out Mr. Pickering's design. Mr. W. E. Frere engaged to collect and prepare for the Press all that could now be recovered of his uncle's Works, and the biographical sketch prefixed to them has been drawn up by Sir Bartle Frere.

Both felt that, other deficiencies apart, thirty-five years of active service in the Tropics, chiefly passed at a distance from all literary and political society, and far away from such books, as well as from such men, as were Mr. Hookham Frere's companions, formed but a bad preparation for the task.

Time had, however, spared few of those who, by personal knowledge and love for the subject, as well as by similarity of tastes and scholarship, were best fitted for the duty. Of Mr. Hookham Frere's early friends or associates not one remained who could be asked to aid; and even those who had known him intimately, in the latter years of his comparative retirement at Malta, were rapidly passing away.

Under these circumstances, none better qualified being able or willing to undertake the task, the advantage of having passed some time under his roof, and in daily intercourse with him, in 1834, 1841-4-5-6, may in some degree compensate for the faults of insufficient or rusty scholarship; and it is hoped that the spirit of filial love in which the work has been undertaken, will make up for serious defects which would not have existed had it been entrusted to abler hands.

Mr. Frere had, in his latter years, a great dislike to the mechanical task of writing, and much that he had composed found no record save in the memory of the few associates of his retired and almost recluse life. Owing to circumstances which need not here be detailed, very few of the letters which he received from his political or literary friends are now forthcoming. Some scattered notices remain of remarks or conversations which happen so to have struck the hearer, that they were written down at the time; but shipwreck and other accidents have caused the loss of many of these imperfect records.

With such scanty materials at command, it can hardly be hoped that the result will be satisfactory to the few now surviving who were amongst his personal friends ; or who know him by the estimation in which he was held by such authorities in politics and literature as Canning and Cornewall Lewis, Coleridge, Southey, and Scott.

But the Editors trust that scholars and men of letters may find among the fragmentary additions to the collected works, however imperfectly edited, some ground for rejoicing that even these brief records have not been allowed to perish ; and though the Memoir bears unavoidable traces of the difficulty experienced in converting what was begun as a simple family record into a sketch of Mr. Frere's political and literary life, all readers may find something to interest them in these memorials of one who Coleridge thought eminently deserved to be characterized as ὁ καλοκάγαθὸς ὁ φιλόκαλος.[1]

---

[1] Coleridge's Will. Athenæum, No. 365.

MEMOIR.

OHN HOOKHAM FRERE was born in London on the 21st May, 1769. He came of an ancient stock, long settled in the counties of Norfolk and Suffolk. A recent French genealogist, writing of those families whose ancestors accompanied the Conqueror from Normandy, professes to find among them the founders of the family of the Suffolk Freres. He traces them to a certain Richard le Frere and his son John, who followed the banner of Robert, son of William Mallett, one of the great nobles who fought under the Conqueror at Hastings. This Robert founded a priory at Eye in Suffolk, in the records of which mention is said to be made of John Le Frere, as " Vavasseur " and tenant of lands in Eye.

On similar evidence the same author identifies with the descendants of this Richard, many of the name of Frere, or Le Frere, who are found mentioned in ancient charters and deeds connected with grants of land in other of the eastern and midland counties.[1]

From John Frere, who lived at Thurston, in Suf-

---

[1] In pedigrees and deeds relating to land in Norfolk and Suffolk, in the 12th and 13th centuries, the name, it is said, is generally written " Le Frere." But in the third year of Ed.

folk, in 1268, there is connected and well-authenticated evidence of successive generations who held lands and bore arms in Suffolk, (at Wickham Abbey, Wickham Skeith, Occold, and Sweffling,) and intermarried with various families of landed gentry in that and the adjoining counties.[1]

Many Freres of previous generations had been buried at or near Finningham, in Suffolk, where a farm called the " Green Farm " was purchased by them in 1598, when the manor and advowson, which still belong to the family, were purchased of Mr. Lambe in 1656, and the hall and lands from the

---

III. (A. D. 1330), " John Frere" is recorded by local antiquaries as having given to the Prior and Brothers of the Carmelites at Synterle (?) in Norfolk, certain lands there for the enlargement of the Manse. Twenty-two years later, " Thos. Frere," described as " Citizen and Fishmonger of London," gave land in the City of London to John Baud, Parson of the Church of St. Nicholas of Colne Abbey. In later times the Suffolk branch of the family dropped the Norman article.

Some of these East Anglian Le Freres held lands near Sawbridgeworth as early as 1197, when it is recorded that, on the day after the feast of St. Mark, in the ninth year of King Richard I., Richard le Frere obtained, on a plea brought before the King's Justices at Westminster from Henstac and others, two virgates of land in Sawbridgeworth, paying therefor 10*s.* sterling; and twenty-three years later Walter le Frere and his wife, with others, sold half a virgate of land in the same township for one marc. About a century later, in 1313, William le Frere is recorded to have bought a messuage, twenty-one acres of land, and half an acre of pasture in Sawbridgeworth " for a hawk."

This branch of the family, with the name anglicised, held lands in the same parish and its neighbourhood up to the last century.

In the records of the 16th and 17th centuries, the name of all branches of the family is variously spelt as Frere, Fryer, and Frier.

[1] The family seems to have shared the passion for foreign adventure and travel which possessed so many Englishmen in the days of Elizabeth and her successors.

The name of John Frier is found among the original 215 adventurers to whom the first charter constituting the East

Cottons in 1657, by John Frere. He died in 1679, and for several generations after him his descendants lived at Thwait Hall, near Finningham, till his great grandson purchased Roydon Hall, near Diss, in Norfolk.

Mr. Hookham Frere's very just estimate of his own obligations to such ancestry may be gathered from his reply to a request, made to him in his later years, that he would write a few lines on his coat-of-arms, of which, as having descended from the time of their first establishment in the county, the family

India Company was granted in 1600, and John Fryer, apparently the same person, subscribed £240 towards the funds of the Company.

In the next generation Dr. Fryer (whose travels in the East Indies between 1672 and 1681, published in 1698, is still one of the most graphic books of Eastern travel we have) is claimed by the family, though not by the Suffolk branch.

The Harleston branch, which divided from the main tree in the 16th century, moved, in the course of the 17th, almost bodily to Barbadoes. In opposition to the politics of the rest of the family, they were strong Parliamentarians. One of them was a member of the Norfolk Committee for Sequestrations ; and another, Tobias, is described in some Royalist lampoons still extant as a vehement partisan of the Parliament. He was member of the Barebones Parliament, and was secretary to the Committee of Sequestrations for the counties of Norfolk and Suffolk. To this branch probably belonged James Frere, the propounder in 1653 of a scheme "for transporting vagrants to the foreign plantations." In Nov. 1655, John Frere and others, "Merchant adventurers to Barbadoes," petitioned the Council of State to the effect "that they can procure but 800 firelocks for the 2,000 old musket barrels formerly granted out of the Tower stores for the use of Barbadoes, and pray that they may pass Custom free." On which an order was passed by the Council to Col. Hooper and Captain Tobias Frere to ship the firelocks custom free ; and the same Captain Tobias, Thomas Frere, and others, obtained in the same year, from the Lord Protector, an order for 200 cases of pistols, 372 carbines, and 600 swords to be delivered out of the Tower for the use of Barbadoes. There may still possibly be representatives of the family in Barbadoes, where members of it have, during the last two centuries, held various offices of honour and responsibility.

were reasonably proud. The verses were asked for by way of preface to a " Parentalia," intended "to preserve, in the spirit of the family motto,[1] traces of kindred and affinity in the relations of a race, the members of which were becoming numerous and widely dispersed."

It was in entire sympathy with this feeling, but with some fear lest future family heralds should be tempted to lay too much store by mere length of descent, unaccompanied by other claims on the gratitude of posterity, that Mr. Frere replied by sending the following verses :—

ON OUR COAT OF ARMS.[2]

THE Flanches, on our field of Gules,
Denote, by known heraldic rules,
A race contented and obscure,
In mediocrity secure,
By sober parsimony thriving,
For their retired existence striving;

By well-judged purchases and matches,
Far from ambition and debauches ;
Such was the life our fathers led ;
Their homely leaven, deep inbred
In our whole moral composition,
Confines us to the like condition.

Among the less remote ancestors of Mr. Hookham Frere, there were some whose example may be supposed to have had considerable influence on the formation of his literary tastes. His great grandfather Edward, born in 1680, was a Fellow of Trinity College, Cambridge, in Bentley's days, and was

---

[1] " Traditum ab antiquis servare." [The motto " Frere ayme Frere " was also used by the family, but it is to the former motto that reference is made, here, and in the following verses.]

[2] Gules, two leopards' faces between flanches, or. It may save the tyro in heraldry trouble to warn him that he will search the text books in vain for the "known heraldic rules" which the poet, following the example of but too many modern heralds, invented for his own amusement.

probably one of the staunch adherents of the great Master in his disputes with the other members of the College; for his name is not appended to the petition which was forwarded to the Bishop of Ely on the 6th of February, 1710, while it appears in the list of thirty-seven Fellows attached to Bentley's reply, which is dated the 13th February in the same year.

Edward Frere's son Sheppard, a Fellow Commoner of Trinity, did not take a degree, but his grandson John, Mr. Hookham Frere's father, went to Caius College,[1] and had the good fortune of contending with Paley for the honours of Senior Wrangler in 1763. The story of the contest is told with characteristic details by Bishop Watson, who was Moderator that year. After recording how, when he took his own degree, he had been placed Second Wrangler, while in justice he ought to have been first, the worthy Bishop relates that when he became Moderator, he prevented such partiality for the future, by introducing the practice of examining rival candidates in the presence of each other, with the happy result which he describes in the following terms :[2]—

"The first year I was Moderator, Mr. Paley (afterwards known to the world by many excellent productions, though there are some ethical and some political principles in his philosophy which I by no means approve), and Mr. Frere, a gentleman of Norfolk, were examined together. A report prevailed that Mr. Frere's grandfather" (this was the Trinity Fellow of Bentley's days) "would give him a thousand pounds if he were Senior Wrangler. The other Moderator agreed with me that Mr.

---

[1] Not Trinity, as inadvertently stated in the first edition of this memoir.

[2] "Anecdotes of the Life of Bishop Watson of Llandaff," 1818, vol. i. p. 30.

Paley was his superior, and we made him Senior
Wrangler. Mr. Frere, much to his honour, on an
imputation of partiality being thrown on my colleague and myself, publicly acknowledged that he
deserved only the second place, a declaration which
could never have been made, had they not been
examined in the presence of each other."

While Paley was slowly working his way to
honours far more enduring than any the University
Moderator could assign him, his competitor had the
good or bad fortune to succeed to his family estate,
and thenceforward devoted himself to his duties as
a country gentleman. In 1768 he married Jane,
the only child of Mr. John Hookham of Bedington, a rich London merchant. She brought with
her, not only fortune and personal beauty, but rare
gifts of intellect [1] and disposition. Her own read-

---

[1] The large collection of her letters, papers, diaries, and
common-place books, still in the possession of various members of the family, all show her to have been possessed of
strong and deep religious feeling, a sound judgment, a passionately affectionate nature, a ready wit, and a vivacious
disposition. The following extracts selected from many
such, with a view rather to their variety than to their literary
merit, may interest some as proofs of her love for metrical
composition.

ETON EPIGRAM ATTEMPTED.

" To holy Henry's fame two Statues rise,
That bears the Sword, but this the Law supplies,
There the rude race an iron rule require,
Here polish'd Law restrains to just desire ;
Those Tyrants awed, and these revere a King,
Yet does this change from his own Eton spring ;
And pious Henry through succeeding reigns
Spreads that true peace, the Sword's subjection feigns,
While this fair age reflects reversed his own,
And Science nurtured here supports the throne,
So Windsor's Tower on Eton's base shall stand—
The honour'd guardian of a grateful land.

2nd ATTEMPT.

" See Henry to thy name two Statues rise,
Whose differing emblems fix our gazing eyes—

ing in early life had been directed by Mr. William
Stevens, the intimate friend of Bishop Horne and
of Jones of Nayland, a ripe Greek and Hebrew
scholar, and one of the most learned laymen of his
day. The catalogue of books which he drew up
for the young heiress, and which she seems, from
her note-books, to have carefully read and studied,
would probably astonish the promoters of modern
ladies' colleges, by the ponderous though varied
nature of the reading prescribed, embracing almost
every branch of what an erudite and pious High
Churchman of Johnson's days would consider sound
divinity and history ; in French as well as in English literature.

That, a rude race with blazing Falchion awes,
This, grants a polish'd age benignant laws,
For our blest time requires no stern controul,
The yielding passions own the ruling soul ;
Health, peace, and joy, the smiling region bless,
The Monarch's is the people's happiness—
Yet does this change from thy own Eton spring,
While Science nurtured here supports the King."

EPITAPH.

" *Begun for Mrs. Edwards.*"

" You who perhaps with heedless step and eye
Approach the place where these dear reliques lie,
Reject not the instructions they impart,
But let my precepts warn and warm the heart ;
Warn'd by my woes, let not thy mind elate
Trust the vain joys of this unstable state—
One beaming morn the tenderest hope inspired,
The next, deprived of all my soul desired,
Saw me, sad victim of relentless fate,
A childless Parent and a widow'd Mate."

Composed in sleep, when dreaming that she could not sleep.

" O come, sweet Sleep, sad nature's soothing nurse,
The greatest blessing left her at the Curse,
Not in fantastic form, with motley hues ;
Come bathe my temple with Lethean dews ;
Gently incumbent close my willing eyes,

Mr. Frere was High Sheriff for Suffolk in 1776, and in 1799 was elected Member of Parliament for Norwich, after a severe contest ; but though a diligent magistrate, devoting much time to county business, he did not neglect the favourite studies of his youth. His son used to regret that so few of his father's óccasional papers had been preserved

---

> And seal my senses, that those busy spies
> Break not thy stillness with abrupt surprise—
> The Rich or Poor on thy soft lap reclined,
> Equal relief and sure Asylum find."

In a little book of "*Early Efforts*" occur the following.

To a Friend on Her Marriage.

> " Length of Days attend my Dear ;
> Happiness, Friends always near ;
>> Health and Pleasure,
>> Joy and Treasure,
>> Plenty, Peace,
>> Love and Ease,
> A good Husband, you Caressing,
> A Hand unseen, you always Blessing ;
> This is the sincere wish of Me—
> Whom Gratitude binds fast to THee."

(In this book she says she was careful not to correct any of the imperfections she noted in these early efforts at poetry—as seeing the faults kept her humble.)

Description of ——

> " Always turning, shifting, changing,
> From Folly still to Folly ranging,
> Ever inconstant, roving, unconfined—
> No rein can guide her, and no ties can bind,
> Never to be restrain'd by reason's rule,
> To seem a Wit, she proves herself a Fool."

It appears to have been her habit to express in verse, spontaneously, the thought of the moment : of such are the following :—

Expectation.
(Waiting for Mr. Frere's return at Roydon.)

> " Swift ye moments, swifter fly,
> Restore him to my longing eye,
> Weary no more my listening ear
> Attentive the wish'd tread to hear,

or published. I have heard my uncle relate with much humour a story of his father's learning, when he was High Sheriff, that a Whig judge, rather a rare phenomenon in those days, was coming on circuit to the Norwich assizes; whereupon the High Sheriff, though not much addicted to theological composition, sat down and composed a High Tory

---

> Or catch the well-known voice ;
> As the loved sound approaches nigh—
> · Each Doubt, each Care and Fear shall fly,
> And I again rejoice—"

THE SAME IN TOWN.

(Waiting for Mr. Frere to return from the House of Commons.)

> " While Coaches rattle, knockers play,
> And Flambeaux cast their glaring ray,
> Each rolling carriage at its sound,
> Makes my impatient Heart rebound,
> With quicken'd pulses throbbing beat;
> The various noises of the Street—
> The Postman's Bell, the Watchman's Cry,
> Th' attentive Ear does listening try,
> When first the dubious murmurs rise—
> And expectation wings surmise."

Often little fragments of three or four lines seem rather the expression of an overwhelming feeling than any attempt at poetical composition.

Thus on a fragment of paper with the date of her husband's death are the lines:—

> "O Life ! O Love, together are ye flown !
> And my heart's treasure thus for ever gone—
> What now awaits me—wheresoe'er I stray,
> A desert, and a solitary way."

" Out of the Deep have I called unto Thee, O Lord. Lord, hear my voice. O let Thine ears consider well the voice of my complaint."

A curious little poem by her great grandmother, preserved amongst her papers (*vide infra*), proves that she was not the first of her race possessed of a taste for versification.

sermon, which he got his chaplain to preach before the judges. It was pronounced, by those of the learned congregation who were not in the secret of its composition, to be "an excellent sermon ; much better than judges usually got from High Sheriffs' Chaplains ;" but whether it did as much to improve the political principles of the Whig judge, as to confirm his Tory brethren in theirs, was more than the real author of the sermon could discover.

Another anecdote of his Father, which Mr. Hookham Frere used to relate was, that one day when Bishop Horne, attended by his Chaplain Jones of Nayland, was staying at Roydon, they were told that Wesley was to preach at Diss; both were most anxious to hear him, but both doubted the propriety of their attending—there was however no such objection to their host going, so he went, and on his return wrote down, for their edification, a full report of the sermon he had heard.

Mr. Frere was an active member of the Royal Society, and of the principal scientific and anti-quarian associations in London, and occasionally contributed a paper to their transactions, or to the "Gentleman's Magazine," then the usual vehicle for publishing the less formal and elaborate class of scientific or literary compositions.

One of these papers, written in 1797, possesses considerable permanent interest. It is an account of some flint implements dug up near Hoxne in Suffolk, and was published in the "Archæologia."[1] This is probably the first notice, in any scientific publication, of the remains left by the pre-historic races in this country, which have of late years attracted so much attention.

Mr. Frere's only surviving sister, Ellinor, married Sir John Fenn, editor of the well-known "Paston

---

[1] Vol. XIII.

Letters," an accomplished and learned antiquary. It is possible that from him, or from some of his antiquarian friends, who were always welcome guests at Mr. Frere's house, his son imbibed that taste and appreciation for English ballad literature which he showed in his early school-boy days, and for which he was remarkable throughout life.

Lady 'Fenn[1] was a woman of strong original understanding and great accomplishment ; though, as she lived at a time when Norfolk was two days' tedious journey from London, her influence was mainly confined to the small country circle in which she moved.

Speaking of her in her later years, Mr. Hookham Frere said, " It is difficult to give any one nowadays an idea of the kind of awe which, in my boyhood, a learned old lady like her inspired, down in the country, not only in us, her nephews and nieces, and in those of her own age and rank who could understand her intellectual superiority, but even in the common people around her.

" I remember one day, coming from a visit to her, I stopped to learn what some village boys outside her gate were wrangling about—they were disputing whether the nation had any reason to be afraid of an invasion by Buonaparte, and one of the disputants said, with a conscious air of superior knowledge—' I tell ye, ye don't know what a terrible fellow he is : why, he don't care for nobody ! If he was to come here to Dereham, he wouldn't care

---

[1] She was herself an authoress of some repute in her own day, and in her own line. There are many now living who can recollect receiving their first reading-lessons in "Cobwebs to catch Flies," and other books for children, which, under the names of Mrs. Lovechild and Mrs. Teachwell, she wrote for her brother's children and grandchildren, and afterwards published. She shares with Mrs. Trimmer and Mrs. Barbauld the credit of founding that school of fiction for children in which Miss Edgeworth afterwards reigned supreme.

that,' snapping his fingers; 'no! not even for Lady Fenn, there!'"

Little that is noteworthy has been preserved of Mr. Hookham Frere's early boyhood. The eldest of eleven children[1] (eight sons and three daughters), he shared in the family migrations from London to Roydon in Norfolk, and Bedington in Surrey, between which places his parents usually divided the year. In 1785, he went from a preparatory school at Putney to Eton. The following are extracts from notes made in 1844 of some of his early recollections.

He had been speaking of the mistake made by a celebrated head master, who tried to keep the boys of a great public school in order by superior physical energy. This was not the way, he said, to attain what should be the object of every head master—to impress every one about him, tutors as well as boys, with a profound respect for his authority. "Davies," he said, "who was head master in my time, was the very incarnation of authority. We boys never dreamed of his condescending to any physical effort other than flogging us. I never shall forget my surprise when my father took me to place me at Eton, and I saw the way in which Davies treated a man to whom I had seen every one else so deferential.

"'Mr. Frere, I believe? Well, sir; is this your son?'

"'Yes.'

"'Well, what can he do? where has he been?'

"'At Mr. Cormick's, at Putney.'

"'Humph! not a bad school; we have had some lads well prepared from him.' And he gave me a passage to read, and away I construed for bare life. Everything about him had the same character, down to his 'Hem!' which might have been heard

---

[1] Two died in early childhood.

at the end of the long walk. He was ordered by his physician, when he got a little infirm, to take carriage exercise. So he had a coach-and-four; but there was something we boys did not quite like, in his riding, even in a coach-and-four, like an ordinary mortal; and this effect was not lessened by his always using, when the horses were restive, the same phrase, and in the same tone, as he was accustomed to address to the prepostors (of the lower school), 'Can't you keep them quiet, there ?'

" When old King George III. came over to Eton, which he used to do very frequently, I remember the jealousy with which we watched Davies, to see that he did not play the courtier too much ; and very well he managed it. The King, too, used quite to understand and humour the kind of feeling we had.

" Davies was preceded by, and, I fancy, caught much of the manner of Foster, who, as I have heard Etonians of his day tell, had almost the same kind of weight in London society that old Thurlow possessed.

" It was a grand idea to have such a school as Eton close under the wing of the royal castle. I have often wished that some one would hunt up the early charters or statutes to find out whether the position was the result of accident or design, like so many of the things which appear accidental in the foundation of Winchester, but which the statutes show, were all provided for, by the foresight of the founder."

At Eton Mr. Hookham Frere formed more than one life-long friendship, and there began his intimacy with Mr. Canning, for whom he cherished a love and admiration, which absence never diminished, and neither age nor death itself could dull.[1]

---

[1] In a " Thucydides " formerly belonging to Mr. Frere, now at Roydon, the following words (i. 138), summing up the character of Themistocles, are underlined, and against them he has written " Dear Canning " :—φύσεως μὲν δυνάμει, μελέτης δὲ βραχύτητι, κράτιστος δὴ οὗτος αὐτοσχεδιάζειν τὰ δέοντα ἐγένετο.

They appear to have become fast friends from
their earliest schoolboy acquaintance. Mr. Canning
was the junior by about a year, but had already
given promise of a brilliancy of intellect, destined,
a few years later, to dazzle the House of Commons,
while the oratory of Pitt and Fox, of Burke and
Sheridan, in their best days, was still matter of
living memory.

In 1786, they joined with a few Etonians of their
own standing,[1] in starting "The Microcosm," a
periodical, the essays and *jeux d'esprit* in which were
supposed to refer primarily to the miniature world of
Eton, though they often contain evidence of views
directed to the great outside world of politics and
literature, where some of the young authors were
destined in a few years to play a conspicuous part.
"The Microcosm" was the first school periodical
which attracted much notice beyond the walls of the
school itself, and to this, perhaps, as much as to the
intrinsic merit of the papers it contained, is due its
great success, which led to numerous literary ventures
of the same kind at other of our great public schools.
Some of the papers in " The Microcosm" contain unmistakeable promise of considerable literary ability,
and one at least, Canning's Essay on the Epic of the
Queen of Hearts, will probably maintain its place in
English literature as a classical specimen of burlesque
criticism.

The first number of " The Microcosm " was published on the 6th Nov., 1786, and forty numbers
appeared regularly every Monday, holidays excepted, till the 30th of the following July, when it
wound up with an account of the deathbed of " Mr.

---

[1] Mr. J. Smith, Mr. R. Smith (brother of Sydney Smith),
Lord Henry Spencer, third son of the Duke of Marlborough;
Mr. Way, Mr. Littlehales, Mr. Capel Lofft, and Mr. Mellish,
were the other principal contributors.

Gregory Griffin," the supposed editor, and a copy of his will, in which he bequeaths to the various authors the papers they had severally contributed. Mr. Hookham Frere's contributions consisted of five papers,[1] the style of which contains but few traces of a school-boy's hand.

"The Microcosm" was subsequently published in a collected form,[2] with a dedication to Dr. Davies, the head master, and went through at least five editions.

Like most Eton men, Mr. Hookham Frere, to his latest years, cherished a warm affection for everything connected with the Royal college, and was never tired of recalling the memories of his school-boy days. Among his companions at that time, he used to say that, "next to Canning, none was expected by his contemporaries to do more in the world than Sydney Smith's brother 'Bobus.'"

"Of Lord Wellesley's" (then Lord Mornington) "future career, the boys," he said, "formed a truer judgment than the masters ; for, while Mornington's school companions had a high opinion of his abilities, and expected him to distinguish himself, the masters underrated him, and used to express surprise at the unsurpassed facility and correctness of his Latin verse."

Much was looked for, both by boys and masters, from Mr. Lambton, the father of the first Earl of Durham. "Lambton was a most amiable, superior man," he said, "and would have made a great figure in public life, if he had not been spoilt by his Whig associates. He was a great favourite with all his schoolfellows, notwithstanding the mortal offence which his father, General Lambton, once gave us. He was a very rough old soldier, and

---

[1] *Vide infra*, p. 3.

[2] "The Microcosm," a periodical work, by Gregory Griffin. Windsor : Printed for C. Knight, 1787.

affronted some of us mightily by inviting us to eat, with 'Come along, ye young dogs! Come and eat this, will ye?'"

Talking of one of his brother Edward's[1] earliest reminiscences of Eton, when eighty boys were flogged for a sort of barring-out, and among them Mr. Arthur Wellesley, afterwards the Iron Duke, he said, "No one who has not seen it can estimate the good Eton does in teaching the little boys of great men that they have superiors. It is quite as difficult and as important to teach this to the great Bankers' and Squires' boys, as to Dukes' sons, and I know no place where this was done so effectually as at Eton. Neither rank nor money had any consideration there compared with that which was paid to age, ability, and standing in the school."

With these recollections he was, not unnaturally, disposed to question the wisdom of the plans which, even thirty years ago, were sometimes propounded, for making fundamental changes in the system and subjects of teaching in our public schools. "It was not," he maintained, "of so much importance what you learnt at school, as how you learnt it. At school a boy's business is not simply or mainly to gain knowledge, but to learn how to gain it. If he learns his own place in the world, and, in a practical fashion, his duty towards other boys, and to his superiors as well as to his inferiors; if he acquires the apparatus for obtaining and storing knowledge, and some judgment as to what kind of knowledge is worth obtaining, his time at school has not been misspent, even if he carries away a very scanty store

---

[1] Next to him in age (born 1770), and educated with him at Eton: a man of rare natural gifts and acquirements, which he devoted to various inquiries connected with physical and mechanical science, especially to all branches connected with the manufacture of iron. He died in 1844, before his elder brother, by whom as by all his family he was greatly beloved.

of actual facts in history, or literature, or physical science. If, in his school-boy days, you cram his head with such facts, beyond what are merely elementary, you are very apt to addle his brains, and to make a little prig or pedant of him, incapable, from self-conceit, of much progress afterwards. Nor can any boy carry from school any great number of facts which will really be useful to him, when he comes in after life to make those branches of knowledge his special study, because they are all, but especially the physical sciences, progressive, and the best ascertained facts, as well as theories, of to-day, may be obsolete and discredited ten years hence. You find many learned men who have been great students and experimentalists, and even discoverers, in very early youth ; but the number of facts worth remembering, which they accumulated in boyhood, always bears a very small proportion to what they have learned after leaving school, and in early manhood."

For these and similar reasons, he held that no physical science, nor even history or literature, taught as separate branches of knowledge, could ever be efficient substitutes for classics and mathematics, at our public schools and universities, by way of mental training, to fit a boy to educate himself in after life : classics as forming style, and giving a man power to use his own language correctly in writing and speaking, and even in thinking ; and mathematics as the best training for reasoning, and as a necessary foundation for the accurate study of physics and natural philosophy.

He once gave me the following illustration of his position that a man might be a great man, in every sense of the word, without even a rudimentary knowledge of the facts of natural science. "I remember one day going to consult Canning on a matter of great importance to me, when he was staying down near Enfield. We walked into the woods to have a quiet talk, and as we passed some ponds I was surprised to find it was a new light to him that tadpoles turned into frogs."

My uncle added—"Now, don't you go and tell that story of Canning to the next fool you meet. Canning could rule, and did rule, a great and civilized nation; but in these days people are apt to fancy that any one who does not know the natural history of frogs must be an imbecile in the treatment of men."

From Eton, Mr. Hookham Frere went to Caius College, Cambridge, where he graduated B. A. in 1792, and M. A. in 1795. His B. A. degree was "allowed," as an ægrotat prevented his going in for honours. But his college career was not undistinguished. He was made Fellow of Caius, and gained several prizes for classical compositions in prose and verse. One of the former still possesses an interest, as showing the views of an ardent young Pittite on such subjects as colonization, free trade, and convict instruction in 1792, and as illustrating the hold which the writings of Adam Smith had already attained on the minds of the young men of his own day. It was an essay which gained the Members' prize in that year on the question—"Whether it be allowable to hope for the improvement of morals, and for the cultivation of virtue in the rising state of Botany Bay?"[1]

After a description of the colonies of Greece and Rome, and of the principles of their management as contrasted with our own American colonies and India, in which our main object had been commercial advantage, the writer refers to the then recent loss of our American colonies, caused, as he argues, by over eagerness to assert sovereign rights, and neglect of the sound commercial considerations which would have dictated a more liberal policy.

---

[1] *Vide infra*, vol. i. p. 41.

Referring to Botany Bay, he insists that no commercial benefit could be expected from the settlement, unless the trade to the East Indies were relieved from the Company's monopoly. He proceeds to warn our government against embarrassing the future growth of the colony, by maintaining too long that strictness of regimen which was needed at first, alluding more particularly to martial law. From the example of our American colonies, from the non-existence in Botany Bay of many temptations met with in older communities, and from the natural tendency of simple habits of life to aid any development of virtuous instincts, he draws a hopeful augury for the wellbeing of the infant community.

He then notices, at some length, and with great surprise, the absence of all mention of religion, both in the published accounts of occurrences in the colony and in the Governor's despatches. He argues that mere fear of death can do little to deter from crime those who have already shown their contempt for it by their acts, and that we ought to think better of human nature than to despair of reclaiming them. At all events, future generations, he insists, might be rescued from contamination, and he adduces our American colonies to prove that, with abundance of fertile land free for their occupation, the children at least might be trained to simple habits and honest industry in field labour.

The essay contains frequent references to Adam Smith, whose great work, published in 1776, was then becoming popular, and after an elaborate eulogy on the author of the "Wealth of Nations:"— as "the man who laid the foundations of peace and concord throughout Europe, opened and guarded the road to Free Trade, enunciated precepts for instructing the people and for colonization, supplied, in short, whatever was necessary beyond the schools of philosophers for the welfare and happiness of mankind, and brought us to all appearance within a near approach to that wealth of the ancients, from which we are certainly now[1] far distant, being excluded not by nature's wrong, but by our own ignorance," concludes with " only let us, according to his advice, not strive by abrupt and headlong courses, but accomplish his ends by following the known and gentle paths which he has pointed out."

On leaving the university, Mr. Hookham Frere entered public life in the Foreign Office under Lord Grenville. He was returned to Parliament in November, 1796, as member for the close borough of West Looe in Cornwall, for which he continued to sit till the dissolution in 1802.[2]

He was from his boyhood a warm admirer of Pitt, who, ten years his senior, had for nearly that period been Prime Minister when Mr. Frere first began to take an active share in politics. Maturer judgment and longer experience in public life, did something more than confirm the young political subaltern's allegiance to a great party leader. His attachment to Pitt was, indeed, a much warmer personal feeling than that which the haughty character of his chief inspired in most of his political adherents, but it was discriminating and enduring; and when the generation of public men, to which they both belonged, had passed away from active political life, and the events which had so passionately convulsed Europe in his youth had become

---

[1] At the time when the essay was written very great and general pecuniary distress prevailed in this country.

[2] I have heard it related, as characteristic of the close borough system, that Mr. Frere never was at West Looe, the borough for which he sat in Parliament, till he accidentally stopped there on one of his journeys to Falmouth to embark for Spain. Nor did he then discover the fact till the bell-ringers, who had learnt that their borough member was at dinner in the Inn set the bells ringing, and called to ask for " something to drink his health."

matters of history half-a-century old, Mr. Frere, who never lost any of his keen interest in the political events of the day, would still maintain that Pitt understood the spirit and force of the French Revolution, as well as the genius and wants of modern English political life, more clearly than any either of his contemporaries or immediate successors in his own party, and that he was a greater and more far-seeing statesman than any of his rivals or opponents.

It cannot be said that this feeling was in any respect the worship of good fortune, for the tide of unvarying prosperity which marked the earlier years of Pitt's administration, had turned before Mr. Frere took office under him.

In 1792 Pitt had been most reluctantly forced into hostilities with France, and however flattering to our national pride may have been the naval successes which from time to time added to our colonial empire, or averted invasion from India or from the British Islands themselves, the brilliancy of these victories did but deepen the gloom which, year after year, seemed settling down on our prospects in our own country and on the continent, as one ancient monarchy after another succumbed to the vigour of the young Republican armies, as our financial and domestic difficulties, especially in Ireland, increased, till in 1800, after eight years of war, the peace of Luneville proclaimed the utter prostration of every one of Napoleon's continental opponents. Nelson's daring at Copenhagen, and the death of the Emperor Paul, averted, for the moment, that combination of the northern powers with France against us, which so seriously threatened our command of the sea ; but it was evident that the danger was but averted for a time, and at no period in our modern history was there so much reason for the grave anxiety of all true patriots—so much necessity for that constancy and courage for which even his worst enemies allowed that Pitt was pre-eminently distinguished.

We who now know how all this ended, and to what it has since led, can with difficulty put ourselves in the position of those who saw the concluding eight years of the last century, and could estimate better than the crowd of their contemporaries the strength of the revolutionary spirit at work, and the weakness, corruption, and divisions of much that was naturally opposed to it. But as we read the chequered chronicle of national success and failure, we can enter into the feelings of those young and ardent followers of Pitt who were, in some sense, behind the scenes of official life, and saw public affairs in something of the same light as he did ; and we can understand the enthusiasm with which they would devote themselves to a leader who, in the darkest hours of our national trials, was still recognized by the instincts of the least reflecting of his supporters as the " Pilot who weathered the storm."

Mr. Frere paid a short visit to France just before the final outbreak of the French Revolution, and brought back with him a strong conviction of the gravity of the crisis which was evidently impending. His intercourse with Mr. Canning, which had been necessarily somewhat interrupted during their college career, when Mr. Canning went to Oxford and his friend to Cambridge, was renewed very much on the intimate footing of their school-boy days at Eton, after Mr. Canning took his B. A. degree in 1793. The following is an extract from a note of some recollections of those days, as described by Mr. Frere nearly half-a-century afterwards (1844-5). The conversation had turned on a Life of Canning, in which his early adhesion to the Tory party was discussed as if it required explanation. Mr. Frere remarked, " Nothing was more natural or less needing explanation than Canning's early adhesion to

Pitt. As schoolboys, while I was by association a Tory, and by inclination a Pittite, Canning, by family connexion and association was a Whig, or rather a Foxite. This was, I believe, almost the only point on which our boyish opinions in those days very materially differed ; but it did not prevent our being great friends, and I am sure that a young man of Canning's views and feelings entering Parliament at such a time, could not long have been kept in opposition to Pitt. Canning's uncle and guardian was a Whig, and at his house Canning met most of the leaders of the Whigs, and they were not slow in recognizing his ability, and tried to attach him to their party. It showed Canning's sagacity, as well as his high spirit and confidence in himself, that he determined to take his own line, and judge for himself. When I went to see him at Oxford he showed me a letter he had received from Mrs. C——, whose husband was a great Whig leader. It enclosed a note from the Duke of Portland, offering to bring Canning into Parliament. The offer was a very tempting one to so young a man. But Canning refused it, and he told me his reason. 'I think,' he said, 'there must be a split. The Duke will go over to Pitt, and I will go over in no man's train. If I join Pitt, I will go by myself.'

" I afterwards, through Lord ——, got Canning introduced to Pitt. He came into Parliament for one of what were called ' Bob Smith's boroughs,' and he very soon became a great favourite of Pitt's. Dundas used often to have Pitt to sup with him after the House rose, and one night he took Canning with him. There was no one else, and Canning came to me next morning before I was out of bed, told me where he had been supping the night before, and added, ' I am quite sure I have them both ;' and I did not wonder at it, for with his humour and fancy it was impossible to resist him.

He had much more in common with Pitt than any one else about him, and his love for Pitt was quite filial, and Pitt's feeling for him was more that of a father than of a mere political leader. I am sure that from the first Pitt marked Canning out as his political heir, and had, in addition, the warmest personal regard for him.

" Some years after, when Canning was going to be married, Pitt felt as keenly about the affair as if he had nothing else to think of and Canning had been his only child. It was a good match for Canning in a worldly point of view, for his own fortune was not adequate to the political position Pitt would have liked him to hold. Pitt not only took a personal interest in the match himself, but he made old Dundas think almost as much about it, as if it had been some important party combination."

In reply to some remark about Pitt's supposed frigidity of disposition, Mr. Frere said, with some warmth, "No one who really knew Pitt intimately would have called him cold. A man who is Prime Minister at twenty-six, cannot carry his heart on his sleeve and be ' Hail, fellow! well met,' with every Jack, Tom, and Harry. Pitt's manner by nature, as well as by habit and necessity, was in public always dignified, reserved, and imperious; but he had very warm feelings, and had it not been for the obligations of the official position, which lay on him almost throughout his whole life, I believe he might have had nearly as many personal friends as Fox."

Speaking (in 1844) of the early years of the French Revolution, Mr. Frere said : " I am certain that, up to the very last, it was Pitt's determination to have kept clear from the European wars consequent on the French Revolution. Nothing was more unjust than the charge constantly brought against him, that he did not do all that a patriotic minister could do to preserve peace. His personal interests and predilections were all in favour of peace, and nothing but the outrageous conduct of the French compelled him to take part in the war, which no English minister could have long avoided, unless by joining the French in their onslaught upon all the old governments in Europe. He had got the funds up from about 64 to something like 93, and had established his Sinking Fund, which, if he had been succeeded by men like himself, would have done all he expected of it; but the inferior men who followed him had not the wisdom to resist the temptation of cribbing from it, to supply the necessities of the day.

"People talk of the Sinking Fund as if Pitt had ever imagined that money had some mysterious reproductive power. He, of course, never imagined anything of the kind. But he knew human nature, and he thought, I believe rightly, that it was a device by which people could be made more patient of taxation to pay off debts than in any other form; and most people, who have an income in excess of their current expenditure, devise some kind of sinking fund for themselves."

In reply to a question whether subsequent events had not shown that Pitt underestimated the strength of the revolutionary spirit with which he had to deal in opposing the French Republic, he added : "I think not in the least. It seems to me that all we have since learnt of the internal history of France during the first ten years of the Revolution, goes to prove that Pitt was much more right in his calculations of what we had opposed to us, than even his followers and admirers at the time supposed. I do not say that anything could have checked the progress of the Revolution. We have not to this day seen the end of it; but the French nation and re-sources were more thoroughly exhausted than we were, which is saying a good deal, and the war would have ended when Pitt expected, and the French have been compelled to let other people alone, for some years at all events, had it not been for the appearance of Buonaparte. He was a phenomenon on which no man could have calculated, and it was mainly owing to him that the final exhaustion of France was deferred for fifteen years. . . .

"A war, like the Revolutionary war, is necessarily one of exhaustion. You cannot end it by a pitched battle, nor even by occupying a capital or overrunning a whole country . . .

"The Republicans had found in history that all great military commanders under a Republic were apt to end by making themselves supreme. They thought to prevent this by chopping off the head of every successful general ; and this system answered very well till they got hold of Buonaparte. I remember when first I read his dispatches from the army of Italy, and saw how completely he understood the Directory and how to manage them, I said to myself, 'Well, here at last is a fellow whose head they will not be able to chop off.' . .

"People who find fault with Pitt's conduct of the war do not consider the difficulties arising from the jealousies of our allies. It is easy to say he might have found a Marlborough and done as Marlborough did. But Marlborough was always doing the work of his allies, and they knew it. It was not till after years of humiliation under Buonaparte's heel, that the continental nations agreed to sink their jealousies under Wellington ; and even he would have had hard work of it if Buonaparte had had a little more time, or if France had been a little less tired of him."

In reply to a question whether he had read Alison's account of the French Revolution in the "History of Europe," he said, "No! I have no wish to read any more summary histories of the French

Revolution. It cost me ten most miserable years of my life; for, from 1794 to 1804, I had but little hope for England. When it first broke out, people in England were beside themselves, and very few men had any notion of what it would lead to. I remember old Lady Fenn, a pattern of a good old-fashioned Tory and High Churchwoman, and a wonderfully shrewd sensible woman too, writing to my father after the destruction of the Bastille. She had been reading Cowper's lines, and was charmed with what had been done. I can fancy his answer was a trimmer; for he saw, more clearly than most men, what mob-rule meant, and that, when once they began to have everything their own way, the mob would not stop, after they had destroyed Bastilles. It is very difficult for any one in this generation to imagine what a struggle it was for existence as the war went on. The first real daylight I saw was when the Spaniards rose and I found that there were people, besides ourselves, in Europe, who were determined not to be swallowed up and converted into French subjects."

Speaking of Burke he said, " I did not know him much personally, and never met him in society; for when I began to busy myself about public affairs, he was old, and depressed, and lived very retired at Beaconsfield ; but I was sitting in the gallery of the House of Commons during his famous dagger speech. I agreed with most of his political views. I well remember getting his first letter on the French Revolution. It was one of the few books which I ever sat up all night to read.

"At the time we were first involved in the Revolutionary war, all Pitt's thoughts and hopes were directed to fiscal and financial and other domestic reforms ; and it is a knowledge of how much his mind was, from choice, directed to such reforms, that satisfies me of the sincerity of his wish to have avoided war at the outset, if he could have done so with honour. He never lost sight of his plans of financial improvement during the whole of the life-and-death struggle which followed ; and it was, I think, his feeling that the opportunity for carrying out his plans was never likely to recur during his own lifetime, which made him towards its close so anxious to put Canning in a position to succeed him as his political heir. Canning fully entered into all Pitt's views on such matters, and would have carried them out, but he never had an opportunity till it was too late ; before he became Prime Minister he had little to say to finance ; and after the war was over, there was for many years great exhaustion, and a kind of lassitude which made men indisposed to entertain projects of reform in finance or in anything else.

"I remember, about that time, asking Canning what had become of many plans of the kind which we used to talk of in our younger days ; and he said, almost bitterly, after naming some of the men with whom he was obliged to act, 'What can I churn out of such skimmed milk as that ?'

"I feel inclined to be angry sometimes when I hear what I know were some of Pitt's early schemes, which he, and Canning after him, hoped to carry out whenever they had an opportunity, spoken of by the Whigs as if they were the rightful inheritance of the Whig party, and as if every one else who took them up was poaching on Whig preserves."

In answer to a remark that assessed taxes were but a bad expedient for raising money, even in a time of war, and that Pitt had very largely resorted to them, he said : "During the war, Pitt was often obliged to raise money by almost any means he could, without much consideration, except for the productiveness of the tax at the moment. The assessed taxes were, I think, necessary evils during the war, but nothing is worse as an ordinary source of revenue. No man was more alive to this than Pitt; and had he lived to see permanent peace, we should not have had any assessed taxes now (1844). They act almost as mischievously and unfairly as a general poll tax. It was the old principle of all English taxation that it should fall mainly on property. The debt incurred during a war is the price of our deliverance from foreign domination. It justly falls on all property in the nation. When a ship is saved, you take the salvage from the value of the cargo, not from the seamen's wages. Our common people gave their blood to maintain the contest, and that is all we ought to expect from them. Nothing is so vexatious as an assessed tax—take what you please out of my income, but let me do as I please with the rest. I believe even now (1844) you must watch that the old paralytic butler, whom you keep as a pensioner, never cleans the plate, lest he should be charged as a house servant. The farm-boy, who is sent off on a cart-horse to fetch Doctor Slop when the good woman is ill, is liable to sur-charge as a domestic servant, and you are obliged to be careful when he pulls turnips and brings them to the kitchen lest the cook-maid should set him to peel them. The assessed taxes keep people living abroad, and encourage every kind of evasion. It would be a good thing if Peel would add sixpence in the pound to the tax on real property, and then do away with assessed taxes altogether.

"I see very little in the real Reforms of late years which Pitt would not have anticipated, had time and opportunity permitted; and he is often most unjustly judged, because he couldn't tell people why he was obliged to postpone his own convictions to the exigencies of the day, or to the opposition of a master like George III., or of some colleague who, in other respects, was indispensable."

Speaking of the conduct of Count Mole, at the opening of the French Session in 1845, he said: "I suspect the secret is a wish on the part of Louis Philippe to show M. Guizot that he can do without him, and that a coalition between Thiers and Mole is not impossible. Guizot seems to me a man of genius, and there is nothing a king of the character and in the position of Louis Philippe finds so irksome as to have for minister a man of genius. Men like Addington are the kind of ministers who are really acceptable to a sovereign who thinks, and wishes to act, for himself."

In answer to a question whether George III. had not a great personal regard for Pitt, he said—"Latterly he had, but certainly not at first. It was a choice between him and Fox, and the King inclined to Pitt as the less obnoxious of the two. Pitt's name was best known, in his early days, as an advocate for Parliamentary reform. I remember, when I was a boy, hearing two High Tories of the old school, at my father's house, talking about Pitt when he first became Prime Minister; they said: 'He is a thorn in our side; but one must sometimes stick to a bramble to save one from a fall into something worse.' The old Tories at first had very little confidence in him. I recollect they were all in great delight when the church at Wimbledon, where Pitt lived, was to be repaired, because he sent a hundred pounds as his subscription, with a request 'that it might be laid out on the steeple, in order that the church might not look like a meeting house.' The old Tories began then to think that there was really some hope of him after that!"

In reply to a question whether Pitt's conduct with regard to the slavery question did not justify the assertion that he had, in his latter years, and in the plenitude of power, neglected to give practical effect to some of the high principles which he advocated so eloquently in earlier life, Mr. Frere said: "No, I have no doubt his sagacity saw obstacles of which we knew nothing. I remember Canning being most eager to get an order in council issued to abolish slavery in the conquered colonies. It could then have been done by a simple order, and none of us could see why the order was not issued. Canning was as vexed as he could be with Pitt. Dundas was against it, and Pitt no doubt saw difficulties on the part of the King. He could not tell us what the obstacles were; and this often happens to a minister when he has one great work, like a war, on hand. He is often forced to postpone some of his favourite projects, and not be able to say why, even to friends like Wilberforce and Canning."

He said, on another occasion, that he felt sure at the time there was some other reason for Pitt's postponement of action with regard to the question of slavery, beyond that which forced him to postpone so many of his favourite measures of reform, and which Windham described as " the impossibility of repairing one's house in the hurricane season. In these days of peace (1845), people forget what an all-absorbing occupation a great national struggle for existence must be. No minister in his senses would have risked divisions of his party during the Revolutionary war, by discussing any controverted questions which admitted of being postponed."

In 1797 Mr. Frere joined with Mr. Canning, and some other of the younger members of their party, in the publication of the " Anti-Jacobin." It was intended to counteract, as far as possible in a weekly paper, the active and persistent efforts of the Republican party to disseminate their principles through the medium of the periodical press. Gifford was chosen editor, and a prospectus published which sets forth at some length, and with becoming gravity, the objects of supporting the existing order of things against the attacks of Jacobins and other secret or declared enemies of the nation and constitution. The first number of the " Anti-

Jacobin, or Weekly Examiner," appeared on the 20th Nov. 1797, with a notice that the publication would be continued every Monday during the sitting of Parliament." At the outset the intention of the projectors appears to have been, to meet the propagandists of the new political and social philosophy with heavy batteries of fact and argument. Authentic news was to be supplied, the misrepresentations of the opposition press were to be refuted under a regularly classified gradation of " Mistakes," " Misstatements," and " Lies ;" and a considerable space was to be devoted to formal essays on historical and constitutional questions. The first number contained a preliminary instalment of an article " On the Origin and Progress of the French Revolution, and its Effects on France and other Countries," with a promise of continuation, which, if it had been fulfilled in the same style, and in the same detail as the introductory chapter, would have required years for its completion.

But the conductors of the " Anti-Jacobin " seem to have become early aware, that it was not by ponderous weapons such as these elaborate essays that the battle was to be fought.

Five years earlier there might have been some use in arguing against those who maintained that the progress of the French Revolution meant no harm to property, morals or religion, as by law established, in any neighbouring nation. There were then many who believed that the war was really caused by the pride, selfish ambition, or obstinacy of the King or Mr. Pitt, or by the class of landowners, the aristocracy, or by the fundholders ; that it might end, as far as England was concerned, whenever the English chose to abstain from it ; and that, if let alone, the French would arrange their domestic affairs their own way, without troubling their neighbours. But in 1797 the conduct of the French nation, and the actions as well as the language of their rulers, had already supplied a sufficient answer to such assertions. With the facts of the past five campaigns in Germany and Italy before their eyes, the great bulk of the English nation had become thoroughly convinced that the war had really been forced on us by the aggressive character of the Revolution ; that the only alternative was to follow the French example, and allow ourselves to be drawn into the Revolutionary vortex ; and that "peace at any price," was incompatible not only with the preservation of our existing laws regarding property, and with the toleration of existing beliefs in matters of religion, but with our separate existence as an independent people. On all these points the mind of the nation was by that time pretty well made up, and an overwhelming and increasing majority in and out of Parliament supported the ministry in the prosecution of the war. Elaborate argument, therefore, on such questions, was superfluous and out of date. But, at the same time, there were dangerous and wide-spread discontents which were often more embarrassing than declared opposition. New opinions on every subject connected with law, religion, and property, were making their way into popular literature, and were spreading among people who had thought little about such questions before ; and the pressure of taxation, felt throughout the country with yearly increasing severity, did not dispose any class to be content with things as they were. Against this kind of feeling, which was rapidly spreading while the actual ministerial majority in Parliament was increasing, the heavy artillery of grave essays on the origin and progress of the Revolution, could do little.

The plan of the " Anti-Jacobin," however, comprised an armoury of lighter weapons, and its projectors soon found that an epigram was, for such a purpose as theirs, often more effectual than an argument.   The first number of the new periodical contained an "Introduction to the Poetry of the 'Anti-Jacobin,'" written by Canning, which indicates the system on which they proposed to avail themselves of this mode of counteracting the effects of the French Revolution, at least as far as the lighter literature of the country was concerned. The humour of the description of the new school of poetry and poetical morality will atone for a long quotation.

" In our anxiety to provide for the amusement as well as information of our readers, we have not omitted to make all the inquiries in our power for ascertaining the means of procuring poetical assistance.   And it would give us no small satisfaction to be able to report that we had succeeded in this point, precisely in the manner which would best have suited our own taste and feelings, as well as those which we wish to cultivate in our readers.

" But whether it be that good morals, and what we should call good politics, are inconsistent with the spirit of true poetry—whether ' *the Muses still with freedom found*' have an aversion to *regular* governments, and require a frame and system of protection less complicated than King, Lords, and Commons :—

> ' Whether primordial *nonsense* springs to life
> In the wild war of *Democratic* strife'

and there only—or for whatever other reason it may be, whether physical, or moral, or philosophical (which last is understood to mean something more than the other two, though exactly *what*, it is difficult to say); we have not been able to find one good and true poet, of sound principles and sober practice, upon whom we could rely for furnishing us with a handsome quantity of sufficient and approved

verse—such verse as our readers might be expected
to get by heart and to sing, as Monge describes the
little children of Sparta and Athens singing the
songs of freedom ; in expectation of the coming of
the great nation.

"In this difficulty, we have had no choice but
either to provide no poetry at all, a shabby expedient, or to go to the only market where it is to
be had good and ready made, that of the *Jacobins*
—an expedient full of danger, and not to be used
but with the utmost caution and delicacy.

"To this latter expedient, however, after mature
deliberation, we have determined to have recourse ;
qualifying it at the same time with such precautions,
as may conduce at once to the safety of our readers'
principles, and to the improvement of our own
poetry.

"For this double purpose, we shall select, from
time to time, from among those effusions of the
Jacobin muse which happen to fall in our way, such
pieces as may serve to illustrate some one of the
principles on which the poetical, as well as the
political doctrine of the New School is established
—prefacing each of them, for our readers' sake, with
a short disquisition on the particular tenet intended
to be enforced or insinuated in the production before
them—and accompanying it with an humble effort
of our own, in imitation of the poem itself, and in
further illustration of its principle.

"By these means, though we cannot hope to
catch '*the wood-notes wild*' of the bards of freedom,
we may yet acquire, by dint of repeating after them,
a more complete knowledge of the secret in which
their greatness lies, than we could by mere prosaic
admiration—and if we cannot become poets ourselves, we at least shall have collected the elements
of a *Jacobin* art of poetry for the use of those whose
genius may be more capable of turning them to
advantage.

"It may not be unamusing to trace the springs and principles of this species of poetry, which are to be found, some in the exaggeration, and others in the direct inversion of the sentiments and passions which have in all ages animated the breast of the favourite of the muses, and distinguished him from the 'vulgar throng.'

"The poet in all ages has despised riches and grandeur.

"The *Jacobin* poet improves this sentiment into a hatred of the rich and the great.

"The poet of other times has been an enthusiast in the love of his native soil.

"The *Jacobin* poet rejects all restriction on his feelings. *His* love is enlarged and expanded so as to comprehend all human kind. The love of all human kind is without doubt a noble passion; it can hardly be necessary to mention, that its operation extends to *Freemen*, and them only, all over the world.

"The old poet was a warrior, at least in imagination; and sung the actions of the heroes of his country in strains which 'made ambition virtue,' and which overwhelmed the horrors of war in its glory.

"The *Jacobin* poet would have no objection to sing battles too—but *he* would take a distinction. The prowess of Buonaparte indeed he might chaunt in his loftiest strain of exultation. *There* we should find nothing but trophies, and triumphs, and branches of laurel and olive; phalanxes of Republicans shouting victory, satellites of despotism biting the ground, and geniuses of Liberty planting standards on mountain-tops.

"But let his own country triumph, or her allies obtain an advantage; straightway the 'beauteous face of war' is changed; the 'pride, pomp, and circumstance' of victory are kept carefully out of sight—and we are presented with nothing but contusions and amputations, plundered peasants, and deserted looms. Our poet points the thunder of his blank verse at the head of the recruiting serjeant, or roars in dithyrambics against the lieutenants of pressgangs.

"But it would be endless to chase the coy muse of *Jacobinism* through all her characters. *Mille habet ornatus.* The *Mille decenter habet* is perhaps more questionable. For in whatever disguise she appears, whether of mirth or melancholy, of piety or of tenderness, under all disguises, like *Sir John Brute* in woman's clothes, she is betrayed by her drunken swagger and ruffian tone.

"In the poem which we have selected for the edification of our readers, and our own imitation, this day, the principles which are meant to be inculcated speak so plainly for themselves, that they need no previous introduction."

Southey's "Inscription for the apartment in Chepstow Castle, where Henry Marten, the regicide, was imprisoned thirty years," is then quoted at length, and followed by the " Imitation," as it is called, an inscription for Mrs. Brownrigg's cell in Newgate, which was the joint production of Canning and Frere.

The parody immediately achieved immense popularity. "It found its way from clubs, drawing-rooms, and literary coteries into the streets." The success of the poetical department of the new periodical was at once secured, and a considerable service was done to the Government of the day. Their opponents were already charging them with straining the law in their prosecutions for political offences. Honest citizens, who believed in and voted steadily for Pitt, were not likely to be carried away by the democratic enthusiasm of the youthful poet, who classed the execution of Charles the First with

> " Goodliest plans of happiness on earth,
> And Peace and Liberty— "

but state prosecutions are never popular, and in the burlesque commiseration for the fate of the prenticide Mrs. Brownrigg, the constitutional defender of law and order found a ready means of confounding the arguments of all over-scrupulous sticklers for the rights of the subject.

The shafts of ridicule told with still greater effect on the more impressible classes, and helped to keep in the ministerial fold many a young literary adventurer or sober dissenter, whose poetical or religious feelings might have been touched by such appeals as Southey's visions of a millennial reign of liberty, or by his description of the beauties of nature, from enjoying which the regicide was debarred.

The promise of the first number of the " Anti-Jacobin " was not belied by its successors. It may reasonably be doubted whether the " leader " with which the second number opens could have been very comforting to the house-keeper of those days, or very successful in convincing the taxpayer that the budget, which trebled the assessed taxes, even " for a limited time," was matter for congratulation ; however much it might, as the writer argued, " demonstrate the vigour and resources of the country in a manner the most likely to shorten the war, and bring our proud enemies to reason."—There was, however, no arguing against conclusions deduced from the Sapphic colloquy between the Friend of Humanity and the needy Knife Grinder, and the best reasoned political essay could produce little effect compared with the imaginary reports of the " meetings of the Friends of Freedom," in which the peculiarities of Fox, and the other great opposition orators, are parodied with such a humorous felicity as would materially impair the effects of their rhetoric in the House of Commons, as long as the clubs were amused by quotations from the burlesque imitations.

Most of the poetical contributions and political squibs took the form either of translation from the French or of imitations of the democratic oratory or literature of the day. Some of them bid fair, as predicted by Sir George Cornewall Lewis,[1] "to be much longer lived than the originals." Many were written in concert by Canning, Ellis, and Frere, so that it was difficult for the authors themselves, in later years, to assign to each his exact original share in the composition. This was especially apt to be the case when the article happened to have been written in the editor's room at Wright the publisher's. The room was the common property of the three who aided Gifford in his labours as editor, and from the anecdotes Mr. Frere used to tell of concurrent authorship, they seem to have suggested, here a line, there a phrase, to one another, very much as they might have done when school-boys at Eton.

Among the contributors whose names possess independent claims to historical record were Mr. Jenkinson afterwards Earl of Liverpool, Lord Clare, Lord Mornington afterwards Lord Wellesley, Lord Carlisle, Chief Baron Macdonald, and Lord Morpeth.

Gifford, besides filling the laborious post of working editor, wrote the articles headed " Mistakes, Misstatements and Lies," which were intended to correct the misrepresentations of fact by the revolutionary writers.

Pitt himself is said to have written one of the earlier papers on Finance, to have contributed a stanza or two to one of the poems, and to have

---

[1] " The Classical Museum," vol. i. 1844, p. 239.

attended one of the earlier meetings of the editors.[1]

It has, however, been asserted that the publication was at last discontinued at his direct instance, from an apprehension not, under the circumstances, at all unreasonable, that the satirical spirit to which so much of the success of the " Anti-Jacobin " was due, might in the long run prove a less manageable and discriminating ally than a party leader would desire.

However that may be,[2] the last number of the " Anti-Jacobin " was issued on the 9th of July, 1798, at the close of the Parliamentary session, after a triumphant career of eight months, in the course of

---

[1] These meetings were held weekly at Wright's, the publisher's, No. 169, Piccadilly. His assistant, Upcott, was employed as amanuensis to copy out the articles before they were sent to the printer ; and the usual precautions appear to have been taken to secure the incognito of contributors. But from the character of the compositions, and the number and position of the contributors, it was hardly possible to preserve secrecy as to the authorship of the more popular pieces ; and many of them seem to have been assigned by rumour to their real authors very soon after publication.

[2] In Mr. Frere's copy of Gillman's " Life of Samuel Taylor Coleridge " (now in the Roydon Library), vol. i. p. 70, at the following sentence—"Chimerical as it appeared, the purveyors of amusement for the reading public were thus furnished with occupation and some small pecuniary gain, while it exercised the wit of certain Anti-Jacobin writers of the day, and *raised them into notice.* Canning had the faculty of satire to an extraordinary degree, etc.," the words italicised are underlined by Mr. Frere, who wrote the following note on the subject in pencil on the margin of the book :—

" Not so. Mr. Canning was at that time Under-Secretary for the Foreign Department, with the certainty of passing, as he did, to a higher office. He had possessed, as everybody knew, the most unbounded influence over the mind of Mr. Pitt—he felt that the office of a weekly journalist was derogatory to the position which he held in society and in the official world—accordingly, as soon as he found that he had succeeded in giving a wrench to public opinion, he closed the publication with the poem of ' New Morality.'"

which its success as a political engine far exceeded the most sanguine hopes of its projectors.

The intrinsic merit of the satirical poetry and lighter literary articles is best proved by their having survived the living memory of most of the circumstances and persons to which they allude, and by their having been frequently reprinted in a collected form.[1]

Much has sometimes been said of the personalities and party spirit, of which they contain abundant evidence. But it must be recollected that they were originally written for purely party purposes, and they are certainly not more open to censure on this account than party writings generally, and the writings of that period in particular. Most readers, on a fair consideration of the circumstances under which the "Anti-Jacobin" was published, will probably feel inclined to agree with Moore, that many of the most pungent articles are " models of that style of political satire whose lightness and vivacity give it the appearance of proceeding rather from the wantonness of wit than of ill-nature, and whose very malice, from the fancy with which it is mixed up, like certain kinds of fireworks, explodes in sparkles."

Nor can there be any doubt that the " Loves of the Triangles," " The Progress of Man," and " The Rovers " conferred on the literature of the day a substantial benefit, by holding up to ridicule offences against sound canons of literary taste and judgment which hardly admitted of any other mode of correction.

In 1799, on Mr. Canning's removal to the Board of Trade, Mr. Frere succeeded him as Under Secretary of State in the Foreign Office. Among the

---

[1] The " Anti-Jacobin " had reached a fourth edition in 1799. Several editions of the poetry were re-published separately ; the last with notes by Chas. Edmonds in 1854.

few of his letters which have been preserved are some which he wrote at this period from the Foreign Office to his brother Bartle,[1] who was attached as Private Secretary to Lord Minto's mission at Vienna. The following extracts are given, not because they throw any new light on the momentous affairs to which the Public Despatches of the Foreign Office at that time had reference, but as specimens of style, and of a humour, which was irrepressible, whatever might be the subject :—

" DEAR BARTLE,

"I have sent you a new box at last, the reason which prevented me from making use of them before was the same which rendered it impossible for Punch to make his appearance in the first scene of the Puppet Show of the Creation, namely, that he was not yet come from the hands of his maker. I trust to Ned, William,[2] and my father, for telling you all family news. The public, I hope, is doing pretty well. But what is most material for me to observe is, that it being now 20 m. past 11 on Saturday morning, it will be as much

---

[1] His fifth brother, Bartholomew, born 1776. He entered the diplomatic service as private secretary to Lord Minto on his mission to Vienna in 1799, the same year in which he took his degree as first Senior Opt., and First Chancellor's Medallist, having been elected Scholar of Trinity, 1797, and gained the Browne medals, 1798. He continued in active employment at Vienna, Lisbon, Madrid, and Constantinople as Secretary of Legation, Chargé d'Affaires or Minister until 1821, when he retired on his pension. He died, reverenced by many beyond his immediate family, in 1851. He will still be remembered by a few who knew him as one of the earliest members of the Traveller's Club, the Royal Geographical and other Societies, where his varied learning, his cultivated taste, playful wit, and most engaging manners, made him a welcome associate, and earned for him the tribute of regard to his memory passed by the President of the Geographical Society in 1852. *Journal R. G. S.*, vol. xxii. p. lxvi.

[2] His fourth brother William, afterwards Serjeant Frere, and Master of Downing College, Cambridge: born 1775, died 1836.

as the messenger can do to get down to Yarmouth
before the packet sails; you say nothing about
Wickham; how do he and Lord M. draw together?

"Yours affte*y*.

"J. H. FRERE."

In another letter he forwards one which he had
received from his brother Edward, announcing his
engagement to be married.   After various humorous
conjectures as to the reason why his brother had
omitted the lady's name, he adds—

"Our *peace*, if we have any (mind I am speaking
seriously and diplomatically), must be jointly with
Austria; preserving her influence with the powers
of Italy and the South of Germany, by dint of
subsidy from England if necessary (as in the case
of Hesse during the last peace), and ready to begin
again if France should stir; with anything short of
this we shall be undone.   Broughton is standing
by me and desires me to say that he has sent your
flies.

"We have fine weather at last, and I hope shall
have a good harvest, the prospect of which instead
of another famine which threatened us, would console us, if anything could, for the miserable news
we have from you.

"By the bye, it seems evident I think, from the
detail of the articles of capitulation, and from the
improbability of an Austrian General taking such
a responsibility upon himself, that the whole must
have been arranged beforehand, and contingent
orders sent from Vienna."

"*May* 18 (1800?).

"I HAVE just a moment while the clerk is bind-
ing up the despatches, to say that we are all well,
which I suppose you may have heard already from
my father and William.   The William above mentioned is, I hope, going on very well.   I do not re-

collect any immediate nonsense which you are not possessed of, except that Lady Laurie [1] has lent us one of our ancestors, in an old frame, which Quinton has been set to copy on a fine old black board, and the copy is now stuck up in the old frame and will be sent to her to find out if she can.

"I have just this morning taken my first lesson in German in the Gazette with all the different stories of Mela's victory.[2]

"You must send us another, for I shall have finished this in two more lessons. It is Mr. Mender who has the credit of my tuition.

"I send you a key for the boxes which Wickham has, and which we shall send you by the next messenger."

"June 3 (1800 ?).

"I OUGHT to take the ten minutes which I shall have before Lord Grenville sends back the despatches to tell you the news, if I could think of any. Oh, I'll tell you, for I have heard of nothing else every day after dinner. We have got a new Divorce Bill, which people are eager about, and more absurd than can be imagined, as my old friend Lord Mulgrave's speeches in the papers may perhaps have informed you already."

After describing the affected indignation of the old "Will Honeycombs," who were anxious to be supposed interested in the subject, he adds—

"You will conclude from this that I intend voting against the *beau monde.* I believe I shall; but it will be more for the spite of the thing than for any

---

[1] Judith Hatley, a first cousin of Mr. Frere's father, married firstly, Mr. Wollaston, of Suffolk ; secondly, Col. Sir Robert Laurie, Baronet, of Maxwellton, Dumfries-shire. Through the Reynolds family, the Calthorps, and De Greys, the Hatleys traced their descent from Gundreda, daughter of William the Conqueror.

[2] Probably his successes against Massena before Genoa, in April, 1800.

good I think it will do. Besides, I do not like to vote against Pitt the moment that he tells one, 'Now here's a question on which you may vote which way you will without being turned out.' I believe you must keep all this nonsense to yourself, for your present society, I apprehend, would belong to what our Norwich friend called the 'obstinate party.' By the bye, nothing can be more kind than Lord Minto's way of speaking of you, and everything about you. I ought to write to him, but it is very late, and if I sit up much longer to-night I shall be knocked up, and look like a devil to-morrow, at the birthday ; and then, what will be the use of my having ordered the light-blue silk coat, with breeches of the same, and steel buttons 'to comply' ? with which I conclude.

"By the bye there are some copies of the Wurtemberg and Mentz Treaties, which will be sent if they come in in time from the printers, and which Lord Minto should present with suitable expressions."

"July 11 (1800).

"DEAR BARTLE,

"It frequently happens between individuals corresponding at a distance, that the very point which the one party considers as too obvious to be mentioned is precisely that which the other is the most anxious about. To illustrate this by a familiar instance. It is not impossible that Lord Minto may at this moment be desirous to know whether his conduct has been approved, and whether we are satisfied with his project and with the expectation of its immediate ratification, and you may still therefore be glad to hear that it was considered as the most welcome intelligence which we could possibly receive. Pray what became of the parole certificates of General Grouchy and Perignan, *vide* your despatch of February 4th ? The French Commissary tells us that his government have

been told that they had been transmitted here—
we have never seen them. They likewise complain
of Collis's detention—as his release, in exchange
for Mack, was a part of the arrangement upon
which Don was released. Item, for family news,
my father is gone out of town. My uncle is coming through town in his way to his new quarters
at Farnham. Sir Robert (Laurie) is getting better,
so is Hatley[1]—he is, or was a week ago, at Cardiff
races, and I am going to get him into the new
Military School, which will just suit him. Ted's
intended spouse is Miss Greene[2]—we are all very
well satisfied with what we hear of her—he has
been in town too, and for some time wore his pan-
taloons over his half-boots [a Whig innovation] in
spite of remonstrance and example. Canning was
married last Tuesday. He dined with me and was
launched into futurity at about half-after seven, by
the Rev. W. Leigh, with great composure. The
clock strikes twelve, and I am very tired, and as I
cannot recollect anything more which I have to tell
you, I take it for granted that there is nothing.
Stop a moment. We are going, I hope, to have a
very good harvest, instead of the continuation of
famine which was generally expected, and moreover, we are not much disheartened by the events
in Italy and Germany, though the rascally funds
had the impudence to rise upon it, taking it for
granted that we must be driven to make peace,
which is all they care about."

Many years after, in 1844, describing Mr. Can-

---

[1] His sixth brother, James Hatley, well known in after
years by his writings on the interpretation of Prophecy, and
as the inventor of one of the most successful systems for
teaching the blind to read : born 1779, died 1866.

[2] Eldest daughter of James Greene, of Turton Tower and
Clayton Hall, Lancashire, M.P. for Arundel, representative of
Humphrey Chetham, the founder of Chetham's Hospital and
Library, Manchester, Sheriff of Lancashire, 1635, died 1653.

ning's marriage, Mr. Frere said—" I was to be best man, and Pitt, Canning, and Mr. Leig , who was to read the service, dined with me before the marriage, which was to take place in Brook Street. We had a coach to drive there, and as we went through that narrow part, near what was then Swallow Street, a fellow drew up against the wall, to avoid being run over, and peering into the coach, recognized Pitt, and saw Mr. Leigh, who was in full canonicals, sitting opposite to him. The fellow exclaimed, ' What, Billy Pitt ! and with a parson too !' I said, ' He thinks you are going to Tyburn to be hanged privately,' which was rather impudent of me ; but Pitt was too much absorbed, I believe in thinking of the marriage, to be.angry. After the ceremony, he was so nervous that he could not sign as witness, and Canning whispered to me to sign without waiting for him. He regarded the marriage as the one thing needed to give Canning the position necessary to lead a party, and this was the cause of his anxiety about it, which I would not have believed had I not witnessed it, though I knew how warm was the regard he had for Canning. Had Canning been Pitt's own son I do not think he could have been more interested in all that related to this marriage."

In a letter of a few days later date, July 15, 1800, he says :—

" I do not send you any news, partly because there is none, partly because I am too tired to sit up to write it if there was any, and partly in resentment for your silence, partly likewise because the messenger is waiting, and as he is an independent gentleman with East India despatches,[1] I do not like to detain him the half hour which it would take

---

[1] We are apt in these days to forget that during the French war, great as was our command of the seas, it was found necessary to organize a regular postal service for India, *viâ*

me to send you a *coup politique et domestique*. I
will try it in an abridged form : Ted is to be married on Monday se'nnight the 28th instant without
fail. William is set out for Roydon *viâ* Cambridge,
with law books and a determination to read them
and to remain there till November next. Sir John
and my lady[1] are setting off for Tenby somewhere
near Swansea, purposing as I apprehend, to turn
Ted's left wing, and to occupy those mountainous
positions [the valley of Clydach in Breconshire]
during the summer.

"I remain here docketing and dispatching as
usual, and as usual,

"Your affectionate Brother,

"J. H. FRERE."

His appointment as Minister at Lisbon was in
contemplation when he wrote on August 8th, 1800:—

"I have written a letter to Lord Minto, which he
will probably show you. If you are at a loss to
know what to make of it, I can only tell you that I
really wish him to determine according to his own
feeling and convenience, and that if he feels you
any way *a charge*, which in his present situation, with
all his family about him, he may very possibly do,
without any fault of yours, he need not be afraid
of throwing you upon the wide world, seeing that I
shall be very glad to have you with me. I ought
to tell you that I shall be able to have you established with me a Secretary of Legation in about

---

Constantinople, Bagdad, and the Persian Gulf. A packet
was sent every six weeks, by whatever route through the
Continent was least liable to be interrupted, to Constantinople,
and thence by Tartar post to the Persian Gulf, where the
Company's cruisers kept up the communication with India.
Ten rupees (£1) was the charge for a single letter from India,
and the signature of the Chief Secretary to the Indian Government was necessary to authorize its transmission.

[1] His sister Jane, who was married to Admiral Sir John
Orde, Bart., brother of the first Lord Bolton.

half a year or a little more. I did not mention this to Lord Minto, because I did not know how to do it without making it bear on one side or other of the question, which I was desirous of leaving in perfect equilibrio. If you should find that Lord Minto, of his own mere motion, is disposed to keep you with him in consideration of your past and expected services, you will of course consider that my convenience is to give way to your improvement and advantage, which may certainly be much promoted by a further continuance at Vienna.

" I have sent you the memoirs of Castle Rack-rent, and have to acknowledge the receipt of Mrs. Bunch. You forgot to tell me your incident for the German play. By the bye Coleridge has translated Schiller's Piccolomini wonderfully well. I have lent it out, or I would send it you."

The next letter enclosed, with a poetical version of his own, a retrenchment which he appears to have been ordered by Lord Grenville to send to Lord Minto, directing the refund of an unauthorized payment of £500 to the Secretaries of his Mission, of whom Mr. Stratton was one.[1]

---

[1] It was formerly customary when a treaty had been signed by a British Minister at a foreign court, to direct him to deliver a diamond snuff-box to the Minister with whom it was negotiated, and to draw on the office in Downing Street for £500, which he was likewise directed to present to him for distribution among his Secretaries. These presents were reciprocal, and when received by the British Minister, the officials in Downing Street were in the habit of claiming them as their perquisites, and in two instances when treaties had been negotiated by Lord Henley, Lord Minto's predecessor, at Vienna, the Downing Street office claim had not been resisted, and the Secretary of Legation, Mr. Stratton, had been deprived of his dues. He stated the case to Lord Minto, who, on signing a treaty with Baron Thurgot in 1800, explained the controversy to him, and requested to be informed expressly what were the Emperor's intentions with regard to the disposal of the £500? and having been told it was intended for the Secretaries of his Mission, in consideration of the extra labour the negotiation

Sep. 2nd, 1800.

" I send you the enclosed little *jeu d'esprit,* which has attracted considerable notice in the official and diplomatic world. You may tell Stratton that I have used him very well, for I was authorized to give him a jobation, as you will see by the enclosed docket, which was returned with Lord Minto's letter.

" Pray assure Lord Minto that I bear no ill-will to his messengers, and that if I give them up to Mr. B——, it is in consequence of a determination (which I made when I came into the office, and which I have always had reason to congratulate myself upon—namely) to give up the whole pandemonium of messengers and couriers to the unrestrained coercion of one single arch-fiend, without check or control on my part. If I had had any taste for such subjects, I might, I believe, have spent a week in hearing complaints and insinua-

---

had thrown on them, he distributed it accordingly. Downing Street retorted by the Under Secretary's writing to Lord Minto (at the same time with Lord Grenville's official directing him to draw for £500) that, as a similar sum would be given him by the Court of Vienna for the Foreign Office, he must apply that to the purpose for which he was directed to draw ; returning it to Baron Thurgot as the gratuity from the British Court to his Secretaries, and abstaining from drawing the bill ; which would leave the Foreign Office in possession of the like sum destined for them. Lord Minto replied he had received nothing for the Foreign Office up to that date, and that in the meantime he would obey his instructions and draw on them. Lord Grenville was then appealed to, and declared in favour of the Foreign Office, as detailed in the *jeu d'esprit.* But they further dishonoured Lord Minto's bill, without consulting Lord Grenville. The bill came back *protested.* Lord Minto remonstrated so effectually that Lord Grenville abandoned the Foreign Office claim, covering his retreat by an order that thenceforward no such presents should be received unless destined for gentlemen of his office. To soften off the asperity of his remonstrance, Lord Minto wrote an eclogue between his Secretaries, and sent it with the original draft to Lord Grenville.

tions, and I might have filled a long letter with what the messengers have said, and how they remonstrated in a body, and reports of the insolent language of the couriers to Mr. B——, and how they refused to take the money, and desired to have despatches and three horses a-piece. There were really materials for an epic poem, if I had collected the whole; but whether I disliked the subject, or saw no chance of getting to the rights of it, the fact is, that except one ineffectual attempt to persuade one of the men that he had no right to complain for being sent home on the same footing with the office messengers, I was glad to keep entirely out of the way, and did so with great success. Seriously speaking, however—for the subject becomes a serious one to me—when Lord Minto appears to be really interested, or to suspect a want of interest on my part in what concerns him, you must, I think, see the utter impossibility of my attempting to interfere in the disputes between the messengers, particularly in opposition to the person who, ever since I have been in the office, has taken the whole trouble of this sort off my hand; the familiar instance of an upper and a lower servant, though not applicable in comparison, may serve as an illustration of the impolicy, and, in this case, the injustice of such a proceeding, and the argument here is certainly an argument *à fortiori.* I must conclude. My mother, I suppose, has sent all family news.

DRAFT TO LORD MINTO.

My Lord, when I open'd your letter,
  I confess I was perfectly stunn'd ;
But I find myself now something better,
  Since I'm ordered to bid you *refund.*

'Tis a very bad scrape you've got into,
  Which your friends must all wish you had shunn'd,
Says Lord Grenville, ' Prepare to Lord Minto
  Dispatches to bid him *refund.*'

Mr. Hammond, who smiles at your cunning,
  On the subject amusingly punn'd ;
Says he, " They're so proud of their funning,
  'Twill be pleasant to see them *refunn'd.*"

As for Stratton, he ought for his sin, to
  Be sent to some wild Sunderbund.
But we'll pardon him still, if Lord Minto
  Will instantly make him *refund.*

Believe me, I don't mean to hurt you,
  But if you'd avoid being dunn'd,
Of necessity making a virtue,
  With the best grace you can, you'll *refund.*

Let the Snuff Box belong to Lord Minto ;
  But as for the five hundred *pund,*[1]
I'll be judged by Almeida[2] or Pinto,[3]
  If his Chancery must not *refund.*

POSTSCRIPT.

There are letters from India which mention,
  Occurrences at Roh-il-cund ;
But I'll not distract your attention,
  Lest I make you forget to *refund.*

Lord Carlisle's new play is the Story
  Of Tancred, and Fair Sigismund,
Our last news is the taking of Gorée,
  But our best is, that you must *refund.*"

In October, 1800, Mr Frere was appointed Envoy
Extraordinary and Plenipotentiary to Portugal.
The following letter was addressed to his brother,
who had in the meantime returned to England
from Vienna :—

" I am very glad to hear of you in England, and
am particularly desirous of having you here as soon
as possible.   You must see Lord Hawkesbury.   I

---

[1] Scoticè pro "pound."—J. H. F.
[2] The Portuguese Minister in London.
[3] The Portuguese Minister for Foreign Affairs, Lisbon,
whither Mr. Frere had just been appointed Envoy.

trust he will appoint you Secretary of Legation. It is an appointment which is absolutely necessary here, where the despatches cannot be entrusted to a common clerk, and where one cannot always have gentlemen to assist one, for assistance' sake, as Ainslie [1] has done hitherto. He has, however, heard accounts of his father's health which make him wish to return. I must not detain him, and I cannot go on alone, and I have no right to ask you to come unless I can get you made Secretary of Legation; therefore, the premises duly considered, I trust Lord Hawkesbury will appoint you. I shall write to him this post."

"P.S. You must come though, at any rate, and directly."

"*July 29th*" (1801 ?).

[Lisbon ?]

While he was at Lisbon a change of Ministry, which took all Europe by surprise, substituted Mr. Addington for Pitt as Prime Minister, and Lord Hawkesbury for Lord Grenville as Secretary of State for Foreign Affairs. Mr. Frere's view of the reasons that induced Pitt so unexpectedly to resign a power still, to all appearance, supreme, was briefly this: In the face of the national distress from deficient harvests, England was left, by the defection of allies, absolutely alone to carry on the contest with all Europe. It was impossible to continue the war unless the country were satisfied that no other course was consistent with our existence as an independent nation. It was necessary, therefore, to test the willingness of France to make and maintain a lasting peace. But Pitt himself had no belief in the sincerity of Napoleon's desire to consent to any real peace without inflicting serious humiliation on the only nation which had proved herself capable of maintaining a contest with France and all the rest

---

[1] Sir Robert Ainslie.

of Europe combined against her.　He felt that to make a transitory and illusory peace would seriously damage his own power to renew the war with effect, and expose him to the charge of having caused the failure which he believed must be the inevitable result.　He therefore determined to leave to other hands the credit of making and, if possible, maintaining such a peace.　Addington's ministry afforded the means of doing this without permanently deranging any of those combinations which were necessary to re-form a strong war ministry, when the hostilities which Pitt believed to be inevitable, should again be renewed by the restless ambition of Napoleon.

Speaking of this period many years afterwards, Mr Frere said :—"When Addington became Prime Minister, Pitt wanted Canning to remain in office ; but, such was Canning's contempt for the whole set, and his dislike to the peace of Amiens, that nothing would induce him to do so, though his refusal led to a temporary coolness with Pitt.　I have no doubt Pitt foresaw what would happen. He did not wish to have to make the peace which was inevitable, and knew he must come in again soon after it was made ; and he wished, on his return, to find Canning in office, where he might have retained him (without difficulty from his aristocratic supporters), but Canning would not let him.

"I was obliged to remind Canning of it afterwards, when he was crusty with Lord Dudley for much the same thing.　I told him, 'Dudley is now doing to you what you did to Pitt—refusing to follow a lead the necessity of which you see, and he does not.'　It is the hardest of a minister's trials not always to be able to acknowledge his own weakness, and give his reasons in such a case."

On the 6th of September, 1802, Mr. Frere was transferred from Portugal to Spain, where he remained as Minister for nearly two years.

To understand his position at this period, and
the circumstances under which he subsequently
revisited Spain, it is necessary briefly to revert to
the course which the Spanish Government had
taken in the great contest with revolutionary
France.

In 1793, when the French Republic declared war
against Spain, the Court and Government of Charles
IV. presented almost every evil feature of effete
despotism.   Corruption pervaded all branches of
the administration, colonial as well as domestic ;
commerce and industry were decaying, unworthy
favourites ruled at a shameless Court, and the disorganized armies and navies of Spain, under the
command of court intriguers, were wholly incapable
of such enterprises as, in earlier days, had raised
her to the first rank among the military powers
of the civilized world.   But all the old forms remained ; the spirit of the people had not yet been
broken by foreign invasion, and the nation at large
still imagined itself as capable of influencing the
destinies of Europe as in the days of its early
glory.

Spain, however, contributed little to the pressure
which the governments of Europe brought to bear
at this time on France ; and the revolutionary
leaders had their hands too fully occupied in other
directions to make any serious efforts against Spain.
In July, 1795, Spain brought her share of the lan-
guid contest to an inglorious close, and made peace
with France.   A year later she entered into an
offensive and defensive alliance with the Republic,
and, as a consequence, war was declared with England.

Spain contributed large sums of money, which
were very acceptable to the exhausted French treasury, and fitted out a formidable fleet, which, on
the 14th February, 1797, was signally defeated by
Sir John Jarvis off Cape St. Vincent.   From that

date to the peace of Amiens in 1802, Spain took but a subordinate part in the contest.

When, after the cessation of hostilities, Mr Frere arrived as British Minister at Madrid, he found little prejudice against England on the part of those who best represented the worthier elements of Spanish character at the Court of Charles IV.; but such men were in a woful minority—all real power was already in the hands of Don Manuel Godoy, the notorious favourite of the King and his worthless Queen.

There was much in Mr. Frere's character and tastes which rendered him peculiarly acceptable to Spaniards who valued their national independence, and were, like all true Spaniards, proud of their national glories. The favourite and his creatures however had little reason to love the English, and there were among the courtiers many traitors to the national cause ready for any intrigue in the interests of France.

Few of Mr. Frere's private letters relating to this period have been preserved, but they bear testimony to the diligence with which he had applied himself to the study of Spanish literature, and the friendships which he formed with men of letters, to more than one of whom he appears to have been a generous and discriminating patron.

From this time, also, dates his friendship with Romana, which was afterwards productive of valuable results to both England and Spain.

Don Pedro Caro y Sureda Romana was born at Majorca in 1761, and had been a soldier from his youth.

Speaking of him in 1844, Mr. Frere said:—"Romana and I were friends from the very first day we met; he was then a Lieutenant-General with the Court, and it was he who enabled me, within a very short time after my arrival at Madrid, to find out exactly how all parties stood, and to

send home a correct account of them. I remember
talking with him over the men who, in the event
of a rupture with France, might have the command
of the Spanish army. Romana, after disposing of
them all, and showing how utterly unfit they were
for command, said :—'Depend upon it, the man
who can command an army of Spaniards is now
coursing the hares in La Mancha, or fighting bulls
in Andalusia.' And so it proved ; for Albuquerque,
who was the only man who could have commanded
the army, was just a country gentleman of the kind
Romana described."

" He once told me, as an instance of the dislike
of old-fashioned Spaniards to parsimony, that when
a young man travelling with his uncle, he locked
the saddle-bag which contained all the money they
had for their journey, and got a severe lecture for
his pains from the old man ;—'to think that any
Hidalgo of Spain should lock up his money!'"

But to return to 1804. Only the first mutterings
of the coming storm were then audible in Spain.
The hollow truce which had followed the peace of
Amiens came to an end when England declared
war against France on the 18th May, 1803, and the
strife was resumed on terms which made it clear
that no real peace could be hoped for till one or
other of the combatants should be thoroughly
humbled.

During the short breathing time which inter-
vened, both nations had rapidly recovered from the
exhaustion caused by the previous contest.

France had in many ways added to her real
strength, and her people were more than ever convinced of the vast increase in aggressive power
which had followed the consolidation of the revolutionary forces under the iron will of the First Consul,
and which almost justified his pretensions to be the
arbiter of Europe.

The English, also, had tasted the blessings of

peace. The proceedings of Napoleon during the cessation of hostilities produced, however, a more general and profound conviction than at any period of the war, that there was no other course open for England, than either to continue the contest till the ambition of Napoleon should be effectually crushed, or to submit to the same sacrifice of independence which had placed all his continental neighbours at his feet.

Thus the war was resumed, with the resolve on both sides that, whatever its cost, it must be fought out " to the bitter end ; " and when once the British nation had made up its mind on this point, it speedily became impatient of the want of vigour which marked the war policy of the Addington Ministry. The conviction gradually gained ground that no man was so able to direct the national efforts as he who, with such unflinching courage, had maintained the contest in its earlier stages, and who had never wavered in his opinions as to the only course consistent with national honour and permanent independence. Mr. Pitt returned to office in May, 1804, but Lord Grenville could not be induced to resume his former post at the Foreign Office, which was filled by Lord Harrowby.

For some time after the renewal of war between England and France, Spain professed her intention to remain neutral. But if any such hope ever really actuated the men who then ruled at Madrid, it must have been speedily dispelled. Indeed the observance of real neutrality seems, under the circumstances, to have been impossible. By the treaty of St. Ildefonso, in 1796, Spain had formed an alliance, offensive and defensive, with France ; and by a secret convention of 19th October, 1803, the subsidy to be paid by Spain to France was fixed at £2,880,000. Thus the action of Spain was virtually identified with that of France. But the English Government was assured that Spain, in agreeing to

the subsidy, the amount of which was at first unknown, was acting under compulsion, and not from
any ill-will to England. It was therefore agreed
that a small and temporary advance of money by
Spain to France should not be considered as en-
titling England to declare war against Spain.
Later in the year, however, when the real amount
of the subsidy was rumoured, the British Minister
intimated to the Spanish Government that any
agreement to furnish a subsidy of such magnitude
would in itself be considered a declaration of hostility against Great Britain. Mr. Frere stated in
his note :—" His Majesty is perfectly sensible of the
difficulties of the situation in which Spain is placed,
as well by reason of her ancient ties with France as
on account of the character and habitual conduct of
that power and of its chief. These considerations
have induced him to act with forbearance to a
certain degree, and have inclined him to overlook
such pecuniary sacrifices as should not be of sufficient magnitude to force attention from their political effects."

He then declares, " That pecuniary advances,
such as are stipulated in the recent convention with
France, cannot be considered by the British Government but as a war subsidy—a succour the most
efficacious, the best adapted to the wants and situation of the enemy, the most prejudicial to the
interests of the British subjects, and the most dangerous to the British dominions ; in fine, more than
equivalent for every other species of aggression."
After adding that imperious necessity compelled
His Britannic Majesty to make this declaration,
Mr. Frere intimated "that the passage of French
troops through the territories of Spain would be
considered a violation of neutrality, and that the
British Government would feel compelled to take
the most decisive measures in consequence of such
an event."

The Spanish minister replied :—" Although the Spanish Cabinet is penetrated with the truth that the idea of aiding France is compatible with that of neutrality towards Great Britain, yet it has thought that it could better combine these two objects by a method which, without being disagreeable to France, strips her neutrality towards Great Britain of that hostile exterior which military succours necessarily present."

In February Mr. Frere presented a further remonstrance on the ground of partiality shown to the French in permitting the sale of prizes, and complained of the naval armaments in the Spanish harbours. His note stated :—" I am ordered to declare to you that the system of forbearance on the part of England depends entirely on the cessation of every naval armament within the ports of this kingdom, and that I am expressly forbidden to prolong my residence here if, unfortunately, this condition should be rejected. It is also indispensable that the sale of prizes brought into the ports of this kingdom should cease, otherwise I am to consider all negotiations as at an end, and I am to think only of returning to my superiors."

It cannot be supposed that a correspondence of this kind rendered the presence of the British Minister at Madrid at all agreeable to Godoy, the " Prince of the Peace," who at that time absolutely ruled the councils of the Spanish Court, and who seemed indifferent to every consideration of national honour, provided his own personal ascendancy were secured. It was rumoured in London that the British Minister would be unable to remain any longer at Madrid ; and, alluding to these reports, Mr. Frere's brother' George[1] wrote to his mother in July :—

---

[1] His third brother, of Lincoln's Inn and Twyford House, Herts : born 1774, and died 1854. He was through life the

"I have great pleasure in assuring you that I hear but one opinion respecting my brother's correspondence with the 'Prince of Peace'—namely, that it establishes his character for spirit and ability, and exposes very completely and very dexterously the stupid pusillanimity of his antagonist. It cannot occasion his recall, though it may very probably, I think, make him desirous of coming home sooner than he otherwise would have done, because a breach of this kind with a great man, with whom he had before maintained the best possible understanding, must render his continuance at the same Court less agreeable. I do not, however, understand that he is expected here at present."

On the 1st August Mr. George Frere again wrote that he had heard at the Foreign Office :—

"My two brothers were well, at Madrid, on the 6th of last month. My eldest brother is coming home immediately, and Bartle remains Chargé d'Affaires. Mr. Wellesley is going to take my eldest brother's place. There is no disapprobation of his conduct that I can learn ; but he has for some time past been desiring permission to return home, and it is obvious that there cannot be that cordiality between him and the 'Prince of Peace,' which is desirable. I hope he will immediately be employed when he does return, and in some ostensible situation, which may serve to mark an approbation of his conduct."

---

trusted friend and counsellor in all matters of business, of his elder brother, who used to say, " George had as much ability, and more perseverance, and better habits of business, than any of us ; if he would have taken, as I wished, to public life, or to the Bar, he might have been a Secretary of State or Lord Chancellor. He always had twice the stuff in him of his old friends and cotemporaries —— and —— " (naming two law lords).

In August Mr. Frere left Madrid to return to England.

On his journey to Corunna to embark he observed unmistakable evidence of preparations for war, which were at variance with the pacific assurances of the Spanish Ministry. From Salamanca he wrote to his brother Bartle, on the 31st of August, as "just setting out from this seat of learning, where I have passed some days not unpleasantly." Arrived at Corunna, on September 10th he writes to his brother:—"I deferred writing to you till I should get to my journey's end; and now I find Admiral Cochrane wants to have me on board immediately . . . My journey has been al- together pleasant, and has furnished me with some curious remarks, which I shall endeavour to write down on board the 'Illustrious.'"

The following is his letter, written next day, from on board the Admiral's flag-ship :—

"'*Illustrious,*'
[Off Corunna]
"*Sep.* 11*th*, 1804.

"Dear Bartle,

"The appearance of things here is very sus- picious and alarming, to say the least of it. An armament is going on, and troops embarking, which is directly contrary to the principle of the *status quo* which was admitted by Cevallos, and which was understood to be settled as the condition to be complied with by Spain as long as England forbore to attack her. We are apprehensive of ships coming round from Cadiz. Duff should be written to to send advices of what is going on [there] both [to the officer] here, and to you at Madrid. You must remonstrate against these pre- parations, and if you will look back to Cevallo's note, you will find one in which he expressly agrees to remain in unarmed *statu quo*.

*   *   *   *   *   *

"It will be a civil thing in you to send the English newspapers to Admiral Cochrane ; he gets the 'Courier de Londres.'"

He subsequently went home in the "Naiad," from on board which he wrote to his brother.—

"Before I go on further, I must tell you what ship I am going on board of ; it is the 'Naiad,' Captain Wallis, who is used to be unlucky with his ambassadors, having nearly drowned Tom Grenville. The 'Illustrious' is to remain here. We expect to be home in two or three days if the wind holds. At this moment it is very fair, and likely to last, as they think. I have opened your dispatch ; the tone of Cevallo's note is, indeed, striking. If you could find any of the little *concioneros*, and an opportunity to send it, it would give me an opportunity of paying an attention to Sir Charles Hamilton, who reads Spanish, and wishes to get one of them. I do not know whether you know that he is captain of the 'Illustrious,' and that I should have gone with him if he had not been detained, and the 'Naiad' ordered home instead. It should be sent to him here."

Later in September, after Mr. Frere had sailed for England, the British Government learnt that detachments of French troops, amounting in all to 1,500 men, had passed from Bayonne to Ferrol, where a French squadron was lying ; and that the Spanish Government had ordered the immediate armament at that port of three ships of the line, and several smaller vessels ; that similar orders had been sent to Cadiz and Carthagena ; that three ships of the line had been sent round from Cadiz to Ferrol, and instructions given to arm the packets as in time of war ; that within a month eleven ships of the line would be ready for sea at Ferrol, where soldiers were daily arriving from France, and there seemed every reason to believe that the Spanish Government only awaited the arrival of the treasure frigates from America to commence hostilities against Great Britain.

Mr. Bartle Frere presented upon this a strong remonstrance to the Government at Madrid, in the following terms :—

"That the total cessation of all naval preparations in the ports of Spain having been the principal condition required by England, and agreed to by Spain, as the price of the forbearance of Great Britain, the present violation of this condition can be considered in no other light but as a hostile aggression on the part of Spain, and a defiance given to England. These preparations become still more menacing from a squadron of the enemy being in the port where they are carrying on. In no case can England be indifferent to the armament which is preparing, and I entreat you to consider the disastrous consequences which will ensue if the misery which presses so heavily on this country be completed by plunging it unnecessarily into a ruinous war."

To this note 'the Prince of the Peace' replied that "the King of Spain had never thought of being wanting to the agreement entered into with the British Government. The cessation of all naval armaments against Great Britain shall be observed as heretofore; and whatever information to the contrary may have been received is wholly unfounded, and derogatory to the honour of the Spanish nation."

In the mean time Mr. Frere had arrived in England. Of his reception there he gives the following account in a letter written to his brother Bartle at Madrid :—

"MY DEAR BROTHER,

"I do not know whether I shall have time to say all I have to say, and I will begin with the most essential. I have been perfectly well received by the King, with an appearance of real kindness and interest about me. I have seen Pitt for a moment only, and not alone, and was very kindly received by him also. He is now out of town. Harrowby would have received me kindly likewise, but I would not let him. I gave him a lecture, but shall admit him to a reconciliation shortly. He is disposed, I believe, to make amends by doing something for you. For myself, I have, after due reflection upon the folly and meanness of people (not three of whom would understand my retirement as anything but an unavoidable retreat from disgrace), and, moreover, being mollified by the King, and thirdly, and more especially, to distinguish myself from ——, and fourthly and lastly, for fear that fellow ——— should be a Privy Councillor before me, I have, I say, determined to become a member of that learned body if it is offered me, which I can have no doubt that it will."

After a number of reasons, in a similar tone of banter, for not seeking the honours of the Bath, which he had reason to believe might have been added, had he expressed a wish for them, as a further mark that his conduct in his very difficult position at Madrid was approved by the King and the Ministry, he proceeds :—

"The only objection to this is that, in Spain— ; but what signifies? I was going to say—that, in Spain, 'Consejero di Estado with a pension,' sounds something like a forced retreat; however, I flatter myself that the thing will be known to be otherwise, especially if Woronzof writes to Moravief. He was at Saltram,[1] when I called there to see that noble and new-married peer, Lord Boringdon ;[2] and

---

[1] Lord Boringdon's seat in Devonshire.

[2] John Parker, second Lord Boringdon, married, June 1804, a daughter of Lord Westmorland. He was, in 1815, created Viscount Boringdon and Earl of Morley.

when I went to Weymouth I found him paying his duty to the real King (you do not know that Boringdon's name, or rather one of them, is King). He happened to be with Harrowby when I called upon him. Wellesley is to go out if anybody goes." *   *   *   *

After some directions regarding his servants, furniture, &c., at Madrid, he proceeds :—

"With respect to your instructions, which I approve of, there is only one point, in the last page but one, which I think would place us in the necessity of giving a declaration of our intention with respect to Spain, in return for the communication of their engagements towards France ; but Hammond and I are both of opinion that this point of your instructions would be effectually fulfilled by confining the demand of explanation to the point of whether any or what assistance, other than money, has been stipulated to be afforded to France during the present war, as by this we may avoid the demand of an explanation in return. I am only returned from Weymouth and Southill (Canning's place) since last night, and have not yet seen either George or my sisters. My last stay here was only one day, and entirely occupied with Cabinet &c. Mulgrave was, as I conjectured, the author of all this *brouillamini*.

"My mother writes me word that my father is very well, and writes herself in good spirits.

"Excuse me to Moravief for not writing to him ; but Hammond is pressing and the messenger waiting.

"Yours affectionately,

"*Sunday*, 30 *Sepr.*, 11 A. M."   "J. H. FRERE."

In a postscript he gives some directions regarding Spanish books and messages to his friends Mr. and Mrs. Hunter, at Madrid, and adds :—

"I saw Lady Erroll[1] last night; she does not give a very good account of herself. I am going to see her again this morning. You are in very high favour."

The misunderstanding with Lord Harrowby appears to have arisen from an unfounded report, earlier in the year, that Mr. Frere had left Madrid after a violent difference with the "Prince of the Peace," and without waiting for recall by his own Government. Under date May 12th, 1804, there is an entry in Lord Malmesbury's diary to this effect :—

"Frere has actually left Madrid, and appointed his brother *chargé des affaires* of his own head, and without any orders from home. His despatches state a conversation in which he differed violently with the 'Prince of Peace;' but nothing can justify such an unauthorized step."[2]

That Lord Malmesbury had been misinformed is clear from the fact that Mr. Frere did not leave till more than four months afterwards, and his position is explained by a further entry in Lord Malmesbury's diary in October :—

"About the end of September Frere returned from Spain, and I had a great deal of very long and interesting conversation with him during the first week in October. He states Spain on the eve of a revolution—not a *French*, but Spanish revolution, so very unpopular are the Court and Government, that is to say, the Queen and the 'Prince of Peace.'"

"I asked him, supposing we had 20,000 dispos-

---

[1] This lady, whom he subsequently married in 1816, was Elizabeth Jemima Blake, daughter of Joseph Blake, Esq., of Ardfry, co. Galway, and sister of the first Lord Wallscourt. She was at this time widow of George, fifteenth Earl of Erroll.

[2] "Diaries and Correspondence of James Harris, first Earl of Malmesbury," edited by his grandson the third Earl. Bentley, 1844, vol. iv. p. 305.

able men, whether such a force would be equal to produce this *Spanish* revolution, and to prevent Buonaparte from availing himself of it. Frere did not doubt it. He said the people were more anti-French than ever, and if they had ministers in whom they confided, and the King left to himself, he was persuaded, with the sort of force I mentioned, Spain might be saved, and become a close, steady, and most useful friend and ally to England. Frere was much hurt at his being recalled ; said he could have effected anything in Spain, and that the ordering him away was as unwise towards the public as unfair towards him. (Allowances must always be made when a man, even an honest and good one like Frere, argues his own cause.)"[1]

In the debate which took place some months afterwards, on the 11th February, 1805, relative to the war with Spain, Mr. Pitt explained the circumstances under which it had, in the year previous, been proposed to recall Mr. Frere; expressing at the same time the sense which the ministry entertained of the ability with which he had acted in a very difficult position.

After describing the hostile character of the engagements into which Spain had entered with France, and enlarging on the unusual forbearance shown by Great Britain to Spain, and on our sincere anxiety not to press hardly on a power which we believed to be acting under a sense of imperious necessity and not from ill-will, Mr. Pitt said :—

" Desirous, however, of affording every facility and removing every obstacle to an amicable arrangement, it was resolved to recall Mr. Frere, in consequence of circumstances having occurred that made it impossible for him any longer to communicate personally with the 'Prince of Peace.' Upon the nature of that difference, which has no relation

---

[1] "Malmesbury Diaries," vol. iv. p. 330.

to the present subject, it is not necessary for me to enlarge. In justice to Mr. Frere, however, I must say that it arose, without any fault on his part, from a most unprovoked, unwarrantable conduct in that person who, though without ostensible office, is known to have the most leading influence in the councils of Spain. Nevertheless, much as Ministers respected the talents and were sensible of the services of that gentleman who had so ably filled the place of Ambassador to the Court of Madrid during a difficult and critical period, they were determined that no collateral obstacles should stand in the way of a friendly termination of discussions in which the public interest was so much concerned. They had reasons of policy for not driving matters precipitately to extremity, and, reserving the right of war should circumstances demand its exercise, they continued to leave an opening for conciliation and arrangement.

"It was intended to send another gentleman to succeed Mr. Frere, the latter returning home on leave of absence. The same vessel, however, which brought Mr. Frere home on the 17th September, brought letters from Admiral Cochrane, which proved in the clearest manner the violation of that condition on which the forbearance of His Majesty's Government had particularly been founded."[1]

Speaking, in after life, of his intercourse with Lord Malmesbury about this time, Mr. Frere said :—

"He was very kind to me as a young man, and when I returned first from Spain. He had seen a great deal of diplomatic life, and gave me some excellent advice, which I afterwards found of great use. Among other things, the use of rascals in doing any dirty piece of work, which it may be necessary to have done. He said 'it was of the utmost importance never to mix up yourself in any

---

[1] "Pitt's Speeches," ed. 1817, vol. iii. pp. 395-6.

such business. You could always meet with foreign adventurers ready for anything of the kind.' It was old advice, and he quoted a Greek proverb, to the effect that you may often have to act—

> ' Not with rascals altogether,
> Nor without a rascal either.'

You must sometimes be connected with such fellows. The great art is to know how far and where you must use them.

"Lord Malmesbury used also to point out a truth which we are very apt to forget, in judging of the feelings of continental nations towards us, that they are jealous of England's commercial ascendancy, not apprehensive of military aggression, with any view to mere extension of our territory. You will find plenty of evidence of this in Lord Malmesbury's diaries and dispatches, whether he is writing of Russia, of Germany, or of France, and of times anterior to the French Revolution. Catherine of Russia had the feeling nearly as strongly as Napoleon. Napoleon's plans for excluding English commerce from the continent would have been generally popular, had his measures for enforcing his decrees not been carried out so despotically that they were almost as insulting to the continental nations as to England."

The Ministry had signified their full approval of Mr. Frere's conduct, in the very difficult and delicate position in which he was placed at Madrid, by making him a Privy Councillor, and granting him a pension. He did not immediately seek re-employment abroad, nor take any steps to re-enter Parliament or public life at home ; and before his successor could arrive at Madrid, hostilities were precipitated by an unlucky accident, which for a time deprived England of her vantage ground as the injured and forbearing party in the precarious neutrality which had with so much difficulty been maintained since the renewal of the war between England and France. The naval armaments were not stopped by the Spanish Government, as promised in their replies to Mr. Bartle Frere, and the orders given by the British Cabinet to their admirals in the Mediterranean and on the Spanish coast, led to the detention off Cadiz of four Spanish treasure frigates, the safe arrival of which in a Spanish port had been long expected, as likely to be followed by an explicit declaration of hostilities on the part of the Spanish government.

The intercepting force of British frigates was barely equal to that of the Spaniards, who consequently refused to submit to detention, and an engagement ensued, in the course of which one Spanish frigate blew up, with considerable loss of life, and the rest were captured. This occurred on the 5th October, two days only after the date of the Spanish note already quoted, which reiterated former promises for a cessation of all naval armaments, and while the British Chargé d'Affaires was still at Madrid.

War was formally declared by Spain on the 12th December ; and the circumstances under which the final breach occurred, gave to it at first more of the character of a contest in defence of Spanish national honour, than if it had been forced on, as must sooner or later have been the case, by French pressure.[1]

The rupture with Spain placed at the disposal of Napoleon a most important addition to his means for carrying on the war against England. At this time, his thoughts and resources were mainly devoted to equip the vast army which he had concentrated round Boulogne, and to provide it with a flotilla, and all other means necessary for the invasion of England. The one thing needed was such a fleet as should enable him effectually to sweep

---

[1] Vide "Alison," vol. v. chap. 38.

the channel, and, "for but fifteen days," to remain master of the sea. This, he felt assured, would enable him to land an army of 150,000 men, complete with all artillery and munitions of war on the English coast; and once there, he never doubted his own power to strike a decisive and mortal blow at the independence of his great enemy.

But hitherto the creation of such a fleet as could give him even a momentary command of the channel, had baffled all Napoleon's energy and resources. Each separate French squadron was hopelessly shut up in its own port by the indefatigable English sea-captains; and while the arduous blockading service created and improved the best class of British sailors, the French seamen lost heart, as every month of enforced idleness debarred them from the practice necessary to give them confidence in the hour of trial.

The Spanish fleet still ranked third in numerical strength among the navies of Europe; and the curse of long misgovernment had told less on its efficiency than on that of other branches of the administration. Spain could recruit her sailors from among hardy mariners, practised in battling alike with tropical hurricanes, and with the fierce pirates of many a distant colonial sea. Her captains were used to long voyages to Manilla and Peru, and round the Horn. She had, in short, all those national resources without which even the genius of Napoleon was powerless to create a navy.

With the marine of such an ally at his disposal, nothing remained but to concentrate the French and Spanish squadrons into one fleet, in order to enable him to attempt the invasion of England. It was not till after this concentration had been frustrated, and the combined French and Spanish fleets had been almost annihilated at Trafalgar, on the 21st of October following (1805), that England realized the greatness of the danger she had escaped, or knew what she owed to the energy and seamanship, as well as to the heroic bravery and self-devotion of Nelson and Collingwood.

Though not actively employed, Mr. Frere was by no means an unconcerned spectator of the great events which took place, and the important questions which were discussed between his return from Spain in 1804, and his second mission thither in 1808.

When Lord Melville's (Dundas) administration of the navy was made the subject of Parliamentary inquiry in 1805, and of impeachment in the year following, he warmly espoused the cause of the Ex-Treasurer. Like many of Pitt's younger and more ardent followers, he had sometimes chafed at the obstacles which Dundas offered, when Pitt would willingly have given effect to his own enlightened views, on such questions as Slavery and Catholic Emancipation ; but Mr. Frere had not only a firm conviction of Dundas's perfect personal integrity, but a strong sense of the debt of gratitude which the nation owed him, as the most sagacious, and most consistent, if not the ablest of all Pitt's personal friends ; and as the man, to whom more than any one in or out of Parliament, the navy was indebted for its high state of fighting efficiency.

He always believed that hostility to Pitt was the mainspring of the impeachment ; and he risked a breach, on behalf of his opinion, with some of his oldest and most valued friends, who objected to strike a balance between the value of Dundas's public services, and the irregularities of practice which had been permitted to pass uncorrected during his administration of the navy.

Again, with regard to the measures for Catholic Emancipation, which were brought forward in the Session of 1805-6, he entirely concurred in the view taken by Pitt. Speaking in later life (1828-30), of Pitt's dealing with the question at this time, he said :—

"It is not true that Pitt ever regarded Catholic Emancipation as a sop to be offered to the Irish to make them accept the Union.   On the contrary, I know that Pitt regarded the emancipation of the Catholics as the more important measure of the two, and he would gladly have carried it at any time.   But, when he first came into power, he saw the danger in bringing it forward, unless Ireland were previously united to England and Scotland. As he could not carry both measures together, which was his own original plan, he was glad to carry the Union, and always regarded it as paving the way for emancipation.

"But Pitt was quite right to resist the Catholic question being brought forward in 1805, when there was no possible chance of its being settled.   No one could have supported it at such a time but those who wished to embarrass Pitt, or who were pedantically determined to discuss it in or out of season.   Pitt knew that if he took it up, it must alienate some of his best supporters,—that the mere discussion would, in all likelihood, quite overset the King, who was not by any means recovered from his attack of the year before ; and the country was to be thrown into all this confusion at the moment when we were engaged in a struggle for bare existence, and when any relaxation of our efforts might lead to immediate invasion.   The blame of the delay in redressing the Roman Catholic grievances rests not with Pitt, but with those who were in power when the war came to an end.

"The state of the King's health was one of Pitt's great difficulties at this time, and contributed almost as much as the defection of old adherents, and the loss of Dundas, to break him down.   I had seen a great change in the King when I had an audience on my return from Madrid ; he was very clear and sensible on all that related to public

affairs, but morbidly inquisitive about other matters.
*   *   *   He was a most extraordinary
man, both in his strong and weak points. After
Pitt's death he was obliged to take in the Whigs,
and he did it with a good grace. But he never got
over his great personal dislike to them ; and the
very first time they gave him an opportunity, he
turned them out. This he did, in spite of all his
mental and physical infirmities, entirely by himself,
and without taking any one into his confidence.

"All the time the Whigs were in, there were
Tory courtiers about him who would have given
the world to have spoken to him on politics, and
who never, even in his rides, could get him to open
his mouth. But the instant the Whigs made a
false move, he saw it, and kicked them out."

Mr. Frere looked on Pitt's labours at this period,
the organization of the national defence against
invasion, and the reconstruction of the European
combination against Napoleon from the renewal of
the war till his death in 1806, as, under all the circumstances, the most wonderful proofs of his foresight and ability, and as ranking among the most
important services he rendered to his country and
to Europe. "It was true," he said, "that, for the
time, all Pitt's plans seemed frustrated by disasters
like Austerlitz and Jena, by the selfish blindness
and indecision of the Allies, and by the extraordinary ability of Napoleon. Still, the principles
of the combination which was at length successful
ten years later, were clearly laid down by Pitt in
1805 ; and all that was good and beneficial to
Europe in the settlement of 1815, was marked out
by him before he died. This he did, too, under the
deepest discouragement. In failing health, and
almost alone ; for, though the nation was with him,
his difficulties in Parliament were greater than they
had been since he first entered office ; and, with the

exception of Canning, hardly one of his immediate followers fully entered into all his views."

In June, 1807, when there appeared some brief hope that Prussia might be able to maintain an alliance with Russia and England in making head against France, Mr. Frere was appointed by the Portland Ministry Envoy and Minister Plenipotentiary to Berlin. But the Treaty of Tilsit in the following month closed the north of Europe against England, and prevented his setting out on that mission.

He used frequently in later life to refer to this period as the gloomiest and most critical in our history since England became a first-class European power. Pitt was dead, and so was his great rival. No one had arisen with genius or authority comparable to Pitt's, or capable of directing the energies of the nation in its great struggle for existence. Canning, whom, as Mr. Frere believed, Pitt had always regarded as his political heir, was still in a comparatively subordinate position, and suffered from the dread with which dull sensible men are apt to regard genius and wit. The short experience of Whig administration had not shown that the ranks of Pitt's old opponents contained the man fitted to take his place in the confidence of the nation.

Had it been possible to believe that Napoleon would rest content with the vast empire he had acquired, the people of England would, in 1807 even more than at any other time, have rejoiced to see an end to the war which had so heavily taxed their resources. But his imperial ambition was continually affording fresh proof of the hopelessness of any such termination of the struggle, and with the light which his own correspondence affords, it is now clear that no permanent peace, on terms honourable to England, would ever have been tolerated by him. The whole continent, it is true, was at his feet. From the Atlantic to the Russian frontier not a cannon could be fired without his leave, and so completely had he fascinated the Emperor of Russia, that the partition of the Turkish empire between France and Russia seemed no improbable or remote result of their alliance. But Napoleon knew that the vast fabric of power which he had raised was not safe while England, his nearest neighbour, was really free and independent. His plans for invading and subjugating his insular rival, which had been delayed by the campaign of Austerlitz, and for the time frustrated by Trafalgar, had never been absent from his mind, and he resumed their active development directly Jena and Tilsit seemed to have placed Germany finally under his yoke. He believed that he possessed all the means required to reduce England to the level, at least, of Prussia and Austria, except such a navy as would make him, if but for a few days, master of the Channel. Spain alone, of all European nations, offered the means of rendering the fleets at his command superior to those of England, and to Spain he turned with the determination to weld the forces of the Peninsula, and especially its marine, into one with those of the French empire. He had already under the treaty of St. Ildefonso, absolute control over all Spanish fleets and armies; but he knew that under such a rule as that of Charles IV. the vast natural resources of Spain and her colonies would be ineffectually wasted, and that even the subserviency of the " Prince of the Peace" was a poor substitute for the vigour with which he could himself act on the administration through a king of his own making, or through his own military commanders. Thus his impatience to apply the power of Spain to further his great purpose of forming an irresistible navy, drove him into what he himself subsequently acknowledged as one of the capital errors of his career. Assured of the connivance of Russia, he was led step by step into the secret treaty and convention of Fontainbleau (May, 1806, and Oct. 1807) with Charles IV., by which Portugal was to be partitioned for the benefit of France and Spain—into the seizure of the Spanish frontier fortresses, and into all the treacheries which followed the meeting of the Spanish royal family with Napoleon at Bayonne, the forced abdications of the king and his son Ferdinand—the Bayonne constitution, the bestowal of the Spanish Crown on Joseph Buonaparte, and the French invasion of the peninsula in support of the usurpation.

In May and June, 1808, all Europe was startled by the explosion which Mr. Frere had foreseen as imminent in Spain two years before, and which he had then foretold to Lord Malmesbury.[1] It naturally, under the circumstances, took the form of an insurrection against the foreign invader, and in favour of Ferdinand, who was regarded by the clergy, the common people, and the great bulk of the nobility, as their legitimate Sovereign. In every part of the peninsula, in the remotest villages, and in the almost inaccessible sierras of the distant provinces, as well as in the great cities, the insurrection broke out with a violence, an unanimity, and a suddenness to which neither before nor since has modern Europe seen any parallel. The French garrisons speedily found that they commanded no more than their guns covered. The people everywhere assembled, seized such arms as they could lay hands on, appointed leaders, organized Juntas as a form of local government, and issued proclamations detailing the wrongs and insults the nation had suffered, and calling on all true Spaniards to join in expelling the invader from their soil. In some cases terrible massacres of the French or their supposed partizans disgraced

---

[1] " Malmesbury Diaries," vol. iv. p. 330, as quoted, *anteà*, p. 68.

the popular cause; but, in general, the people be-
haved with wonderful self-command, and with a
dignity which added greatly to the moral effect
produced by the insurrection on the rest of Europe.
The leading Juntas took prompt and effectual steps
to appeal for sympathy and aid to all foreign
nations, and especially to England, the only power
which had never either succumbed to the force or
yielded to the seductions of the Arbiter of Continental Europe.

Spain was peculiarly fitted for the part she thus
took in an insurrection against the imperial despotism of France. The people were, as Napoleon's
sagacity had before pointed out, "unexhausted by
revolutionary passion." Peculiarities of race combined with the physical features of the country,
and with the history and traditions of the many
nations which make up its population, to render the
Spaniards a people dwelling apart not only from
the rest of Europe, but divided very distinctly
among themselves into separate communities independent of each other; so that the subjugation or
destruction of one province would have little effect
in ensuring the submission of its neighbours. The
consequent division of interests, feelings, and action,
which so often led to subsequent disaster, at first
greatly promoted the spread of the insurrection.
On a few vital points—their national pride, their
devotion to their national religion, their obedience
to its ministers, and their indignation at the treatment the nation and the royal family had received
at the hands of Napoleon—the mass of the population felt as one man, and all determined to resist
the invader. But each city and province took its
own measures for organizing resistance; and, till
bitter experience taught them some of the evils of
disunion, each acted as if it had been a separate and
perfectly independent power.

By the end of May, or early in June (1808), the

Juntas had been organized in most of the provinces; that of Seville had secured the co-operation of the Spanish divisions under Castaños in the south of the peninsula, and through him had opened friendly relations with Sir Hew Dalrymple, the English commander at Gibraltar ; had formally declared war against France, and had issued a manifesto which was accepted by England and other powers of Europe as the national declaration of Spain against Napoleon. By the middle of June the French squadron in Cadiz was captured, and the garrisons of Ferrol and Corunna had already declared for the national cause. Before the end of July, Dupont, with 20,000 excellent French troops had been confronted in his march on Cadiz, and forced to lay down his arms to Castaños at Baylen— the first great and decided reverse which had befallen the French armies in a fair field since the revolutionary wars began. Joseph Buonaparte upon this hastily quitted Madrid, and the capital was once more left in the sole possession of Spanish troops.

Napoleon had clearly foreseen the danger. Writing from Bayonne to Murat at Madrid, in March, 1808, before he had entirely thrown off the mask, he said :—" Never suppose that you are engaged with a disarmed nation, and that you have only to show yourself to insure the submission of Spain. * * * They have still energy. You have to deal with a virgin people. They already have all the courage, and they will soon have all the enthusiasm which you meet with among men who are not worn out by political passions.

" The aristocracy and the clergy are the masters of Spain. If they become seriously alarmed for their privileges and existence, they will rouse the people, and induce an eternal war. At present I have many partizans among them. If I show myself as a conqueror, I shall soon cease to have any." * * *

After pointing out how effectually England might act on the coast, and discussing all possible plans for governing the country under French dictation, he winds up with the emphatic declaration,—" If war break out, all is lost."

In exile at St. Helena, he very truly said :—" It was that unhappy war in Spain which ruined me. It was a real wound, the first cause of the misfortunes of France." When the insurrection did break out, he never underrated its importance, but determined to crush it at once. In his earliest instructions he had charged his generals, "above all, take care to avoid any misfortune in Spain ; its consequences would be incalculable." Dupont's surrender, and Joseph's consequent retreat from the capital, were two misfortunes regarding the gravity of which there could be no mistake. The Emperor well knew that the Assembly of Notables at Bayonne were no true representatives of the Spanish nation, and that their assent to his usurpation was of little practical value. But he had confidence in his own power to carry out a thoroughly effective military occupation of the peninsula. He ordered his best troops and most trusted marshals to march for Spain. The better to organize operations, he returned to Paris in August. In September he met the Emperor of Russia at Erfurth ; made a favour to Prussia of withdrawing from the military occupation, which had lasted since Jena, the veteran troops he needed in Spain ; did his best to overawe Austria, already showing signs of impatience under his yoke ; and, having confirmed his influence over Alexander, attempted, with the help of Russia, to negotiate with England, and to neutralize her hostility that he might deal with Spain single-handed. But England had already determined to make common cause with the Spaniards. The deputies from the Asturian Junta had arrived in London early in June, and each successive post brought news of the spread of the insurrection. The general enthusiasm of the Spaniards left no room for doubting that it was a really national and popular movement, essentially different in its origin, character, and extent, from anything which had previously occurred on the Continent to check the uninterrupted success of Napoleon's career. Sheridan vied with Canning in eulogizing the conduct of the Spanish patriots, and the Opposition cordially supported the Ministry when they declared their intention of sending British troops to aid the Spaniards in asserting their independence.

There are few portions of modern history with which Englishmen are better acquainted than with the details of the contest on which England thus entered. The story has been told in the stately periods of Southey, and by the burning eloquence of Napier. In the two wonderful series of volumes more lately published, containing the correspondence of the great soldiers who directed the armies of England and France, Wellington and Napoleon have themselves recorded for posterity the minutest details of their own plans, and much criticism of their opponents. In this short biographical sketch it is only necessary that I should very briefly allude to those events of this well-known history with which Mr. Frere was officially connected.

His previous services in Spain, his warm sympathy with all the nobler traits of Spanish character, his intimate acquaintance with the Spanish language and manners, and, above all, the esteem and respect in which he was held by all the best among the leaders in the Spanish national cause, to many of whom he was personally known, pointed him out as eminently fitted to represent England in Spain at a juncture of such importance, and on the 4th of October, 1808, he was accredited as British Minister Plenipotentiary to Ferdinand VII., then represented by the Central Junta, at whose place of assembly Mr. Frere had instructions to take up his residence.

He had already been partly instrumental in restoring to the armies of Spain a very important reinforcement. The story of the mode in which a Spanish division under the Marquis de Romana was released from Denmark and transferred to Spain has been repeatedly told ; but Mr. Frere's connexion with the enterprise will justify a recapitulation of some of its romantic details. It had been a part of Napoleon's policy in Spain, as in most other countries which he occupied, to weaken the national power of resistance to his encroachments, by transferring the flower of the regular army to distant foreign service ; and one of the first uses he made of the control he acquired over the Spanish armies in 1807 was to march Romana's division of about 14,000 men to Hamburg and thence into Denmark, where it was destined to join the Franco-Danish army which Marshal Bernadotte was collecting for the invasion of Sweden. Here they were closely watched and cut off from all intercourse with Spain. In March, 1808, the Spanish division had commenced crossing the Belts, when their movement was interrupted by the appearance of British cruisers, which captured a Danish ship of the line, and for more than three months prevented the transit of the invading force to the shores of Sweden. The oath of allegiance to Joseph Buonaparte and to the Napoleonic constitution in Spain had previously been tendered to the Spanish troops ; but their suspicions were aroused by the circumstance that no private or other letters accompanied the public despatch forwarding the oath of allegiance, and that no intelligence was allowed to reach Spaniards in Denmark except through the French press, or through channels controlled by the French Government. Some of them, however, took the oath without much demur. Others, including the troops nearest Romana's head quarters, took it conditionally, with a proviso that their oath should be null unless the Revolution were confirmed by the general consent of the Spanish nation ; and two regiments' absolutely refused the oath, rose on their French commandant, and planting their colours knelt round them and swore to be faithful to their country.

When the insurrection against the intrusive government in Spain spread to the army under Castaños, it was one of his first requests to Sir Hew Dalrymple, at Gibraltar, that the Spanish troops in the Baltic might be apprised of the turn affairs had taken in their native country, and that the English would open communication with Romana. But watched as the Spaniards were by the French, and in Denmark, with which we were then at war, this was a matter of the utmost difficulty and danger. The task was undertaken by a priest named Robertson, an accomplished linguist ; and, as it was impossible to risk the danger attaching to written credentials, he was instructed to use, as his passport to Romana's confidence, a verse from the Gests of the Cid. Mr. Frere, when at Madrid some years before, had suggested to Romana a conjectural emendation in a verse,[1] the mention of which, as it could only be known to the two friends, would satisfy Romana that Robertson had communicated with Mr. Frere, and that his intelligence might be relied on.

Robertson started for Heligoland with Mr. Mackenzie, who was charged to aid him in landing on the continent. Throughout the war the little island was used as a rendezvous for our cruisers and an entrepôt for the British commerce, which was ex-

---

[1] "Aun vea el hora que vos *merezca dos* tanto," v. 2348, where Mr. Frere proposed to read *merezcades*, an emendation of which Romana at once perceived the propriety.

cluded by the decrees of Napoleon from direct
admission to any continental port. On their arrival, the Governor placed an embargo on all the
shipping there, and Robertson started in a boat to
the nearest shore ; but it was found impossible for
any one unprovided with a passport to elude the
vigilance of the French and Danish officials, and
after three days he returned without effecting a
landing. Mackenzie, however, found the master of
a captured Bremen vessel, who promised, if his
vessel were released, to land Robertson in safety
and provide him with a passport. The Bremener
had a near relation among the city officials, with
whose help he fulfilled his engagement. Robertson, in the character of a German schoolmaster,
made his way to Romana's presence ; and having
accredited himself by his verse from the Cid, detailed to him in Latin the course which events had
taken in the Peninsula. Romana at once resolved
to effect his escape from Denmark, with his whole
force, provided he could obtain the assistance of
the British naval and military commanders, who
were then in the Baltic supporting the Swedes in
their resistance to the threatened French invasion.
Robertson returned to Heligoland with this assurance, and with a request that Mackenzie would
communicate with Sir John Moore, who then commanded the British Auxiliaries in Sweden, and
procure his aid in covering the retreat and embarca-
tion of the Spaniards. The requisite orders were
issued by the British Government, and within a
week Mackenzie received letters for Sir John
Moore, which he determined to carry himself to
Gottenburg. But when he arrived on the Swedish
coast, the British troops had already sailed for
England. Returning to Heligoland, the packet in
which he sailed was driven by a gale on to the
Danish coast. There he fell in with a Danish pri-
vateer of greatly superior force, and after a running

fight of four hours, escaped with difficulty back to Gottenburg. He then determined to communicate with Sir James Saumerez, the British Admiral in the Baltic. This he at length accomplished. Sir James at once determined to effect the release of the Spaniards. Under his orders Sir Richard Keats had commenced the necessary arrangements, when Sir James received despatches from his own government suggesting the course he had already adopted; and a Spanish courier brought from London letters from the Junta of Gallicia and others in Spain, for Romana and his second in command.

To convey these to the Spanish camp, and when all was arranged with the leaders to keep the contemplated movements secret; to concentrate and embark the scattered Spanish troops from an enemy's country and in the presence of the hostile forces of France and Denmark, was still an operation of the greatest difficulty. The Spanish regiments were quartered, widely apart, in various towns on the mainland of Jutland, and in several islands in the Baltic. A young Spanish officer crossing from one island to the other was taken prisoner by the British squadron, enlisted in the cause, and sent on with letters for Romana. But the fact that he had communicated with the British squadron was discovered by the French Commandant, whose suspicions had been already aroused, and Romana resolved to prevent interruption from the Danes by seizing Nyborg. This was effected with Admiral Keats' help, after a determined resistance on the part of some of the Danish officers, who, faithful to their French allies, refused to aid the Spaniards. The captured gunboats and coasting craft afforded the means of collecting and embarking such of the Spanish regiments as could reach the coast near Admiral Keats' squadron. One regiment marched eighty miles in twenty-one hours, and all made incredible exertions to rejoin

their countrymen.   Many hair-breadth escapes and
romantic incidents occurred while the Spaniards
and their English naval allies were engaged in this
perilous service.   At length nine thousand men,
besides followers, were landed on the Swedish
shore, and there first learnt the details of the wonderful success which had attended the early efforts
of their countrymen to eject the French invaders.
By the end of August transports arrived from England to embark them, and they sailed for Spain.
Romana, on his way to Corunna, visited England
to confer with the Ministry, and learn their views
regarding the future conduct of the war, and did
not reach Spain till later in the year.

The British Government meanwhile had not been
idle.   They had from the first resolved to support
the insurrection vigorously.   Mr. Canning and Lord
Castlereagh at this time held the seals of the Foreign and the War Departments in the Duke of
Portland's Ministry.   When the news of the Spanish insurrection first arrived in England, an expedition of about 10,000 men, organized by the preceding administration, was about to sail from Cork for
South America.   It was determined to divert to
Portugal this force under command of Sir Arthur
Wellesley; and Sir John Moore, who had been
sent to Sweden to assist in repelling the French
and Russian invasion, and whose aid had been declined by the King of Sweden, was recalled and
directed to sail for the Peninsula.   Sir Arthur
Wellesley's expedition left Cork on the 12th July,
1808.   The General himself reached Corunna on
the 20th, and learning there that the Junta of Gallicia did not wish for the aid of his troops, he supplied them with arms and money and proceeded to
Portugal, the liberation of which was the first object
of his instructions.   Off Mondego Bay he learnt
that he was to be superseded as soon as Sir Harry
Burrard should arrive, and that Burrard again was

to give place to Sir Hew Dalrymple as soon as he could come round from Gibraltar. But hearing at the same time of the surrender of Dupon's army to Castaños, and seeing the opportunity, if no time were lost, for striking an effective blow against the French under Junot at Lisbon, Wellesley landed on the 1st of August with less than 10,000 men to face the 25,000 French soldiers, who then garrisoned Portugal. Being opportunely reinforced by General Spencer, who had anticipated his orders to join him from the south of Spain, Wellesley, undeterred by the delays of the Portuguese, pushed on to attack Junot. On the 15th of August the first British blood was shed in a skirmish with the French advanced guard. At Roliça, on the 17th, Sir Arthur gained his first victory in the Peninsula, and captured three guns. Junot advanced from Lisbon with all his disposable force to meet him, and Wellesley, who had been reinforced by further arrivals from England, ordered a movement to cut off Junot from the capital. But the reinforcements brought also a senior officer, Sir Harry Burrard, who, before he landed, forbade the move as attended with too much risk. Meantime Junot had attacked Wellesley at Vimiero on the 21st August, and was beaten, with the loss of thirteen guns and 400 prisoners. The victory would have been still more complete had Wellesley been allowed to follow it up. He was, however, superseded on the field by Sir Harry Burrard, who ordered a halt; and Junot, by a forced march, regained the capital unmolested. On the 22nd August, Burrard was himself superseded by Dalrymple. The next day further operations were suspended by a French flag of truce. The Convention of Cintra ensued, and the French army evacuated Portugal, including the strong frontier fortresses of Elvas and Almeida. By the middle of October not a French soldier remained, and the Russian fleet in the Tagus had been surrendered to

English custody. These were great results. They might, however, no doubt have been greater, had Wellesley been left in undisturbed command, to carry out his own plans either before or after the battle of Vimiero. The English nation was profoundly dissatisfied, and directed its anger not against the Minister who sent three Generals to supersede one another on the same field, but against the Generals who signed the Convention. They were all summoned to England to defend their conduct before a Court of Enquiry, and Wellesley was thus prevented from having any chance of testing his opinion that, within a month after the Convention, he could have been at Madrid with 20,000 men.[1] In judging of these operations, as well as of all others that followed them in the Peninsula, it should be borne in mind that Wellesley's difficulties from deficiency of information, of carriage, of roads, of regular supplies, and of cavalry—from uncertain, over-confident, or half-hearted friends, and from concealed enemies, and above all from numerical inferiority of trained soldiers, were the same in kind, and hardly less in degree, than those which he and Moore and every other English general in Spain experienced up to the end of the war. We may thus appreciate the qualities which enabled him from the first to understand the real conditions on which alone he could hope to war successfully in such a country, and the cautious boldness with which he pressed on, till he finally expelled the French from Spain.

Dalrymple, Burrard, and Wellesley, having left or been superseded, Sir John Moore, who had arrived in Portugal some time before, was appointed[2] to command a force of 30,000 infantry and 5,000

---

[1] Gurwood's "Wellington Dispatches," vol. iv. p. 121.

[2] Vide Letter from Lord Castlereagh to Sir J. Moore, dated 25th Sept. 1808.

cavalry, to be employed in the north of Spain, to co-operate with the Spaniards in the expulsion of the French ; and of this force about 15,000 men, expected from England, under Sir David Baird, were to land at Corunna and to join him. Moore's instructions directed that his army was not to be partially committed against the enemy. He was to consider the points in Gallicia or on the borders of Leon, where it could be most advantageously equipped and concentrated, and the routes by which it was to be assembled were left to his discretion. He was to open communications with the Spanish authorities, and to frame a plan of the campaign.

On receipt of these instructions, Moore divided his forces to facilitate their movements, going himself direct to Salamanca, which he reached on the 13th November, and sending the reserves and most of the artillery by a more circuitous route. Baird had landed at Corunna on the 13th October, but was still four marches from Salamanca on the 20th November.

A Central Junta for Spain had been installed at Aranjuez about the end of September. The practical incapacity of most of its members, their irreconcileable jealousies and divisions, and other inherent faults of its constitution, rendered it from the first, incapable of anything like efficient administration. Spain, in fact, up to the end of the Peninsular War, had barely the semblance of an effective central government.

This was, however, the body to which Mr. Frere was accredited as British Envoy and Plenipotentiary. He arrived at Corunna on the 20th October, accompanied by Romana, whose troops, released from Denmark, had already been disembarked.

Mr. Crabb Robinson, who had gone out to Corunna as Correspondent to the "Times," after an account of the landing of Baird's troops on the 13th October, 1808, and their march to the interior on the ex-

pedition which he " understood was ill-planned,"
says :[1]—

"On the 20th there was an arrival which, more
than that of the English, ought to have gratified
the Spaniards. I witnessed a procession from the
coast to the Town Hall, of which the two leading
figures were the Spanish General Romana and the
English Minister Mr. Frere. Few incidents in the
great war against Napoleon can be referred to as
rivalling in romantic interest the escape of the
Spanish soldiers under General Romana from the
North of Germany."

He was disappointed in Romana's appearance,
but adds :—

" I received a favourable impression from the person and address of Mr. Frere ; and when, in a few
months, the public voice in England was raised
against him as the injudicious counsellor who im-
perilled the British army by advising their advance
on Madrid my own feeling was that he was unjustly
treated."

Napoleon's meeting with the Emperor Alexander
at Erfurth, already referred to, had arranged what
was in effect a virtual division of the supremacy of
Europe. Russia was to get undisturbed possession
of Finland, Moldavia, and Wallachia, with great
prospects in Poland and Asia, so as to threaten the
British Indian Empire. Napoleon obtained Russia's
recognition of his conquests in Italy, the Peninsula,
and Germany. The severity of his grasp on Prussia
was to be relaxed in the interests of Russia.

Alexander, on the other hand, was to aid France,
should Austria prove troublesome. Regarding
Turkey only they failed to agree. Neither Emperor could consent to see the other master of Constantinople.

Thus secured for a time against diversions on his

---

[1] "Crabb Robinson's Diary," vol. i. p. 275.

other frontier, Napoleon returned to Bayonne, November 3rd, determined to devote his whole power to crush Spain and Portugal, and to drive the English out of the Peninsula.

He had already drawn to the frontier, from France, Germany, and Italy, 300,000 men, the flower of his veteran army. About 180,000, concentrated under his own eye, were ready for operations west of the Ebro.

To these the Spaniards could oppose less than 75,000, most of them untrained recruits, widely divided, ill-organized, imperfectly armed, under inexperienced and almost independent commanders.

Their British allies, coming up to their aid, were marching on Salamanca by several lines wide apart, and all far in the rear of the Spanish armies.

Early in November, Napoleon let loose "the hurricane of war" which he had so carefully designed. In the course of that month, his Marshals had met and utterly defeated the Spaniards in three decisive battles, driven their divided armies still further asunder, carried the formidable Somosierra pass, and by the 4th of December the Emperor was in possession of Madrid.

Thus, before the end of November, it had become clear that the English were too late and too few to support the Spaniards in holding the line of the Ebro against Napoleon's overwhelming advance. Moore saw the possibility and great political advantages of an advance on Madrid to support the Spaniards in their defence of their capital. But this movement was one of great risk. His own judgment inclined to a retreat and re-embarcation in Portugal, and a renewal of operations in support of the Spanish armies in Southern Spain.

Under these circumstances he, on the 27th November, asked the British Envoy's opinion as to which of these two courses he thought best, with reference to the Spanish nation's power of resistance, and to the probable wishes of the English Cabinet and people, could they know all the circumstances.

Mr. Frere replied on the 30th November, recommending a retreat on Gallicia, or on the strong country about Astorga, as preferable to a retreat on Portugal, if retreat were inevitable. With regard to the temper of the Spanish people, he urged that the spirit of resistance was much stronger in almost every other province than in the open plains of Leon and in Castile.

Recognizing the greater hazard of the forward move, he spoke decidedly of the good spirit of the Spanish people, and hopefully of the Government, adding, " I cannot but think, therefore, that considerations both of policy and generosity call upon us for an immediate effort.

" If, however, this view of the subject should not appear to you sufficiently clear or conclusive to induce you to take a step which would, I am well convinced (since you do me the honour to refer to me on the subject), meet with the approbation of His Majesty's Government, I would venture to recommend retaining the position of Astorga. A retreat from that place to Corunna would (as far as an unmilitary man may be allowed to judge of a country which he has travelled over) be less difficult than through Portugal to Lisbon ; and we ought, in that position, to wait for the reinforcements of cavalry from England, which would enable the army to act in the flat country which opens immediately from that point, and extends through the whole of Leon and Old Castile. My political reasons on this head I have already troubled you with.

" I mention this, however, merely as in my humble opinion the least objectionable of the two modes of retreat. Our first object, as it appears to me, ought to be to collect a force capable of repulsing the French before they receive their reinforcements.

"The covering and protecting Madrid is surely a point of great moment for effect in Spain, and still more in France, and in the West of Europe. It would be a point of the utmost importance for Buonaparte to be able to publish a decree, or to date a letter from Madrid.

"The people of that town are full of resolution, and determined to defend it, in spite of its situation, which is judged to be an unfavourable one. This determination ought surely to be encouraged by some show of support.

"The siege of Madrid by a Pretender to the throne would be a circumstance decisive against the claim, even if in other respects it were a legitimate one."

On the 3rd of December, Mr. Frere wrote again from Talavera, detailing the reports he had received of the spirit of resistance evinced by the populace at Madrid, and strongly urging the necessity of supporting the determination of the Spanish people by all the means in his power.

This letter reached Sir John Moore on the 5th. Baird, on the 29th of November had, in obedience to Moore's orders, commenced a retrograde movement to Villa Franca. Moore now ordered him to stand fast, and to prepare to return to Astorga.

The next day he repeated his orders to return to Astorga, adding, "What is passing at Madrid may be decisive of the fate of Spain, and we must be at hand to aid, and to take advantage of whatever happens. The wishes of our country and our duty demand this of us, with whatever risk it may be attended. I mean to proceed bridle in hand, for if the bubble burst and Madrid fall, we shall have a run for it;" and in view to such a contingency, he desired Baird to continue his preparations for retreat on Corunna.

On the 9th of December, he received certain information that the French had possession of the suburbs of Madrid, but hopes were still held out that the city would resist.

On the 13th, Moore advanced towards Valladolid to join Baird. But learning on the 14th that Madrid had already fallen, he determined to strike a blow against Soult, who in the valley of the Carrion covered the right flank of Napoleon's communications, and then to retreat on Gallicia. On the 20th, he effected a junction with Baird's force at Mayorga, and the next day the British cavalry under Lord Paget surprised the French cavalry, who believed the British to be far off, and in full retreat to their ships. Two colonels and 160 men were made prisoners ; and the French, though greatly superior in force, were utterly routed.

This advance completely paralyzed the southward movements of the French armies. Every other important operation was immediately suspended, and 50,000 men, the flower of the French troops, were ordered, under the Emperor in person, to check the progress of the British. Urging his men, by his own example, in the teeth of a violent wintry hurricane over the Guadarrama Pass, Napoleon, on the 26th of December, established his head quarters at Tordesillas.

Ney meantime was moving from Zamora northwards to cut off Moore's retreat first on Portugal and then on Gallicia ; but Moore had suspended his advance on the 23rd of December, and retiring, reached Benevente before the enemy. There he halted for rest, behind the Esla, swollen and impassable from wintry rains. On the first of January (1809), the Emperor had united at Astorga 70,000 men and 100 pieces of cannon under Soult and Ney. In ten days he had brought 50,000 men 200 miles from Madrid, over mountain ranges and rivers almost impassable, in the depth of winter ; but before arriving at Astorga he was arrested by the news of Austria having joined the confederacy against him; and believing that he had now virtually performed his threat of driving the English into the sea, he left Soult and Ney with 60,000 men to continue the pursuit, and returned with his guards, to meet what he deemed the more pressing dangers threatening him in Germany.

The English continued their retreat, hard pressed by their active and numerous enemies, and suffering almost as much from relaxed discipline as from the terrible severity of the march through inhospitable mountains in the depth of a severe winter. But whenever battle was offered, the old spirit revived. Corunna was reached on the 11th of January. On the 16th, Soult with 20,000 French, and strong in artillery, attacked the British force, reduced to 14,000, weak in artillery, and not advantageously posted. The attack was repulsed with great loss to the enemy, and the British remained masters of the field. But Sir John Moore was mortally wounded in the moment of victory; Baird also was severely hurt, and the command devolved on General Hope, under whom the troops were embarked without further molestation, and sailed for England. Corunna and Ferrol, with seven sail of the line and great naval stores, surrendered to the French a few days afterwards.

Such, in brief, were the events of the first Peninsular campaign. The army under Sir John Moore was the strongest and most complete which England had ever been able to land on the Continent since the Revolutionary wars began. The public in England, with a very inadequate notion of the task before it, had formed the most extravagant expectations of what that army was to do; and their disappointment and anger knew no bounds when the remnant returned home,—so toil-worn and disorganized by exposure and privation, that almost

every corps required complete renewal before it was
fit for further active service.

A victim was required to appease popular discontent. The General who commanded had died
a hero's death on the field of victory, and of those
who took part in the events connected with the
campaign, the next most prominent actor was the
British Minister whose opinions throughout these
operations had been frequently opposed to those of
the General. It was not to be expected that the
Government or their supporters would admit that
the blame of failure was fairly attributable to any
fault in their plans or administration. Contemporary hostile criticism of the General, or his proceedings, was virtually precluded by his death. So upon
the Envoy was cast, by the public and the press, a
share of blame which, under the circumstances,
could hardly fail to be far in excess of what was
deserved.

When Parliament met, a motion was brought
forward by Mr. Ponsonby in the House of Commons (February 24, 1809) "that it is indispensably
necessary that this House should inquire into the
causes, conduct, and events of the late campaign in
Spain." The debate was long remembered as
having been interrupted by the news that Drury
Lane Theatre was on fire, and by a discussion
whether the House should proceed with business
when so much property, in which members and
their constituents were interested, was in jeopardy.
The motion for inquiry was resisted by the Ministers, and after much debate finally rejected on a
division by a majority of 93 in a House of 347. The
Government, however, so far yielded to the popular
feeling of the day, that they determined to recall Mr.
Frere. The appearance of censure was technically
avoided by selecting as his successor the Marquis
Wellesley, fresh from the glories of his Indian
administration, and by appointing him (on the 29th

H

April, 1809,) Ambassador to the Court of the King of Spain, a grade higher than that of Envoy, which was the rank Mr. Frere held. But the supersession was regarded as an unmistakeable censure, which Mr. Frere felt he had not deserved. He thenceforward renounced public life, and when it was proposed to send him as Ambassador to St. Petersburg, and, twice in after years, to raise him to the Peerage, he declined both offers. It was natural he should feel that what he had deserved from the Government, if they approved his conduct, was support and approbation when he was unjustly attacked ; and that no subsequent honours or promotion could compensate for his having been left a mark for public obloquy, when he had under most trying circumstances performed an important service to his country.

It would perhaps have been hardly reasonable to expect from their cotemporaries a perfectly impartial apportionment of praise or blame to the chief actors in these events. It is possible, however, for this generation with a much fuller knowledge of facts than was then accessible to the English public, and after the lapse of sixty years has mitigated personal and party animosities, to form a more dispassionate judgment. It is now clear from Napoleon's correspondence that, in his opinion, the results of the campaign were far more important to the final issue of the great continental struggle, than most of Moore's countrymen at the time believed ; and, what is more, that this opinion of the Emperor's was so well founded, that those results would have justified almost any sacrifice which the British forces employed could have made. With the more complete evidence now available, we are better able to judge whether the Envoy or the General was right where they differed, and to decide how far the Envoy was answerable for the results of the campaign not having been yet more considerable, or for the cost of attaining those results having been so great.

What was the object aimed at in sending a British army to Spain?

It was not merely to secure the independence of Spain or Portugal. The expulsion of the French from the Peninsula would have been but one step towards attaining that security for the independence of every separate state in Europe, which had for years been the avowed purpose of all our efforts against Napoleon. This was well understood in Austria and Prussia. Germany watched the Peninsular contest with the conviction that her immediate prospects of freedom from the foreign thraldom under which she had so long groaned, depended on the results of the Spanish insurrection. The gigantic preparations made by Napoleon to crush all opposition in the Peninsula, sensibly diminished his powers of repression in Germany; and whatever prolonged the necessity for engaging the attention of the Emperor himself and of the flower of his armies in Spain, became nearly as important to the general cause of freedom in Europe, as any repetition of such a demoralizing defeat as Baylen could have been.

In no part of the wide area of the European contest could the power of England be used to so great advantage as in Spain. It was a true instinct which directed thither the scattered expeditions previously detached in various directions towards America, Sweden, and to different points in Europe. But the English Government and people were still tiros in such a struggle as that in the Peninsula. They had made a greater effort than in any of our previous continental enterprises to equip the army entrusted to Sir John Moore; but it was wholly inadequate to cope single-handed with the vast hosts of France, concentrated under the Emperor in person.

What, then, might reasonably have been expected of Moore and his army ?

His instructions indicated concentration in the north of Spain, at some point in Gallicia or on the borders of Leon : after which he was to act on such a plan of campaign as he might concert with the Spanish authorities, and he had the most ample discretion left him to make the best use he could of the forces placed at his disposal.

Subsequent events proved that it would have been difficult to give any better instructions to the British General than to leave him thus free to devise his own plan of operations for aiding the Spaniards to expel the French.

Moore's campaign, as far as it was in accordance with these instructions, was a decided success. It saved Portugal and the south of Spain from being overrun. It inflicted great loss on the French armies, by forcing them to act on a vast scale in the most unfavourable season, and in a country where their movements cost the heaviest sacrifices of men and resources. Above all, it occupied Napoleon's personal attention till the critical moment arrived when the action of Austria obliged him to turn to Germany, and to leave to other hands the task of crushing the Spanish nation ; an undertaking in which nothing short of his own genius had a chance of success. The campaign has been criticised on various grounds, some military, some political, and some of a mixed character ; partly military and partly political. Into the purely military questions it would be out of place here to enter. Whether Moore should have moved from Portugal by one line, or, as he did, by several; —whether he might not have concentrated, and moved from Salamanca more rapidly, or done more, by previous preparation, to facilitate his own retreat on Corunna, and to impede the advance of his pursuers ;—these, as far as they are military points, may be left to military critics.[1]

But the questions on which he differed from the Envoy were, in the main, political, and though few, most of them were of vital importance.

The Envoy thought that the General should, by an earlier move forwards, have attempted to save Madrid, or at least to delay its falling into the hands of Napoleon.

Whether this would at any time during the campaign have been possible, is, and must ever remain, matter of opinion. It is vain now to speculate whether the populace of Madrid, if they had been led by a Palafox and not by a Morlà, would or would not have emulated their brethren at Saragossa; or how far Napoleon would have been successful in overcoming a form of national resistance which elsewhere baffled the ablest of his lieutenants. This at least is certain, that with all his genius, and all the force at his command, the Emperor found it a matter of extreme difficulty to obtain possession of Madrid without a siege; and that he might have failed had he not been aided by the treachery and cowardice of those to whom the populace looked as leaders.

But there can be no doubt of the importance, at such a juncture, of delaying by even a few days Napoleon's occupation of Madrid, and of making it clear to all the civilized world that the submission of the Spanish capital was the result of force, and not of national preference.

Nor was there ever any reason to believe the

---

[1] *Vide* Napier, book iv. chap. vi. ; Alison, chap. l. p. 805, note, and p. 857 of vol. vi. edit. 1837 ; "Castlereagh Correspondence," vol. vi. ; " Life of Sir David Baird," vol. ii. ; Lord Londonderry's " Narrative of the War in Spain and Portugal," 1829, vol. i. pp. 149 to 289 ; Col. Sorell, " Notes on the Campaign of 1808-9," 1828.

difficulty or risk of an attempt to support any effort
of the Spaniards to defend Madrid would have been
so great as to put it out of question as a possible
move, which a military commander in Moore's position might prudently attempt, and which, therefore,
it would have been the duty of the British Minister
to urge on him, as most desirable on political
grounds.   Not to insist on the opinion of the Duke
of Wellington that it was possible for the force to
which Junot surrendered at Lisbon to have been at
Madrid in a month from the convention of Cintra,
it is clear that Moore himself, up to the 27th of
November[1] (1808), five days before Napoleon summoned Madrid to surrender, did not consider it a
hopeless enterprise "to march upon Madrid, to
throw himself into the heart of Spain, and thus to
run all risks, and share the fortunes of the Spanish
nation."   He then considered such a move, though
of "greater hazard" than a retreat on Lisbon,.
"perhaps worthy of risk, if the Government and
people of Spain are thought to have still sufficient
energy and means to recover from their defeats,"
and he formally asked the Envoy's opinion as to
which of the two courses before the General, he, the
Envoy, considered, on political grounds, the more
eligible ?

Even, then, if it be admitted that it never was in
Moore's power to save Madrid, it cannot be said
that the Envoy was wrong in pressing on him the
importance of the attempt up to the time when the
question was settled by Napoleon's masterly occupation of the capital—an operation which, even in
his biography, stands conspicuous as an instance
of the wonderful success of "a judicious mixture of
force and policy."

The next important point on which the General
and Envoy differed was, whether, in the event of its

---

[1] *Vide* his letter to Mr. Frere of that date.

being impossible to save Madrid, the retreat of the British army should be by Gallicia on Corunna, or through Portugal on Lisbon? The General, up to the 27th Nov. preferred the latter, the Envoy strenuously urged the former, not merely on the military grounds of its being the shorter, the safer, and the more defensible, the less liable to interruption from the enemy, and the more threatening to his communications; but on the political grounds that it enabled us to keep our hold on a most important province of Spain, to avoid even the appearance of deserting the Spanish cause, and afforded means of obtaining supplies and reinforcements to any extent by sea from England, and of issuing forth in renewed strength to resume the contest whenever opportunity offered. It is unnecessary to examine at length the reasons each gave for his opinion, since ultimately the line which the Envoy preferred was adopted by the General, and was an essential part of a movement which, as the event proved, saved the south of Spain, had the most important bearing on the final issue of the great continental struggle, and won from Napoleon himself the tribute of unqualified approval, as the only move which could have arrested the southward progress of the French armies, and for the time, to use his own phrase, "given the lock-jaw" to their other movements in Spain.

It was in the discussion on this point that most fault was found with the Envoy, both as regarded the advice he gave, and the terms in which that advice was given.

If, however, as is now clear, the advice itself was, in the main, so sound that the course recommended was ultimately adopted by the General, in opposition to his own previously expressed decision, and if the course so adopted proved most successful at an important crisis in a great contest, some passionate eagerness of expression might be forgiven in urging that course, on the part of one who clearly foresaw both the magnitude of the interests at stake, and the only mode to secure them.

But in truth, in now reading the correspondence, it is not easy to select expressions to which fair exception might be taken, though at the time, no doubt, some natural irritation must have been felt, not the less keenly when it became apparent that the arguments used had such strength of reason as to carry conviction.

Up to the 5th December, Moore had adhered to the opinion he had expressed to Mr. Frere, that a retreat on Portugal, with a view to ulterior operations in the south of Spain, was the only alternative open to him, if an advance on Madrid should prove too dangerous to be attempted. Mr. Frere had, in reply to the General's request for his opinion, very strongly urged, in a letter already quoted,[1] the superior political advantages of adhering to the original scheme laid down by the British Government of operating in the north of Spain. As the French armies advanced, every day brought some fresh confirmation of the soundness of the latter view, and at length, on the 5th December, Moore's own opinion underwent a change, and he determined to give up his previous plan of a retreat on Portugal, to advance against Soult on the Carrion, and as soon as he had effected the diversion of the enemy's forces, which he knew must ensue in order to avert the danger threatened to their communications, he prepared to retreat on Gallicia.

This was precisely the course the necessity and advantages of which Mr. Frere had been pressing on the General's notice.[2] The determination to

---

[1] *Vide* pages 93-94.

[2] This appears to have been in accordance not only with the views of the Envoy, but of Baird and of other officers about him, who had every claim to the General's confidence. *Vide* "Baird's Life," vol. ii.

adopt it was taken at Salamanca on the 5th December, but intimation of the change of plan had not reached Mr. Frere at Truxillo, when on the 8th December he despatched a letter by Mr. Stuart (afterwards Lord Stuart de Rothsay), whom he commissioned to press on Sir John Moore the arguments used in his letter, pointing out, in the strongest terms, the ruin to the Spanish cause, and the disgrace to the British arms, which must follow a retreat on Portugal without any attempt to arrest or divert the French advance, or to defend Gallicia.

This letter reached Sir John Moore at Toro on the 16th, when he had already adopted the course which had always been advocated by the minister. Read by the English public after Moore's death, the strong terms in which the letter was expressed doubtless appeared unnecessarily harsh and severe. But it is only just to the British minister to bear in mind that the letter is but one of a series, all urging the adoption of the same course, and that, had the retreat on Portugal not been abandoned (a timely change of purpose of which Mr. Frere was not aware when he wrote), the terms used in the letter would not have been at all too severe to characterise a movement which, as the event proved, would have been as fatal a mistake in a military as in a political point of view.

The channel through which this letter was conveyed was not open to objection, as Mr. Stuart was a personal friend of Sir John Moore's, and like all his friends warmly attached to him ; but Sir John Moore had felt much hurt at a former communication on the same subject having been sent him by a French emigrant officer in the English service, whose employment by the minister on so confidential a mission, was described at the time, and after Sir John Moore's death, as not only an act of extreme imprudence, but as an intentional insult to the British general.

So much blame has been attributed to Mr. Frere in this matter that the transaction may be described in greater detail than would be otherwise necessary. Colonel de Charmilly, a French Royalist, naturalised in England, married to the sister of a British nobleman,[1] and holding a British commission as Colonel in a colonial corps, had gone to Spain with the avowed intention of raising a Spanish regiment, for service against Napoleon; having, like many other French Royalists of that day, devoted his whole life to oppose the Revolution, and Napoleon as the embodiment of revolutionary ideas. On his way to Madrid he was introduced to Sir David Baird and Sir John Moore, stayed some days at their head-quarters, and seems to have had more than casual communications regarding his plans with them both. Though not previously acquainted with either general, his introductions left no ground for mistrust. A nephew of his wife's was an officer in Sir John Moore's own regiment, favourably known to the General, and present at the time with his regiment at head-quarters.

Reaching Madrid the 28th November, and finding the city carelessly lulled in the belief that the French were still at Burgos, de Charmilly went to Aranjuez, to present his letters of introduction to the British Envoy, to whom he was personally unknown; and there heard for the first time that the French, having forced the Somosierra Pass, threatened Madrid; and that the Supreme Junta had determined to retire to Toledo. Returning to Madrid, for his arms and baggage which he had left there, de Charmilly found the capital, not, as might have been expected, cowed or panic-stricken by the unexpected apparition of the Great Emperor

---

[1] Dorcas, sister of Sir James Blackwood, Bart., Baron Dufferin and Clandeboye.

with such overwhelming force, but in a ferment of popular and patriotic enthusiasm, reminding him strongly of the scenes he had witnessed at Paris in the first fervour of the Revolution of 1789. The mob, hearing he was a British officer, led him through barricaded streets and a populace working by torchlight at works of defence, to the palace where the Junta of defence organized that day, and the Spanish commander-in-chief, were in conference. The Duke of Infantado, as president of the Junta, received him, described their means of resistance, expressed in the strongest terms their determination to use them to the last extremity, and urged him to communicate to Moore his conviction of the paramount importance of the English army manœuvring to divert the attention of the French and allow time to organize the defence of Madrid. Finally the Duke gave the Colonel a passport for the express purpose of his going to Salamanca to communicate to Moore the state of affairs of which he was an eye-witness. On his way by the circuitous route indicated to him as the only one safe from the patrols of the French cavalry, he met the peasantry flocking to the capital with such arms as they had, and found the people and the Junta at Toledo equally enthusiastic in the national cause. At Talavera he, on the 3rd December, accidentally learnt that the British Envoy, in following the movements of the Supreme Junta, had just arrived there, and waiting on him to pay his respects, de Charmilly found that the Envoy had not heard of the popular rising at Madrid, nor of the establishment of the new Junta of defence, with the Duke del Infantado, a nobleman believed to be a real patriot and sincere friend of the British, as president. Colonel de Charmilly's intelligence was so unexpected and important that Mr. Frere hoped it would satisfy Sir John Moore that there was yet a chance of directing the British army to some better purpose than a retreat on Portugal; and he made de Charmilly the bearer of letters strongly expressing this view, and representing the necessity of supporting the determination of the Spanish people by all the means which had been entrusted to the British General for the purpose, adding that he considered the fate of Spain as depending absolutely, for the present, upon the decision which Moore might adopt.

The intelligence thus conveyed reached Moore on the 5th December, and decided him to recall Baird, who was already moving on Corunna, to change his own line of retreat, falling back through Gallicia instead of on Portugal ; and meantime to advance towards Soult on the Carrion, and thus threaten the French line of communications.

Had Mr. Frere's dispatches been confined to the letter given to Moore on the 5th, no offence apparently would have been taken at the employment of Colonel de Charmilly as the bearer of the communication. He was better known to the General and his officers than to the Envoy, and any suspicions Moore may have previously entertained had been removed. The intelligence he brought indicated a turning-point in the conduct of the Spanish people and Government ; of the accuracy of his information there could be no doubt; and it impressed the General, as it had the Envoy, with a conviction that it justified and required an entire change in the plan of operations.

But Mr. Frere had entrusted to de Charmilly a second letter, to be delivered only in the event of the General persevering in his determination to retreat on Portugal, after he had received the first dispatch, and heard de Charmilly's account of the popular rising at Madrid. This second letter, de Charmilly, ignorant of the effect which the first had produced on the General's mind, and the consequent alterations in his plans, presented the next day. In it Mr. Frere requested that if the General adhered to his determination to retire, Colonel de Charmilly might be examined before a council of war.

Under the circumstances there can be no doubt that this must have appeared to Moore a very unnecessary interference with his functions as a military commander, personally and solely responsible for the movements of his army; and it is not surprising that he should have felt and expressed much indignation at what must have appeared to him a most unwarrantable proceeding, and that it was thus represented by his friends after his death.

But unfortunately for all parties, the General's natural indignation at what he imagined to be an intentional act of disrespect did not permit him to hear the explanation which Colonel de Charmilly could have given.[1] Had he been allowed to state the circumstances and instructions under which the second letter was entrusted to him, Sir John Moore would have learnt that, whatever might be thought of the course adopted, Mr. Frere's object had been misunderstood. The Envoy knew that a retreat on Portugal had been ordered, and he could not know that the order had been recalled. But he believed that if the General were unwilling to incur the responsibility of recalling that order, a council of war might facilitate the adoption of the only course which the Envoy believed, and which the result proved, could ensure the honour and safety of the army.

The step was one which, according to the ordinary rules of official intercourse, nothing short of a most clear and urgent necessity could excuse. Any justification of it must rest on the momentous

---

[1] *Vide* De Charmilly's Narrative, 3rd edit. 1810, pp. 42 to 52.

character of the interests at stake ; and judged by this light there can be no doubt that the occasion was one of importance sufficient to justify almost any infraction of the limits which custom and reason prescribe to such advice as the representative of the Sovereign may offer to a General commanding that Sovereign's forces in the field.

Under ordinary circumstances it would, of course, have been out of the question to employ, in an office of such importance and delicacy, a comparative stranger, and a foreigner. They, however, who have insisted on Colonel de Charmilly's disqualifications in these respects appear to forget that the Envoy, unexpectedly met by him during a hurried retreat, had, in the absence of all other trustworthy means of conveyance, absolutely no choice but either to leave the General in ignorance of the rising of Madrid, the most important intelligence he could receive, and which was certain to influence all his operations, or to send him the information through Colonel de Charmilly. Moreover, the whole importance of the despatch was derived from the news which the Colonel himself had brought, of its truth and momentous import there could be no doubt ; it was imperative to send it across plains scoured by hostile cavalry ; hence the necessity for providing against risk of the despatches having to be destroyed, to prevent their falling into the enemy's hands, will explain the reason for Mr. Frere reading them over to Colonel de Charmilly, and making him acquainted with the view he had himself taken of the important news which the Colonel had been the first to convey.

That he should unnecessarily have wounded the feelings of a brave and devoted soldier was a subject of the deepest regret ; but nothing could have excused the Envoy had he at so grave a crisis omitted any possible precaution for ensuring the fullest consideration for facts on which he believed that the honour and existence of the British army depended.

Upon the whole, posterity will probably be inclined, in the matter of these letters sent by Colonel de Charmilly, to join in the opinion which appears to have been formed at the time on the subject by Sir David Baird, and which is very clearly expressed by the late Lord Londonderry, that while the advice given was sound and salutary, and while the Envoy was not only justified, but in duty bound to have tendered it, the proposal to examine de Charmilly before a council of war was one to which the General could under no circumstances have acceded, and which he naturally resented.[1]

---

[1] *Vide* "Life of Sir David Baird," by Theodore Hook. 1833, vol. ii. pp. 214 to 288 ; Lord Londonderry's " Narrative of the War in Spain and Portugal," 1829, vol. i. pp. 149 to 289.

Hook says of Mr. Frere's first letter by de Charmilly, that the tone and style assumed appeared to many officers on the spot, fully competent to form an opinion, " not exactly suited to his official situation ;" and that the second letter by de Charmilly " naturally irritated " the General ; but of the change of purpose to which the letters contributed, Baird seems fully to have approved.

Lord Londonderry says : " Mr. Frere was doubtless fully justified in writing in this strain ; as minister from the court of England he was perfectly authorized to give advice respecting the course to be pursued by the English general, even if that officer had abstained from requesting it. But Sir John Moore having repeatedly solicited his opinion as to the prudence or imprudence of schemes in agitation, his right to speak or write strongly became increased fourfold.

" Mr. Frere, however, in my humble judgment, erred in desiring Col. Charmilly should be examined before a council of war prior to any movement being made. . . . It would have been not only insulting to the commander of the forces to have the judgment of a non-official emigrant set up in opposition to his own, but the consequences might have been every way ruinous.

" Sir John Moore dismissed that person with marks of dissatisfaction ; and I think I should have done the same.

" In spite of all this, however, and in spite of the excessive timidity of the Supreme Junta . . . only one opinion can, I

It is not, however, by isolated acts or expressions that such a controversy can be decided. The question was, what a powerful army of a great nation might do or ought to attempt; and the parties to the controversy must be judged by what may ultimately prove to be the intrinsic soundness of the views each advocated. It was not thus, however, that contemporaries could judge. They could not but feel that the General, whose views and acts were criticized, had subsequently fallen in his country's cause; and opinions which, if the fate of the correspondents had been reversed, would have been regarded as inspirations of prophetic statesmanship and of the truest patriotism, were often misread at the time as intentional insults to a dying hero.

Have, then, subsequent events shown that the Envoy expected too much from the British army under Moore, or urged him to undertake impossibilities? If we look only to the experience of Moore's campaign it is clear that, as far as the General was swayed by the Envoy's advice to advance so as to threaten the French communications, and then to retreat on Gallicia rather than on

---

conceive, be formed as to the soundness of the views taken by Mr. Frere on this occasion."

Southey, who alone of the contemporary historians does full justice to Mr. Frere's services in the Peninsula, seems to except from the general commendation of his views and conduct, his desire that de Charmilly should be examined before a council of war.—"Peninsular War," vol. ii. chap. xxi. p. 279.

Some writers at the time wrote of de Charmilly as a creature of Morlà's, employed to decoy the British army to destruction, with a view to obtain favour for Morlà from Napoleon. De Charmilly appears completely to have cleared himself of all suspicion of any communication whatever with Morlà; and there is abundant evidence to prove that the information he conveyed as to the state of affairs in Madrid was strictly accurate.

Portugal, the campaign was a great success, and the cost, heavy as it was, not out of proportion to the results.[1] It was no fault of the Envoy's that the loss was not further reduced by earlier and more complete preparations on the line of retreat to Corunna,[2] or the results enhanced by the transports, which subsequently embarked the army, being sent to reinforce it instead of to bring it away from Spain.[3]

Still clearer is the testimony which the later campaigns in the Peninsula bear to the general soundness of Mr. Frere's views on the principal points regarding which he had the misfortune to differ from Sir John Moore.

---

[1] " Notwithstanding the clamour with which this campaign has been assailed, as if no army had ever yet suffered such misfortunes, the nominal loss was small, and the real loss smaller, sinking to nothing when compared with the advantage gained."—*Napier*, bk. iv. ch. vi. p. 356, 8vo. ed. of 1851.

[2] Ibid. p. 358.

[3] Thirteen thousand men, intended as reinforcements for the army in Spain, were actually re-landed in England, after being shipped, and the transports sent out empty. There can be no doubt that the ministry were prepared to reinforce Moore ; and there were means at hand, as the Duke of York showed, of raising the force in Spain to a strength of 60,000 rank and file. But Moore did not see any paramount necessity for augmenting the force in Spain. As late as the 13th November, writing to Lord William Bentinck, who had been acting as British Envoy up to the time of Mr. Frere's arrival, he said : " I have no objection to you or Mr. Frere representing the necessity of as many more British troops as you think proper." But he differed from the view they had taken, and which subsequent experience proved to be correct, that on the English, and not on the Spanish armies, must fall the main burden of the task to be executed. " I differ," he said, " only with you in one point. When you say the chief and great obstacle, and resistance to the French, will be afforded by the English army. If that be so, Spain is lost." And after expressing his conviction that the salvation of Spain depended mainly on the Spaniards, he added : " I am, therefore, much more anxious to see exertion and energy in the Government, than to have my force augmented."—*Vide* " Moore's Narrative," p. 24.

I do not, of course, refer to any comparison either in conduct or results between the one campaign which it was Moore's fortune to conduct, and the series of campaigns under Wellington. Napoleon's absence from among Wellington's immediate adversaries in Spain, would alone render any such comparison impossible. I refer simply to those characteristic and peculiar local difficulties in carrying on the war in the Peninsula, which appeared to Moore so great as to render any efficient action by his army almost hopeless; and which it has been said by many historians of high character as well as by party writers of the day, that Mr. Frere failed either to see or to estimate at their proper value. The list extends to nearly all the shortcomings and failings of the Spaniards as a nation, and even the deficiencies of their country in roads or resources. One of the complaints most frequently implied as well as directly urged, is the omission to supply the accurate intelligence on which so much of the success of military operations depended.

It is unnecessary to dwell on the obvious fact that no Envoy could get from the Junta more than they knew, and that they were generally as ill-informed as their allies regarding what was really going on in other parts of Spain. Perhaps, now that the Spaniards and their peculiarities are better understood by their neighbours than they were a generation ago, our surprise at this national characteristic of their public life may be less than was felt by our forefathers. At any rate, it is clear that then, as now, he who would possess accurate information regarding political affairs in Spain, must gather his facts for himself, and not trust to the Government for them—and for such a task the General had as great facilities as the Envoy. The latter had only landed at Corunna towards the end of October, and did not reach Aranjuez, where the Junta was assembled, for several weeks afterwards.

The General, on the other hand, had been in the Peninsula since the latter end of the previous August, and in supreme command of the British forces during the greater part of the time. He had halted at Salamanca from the 13th November to the 12th December, and had there better opportunities than the Envoy could possess at Aranjuez, of learning for himself everything essential to the conduct of the war.

But as regards this and all other difficulties arising from local peculiarities, whether of national character or of a political or physical nature, it is obvious that they were not less obstacles to the later than to the earlier campaigns ; why then were they not found as formidable by Wellington as they appeared to Moore?

The difference clearly was not merely or mainly in the genius or temperament of the two commanders. It was greatly due to their previous training and experience.

For an English general with British troops to conduct active operations in Spain, at the beginning of this century, meant to carry on war in a country with the language and manners of which few of the soldiers, or even of the best educated and accomplished of the officers, had the slightest acquaintance—to disarm the hostility of a proud, jealous, sensitive, and high-spirited race—to avoid affronting the prejudices of an uneducated populace, or the bigotry of a fanatical and all-powerful priesthood—to draw supplies of money and food from a country where internal commerce was nearly extinct, and which was almost destitute of roads passable by wheeled carriages—to depend on a maritime base of operations many hundreds of miles distant, and to use as auxiliaries the armies of a people possessed indeed of many soldierlike qualities, but unaccustomed to united and systematic subordination ; and who required, in order to turn them to the best account, sometimes to be provided with an independent field of action for themselves, under their own commanders; and sometimes to be assimilated to our own troops, under British discipline and officers.

Most of the superior officers in Napoleon's army had acquired, more or less, by long experience in foreign war, the art of performing some portions of such a task as this; but it is no exaggeration to say that, at the commencement of the Peninsular War, it was impossible for any English general, with merely European experience, to have learnt such a lesson, except by instinct or theoretical reading. Moore had not, in this respect, been more fortunate than his contemporaries.   He undertook the charge of the expedition as a matter of duty, with a sad foreboding of the certainty of failure,[1] and nothing in his previous experience gave him much help in overcoming the peculiar difficulties of his position.

But no part of the task presented any untried or

---

[1] Stapleton thus describes Moore's last interview with the secretary at war : "Lord Castlereagh disclosed to the Cabinet the parting words addressed to him by Sir John.   After the latter had had his final interview, had taken his leave, and actually closed the door, he re-opened it, and said to Lord Castlereagh, 'Remember, my Lord, I protest against the expedition, and foretell its failure.'   Having thus disburdened his mind, he instantly withdrew, left the office, and proceeded to Portsmouth to take the command of the expedition.   When Lord Castlereagh mentioned this circumstance to the Cabinet, Mr. Canning could not help exclaiming, 'Good God! and do you really mean to say that you allowed a man entertaining such feelings with regard to the expedition, to go and assume the command of it?'   It was in consequence of what passed in the Cabinet respecting this interview, that an official letter, which is described as equivalent to one demanding his resignation, was sent after him.   But Sir John did not take the hint, sent a dignified reply, and sailed with the expedition."—STAPLETON'S *George Canning and his Times*, 1859, p. 160.

insuperable difficulty to one who, like Wellesley, had practised war on a large scale, and in independent command, in India; and the reader who will carefully study "Sir Arthur Wellesley's Indian Despatches," will find every one of the characteristic difficulties of Peninsular warfare faced and overcome in the Deccan, by exactly the same qualities and management which were subsequently so successful in Spain.[1]

It is a matter of more than personal or passing

---

[1] A striking example will be found in one of his earliest letters to Lord Castlereagh, dated Corunna, 21st July, 1808. His correspondence at that time not only shows a sound appreciation of the state of affairs in Spain, but is full of practical suggestions for the conduct of the war, which could not then have been the result of Peninsular experience; *e. g.* the recommendation that 30,000 Portuguese troops should be raised by Great Britain, as auxiliaries to 20,000 British troops.—*Vide* "Despatches," vol. iv. pp. 24-43.

In a subsequent letter, written Oct. 19, 1808, after his return to England, and when he had no command in the Peninsula, he offers to Lord Castlereagh advice which is not less remarkable for its substance than from its being volunteered by one so constitutionally averse from offering advice unasked. After pointing out the importance of magazines, he observes: "All these difficulties of communication, and supply of magazines to which, as I told you in a former [letter], scarcely one of us has turned his mind, render it most desirable that our army should be employed on the enemy's flank and on the coast. . . . . ."

In a PS. he adds: "I recommend to you to make all your arrangements for forming a magazine in the heart of Spain, whether the General will call for it or not. After what has passed lately [relative to the convention of Cintra], the general officers will be disinclined to take upon themselves anything excepting the performance of their military duty under their instructions, and Sir John Moore will be unwilling to throw himself into the heart of Spain unless he is ordered to do so, or to make arrangements preparatory to that operation till it will be ordered by Government, when such arrangements will be too late."—*Castlereagh Correspondence*, vol. vi. pp. 476-481.

interest to note this essential difference in the experience and opportunities of the two generals. For if our officers can have no brighter example than Moore in all the moral and personal qualities which go to form the perfect soldier, it is certain that they will never, as Wellington did, lead to habitual victory the armies of an empire so extended and composed of such varied materials as that of England, if they lack the practice and experience in warfare in ruder countries, which gave to the genius of Wellington its early development.

Much of the blame which was at the time so freely thrown on Mr. Frere by those who asserted that he did not see, or failed to appreciate, the obstacles to be overcome by the British general, was due to the fact that he saw more clearly than a large proportion of the British public then did, the essential points wherein the contest in Spain differed from the other continental wars in which we had previously taken part against Napoleon, and the vastly superior importance of the issues at stake. It was not a dynastic, but a national struggle for independence, and its peculiar significance was the greater, because the Spaniards had not the advantage, which the Germans and Russians afterwards possessed, of a settled government, able to share and direct their patriotic enthusiasm. The great Whig party had, in many respects, altered the position which it had held, during the earlier years of the French Revolution, in all discussions with regard to the duty and interest of England. Many of those who had ceased to look on a contest with Napoleon as war against the liberties of mankind, were, nevertheless, so dazzled by his achievements, that they regarded hostilities against him almost as if waged against an irresistible fate; and they failed to see that the cause of the Spaniards was not only the cause of national liberty against foreign tyranny, but that it contained within itself elements of success which could not be looked for in any purely dynastic contest.[1]

Thus to the amount of obloquy which would naturally have fallen on all who had any share in what was then regarded as a most unfortunate expedition, was added much of party bitterness ; and the circumstances of Sir John Moore's death precluded such defence of those who differed from him, as might have been possible had all lived to receive their fair award of praise or blame from their countrymen. When urged in after years to leave on record an answer to the calumnies and unjust criticism to which he had been subjected, Mr. Frere replied that the time for his doing so for himself had gone by, and that as one who was long since passed from political life, he was willing to leave it

---

[1] The position of the Whigs at this time, and their mistaken course regarding the Peninsular War, have been well described by Lord Russell, who speaks with unusual authority, both on account of having been in early life an eye-witness of the state of affairs in the Peninsula, and from his intimate lifelong acquaintance with all that concerns that party.

After describing the character of the Spanish insurrection, and the obvious duty and interest of England with regard to it, Lord Russell comments on the inability of Lord Grenville and the leaders of the Whigs to comprehend the true nature and bearing of the contest, and quotes Mr. Horner's opinion, in 1813, as to the serious character of the mistake they had made in 1808-9, which Horner said he had never "ceased to lament," as "so inconsistent with true Whig principles of continental policy, so revolting to the popular feelings of the country, and to every true feeling for the liberties and independence of mankind."—*Selections from Earl Russell's Speeches and Despatches*, Longmans, London, 1870, vol. i. p. 4.

Speaking of Lord Holland as he saw him at Corunna, Crabb Robinson says : "Lord Holland was known to be among the warmest friends of the Spanish cause ; in that respect differing from the policy of his Whig friends, who by nothing so much estranged me from their party as by their endeavour to force the English Government to abandon the Spanish patriots."—*Crabb Robinson*, vol. i. p. 278.

to history to judge whether he or those from whom he differed had best estimated what an English army in Spain could be fairly expected to achieve. He added, that the manner of Sir John Moore's death had prevented him from answering at the time, in any hostile or controversial tone, what Moore's family and friends had written and published — "but," he added, "I have often been tempted to answer what others said of my having been deceived by Morlà. This was utterly false; I never saw Morlà; I was only in Madrid at that period for a few hours, on my way through to Aranjuez; and so far from being deceived by Morlà, some of the leading men at Madrid with whom I was acquainted, came to me at Aranjuez, and communicated to me their suspicions of his fidelity; and I went so far as to say that I would, in my communications with the Junta, act on their belief of his infidelity, if they were prepared to take the steps necessary to justify my so doing."

In speaking of these events, Mr. Frere never under-estimated the difficulties of defending Madrid against Napoleon; but he referred to the effect of Moore's diversion, late as it was, to prove that the difficulties were not all in Napoleon's favour, and to the experience of subsequent years, as proving that it was impossible to calculate the effect on the French of the slightest reverse at that particular moment, or the degree to which the Spaniards would have been encouraged to resistance, by knowing that the English were not going to desert them. He said, " I certainly did expect much from them at that time, but not so much as their subsequent conduct justified. It is almost impossible to give an adequate idea of their intense hatred of the French, or of the kind of fellow-feeling which banded Spaniards of the most discordant opinions, to act for the one object whenever they had anything to do against the French; and it is equally impossible for any one who does not intimately know the Spanish character to appreciate the extent to which their hatred of the French interfered with all the French operations. There was no beggar so poor that bribery could induce him to carry the French despatches. These were brought to our officers to an extent incredible to those who have not experience of a war carried on against the national feeling of the country which is the scene of operations. I had an intercepted despatch of Soult's when he was on the Douro, complaining that for two months he had had no despatch from Madrid. This was brought to me by a simple countryman, who gave this account of the way in which he came by it. He told me he was coming along a narrow road when he heard the clatter of hoofs behind him, and some one calling to him to get out of the way. He turned, and saw a French trooper riding after him, and stepping aside, as the Frenchman passed, he picked up a stone and threw it with such force at his back, that, as he said, ' I brought him to the ground, and killed him with my knife.' He described the action just as he would have related the killing of a weasel, or any other vermin in a hedge, and seemed to take it quite as a matter of course that he should have killed the Frenchman as soon as he saw that he had the power to do so. ' And there,' he said to me, ' is what I found upon him,' showing the despatches. Some of the reports of the French medical staff, which I saw at the time, were occupied with the description of cases brought into hospital at Madrid, where the men were supposed to have been poisoned in the wine-shops in the city. This the medical author of the report discredited, but knowing how intense and bitter was the hatred of the common people against the French, and how meritorious they believed the destruction of a Frenchman to be, I doubted at the time whether the horrible suspicion was as unfounded as the French medical officer supposed. Whatever else might have resulted from Moore's having been able to hold a position in the north of Spain, instead of embarking, there can be no doubt that the national spirit which would have been roused against the French would have most seriously impeded their operations in other parts of the Peninsula, and rendered it almost impossible even for the military genius of Napoleon to have maintained and fed in the mountains, or the north coast of Spain, such an army as would have been necessary to have forcibly ejected the English from a stronghold on the coast."

Fortunately for England, for Spain, and for Europe, the British Government, though hard pressed, in and out of Parliament, during the spring of 1809, to abandon the contest in the Peninsula, had resolved to continue it, and to entrust its conduct to one who had already shown how thoroughly he understood the conditions on which it must be fought out.

But the interval between the re-embarkation of the last of Moore's army at Corunna, in January, and Sir Arthur Wellesley's arrival at Lisbon in April, was a period of unexampled trial and sore discouragement to the Spaniards; and if anything did, from time to time, occur during those winter months to cheer their hopes of ultimate victory, it was less often in the shape of success, however small, than in some fresh proof of the unconquerable spirit of the people, when contending against the heaviest odds, and under every circumstance of discouragement.

Thus, the second siege of Saragossa, though it ended in the reduction of the illustrious city (February 22nd, 1809), read many a memorable lesson, alike to the Spaniards, their enemies, and their allies.

On the Catalan coast, British naval captains like Lord Cochrane, showed how much might be done by enterprising officers to aid the Spaniards in impeding the operations of the French generals in the maritime districts.

At the other extremity of the French line of operations, Romana, with not less courage and enterprise, and with better fortune than Palafox, maintained an unequal contest against Soult and Ney, amid the mountains of Gallicia. Nothing could well have been more desperate than his position after the embarkation of Moore's army and throughout the winter. He appeared destined to certain destruction or capture, with no prospect but that of an ignominious death if he were taken. Yet routed, and, as the French believed, practically annihilated at Monterrey in February, he re-appeared in March to surprise the garrison of Villafranca, to make prisoners of 800 of Soult's best soldiers, and to contribute more than any other single cause to arrest Soult's progress southwards from Oporto.

Sir John Cradock, on whom had devolved the command of the British troops left in garrison in Portugal after Moore's death, was a brave and capable officer ; but he was necessarily unacquainted with the effect which the results of Moore's campaign might have on the views of the British Government ; and he had neither the means nor the authority required for any but temporary dispositions of the force at his command. Many measures were, however, taken by him, or with his consent, which had an important bearing on the success of after-operations. English officers were employed to discipline and command Portuguese troops, and though the full effects of this system were not realised till Beresford was placed in supreme command of the Portuguese forces later in the year, the services rendered by men like Colonels Trant and Patrick, and Sir Robert Wilson, in organizing and leading Portuguese levies during the winter and early spring, formed a bond of union between the English soldiers and their allies which was turned to most valuable account by Wellington in his subsequent campaigns.

Sir Robert Wilson's position, in particular, speedily became one of great importance. Endowed with great natural abilities as a soldier, and with unusual powers of influencing and commanding men, he speedily extended the sphere of his operations across the Spanish frontier to the country round Ciudad Rodrigo, where his presence was of the utmost importance, as threatening Soult's flank should he move southwards towards Lisbon, and interrupting his communications with Ney and with Madrid. Mr. Frere had prevailed on the Supreme Junta to confer on Sir Robert the rank of a Brigadier-General in the Spanish army, and thus gave equal scope to his enterprise on both sides the border.

It was well that the formidable obstacles they encountered at either extremity of the line of their invading armies, disinclined the French to advance southwards ; for the Spanish armies which nominally covered the provinces south of the Tagus, were not in a condition to offer any effective resistance.

There is a dreary uniformity about the description of all the Spanish forces at this time, between the Portuguese frontier and Catalonia. " In such miserable circumstances that increase of numbers brought no increase of strength." " Arms, clothing, and provisions were wanting." " The army was alike without resources, discipline, or system ; in want of efficient officers of every rank, and those which there were, divided into cabals and factions." And worst feature of all, neither the superior officers nor the central Government were aware of their military deficiencies. When prudence would have dictated an entirely defensive policy, and the devotion of their whole time and resources to organisation and discipline, each general as he succeeded to supreme command, planned extensive and combined operations on the largest scale, such as required for their successful execution the best of troops, of officers and means ; as a natural consequence, one commander after another incurred speedy and ignominious defeat, whenever a general action was risked. It has been truly said by Southey, that this national incapacity for seeing their own defects, which always exposed their armies to defeat, nevertheless, as a nation, rendered the Spaniards invincible ; and that the French could have invaded no people whom it was so easy to rout, none whom it was so impossible to subdue.

Throughout the winter, Mr. Frere continued at his post, with the Supreme Junta, which had established itself at Seville ; and, in every way by his influence and advice powerfully aided the common cause. It was greatly owing to the confidence with which his personal character inspired the Junta, that they seem never for a moment to have wavered in the trust they reposed in the good faith of the British Government, and the certainty of its continued hearty support ; and that they turned a deaf ear to the reports industriously propagated by the French that the British Government was withdrawing its troops from the Peninsula, and that they would never return. To Romana and Sir Robert Wilson, Mr. Frere's correspondence and his energetic support of their views with the Supreme Junta, were of the utmost value. In his communications with that body, he exposed with just and unsparing criticism the defects of the Spanish armies, and the short-comings of their generals ; and exerted himself incessantly, though unfortunately with but partial success, to have the commands of the scattered corps combined, and entrusted, with full powers as commander-in-chief, to a single competent officer.

A good illustration of the difficulties of his position, and the extent of the personal influence he had acquired, was afforded in February. Sir George Smith had been sent to Cadiz, without previous reference to the British Minister, to provide for the possible case of British troops being needed there. Through excess of zeal Sir George considerably exceeded his instructions. He informed the Spanish Governor that he was empowered to require that British troops should be permitted to garrison Cadiz ; and without even waiting for the consent of the Spanish authorities, or communicating with the British Minister, he wrote to Sir John Cradock to send troops from Portugal. The Spaniards naturally took alarm, which was increased by the secrecy and suddenness of the move, and by its taking the British Minister as well as themselves by surprise. The Supreme Junta, sharing the popular feeling, had further cause for uneasiness on its own account, for the local authorities of Cadiz, jealous of the central Government, spread reports that its members were in league with traitors to deliver up the last remaining arsenal of Spain into the hands of foreigners. In the course of the discussion Mr. Frere appealed to the Junta in the following terms : "The members of the Junta will do me the justice to admit that I have never endeavoured to promote the interests of my nation but as being essentially connected with those of their own. If, however, I have always been guided by the same sentiments and the same views which a Spanish politician might have, I do not think it is to depart from them, if I deliver the same opinion which I should give had I the honour of occupying a place in the council of your nation, viz., That the whole policy of the Spanish Government rests essentially on a persuasion of perfect good faith on the part of England, and that it is important to confirm it more and more, by testimonies of mutual confidence, and by

avoiding the slightest appearance of distrust between Government and Government." This appeal
had the desired effect. Leave was given that any
British troops which had arrived or might arrive at
Cadiz should disembark, and the mode of best
employing them was discussed. Ultimately the
British Minister was asked to select the Spanish
Governor of Cadiz; and though he of course declined the responsibility involved in such an unusual
mark of confidence, the correspondence ended in a
manner which marked unequivocally the extent to
which the Spaniards trusted to the honour of their
English allies.

While these discussions were going on at Seville,
an incident had occurred during a popular tumult at
Cadiz, which showed that the feeling of confidence
in the English was not confined to the ruling
authorities. The people had risen in insurrection
on an alarm that the fortifications were to be
entrusted to traitors and foreigners, and, at the
instance of the Governor and the Guardian of the
Capucins, some English officers who could speak
Spanish were permitted to assure the populace that
the British troops would not interfere in the
internal affairs of the city, but would assist in defending it. So powerful was the impression produced on the popular mind by what the British
officers said, that the mob proceeded to demand
that the fortifications should be examined and
reported on by them; and the English general
having appeared on a balcony with some of the
authorities, and declared his satisfaction with the
arrangements made, the mob dispersed with loud
vivas "for King George and King Ferdinand!"

On the 22nd April, 1809, Sir Arthur Wellesley
landed at Lisbon and assumed the command of the
British and Portuguese troops in the Peninsula. In
less than a month he had concentrated his disposable force at Coimbra, forced the passage of the

Douro, and driven Soult, with the loss of all his artillery, baggage, and one fourth of his men, into the mountains of Gallicia. Suspending the pursuit on the 18th of May, he turned to join the Spanish General Cuesta, in operating against Victor in the valley of the Tagus. Having received the full permission of the British Government to extend his operations into Spain, by the 20th of July he had marched the greater part of his force more than three hundred miles, effected a junction with Cuesta at Oropesa, within five marches of Madrid, and had it been possible to induce the obstinate old Spanish general to move at the critical moment, he would have attacked Victor on the 23rd in such a position and with such superior force, that the defeat of the French seemed inevitable.

Cuesta's obstinacy enabled Victor to extricate himself and to effect a junction with King Joseph and Sebastiani, but did not save the French from defeat when, disregarding the sounder advice of Jourdan, Victor assumed the offensive, attacked the combined English and Spanish armies at Talavera on the 27th and 28th of July, and, after two days of desperate fighting, was forced to retreat, leaving seventeen pieces of cannon in the hands of the allies.

The utter want of effective co-operation from the Spaniards disabled Sir Arthur from following up his victory, and the experience of the whole campaign taught him that with such a small force of British troops as had been entrusted to him, and with such inefficient allies, no skill or energy on his part could enable him to act on the offensive, against the vastly superior French force, with any chance of ultimate and permanent success. Thenceforward he laid down for himself and rigidly carried out an entirely different system. Acting strictly on the defensive, he patiently built up that army of English and allied troops with which, as he afterwards said, he "could go anywhere, and do anything."

But the task required for its successful execution not only every quality of a great commander, but time ; and it was not for a year and a half after his victory at Talavera, nor till he had forced the wave of invasion to break itself against the rocks of Torres Vedras, that he was able to resume the offensive, in that series of masterly campaigns which, in the course of four years of incessant fighting, drove the French armies out of Spain, and enabled him to carry the war into France.

On the 1st of August Mr. Frere's functions as British Minister in Spain were terminated by the arrival of the Marquis Wellesley. He had been appointed Ambassador early in April, but had been disabled by illness from leaving England till the 24th of July. He landed at Cadiz on the fourth morning after the battle of Talavera, in the midst of the excitement consequent on the news of his brother's great victory, and was received with every mark of public honour and popular enthusiasm.

Mr. Frere carried with him into his retirement the personal esteem, respect and entire confidence of all the best men belonging to the Spanish Government and armies with whom he came in contact. When he had laid down his office, the Supreme Central Junta, who, with all their faults, had never shown themselves indifferent to services rendered to the Spanish cause, applied to his successor to obtain the sanction of the King of England for their bestowing on him, in the name of the Spanish Sovereign, a Castilian title of honour, that of ' Marquez de la Union,' as " a mark of their acknowledgment of the zeal with which he had laboured to promote the friendly union and common interest of the two countries." Such honours have never been lightly granted to foreigners of even the highest rank in Spain, and never without the ostensible reason of great services rendered to the Spanish crown or nation. In conveying to Mr. Frere the

King's permission to accept the title, Lord Wellesley wrote :—

"I am further commanded to communicate to you that His Majesty's condescending goodness, in permitting you to accept this mark of the esteem and gratitude of Spain, is intended as a proof of His Majesty's most gracious acceptance and approbation of your general conduct in the discharge of the duties of your mission in Spain.

"I beg leave to offer you my congratulations on this distinguished mark of His Majesty's royal favour and approbation, and to express the peculiar satisfaction with which I obey His Majesty's most gracious commands on this occasion."

From the few words of cold and rather formal courtesy in which this letter was acknowledged, it does not appear as if Mr. Frere thought that the permission of his Sovereign to accept a Spanish title, or the stately periods of the Ambassador's congratulations, were in themselves a suitable recognition of the services he had rendered his own country. But, as far as the Spaniards were concerned, he felt then, and ever retained, a deep sense of the only mark it was in their power to bestow of their gratitude for his exertions in the common cause of national freedom.

Some weeks later, in a private letter, Lord Wellesley, referring to the formalities connected with the grant of the title, added "amidst all the delays and omissions of this (the Spanish) Government, it has at length performed its duty towards you." Two months' severe experience had shown him how trying were the responsibilities of the office in which Mr. Frere had laboured, under peculiar disadvantages. In a letter to his brother dated about the same time, Lord Wellesley said with unaffected bitterness, "I am worked like a galley-slave, and can effect nothing." He had already realised the truth of the warning previously received from that brother, when Sir Arthur, referring to Lord Wellesley's acceptance of office as Ambassador to Spain, wrote to him, "You have undertaken an Herculean task ; and God knows that the chances of success are infinitely against you."

In truth, arduous as had been the duties of British envoy in Spain before Sir Arthur Wellesley's arrival, they were in no respect rendered more easy to discharge when the contest was renewed in the valley of the Tagus. During the winter, with little external support, and mainly by personal influence and character, Mr. Frere had had to meet all the obstacles created by the suspicions of the Spaniards, to encourage them under reverses the most disheartening, and, what was far more difficult, to moderate their inordinate self-confidence, on the slightest return of good fortune. All this was not impossible to one who thoroughly understood and ardently sympathised with the Spaniards ; but the case was far different when, as Envoy whose successor had long since been appointed, and whilst holding office, as he himself expressed it, "only from day to day—looking for the arrival of his successor by the first fair wind," Mr. Frere had to face all the obstacles so graphically described in the Wellington despatches written during the Talavera campaign.

The tone of those letters which are addressed to Mr. Frere, shows how fully Sir Arthur appreciated the departing Envoy's efforts to aid him, and even when smarting under the disappointment of losing the fruits of his victory at Talavera, through the obstinacy of Cuesta and the supineness of the Spanish authorities, he wound up a letter to Lord Wellesley, full of bitter complaints of the Spaniards, by adding, "I must do the late British Minister the justice to declare that I do not conceive that this deficiency of supplies for the army is at all to

be attributed to any neglect or omission on his part."
Their relations had indeed from the first been of
the most cordial and confidential character.[1] The
General had at his disposal every advantage that
Mr. Frere's experience, or his authority and position as Envoy could afford. The British officers
attached as agents to the Spanish generals, who
had in the first instance been directed to report
to the Envoy, were instructed by him to consider
themselves under Sir Arthur's orders. These instructions, after Mr. Frere's departure, were for
some time suspended; with effects the reverse of
beneficial to the public service.[2] Finally, all the
influence Mr. Frere possessed with the Supreme
Junta, had been used to obtain for Sir Arthur
Wellesley the rank of Captain-General of the
Spanish forces,[3] and to substitute for Cuesta a
younger and less impracticable commander of the
main Spanish army in the south of the Peninsula.

Neither of these two latter measures was formally
completed till Mr. Frere's successor had arrived,
but both were carried mainly by his influence with
the Supreme Junta, and had they been adopted
at the time when he first recommended them, there
can be little doubt but that they would materially
have altered the results of the campaign.

At such a moment the supersession of the Envoy
by any one possessing the higher office and authority of Ambassador, made a considerable change in

---

[1] Mr. Frere "not being deterred from the performance of
his duty by the clamour raised against him in England, but
delivering his opinion to the British General, upon the same
footing, he said, as he should have done, had he been holding a private conversation with Sir Arthur, and as he should
equally have ventured to do had he been residing casually in
Spain in a private character."—*Southey*, vol. II. chap. xxiv.
p. 399.

[2] *Vide* "Whittingham's Memoirs," p. 100, ed. 1868.

[3] This office had been offered to and declined by Moore.

the position of the general. In many cases it would have been a decided advantage to him to have such a post filled by a brother ; but, in this instance, such relationship was not needed in order to secure entire cordiality of feeling and unity of action ; and Lord Wellesley's appointment tended to place his younger brother in a position of relative subordination, so similar to that which he had previously held under the great pro-consul in India, that it could hardly be entirely agreeable to one of Sir Arthur's energy and force of character. It is not therefore improbable that the young general was "uneasy at his brother's advent into Spain," and that he would have been well pleased to retain Mr. Frere as his coadjutor.[1]

Regarding his own services at this period Mr.

---

[1] *Vide* "Whittingham's Memoirs" as above. The position which General Whittingham occupied while Lord Wellesley remained in Spain, and the confidence with which he was regarded by all the parties referred to, gave him peculiar facilities for judging correctly as to the views and feelings of the two illustrious brothers on such a subject. There are many indications in their published correspondence which tend to support the view expressed by the author of the Memoirs ; and though with such men the feeling could never wittingly have interfered with duty, there can be no doubt that Lord Wellesley, as Ambassador in Spain, was placed in a false position, and might have greatly increased his brother's difficulties, had not his mission been terminated by other considerations, after a little more than three months' tenure of the post.

It may not be out of place here to remark that, except by Southey, and in some of Wellington's despatches, scant justice has been done to the great services of General Whittingham throughout the war, and notably at a very critical juncture of the battle of Talavera. His Memoirs, as far as they relate to his own proceedings in Spain, contain many valuable contributions to the history of the great struggle, illustrating the career of one of the most active and distinguished of the British military agents employed with the Spanish armies, and the effect which their labours had on the condition of the Spanish troops, and through them, on the later operations of the war.

Frere never could be induced to publish a line, in
addition to the official despatches which were laid
before Parliament. But long after these events had
become matters of bygone history he would sometimes dwell on his recollections of the men who
had taken part with him in them.

Of Wellington's military genius it is hardly
necessary to say that he had anticipated the estimate which history has recorded. Speaking afterwards of him he said, "I never met Wellington in
Spain but once in Seville, when he came to meet
the Junta—but I saw directly, what I had gathered
from his letters, that he thoroughly understood the
Spaniards—that he took a right view of the nature
of the contest, and I never had a doubt but that,
if he were allowed by the people at home, he would
carry it to a successful issue."

"He never had the same means which Moore
had, nor the same power of calling for reinforcements which Moore might have had. The first intention of the English Government was to confine
his operations almost entirely to Portugal, and leave
to act in Spain was given him later, and with some
hesitation."

In reference to some criticism on the Talavera
campaign, Mr. Frere said, "It did not seem to me
at all rashly undertaken. In fact, had almost any
one of the generals except old Cuesta been in command, it must have been a great success. Wellington's combinations were so good, and his movements so rapid, that had Cuesta supported him
Victor must have been crushed, before Sebastiani,
Joseph or Soult could have come to his aid ; after
defeating Victor, Wellington would have been able
to deal with the others in detail, and the French
must have evacuated Madrid. It was impossible to
calculate what would have been the moral effect of
such a blow. Wellington's critics forget how de-
moralized and hampered the French army had at

that time become, by their habits of plunder, by the divisions among their commanders, and above all by their experience of the hatred of the country people, and the consequent difficulty of communicating, and getting intelligence.

" The aid Wellington expected from Cuesta and his army was nothing more than the Spaniards could have rendered under almost any other of their generals.   It was a conviction of this that made me so anxious to have old Cuesta superseded, and to get Alberquerque appointed in his stead.   I felt then, and am sure now, that had Romana or Alberquerque been in command in place of Cuesta, the whole character of the subsequent contest would have been altered." * * * " Cuesta was not lukewarm nor disaffected, but utterly worn out, and retaining little of his former character but his extraordinary obstinacy and self-will, and his contempt for all opinions and orders of the Supreme Junta.   Yet in England it was one of the many faults charged against me, that I had pressed on the Junta the old man's removal."[1]

---

[1] This estimate of Cuesta is very fully borne out by the ample details given in the Wellington Despatches.   On the 13th June, 1809, Sir Arthur wrote to Mr. Frere : " The obstinacy of this old gentleman (Cuesta) is throwing out of our hands the finest game that any armies ever had." (Gurwood, vol. iv. p. 394.)   A month later (13th July) he wrote to Mr. Frere a curious account of his interview with the old Spanish general, who would not speak French, the language of the hated invader, while the young Englishman could not express himself fluently in Spanish.   He notes the prevailing contempt which Cuesta evinced for the Junta, and the evidence that the Junta were afraid of Cuesta.   (Ibid. p. 478.)

For the time Wellington thought he had sufficiently secured the hearty co-operation of Cuesta's army, through the influence of the Spanish adjutant-general.   But this hope proved fallacious ; for he complains (p. 488) that the treatment of his army by the Spaniards was worse than if they had been in an enemy's country.   And soon after (24th July), just before the battle of Talavera, he wrote to Mr. Frere :

Of Alberquerque's natural capacity as a general
Mr. Frere always expressed a very high opinion.
" Had he lived and been continued in command in

" Cuesta more and more impracticable every day.   It is impossible to do business with him, and very uncertain that
any operation will succeed in which he has any concern."
(Ibid. p. 498.)   It was by this time apparent that Cuesta's
own army had become quite tired of him.

To Lord Castlereagh Wellington wrote (1st August), a few
days after the battle : " I certainly could get the better of
everything if I could manage General Cuesta ; but his temper
and disposition are so bad that that is impossible."   (Ibid.
p. 523).

Southey says, " The necessity of removing Cuesta from the
command, appeared so urgent to Mr. Frere, that he deemed
it his duty to present a memorial on the subject, though
Marquis Wellesley was expected two days afterwards (August
9th) at Seville."   Having detailed the evils consequent on
Cuesta's neglects and omissions, he urged the appointment
of another commander, " either the choice being left to Sir
Arthur, or the Junta itself appointing the Duke of Alberquerque, who possessed his confidence, and that of the army ;
and whose abilities had been tried and approved." * * " This
was the last act of Mr. Frere in his public capacity ; and it
was consistent with the whole conduct of that Minister, who,
during his mission, never shrunk from any responsibility, nor
ever, for the fear of it, omitted any effort which he thought
requisite for the common welfare of his own country and of
Spain."   Southey remarks, that the presentation of this memorial, at such a moment, might seem irregular in a public
point of view, and, in a private one, might alter the feelings
with which Mr. Frere would wish to take leave of many
friends in Spain.   But in addition to the urgency of the case,
he considered it would be peculiarly unpleasant for Lord
Wellesley to begin his mission with a discussion in which his
brother was concerned.   In fact, the Marquis did not, on his
arrival, think it necessary to follow up the memorial by insisting on Cuesta's removal, and limited his interference to a
strong expression of his own sense of Cuesta's misconduct.
A few days later, after further communication with the Junta
and his brother, he came round to Mr. Frere's view, and presented a note, which enforced his predecessor's suggestion.
But, in the meantime, a paralytic stroke had rendered Cuesta
physically incapable of command, and he had resigned.—
Southey, vol. II. chap. xxx. pp. 456-8.

the field, he would have effected a great deal. He had not Romana's education or experience, nor would he, on the whole, have been as good a general-in-chief—but he had great courage and energy, and his high rank and popularity would have enabled him to do many things no one else could have attempted. He had the reputation too of being extremely lucky, which goes a great way with the common people in Spain and every where else. He thoroughly understood his soldiers, and could make them do anything for him, and especially he could make use of their extraordinary powers of endurance and marching, for which the Spaniards have been famous since the time of the Carthaginians. Nothing could have better shown what he could do with such troops as he had than his march to cover Cadiz when threatened by Mortier. Alberquerque marched from near Cordova to Cadiz, with 8000 infantry and artillery, as well as cavalry, more than 260 miles in eight days, and saved Cadiz. It was after I had been relieved, but I was at Cadiz at the time. I was so surprised, when a man brought the news of Alberquerque's approach, that I could not believe it till the man told me he had spoken to the Duke and given him a light for his cigar, and described him so minutely that I felt sure he had seen Alberquerque." * * " He had in perfection some of the faculties in which Cuesta and all the old generals were most deficient, and had he commanded earlier, and been better supported, he would have given Wellington exactly the kind of aid he needed, and the war might have been materially shortened ; but after I left, Lord Wellesley did not know his value till too late, and did not support him as he should have done. The Junta were always jealous of him, and anxious to get rid of him, so they sent him to England as Ambassador, by way of an honourable exile, and he afterwards died of vexation and a broken heart."

Of Romana, Mr. Frere had, on the whole, a higher opinion than of any of the Spanish generals; and, making every allowance for their early and intimate friendship, Romana's career justified his estimate, which was in the end fully confirmed by the judgment of Wellington.

The following letters are given, as illustrating the character of the intercourse Mr. Frere kept up, and the manner in which he endeavoured to support the Spanish General.[1]

After Soult had been driven by Sir Arthur Wellesley from Oporto into the mountains of Gallicia, in May, 1809, Romana, having disposed the forces under his immediate command to harass and watch the French, paid a flying visit to Asturias, for the purpose of rousing that province to a better use than had been previously made of their resources. Finding the Junta both inefficient and corrupt, he used his authority as Captain-General to suppress them, and nominated a fresh Junta, composed of men of greater energy, and undoubted devotion to the national cause.[2] The measure seems to have been wise and necessary; but, under the pressure of more urgent calls on his attention, Romana neglected to justify or even report it to the Supreme Central Junta.

This omission gave great offence to that body, and led to Mr. Frere addressing the following letter to Romana :—

"SEVILLE, *June 4th*, 1809.

"MY DEAR ROMANA,

"I HAVE for a long time deferred writing to you upon a subject which is very disagreeable to

---

[1] The limits of a slight biographical sketch do not admit of the insertion of Mr. Frere's longer and more important despatches, which have been already published.

[2] See Southey, vol. ii. chap. xxii. p. 322, ed. 1827, for a full account of the romantic incidents of this visit of Romana to Asturias, and of its causes and results.

me to mention; but which I cannot, I think, any
longer delay, without being wanting in that friendship with which you have honoured me; but I cannot conceal from you, that the effect which has been
produced by the interruption of your correspondence, has been extremely unfavourable.

"If you wish to remain upon fair terms with the
Junta, and not to be understood as treating them
with voluntary disrespect, it will be necessary to
send a complete and most careful explanation of
your motives for suppressing the Junta of Asturias,
in which I have not the least doubt that you were
right, and I have lost no opportunity of saying so.
But when it is merely objected, that whatever might
have been the *necessity* for suppressing an ancient
constituted body, that *necessity* ought to have been
made evident to the Government at least after the
measure was taken, I feel myself at a loss for an
answer. The expression of their being *a Junta
nominated by intrigue*, has given great offence to
their countrymen here, and will require particularly
to be accounted for, or qualified.

"It will be necessary likewise to enter into a
general review of your military operations since
your return to Asturias, and their motives. That
you must have had great difficulties to encounter
cannot be doubted; but while this is only known
or felt in general, and without any knowledge of
the particulars, it must lead to a very false estimate of your merits, while the Asturians are exag-
gerating the means which they say they are ready
to put at your disposal.

"I have not the least idea that they could have
given you two regiments in a state fit to leave the
province; but, till this is explained and made evident, people here will think that you had nothing
to do but to march into Gallicia with the force which
was offered you, and destroy General Ney."

Mr. Frere then refers to his own recall, and proceeds :—

"You will undoubtedly have heard from England, that General Moore's business has ended in my recall. I cannot deny that I feel it very sensibly, though I knew at the time that I ran the risk, and exposed myself to it voluntarily."

He speaks of his own determination, "at any rate, and by any means," to urge Moore to what appeared to him to be the duty of a general in command of such an army, and adds :—

"This is among the other reasons which induce me to write to you. My successor is immediately expected. He is a man of talents, but cannot be expected to feel for you the same interest as your very faithful and sincere—J. H. FRERE."[1]

On the eve of quitting office, and after his successor had arrived at Cadiz, Mr. Frere, feeling how necessary to Romana would be the support he had always received from the British representative, addressed the following letter to Lord Wellesley, inclosing a copy of a note which he had addressed to the Supreme Junta regarding Romana's services, and the mode in which they might be made of most avail to the common cause.

"*Private.*"　　　　　　　　　　"*August 8th*, [1809].

"MY DEAR LORD,

"YOU will have seen from my last dispatch the situation of the M. Romana, against whom the Asturians have been driving a most furious intrigue, which has been assisted by the total want of attention to correspondence on his part ; the consequence

---

[1] Lord Russell, then a very young man travelling in Spain with Lord and Lady Holland, lived for some time with Mr. Frere at Seville. He told me that Romana, who was also living in the house, would often join Mr. Frere in the afternoon, and the two friends would set out without their hats whilst waiting for dinner, and sometimes ramble so far absorbed in their conversation that they forgot the dinner and the other guests waiting for it.

was, that a general idea prevailed here that his faculties were impaired; and so universal was the consent upon this point, that I hardly felt myself authorized to stand out against it, when the determination was taken by the Junta to recall him.

" These ideas have since vanished, and I accordingly directed a note to Mr. Garay.

" I would not, however, communicate it to him (the Marquis Romana), having nothing but conjecture as to the sentiments of the Government at home, and being in expectation of your almost immediate arrival by every dispatch that I received; and being apprehensive that those sentiments might not be in unison with the conduct which he may probably hold, and which is insinuated at the end of my dispatch (I think No. 93). But if Government are disposed to continue to him their support, I think that no time should be lost in informing him of the interest which is taken by them in his situation, and I would in that case forward my note to him."

Romana had shortly before this been summoned to take a seat in the Supreme Central Junta at Seville. The promotion was ostensibly an honourable recognition of his great services; but he regarded it, with feelings which the event seemed to justify, as a mistake to remove him, at such a moment, from the province where he had so well organized the most effective form of national resistance to the invader. In a touching and spirit-stirring general order,' he took leave of the companions-in-arms many of whom had followed him in his escape from Denmark. At Seville he soon found fresh proof of the utter incompetence of a body constituted as the Junta was, to rule Spain at such a juncture ; but it was not easy under the circumstances to devise a better form of government. Many plans were discussed, and Romana submitted to his colleagues a note, strongly advocating, on

constitutional grounds, as well as on considerations
of present expediency and general policy, an entire
change in the form and machinery of administration ; so that the Government should represent
more distinctly a regency acting for the lawful
Sovereign and for the Cortes, as, by ancient right,
the representatives of all estates in the realm.[1]

It is apparently in reply to a letter from Mr.
Frere, forwarding a copy of this note, which he had
received from Romana, that Lord Wellesley several
weeks afterwards wrote to the former :

"*Private.*"   "SEVILLE, *Oct.* 17*th*, 1809.

"MY DEAR SIR,

"I RETURN the Marquis de la Romana's
note, with many thanks to you for this very interesting communication.

"I request you to express to him my particular
gratitude for the perusal of a paper containing so
much real wisdom and public spirit, conveyed in
the most powerful and eloquent language.

"The general sentiments and ideas expressed by
M. de la Romana are entirely conformable to my
opinions, and I sincerely hope that he will urge,
with his characteristic energy, the instantaneous
accomplishment of the two great objects of his proposal—the appointment of a Council of Regency,
and the proclamation of a fixed and early day for
the assembly of the Cortes.

"In some of the details of his plan, I should perhaps differ with him, and I should certainly be
disinclined to insist on any point of the detail, or of
mere theoretical perfection, which might delay the
concentration of the executive power, or the meeting of a regular representation of the estates of the
realm.

---

[1] The substance of the note is given by Southey, vol. II.
chap. xxv. p. 492.

"In one point, however, I agree completely with M. de la Romana, in the absolute necessity of rendering the executive power, now to be formed, as exact an image as can be constituted, of the legitimate sovereignty of the absent King.

"Its form, constitution, character, and even its name, should be so framed as to recall to the nation the actual existence of the lawful monarch—a circumstance which the present Government is ill calculated to preserve in the memory of the people.

"The Marquis de la Romana's note is so admirable in many respects, that I should be much obliged to him for a copy of it, with permission to translate, and to lay it before His Britannic Majesty, who would not fail to approve a composition which unites such animating sentiments of loyalty and freedom.

"Believe me to be, with great esteem, dear sir, your faithful servant,   WELLESLEY." [1]

---

[1] When this letter was written, Lord Wellesley was on the eve of returning to England, and nothing effectual was done to improve the constitution of the body which represented the central authority of the Spanish Government. Shortly afterwards, in January, 1810, when the incompetence of the Junta had brought the enemy to the gates of Cadiz, Romana was nominated to command the army in Estramadura. After rendering important service by securing Badajos against being surprised by the French, he, with very inadequate means, made effectual head against them for several months in his own province, whilst Wellington was maturing his plans and organizing his troops for the defence of the lines of Torres Vedras. After Wellington retired within the lines, at the end of 1810, Romana joined him with 6000 men of the Estramaduran army. When Massena was forced to retreat, and Wellington issued from his lines to follow up his baffled opponent, it was arranged that Romana should employ his troops on the enemy's flank. He was to have set out the next day to rejoin his army, which had re-crossed the Tagus, with a view to keep open communication with the rich corn country of Alemtejo and Badajos, when he was seized with a heart complaint, and died suddenly at Cartano on the 23rd of January, 1811. Wellington had learnt thoroughly to appreciate

Mr. Frere used to refer to the bitter and most unjust opposition to Wellington, and especially to the clamour in Parliament, in the Common Council of the City of London, and by a portion of the press, against the grant of a peerage and pension to him, after the battle of Talavera, as striking proofs of the errors to which popular contemporary views and opinions are liable, and as illustrating the dangers of entrusting executive power to an assembly too exclusively composed of what are called "practical men." "They are apt," he said, "to undervalue or ignore the teachings of history, and always distrust any suggestion of that foresight which requires somewhat of the poetical faculty and imagination. If the 'practical men' who were always inveighing against the war had had their way, Wellington would have been recalled, and Spain delivered over to France in 1810. The instinct of the English nation was right, as it often is, without knowing why; but comparatively few men, in or out of Parliament, really understood why it was certain that in the long run the Spaniards must succeed if they persevered, and why it was wise and safe for England to support them to the utmost. The greater part of the Whigs shut their eyes to the fact that the cause of the Spaniards was really the cause of national freedom and liberty. They were so charmed with the Revolution for de-

---

the great qualities of the Spanish soldier under every form of trial; and unused as he was to lavish praise, he recorded his sense of Romana's services in the following tribute to his memory:

"In Romana the Spanish army have lost their brightest ornament, his country their most upright patriot, and the world the most strenuous and zealous defender of the cause in which we are engaged; and I shall always acknowledge with gratitude the assistance which I received from him, as well by his operation as by his counsel, since he had been joined with this army."—*Wellington Despatches*, 26th January, 1811, vol. vii. p. 190.

stroying absolute monarchy, that they continued to worship it after it had, as violent revolutions generally do, erected another and a worse tyranny."

In the revulsion of feeling consequent on Wellington's splendid successes in the last four years of the war, the very essential services of men like Sir Robert Wilson, Col. Trant, Sir Samuel Ford Whittingham, and of many individual Englishmen, as well as Spaniards, were in danger of being altogether forgotten. Few officers suffered more from this forgetfulness than Sir Hew Dalrymple. Of him Mr. Frere said—"He had the rare merit of seeing from the first the real character and importance of the Spanish insurrection against Napoleon, and of always doing or advising the right thing to aid it. Yet he is chiefly remembered as if he had been responsible for stopping Wellington's career of victory by the convention of Cintra. Whereas the truth is, all the mischief was done before he arrived, and the convention was, as many excellent military judges believed, the best thing he could have done under the circumstances. However that may be, but for him the Spanish insurrection might have been nipped at the outset."

The following memorandum expresses these views more fully :—

"I consider Sir Hew Dalrymple to have been the most active agent in promoting the insurrection in the south of Spain.

"Had not Castaños relied upon the promises of support given him by Sir Hew, it is much to be feared that he would not have moved from Algeziras, for he could by no means rely at that period either upon Pena or Morlà.

"Castaños had under his command 10,000 regular troops ; with them were incorporated at Utrera 15,000 peasants ; *the whole of the Spanish force at the Battle of Baylen.*

"After the capitulation, 17,000 Frenchmen filed

through the ranks of the Spanish army, and laid down their arms.

"The number of killed and wounded on the part of the French at the Battle of Baylen amounted to 4,000. Dupont was therefore defeated, and obliged to capitulate, by a force very little superior in number to his own, and three-fifths of which had only learned to load and fire a few days previous to the battle.

"It should however never be forgotten that Sir Hew Dalrymple's enlightened view of the grand movement of the Spanish nation induced him, upon his own responsibility, to engage Castaños to take the field, in spite of the lukewarm support of his friends at Cadiz; and that without the co-operation of Castaños, the Battle of Baylen could not have been fought, and the war would, in all probability, have been crushed in its infancy.

"So important, however, and well-timed was the capitulation granted by Castaños to Dupont, that one battalion of Reding's force was actually surrounded and taken prisoners by Vedel, before Vedel was informed of the capitulation, and he was at last driven to agree to it by Dupont's threats."

On his return to England, Mr. Frere found the position of parties materially changed, by the differences between Mr. Canning and Lord Castlereagh, which had ended in a duel, in the retirement of both from office, and in the complete breaking up of the Portland ministry. Many years after, in reply to a question as to the original cause of the divergence of opinions which had ended so disastrously, Mr. Frere said : "Canning told me he had written me a very full account of the quarrel, and of all that led to it. It happened while I was in Spain; and the letter was lost with the vessel which carried the mails. I have no doubt the cause was something of the same kind as occurred very often to me. For instance : it was a great object for us to occupy

Cadiz ;[1] the difficulty was to overcome the jealousy
of the Junta.   I was working, by the aid of Garay,
the secretary to the Junta, to get the proposition
that an English garrison should be sent to occupy
Cadiz, to come from the Junta themselves.   We
had so far succeeded, that I had every reason to
believe that such a proposition would in a few days
be made to me ; when, without any warning, I got
a despatch from Lord Castlereagh (who was then
Secretary at War), telling me that he had sent an
agent of his own to arrange for the landing of an
English force, and desiring me to assist him.   This,
as far as I could learn, was without any previous
communication with the Foreign Office, or any
notice to me.   The jealousy of the Junta was
instantly aroused, and it was with the greatest
difficulty I pacified them, pointing out what had
happened with Madeira, which had been occupied
while I was at Lisbon by an English force, to prevent its falling into the hands of the French, without previous notice sent to Portugal ; but it was,
at the time I spoke, again safe in the hands of the
Portuguese.   I have no doubt things of this kind
were of constant occurrence.   This want of fore-
thought, and of consideration for his colleagues in
the Cabinet, was of course very galling to a man of
Canning's temperament." . . . . Of Lord Castlereagh, he added : " When he got among the
princes and sovereigns at the Congress, to settle
Europe after the war, he thought he could not be
too fine and complaisant ; the consequence was,
the sacrifice of many points on which we ought
and might easily have insisted.   The first thing I
heard of his doing at the Congress made me feel
that he was not up to the work.   It was some
arrangement which he had much at heart for some
accession of territory to Hanover.   This satisfied

---

[1] *Vide ante*, p. 126.

me that he did not understand his position, for it was in direct opposition to what our Government had always declared to be our own intentions with regard to Hanover. The surrender of Java was another instance of great interests of our own sacrificed to a wish to please other potentates at the Congress. It did not seem to me that he ever clearly saw what of real good had resulted in various ways from the convulsions consequent on the Revolution, and the long war ; and how much there was in the former state of things which it was by no means desirable to restore. Where, for instance, was the necessity for picking up the poor old Pope and all the little Italian princes out of the mire, and brushing them, and setting them up again ? It only turned good men into Carbonari."

With his mission to Spain Mr. Frere's active political career ended, and his subsequent life of comparative retirement is marked by few events. His father had died in 1807, leaving him landed estates in the eastern counties, the management of which afforded him for a time ample occupation and amusement. A letter from his mother, written just after he set out on his second voyage to Spain, gives a glimpse of the home to which she was prepared to welcome him on his return from his eventful mission.

"October 31st, 1808.

"My Dear Son,

"The letter I received from Bartle containing the account of your safe arrival at Corunna, gave the greatest satisfaction to all your relations here, especially to me, who have listened to all the wind and stormy rain since you sailed with much fear, mixed with a little hope that you might have escaped from them. We had continual accounts of wrecks, but I had no idea of having more than two sons exposed to that danger till I received a scrap, in pencil writing, from Temple,[1] dated 'Commerce,' Yarmouth Roads. You must have had a full gale in your favour to be only one day without seeing land between the English and Spanish coast, and it was no slight rolling of the vessel that would have had an uncomfortable effect on you, which Bartle says he felt in an inferior degree. I am truly thankful your perils from the sea for the present are ended. Temple hurried to London to catch a glimpse of you both, and was too late; and with his voyage, disappointment, and journey, was more fatigued than ever I saw him before."

After a chronicle of family news, she returns to business at Roydon, his country house in Norfolk, details the arrival of the boxes of books, pictures, and painted glass, which he had brought home after his first missions to Lisbon and Madrid, and her deliberations as to the particular windows in which he might think the painted glass could be put up to the best effect—then reverts to the account his brother had given of their landing at Corunna:

"Your reception in Spain was both splendid and affectionate; honourable to your country and to your former representation of it. I hope the close of your mission, whenever it happens, will be fully answerable to the commencement. Susan" [his sister] "is looking for me. As I cannot look at you, I will fold this up, for when your Aunt Fenn comes, whom I am expecting every minute, I must go instantly."

At a less hurried moment she adds a—

---

[1] Her youngest son: born 1781; died 1859. Rector of Finningham, Roydon and Burston, and subsequently Speaker's Chaplain and Canon of Westminster. Like his brothers he was a tall striking-looking man, whence arose the name given him by his friends, "The Beauty of Holiness."

"P.S.—Write often. Tell Bartle we thank him for his letters. Answer the painted glass queries."— and ends with a quiet suggestion, such as becomes a good church-woman, even in the days when church restoration was little thought of:

"N.B.—Is any of the glass designed for Roydon church?"[1]

A letter written by a lady who was staying at Roydon in 1813 describes him as "a very odd creature, but very good and very entertaining;" getting up early in the morning to teach two little nephews grammar, taking one still smaller a walk, during which he completed teaching him his letters, and "spending an hour after dinner in reading to them the ballad of William of Cloudesley, which delighted them very much."

One of their school books bears marks of a visit the same boys had just before paid him at Eastbourne. Under a picture of a child gathering crabs, he had written:

> "By cruel uncles harassed and perplexed,
> First taught to read and to count figures next,
> His only pastime, when his task is o'er,
> Is picking Crabs and Sand-eels on the shore."

---

[1] His mother died in 1813. She lived a life of unobtrusive charity and good deeds in a quiet country home ; but her own poetical powers (for one or two short specimens of which *vide* pp. 6—9) were above the average of authoresses of that day, and her extensive reading, correct taste, and capacity for entering into all the literary and political pursuits of her children made her always their trusted friend and companion. When she felt her strength failing, she summoned to her bedside her eight children who were in England, and after talking calmly and cheerfully of that their last meeting on earth, "bade them go to dinner, which she trusted they would enjoy, and never to let their sorrow for her make them neglect their own health ; and she promised she would send them down a toast," after the fashion of the day. This she did in the words "Our union ;" which, in memory of the occurrence, and in accordance with her wishes,

There are many passages in his writings which show how well Mr. Frere could appreciate the characteristic features of such East Anglian scenery as Crabbe and Bloomfield have described, and Crome and Constable have painted. The lines headed " Modern Improvements,"[1] which Byron admired as a fragment of "real English landscape painting," were inspired by some rough unimproved fields, near the Hall at Roydon. The " Journey to Hardingham" is a versification of an actual reverie on a wintry ride to visit his friend Whiter, and his imitation of "Quid tibi visa Chios," describes the scenes and thoughts of his everyday life at Roydon. But while not insensible to the charms of the country, his favourite pursuits and early friendships all conspired to draw him to the capital. In London society his polished wit and playful fancy, his varied learning and great powers of conversation, joined to the easy courtesy of a travelled English gentleman of the old school, made him everywhere a welcome guest. He had many qualifications for the highest success in almost any branch of literature, but he wanted the stimulus of ambition or of necessity to write, whilst his extreme fastidiousness disinclined him to regard anything he composed as finished, and his wonderfully accurate and retentive memory tempted him to avoid the mechanical

---

her youngest son Temple afterwards had engraved as the motto on signet rings, bearing the device of the seals which Walton tells us were given by Dr. Donne " to many of his friends"—a Cross as the stock of the Anchor of Hope.

[1] The same feeling which runs through " Modern Improvements " is more tersely expressed in the following lines, scratched by Mr. Frere with a diamond on a dressing-room window in the east turret of Holland House, in 1811. They are now hung up as a souvenir in one of the boudoirs :

" May neither Fire destroy, nor Waste impair,
Nor Time consume thee, till the twentieth heir :
May Taste respect thee, and may Fashion spare."

labour of noting down either his thoughts or the results of his reading.

For this he paid a penalty, which is more or less rigorously exacted from all who prefer the pleasures of living society to the task of writing for the future. The most characteristic and valuable results of his reading and thinking were lost in every-day use; what little remains owes its preservation to contemporary friends, and the care of their biographers, who have noted a few of the sayings and anecdotes which survived in the memory of his companions long after Mr. Frere had ceased to be among them.

Such are the anecdotes preserved by Moore, in his faithful record of the meetings at which he was the petted guest of those who, a generation ago, gathered round them all that was distinguished for literary or political ability in London.

At one time he is pleased with Frere's comparison of O'Connell's eloquence to the "aërial potato" described by Darwin in his "Phytologia," and with his severe criticism on Erskine's verses, "The Muses and Graces will just make a jury." Another time he refers to "Frere's beautiful saying that 'next to an old friend, the best thing is an old enemy,'" and again he relates how "Madame de —— having said in her intense style, 'I should like to be married in English, in a language in which vows are so faithfully kept,' some one asked Frere 'What language, I wonder, was she married in?' '*Broken* English, I suppose,' answered Frere."[1]

Canning and Frere being invited by a clerical friend to come and hear his first sermon, asked them afterwards how they had liked it? Canning, to avoid saying it was uninteresting, promptly replied, "I thought it rather—short." "Ah," said the com-

---

[1] "Life, Letters, and Journals of Thomas Moore," edited by Lord John Russell, vol. iv. p. 302; vol. v. p. 102; vol. vi. p. 345.

poser, "I am aware that it was short, but I was afraid, if I made it longer, of being tedious." He paused for an answer. "But you were tedious," replied Frere *sotto voce*.

One night he had returned to Holland House to supper, with Lord and Lady Holland, after the play. They found that Mr. Shuttleworth[1] had already retired to rest. Whilst at supper they were disturbed by strange unearthly sounds at regular intervals, concerning the origin of which Frere expressed some curiosity. "Oh! it's only Shuttleworth snoring," said Lord Holland. "Ah," said Frere, "now I understand. He has not got that large nose for nothing."

The list might be enlarged by references to the works or memoirs of Scott, Byron, Southey, Gifford, Rose, Coleridge, Moore, Windham, Rogers, and others of his literary or political friends ; but except occasionally in the case of a careful chronicler like Moore, the wit or the wisdom which charmed are generally only to be inferred from the impression noted as produced on the hearer.

His letters, on the most trivial incidents of every day life, bear the impress of the same qualities which at all times lent a peculiar grace to his conversation. From the nature of the topics it is not easy to select what would give to the general reader a fair idea of the charm they had for the intimate friends to whom they were addressed.

A few extracts may, however, serve as specimens. The first is to his brother Bartle, who after serving with him for some years, and repeatedly acting as Envoy in Portugal and Spain, had been sent as Secretary of Legation to Constantinople.

---

[1] Rev. Ph. Shuttleworth, "a good scholar and most amiable man," tutor to the late Lord Holland, and subsequently Bishop of Chichester. The story is also told of Mr. Allen—but I am informed on undoubted authority that this was incorrect.

"ROYDON, *March 27th*, 1812.

"MY DEAR BARTLE,

"THOUGH I am not well to-day, and my views of things partake of the sort of physical anguish I feel, which I attribute to having sauntered about yesterday in the wind and sun with William, yet as to-morrow is not post-day, and my letter, though it does not enliven you, will show at least that I have not begun to forget you, I would not omit writing while Mam, William, and George were all employed in the same way. It will be no satisfaction, I believe, to you to know that your going makes me very melancholy; but I am still fully convinced that it was the only thing for you to do, and I think that you can never repent of having done so, and might very much of having refused it. After all, it will not be an unpleasant circumstance in your life to have seen those same Turks, of whom I would endeavour to know everything that could be known, and that my opportunities of leisure would allow me to learn. This cannot but be creditable, and may be very advantageous to you, let alone the satisfaction of one's own curiosity in the history and modes of thinking of so singular a race; I would, therefore, if possible, acquire the language, or, at least, as much of it as I could. I propose, in return, to task myself to write you long letters of what is going on here, such as if you think them worth keeping, which I hope you will, it may be a satisfaction to me, and perhaps at a more distant time to others, to look over. Above all, believe me, dear Bartle, ever affectionately yours, J. H. FRERE."

"If you have any commission for books or anything else to be sent after you, *I will* look to it."

"BLAKE'S HOTEL, *May 10th*, 1812.

"MY DEAR BARTLE,

"MR. MEYER, Secretary to the Commission to Malta, and a student of this Hotel, has sent his name to me very civilly, with an offer to take any letter or commission for you. Accordingly, I think it a good and safe opportunity for forwarding Birch's recipe with my compliments to the part affected. If it were not Sunday, I would get over the repugnance which I have felt hitherto in presenting myself as a customer at Mr. Weis's magazine, and dispatch the artillery by the same conveyance. Mr. Meyer is going within an hour or two, and therefore I will only set down, summatim, the history of the family since your departure. William [his brother, Sergeant Frere,] was made Master of Downing[1] on Friday last, by the votes of the two Archbishops and old T——; the two first procured by his own merits, and the third by H——, who had been himself a candidate, but seeing no chance of success, chose to secure it to William instead of leaving a doubtful election, which, as it might have left the business to the Chancellor, would in that case have been a decision in favour of his old antipathy, C——. Little D—— has been in town, and has been very strenuous and acute in the business, as he himself seems to allow. I have just this moment written a note to him to return me 'Childe Harold,' which I had lent him, and which I wish to send you. His (not D——'s, but Lord Byron's) love is Mrs. ——, as appears by the passage in which he mentions her having been born at Constantinople, and expresses the pleasure which arises from the reflection that the spot in which we are, has been before visited by other friends.

"Having just recovered from a fit of coughing, I will only say that William will not feel himself obliged to give up the law, and will continue to do as much business as he can get, and that the College in his hands will, I really think, be an ornament and an advantage to the University, instead

---

[1] Downing College, Cambridge.

of being (as it would otherwise have been made) a nuisance and a job, and (what you would feel most) a Johnian job."

Then after some family news :

" As for myself, I am thus far advanced since I left you in my way for Roydon, after having a *tête-à-tête* in my way here with old Admiral B—— at Godalming. Before I set off I went to buy a book (to take with me in the chaise), and pitched upon a pocket Pope's Homer. This has since led me to look at the original of that celebrated work. The result of my enquiries is that the second book has nothing to do with the first, and that the catalogue, together with the third and fourth books, at least, belong to some poem which related to the first events of the war. The author of the first book does not appear again distinctly till we see his Jupiter thundering against Nestor and Diomed. Such are my opinions, more amply detailed in a red book which I wish I could send you ; but if you partake of Lord Byron's feelings and would like 'to read what I have read,' I think you will agree with me. They begin to tell me that it is half-past twelve, and that Mr. Meyer was to set off at twelve. So adieu, my dear Bartle, and, believe me, ever affectionately yours, J. H. FRERE."

His unmarried sister, Susan, had made her home with him after their mother's death, and her letters to their absent brother at Constantinople form a very faithful chronicle of home doings. The difficulty and uncertainty of the communication during the last years of the great war may be judged of from the fact that letters every three or four weeks are spoken of as a " great luxury," though they took from two to five months in transit, and the later-written letters sometimes outstripped their predecessors by a month or two. Mr. Frere, in March, 1814, is described by his sister as joining her on a visit to their cousin, Lady Laurie, at Dover,

and there entertaining them with some verses of
"excellent nonsense," the recital of which is accidentally interrupted. The chronicle further records
the departure of Louis XVIII. and the Duchesse
d'Angoulême from Dover on the 24th April, 1814,
and the arrival of the allied sovereigns on the 6th
June : " Not a prince, potentate, or hero can visit
England without passing through Dover, and we
are waked out of our sleep in the night by the con-
cussion of the guns from the cliff above our house,
for these great people have so inured themselves to
hardships that they travel without respite, and their
greatest indulgence seems to be a truss of straw to
lie on when they stop to collect the train of their
followers ; the Emperor would have no other bed
at Mr. Fector's, and his sister the Grand Duchess
desired not to have a bed but a sofa to sleep on.
This trait, I find, raised them in the estimation of
my lady's maid and the housekeeper to an order
of beings much above the common race of mortals."
She describes the emperor's "ingenuous benign expression, and his look and personal together much
like a good English country gentleman, who knows
he is surrounded by people who respect him." The
Grand Duchess as "pretty, like her brother, with a
sweet expression." The Duke of Clarence had
determined on escorting the imperial party across
the Straits, but the Grand Duchess insisted on
Admiral Foley providing her another ship. She
had her little son, about four years old, with her,
and Mr. Fector's little boy, rather younger, was invited to pay him a visit, which was most graciously
received ; for, though his little Imperial Highness
made light of a warning that "it was not right to
stand on the hearthstone," he would not eat till his
young guest was first served ; and when they were
running about he stopped, and holding up his hands,
went softly for a minute aside, and in reply to a
question, What he was doing? replied, "He was

begging of God that he would let that nice little boy live." There are also descriptions of "Blücher shaking hands with everybody. The King of Prussia looking grave, dignified, with a handsome and agreeable countenance, though somewhat melancholy. Platoff bent with the fatigues he has gone through, and looking quite aged. The Duke of Wellington, who landed at five in the morning, and had at nine a levée of ladies to see him at breakfast, when they were most graciously received. The only unhappy-looking person of the party being the Prince of Orange (the unsuccessful suitor of the Princess Charlotte), who had come from London to meet the Duke."

Mr. Frere had been to Portsmouth to the great naval review given to the allied sovereigns by the Prince Regent, "who ingratiated himself much with the naval officers, who had before all a strong impression of his being very unfavourably disposed towards them. The Prince said 'he had never known till then what a glorious thing the British Navy was, and that he should never be satisfied without having Naval aides-de-camp as well as Military.'" The promise, however, was not fulfilled till after his brother came to the throne.

The following is from Mr. Frere to his sister, from Roydon :

"August 14th, 1815.

"MY DEAR SUSAN,

"I HAVE to thank you first for three letters.

"Secondly, for certain lobsters which came very opportunely when I was wanting to mend my dinner for Mr. Carter.

"Thirdly, for some picture frames, which are very handsome, and fit the pictures very exactly.

"Lastly, I have to thank my cousin for recollecting that I should like to see Made. Suffrien's letter, which is indeed a very curious one, and shows that unless a Royalist party is formed quickly, there will be only one party in the country, which will reduce it to a situation worse than that of Spain four years ago."

*　　　　　*　　　　　*

Then after some amusing country gossip, and details of his every-day life, he adds :—

"I am now thinking what I can do in return for the favours above enumerated.

"First, this letter contains all that I could have had to tell you if I had written regularly in answer to yours, for it is all that has happened of any kind.

"Secondly, I send you some apricots.

"Thirdly, Mr. Bett's cart is agreeable to take your chair, which I send herewith.

"Fourthly, I transmit half the remainder of the Stilton cheese, which I hope will meet with your favourable construction.

"Fifthly, I return my cousin's letter with many thanks, and desire you to give my love to her, and to believe me, &c.

"I must send back my cousin's carriage, and I believe when it goes I shall slip into it, *but I have so much to do*, as Mrs. B—— says."

In one of his letters, when urged to "mention news, literature, or the ordinary topics of the day," to a relation who was suffering from the severest of domestic afflictions, and to whom he had just written several pages of grave, thoughtful, earnest reasoning, he excused himself from attempting lighter topics by saying, "It would be too much like the story in St.-Simon of the old Abbé at Versailles, who finding a man in the forest with his leg broken, being unable to do anything better for him, stood by him and offered him pinches of snuff from his box."

A letter written in the autumn of this year by his sister gives an amusing account of the party assembled at Roydon. The prospects of a secure and prolonged peace were supposed to promise a fall in the high rents of war time. Lady Laurie, the "cousin" of the letter just quoted, had been suggesting various household reforms, and Mr. Frere, his sister says, had gone to London and "amused himself just as he was going in contriving retrenchments of expense, in the prospect of having large deductions of receipts the next rent day. I told him it would end in some nightly visitation of the Muse; and accordingly, one morning were produced some verses, which I saved to divert you with, though the fragment will never be finished, and my cousin's occupations of making wines and preserves, which were to have been immortalized, are not yet sung :—

> " In the old cupboard with the fluted key
>   To hoard the sugar and secure the tea;
>   To purchase groceries at a cheaper rate,
>   To teach old liveries to outlive their date,
>   To count the fowls, to cater for the hogs,
>   To calculate the coals, to hoard the logs;
>   In yearly brewings to retrench the malt,
>   To reckon and secure the pork in salt,
>   By just restraint of economic law
>   To curb the roaring oven's ravening maw,
>   To watch the dairy's ever-varying ways
>   With timid censure, or with temperate praise;
>   Nor seek to scrutinize the wondrous plan,
>   Unfathomable by the mind of man,
>   The mysteries of that secret sphere are known
>   To female spirits, and to them alone.

" And here end the verses, which are marred in the transcribing by some absence of mind caused by my cousin's discourse about the fog, which is coming by solemn approaches up to our windows; Marshal Ney's trial; a round of beef that I am contriving how to pickle and send you, that you may have some use for that mustard pot she gave you; and Patience herself, you know, when represented as tried to the utmost, has been described as seated upon such a throne, watching for the arrival of the desired round, and therefore we are uneasy at your being under so long and severe a trial, for we had no notion of the impossibility of getting good salt beef at Constantinople. These topics, and many others have been discussed whilst I am writing, and left me I do not know where in my letter." And then, after an ample family chronicle of the doings of distant branches, she ends with—" Here is a bulletin that you will scarcely have patience to go through at once; but, as a gentleman observed to Mrs. C——, who proposed reading to him her own poem on the Battle of Waterloo, 'he would have it to read to himself, and take as much as he liked at a time.'"

The letters dated 1816 contain numerous references to the agrarian disturbances which in the spring caused much alarm throughout the country. The details read much more like letters from a proclaimed district in Ireland than the chronicles of quiet Norfolk and Suffolk villages. The poor had suffered greatly through the winter; and though in parts wages had been raised in proportion to the rise in the price of wheat, "to 1*d.* more than the magistrates' order," this had not been done generally, and the poorer people, "persuaded that there was some design to wrong them," were inclined to all sorts of outrages. There are daily records of barns and ricks fired, shrouds and threatening notices sent to obnoxious employers, and crowds of pauper labourers "parading the country with horns blowing and threats of violence."

On the 12th of Sept. 1816, Mr. Frere married Elizabeth Jemima, Dowager Countess of Erroll. At this time, and indeed throughout his life, his friends had many anecdotes of his habitual abstraction of mind, when following out any absorbing train of thought. One of the best authenticated related that the late Mr. John Murray having for once relaxed his usual rule never to allow an author

to read or recite in the sanctum in Albemarle Street,
got so interested in some verses which Mr. Frere
was repeating and commenting on, that his dinner
hour was at hand.   He asked Mr. Frere to dine
with him, and continue the discussion ; but the latter, startled to find it was so late, excused himself
on the plea that "he had been married that morning, and had already overstayed the time when he
had promised Lady Erroll to be ready for their
journey into the country."   Another story rested
on Lady Erroll's own authority, and related to
their first acquaintance, some years before, when she
was in the zenith of her beauty, as Cosway and Sir
Martin Shee have painted her.   Mr. Frere had just
been introduced to her at an evening party, and
offered to hand her down-stairs and procure some
refreshment ; but getting much interested in conversation by the way, became so engrossed in the
train of thought he was pursuing, that he drank
himself a glass of negus that he had procured for
her, and then offered his arm to help her upstairs
without any idea of their not having achieved the
errand on which they came; and was only reminded
of his mistake by her laughing remonstrance with
him on his forgetfulness of her existence.   "This,"
she added, "convinced me that my new acquaintance was at any rate very different from most of
the young men around us !"

Whatever foundation there may have been for such
anecdotes, it is certain that long acquaintance deep-
ened his admiration of her into a devoted attachment.   Except in later years, from her failing
health, there was little of earthly sorrow to cloud
their married life, the character of which is aptly
foreshadowed in the closing verses of the lines he
addressed to her in the earlier years of his court-
ship.   To the charms of personal beauty and engaging manners she added those of deep and refined
feeling ; and his reliance on her good sense and

judgment is shown by constant reference in his letters to her fiat as decisive not only in questions of every-day life, but of literary taste and fitness.

The first part of "The Monks and the Giants" was published by Mr. John Murray, in 1817, as the " Prospectus and Specimen of an intended National Work, by William and Robert Whistlecraft, of Stowmarket, in Suffolk,[1] harness and collar makers, intended to comprise the most interesting particulars relating to King Arthur and his Round Table." A second part was subsequently sent to Mr. Murray, who published both together in 1818, with the title of " The Monks and the Giants."[2]

In this *jeu d'esprit*, Mr. Frere revived[3] in English poetry the octave stanza of Pulci, Berni, and Casti, which has since been completely naturalized in our tongue. Men of letters were not slow to recognise the service thus rendered to English literature, and Italian scholars especially were delighted to see one of the most beautiful of their favourite metres successfully adopted in a language so different from the dialect in which it was first used. Its value was immediately recognized by Byron. He wrote

---

[1] A lady residing in that part of Suffolk amused her friends much, at the time of the publication, by making a pilgrimage to Stowmarket, for the purpose of seeing "*those very intelligent Harness-makers.*"

[2] The late Lord Lansdowne, speaking on one occasion of Mr. Frere, to his nephew the Rev. Constantine Frere, said— " All his friends liked him all the more for his originality in everything"—and mentioned as an instance, that when he gave him a copy of "Whistlecraft," he did not formally present it, but, happening to be dining that night at Lansdowne House, said, as he got up to go away, " O, Lansdowne, where I left my hat and stick, in the hall, you'll find something, I think, you may like to see." " I looked," said Lord Lansdowne, " and found Whistlecraft."

[3] Fanshawe's "Lusiad," Fairfax's Tasso, Harrington's Ariosto, and other English works had previously been written in this metre. *Vide* " Notes and Queries" on this subject,— January 27th, 1872.

to Murray, from Venice, in October, 1817, announcing " Beppo," and said, " I have written a poem of eighty-four octave stanzas, humorous, in or after the excellent manner of Whistlecraft (whom I take to be Frere)." And ten days later, " Mr. Whistlecraft has no greater admirer than myself. I have written a story in eighty-nine stanzas, in imitation of him, called 'Beppo.'"[1]

Mr. William Stewart Rose, himself one of the most elegant Italian scholars of his generation, thus addressed Mr. Frere two years afterwards—

> " O thou that hast revived in magic rhyme
> That lubber race, and turn'd them out, to turney
> And love after their way ; in after time
> To be acknowledged for our British Berni ;
> Oh send thy giants forth to good men's feasts,
> Keep them not close."[2]

And in 1837 Mr. Rose wrote,[3] " Lord Byron is usually considered as the naturalizer of this species of poetry, but he had seen Mr. Frere's work before the publication of 'Beppo.' He made this avowal to me at Venice ; and said he should have inscribed 'Beppo' to him that had served him as a model, if he had been sure it would not have been disagreeable. Supposing (as I conclude) that some passages in it might have offended him."[4]

Southey, writing to Landor, who was residing

---

[1] A few months later (March 26, 1818), again writing to Murray of " Beppo," he says, " The style is not English, it is Italian ;—Berni is the original of *all;* Whistlecraft was my immediate model." Further acquaintance with Italian literature showed him Berni's obligations to his predecessors ; and on February 21st, 1820, writing of Pulci's Morgante Maggiore, he said, " It is the parent, not only of Whistlecraft, but of all jocose Italian poetry."

[2] " The Court and Parliament of Beasts. Translated from Casti." London, 1819.

[3] " Rhymes." Brighton, 1837.

[4] See also Miss Cornwallis's account of her conversation with Mr. Frere on the subject in May, 1819. " Letters of C. F. Cornwallis." Trübner & Co. 1864, pp. 22 and 23.

abroad, in February, 1820, said, "A fashion of poetry has been imported which has had a great run, and is in a fair way of being worn out. It is of Italian growth—an adaptation of the manner of Pulci, Berni, and Ariosto in his sportive mode. Frere began it. What he produced was too good in itself, and too inoffensive, to become popular ; for it attacked nothing and nobody; and it had the fault of his Italian models, that the transition from what is serious to what is burlesque was capricious. Lord Byron immediately followed, first with his ' Beppo,' which implied the profligacy of the writer, and lastly with his ' Don Juan,' which is a foul blot on the literature of his country, an act of high treason on English poetry. The manner has had a host of imitators."

There are passages in the " Monks and Giants " of great poetical beauty, and it is full of the humour which twenty years before had been so effective in the pages of the " Anti-Jacobin." But it did not achieve the popularity which might have been expected from these circumstances, joined to the complete mastery of metre and delicate sense of rhythm which the versification evinced. This was due not only to the reasons mentioned by Southey, but because people generally looked in it for political satire, and were disappointed when they failed to discover the meaning which they fancied must be hid under every name and allusion.

Among men of literary taste, the reception of the poem was sufficiently flattering to render it a matter of surprise to his friends that he never completed the continuation promised in the parts published, and of which he was known to have composed a great number of stanzas; these he would willingly recite to any appreciative listener, though he never wrote them down. Many years after (1844), in reply to a question as to the reason why he never completed the work, he said, "You cannot go on joking with people who won't be joked with. Most people who read it at the time it was published, would not take the work in any merely humorous sense; they would imagine it was some political satire, and went on hunting for a political meaning; so I thought it was no use offering my jokes to people who would not understand them. Even Mackintosh once said to me, 'Mr. Frere, I have had the pleasure of reading your "Monks and Giants" twice over,' and then he paused; I saw what was in his mind, and could not help replying with a very mysterious look, 'And you could not discover its political meaning?' Mackintosh said, 'Well, indeed, I could not make out the allegory;' to which I answered, still looking very mysterious, 'Well, I thought you would not.'

"I wished to give an example of a kind of burlesque of which I do not think that any good specimen previously existed in our language. You know there are two kinds of burlesque, of both of which you have admirable examples in Don Quixote. There is the burlesque of imagination, such as you have in all the Don's fancies, as when he believes the wench in a country inn to be a princess, and treats her as one. Then there is the burlesque of ordinary rude uninstructed common sense, of which Sancho constantly affords examples, such as when he is planning what he will do with his subjects when he gets his island, and determines to sell them 'at an average.' Of the first kind of burlesque we have an almost perfect specimen in Pope's 'Rape of the Lock;' but I did not know any good example in our language of the other species, and my first intention in the 'Monks and Giants' was merely to give a specimen of the burlesque treatment of lofty and serious subjects by a thoroughly common, but not necessarily low-minded man—a Suffolk harness-maker. Of course it was not possible always to adhere to such a plan, and I have no doubt I did occasionally diverge into something which was more akin to one's own real feeling on the subjects which turned up, and thus misled my readers; but for some time after the work was first published I was very fond of pursuing the idea, and used to finish a couple of stanzas every day.

"Another thing which disinclined me to go on with the work was the sort of stigma which at first attached to the metre after the publication of ' Don Juan.' I had a sort of parental affection for the metre, and knew what it was capable of in English as well as in Italian. Byron took a great fancy to it, and used it in ' Beppo,' which was all very well, and so were parts of ' Don Juan,' but there were other parts of ' Don Juan ' which could hardly be read *virginibus puerisque*, and there was such an outcry that if I had gone on writing in the same metre, and any one had misunderstood me, I should have been suspected of meaning something very improper."

I asked him if he could remember any of the stanzas of the continuation, and he repeated a good many, of which I am sorry to say the following are all of which the notes have escaped shipwreck. They were from the description of Ascopart, a young giant, who having been found by the monks, forsaken by his companions, and powerless from a broken limb, is taken into the monastery, cured, baptized, and, as far as the good brethren were able, civilized and rendered "a useful member of society;" though his giant nature perpetually breaks out in a manner which rather discomfits his reverend instructors. As soon as he can get about, the monks lead him round the convent, and show him all the wonders of civilization. Some things he understands, others are an inexplicable puzzle. All the arrangements for storing and providing food are easily enough understood, but—

" The mystery of the Turnspit in the Wheel
He understood not but admired with zeal.

    *   *   *   *   *

" No longer he regrets his native groves,
  His wonted haunt and his accustom'd rill ;
He views the bake-house, scullery, and stoves,
  And from the leathern jack delights to swill.
He saw the baker putting in some loaves,
  And, being quick and eager in his will,
He thrust him in, half-way, for an experiment—
It was not malice, it was only merriment.

    *   *   *   *   *

" The monks had purchased for their chapel floor
  Some foreign marbles, squares, of white and black ;
It lay where it was left, upon the shore,
  Till Ascopart convey'd it, on his back,
Through miry roads, eleven leagues and more,
  Poked, like backgammon men, into a sack ;
Went to the wood and kill'd a brace of bears,
Then drank six quarts of ale, and so to prayers.

" Besides all this he mended their mill dam,
  Digging a trench to turn aside the flood ;
And brought huge piles of wood to drive and ram,
  Jamm'd in with stones to make it sound and good.
The story looks a little like a flam,
  But in five days he built five stacks of wood,
To serve the convent for five winters' fire,
As high as their own convent-church or higher.

" But most he show'd the goodness of his heart
  In slaughtering swine and oxen for the year ;
From dawn to sunset there was Ascopart,
  With sweat, and blood, and garbage in a smear.
The butcher pointed out the rules of art—
  ' I'll smite 'um,' quoth the Giant, ' never fear.'
The clapper of the great old broken bell
He bang'd about him with, and down they fell.

" Pigs, when their throats were cut, amused him most—
  All cantering and curvetting in a ring ;
To see them as they jostled and they cross'd,
  He swore it was a pastime for a king.—
Laugh'd and laid wagers and cried out, ' ware post !'
  And as the monks were teaching him to sing,
He criticized their squeaking, and found fault—
' Come Pig ! now for a holding note in Alt.'

> " With such a size, and mass of limbs, and trunk,
>   And his loins girded with a hempen string,
> He look'd, and might have been, a lordly monk ;
>   Therefore I think it an unlucky thing
> That at their vespers he was always drunk,
>   And that he never would be taught to sing,
> But only saunter'd from the kitchen fire,
> To howl and make a hubbub in the quire."

*   *   *   *   *

" I put a good deal of this description of the young giant into Latin monkish verses. Here is one of them—

> " Notandum quod Asquibardus, Gigas et Paganus,
>   Tres menses in cœnobio sejurnavit,
>   Et gratam mentem monachis monstravit,
> Ad opera monasteria præstans manus ;
>   Ad salinandum bestias mactavit ;
> Eodem die, viz. Novembris tredecem
> Comedit salsasorum ulnas sedecem.

NOTA. " ' Campanæ magnæ funis tenet
>   Dimidium ulnæ minus,' says the margin ;
> A learned antiquary that had seen it
>   Transcribed the passage for me, strictly charging
> That I should keep his secret—and I mean it ;
>   His praises otherwise I should enlarge in—
> Encouraging and affording me facilities,
> In order to display my poor abilities."

" I thought the feats of pig-killing, and of eating so many ells of sausages, were not bad achievements for my harness-maker poet to admire in his gigantic hero."

One of the events was the tossing of King Ryance in a blanket ; his tormentors of course sing a song, the chorus of which was to this effect :—

> " This is King Ryance of high degree,
> Who sent the defiance so saucily ;
> Give him a lift, a turn, and a shift,
> And a flight in the air, hurra ! hurra !"

In a letter to his brother Bartle, dated May 24th, 1818, he wrote regarding the publication of the second part of the poem :—

"My Lady[1] is very anxious to have it published and very peremptory. My own impulse and resolution was to leave the thing unpublished, at least for the present.

"In my notion, a mere *jeu d'esprit*, such as the first, is pardonable if good judges think it good, even if the populace should not like it, and if the poem were a serious one there would be no harm in going on for the sake of the good judges before mentioned; but to persevere in a nonsensical work merely for the sake of the good judges of nonsense is a different business. Besides that, people are always ready to say that a continuation is not so good as the first part. I wish you would look it over to see whether there is any room for such an observation."

Fortunately his brother's judgment concurred with Lady Erroll's; and the second part, which contains some of the best passages in the poem, was not lost. The following recent criticism by a distinguished American scholar may be quoted, as showing that something more than personal friendship or the fashion of the day actuated his contemporaries in the estimate they formed of the work at its first appearance :—

"There are few books of its size which contain as much genuine wit, humour, and fancy, or which display greater skill in the management of both light and serious verse, or indicate fuller resources of culture. It is a fresh and unique *jeu d'esprit*, which exhibits a quality of cleverness as rare as it is amusing. The form and method of the poem, the structure of its verse, its swift transitions from sprightly humour to serious description or reflection, its mingling of exaggeration with sober sense, its heroi-comic vein, are all derived from the famous Italian romantic poems, especially from the *Mor-*

---

[1] Lady Erroll.

gante Maggiore of Pulci, and in a less degree from the *Animali Parlanti* of Casti. It has no moral object, and does not confine itself to a single continuous narrative, but is a simple work of amusement, free in its course, according to the whim and fancy of the writer. It is the overflow of an abundant and lively spirit, restrained only by the limits imposed by a fine sense of the proprieties of humour, and a thorough acquaintance with the rules of art. Its execution displays a command of style so complete in its way that it may be called perfect. The imaginary authors, the Whistlecrafts, appear in the poem only as giving a natural propriety to some of its simplicities of diction, and humorous absurdities of digression. Frere created the fiction of the 'harness and collar makers' simply to gain a freër swing for his mirth, and is at no pains to preserve an absolute consistency of tone. The bland conceit of the pretended illiterate poet and prosaic tradesman add point to the keen wit and delicate appreciation and expression of one of the finest of literary masters, of a scholar who quotes Æschylus, transcribes professed rhyming Latin monkish chronicles, explains the fable of Orpheus, and on every page shows—

"'Traces of learning and superior reading.'"

Speaking of the third and fourth cantos, the reviewer says: "The same qualities of style distinguish them,—the easy flow, of verse, the perfect command of natural language, the control of rhyme (the poet never seeming to be mastered, as Pulci and Berni often are, by the difficulties of the line), the rapid transitions, the playful humour, the happy strokes of satire, the characteristic delineation of personages, and the charming descriptions of scenery, display the genius of the author in even fuller measure than it is shown in the earlier episode of this delightful poem. . . . . . And thus ends one of the most playful, humorous, and original poems

in English, a perfect success in its kind, and that
kind one of the rarest and most difficult."[1]   He
then quotes Miss Cornwallis' account of her conversation with Mr. Frere on the comparative merits
of " Beppo " and "Whistlecraft," and Coleridge's preference for the superior metrical skill of the latter
poem, as shown in the greater ease and rapidity of
the verse.[2]

Byron's own opinion of Mr. Frere's taste and judgment is shown by his desiring Mr. Hobhouse to
send the first canto of " Don Juan " to him, and to
consult him, with Mr. Stewart Rose and Moore, as
to the propriety of publishing it.   The incidents of
this interview are thus described by Moore :[3]

" Met Hobhouse. . . . Asked him had I any
chance of a glimpse at 'Don Juan'? and then
found that Byron had desired it might be referred
to my decision ; the three persons whom he had bid
Hobhouse consult as to the propriety of publishing
it being Hookham Frere, Stewart Rose, and myself.   Frere, as the only one of the three in town,
had read it, and pronounced decidedly against the
publication. . . . . .

" Frere came in while I was at Lady D—'s ; was
proceeding to talk to him about our joint umpire-
ship on Byron's poem, when he stopped me by a
look, and we retired into the next room to speak
over the subject.   He said he did not wish the
opinion he had pronounced to be known to any one
except B. himself, lest B. should suppose he was
taking merit to himself, among the righteous, for
having been the means of preventing the publication of the poem.   Spoke of the disgust it would
excite if published ; the attacks in it upon Lady B. ;

---

[1] Article on John Hookham Frere in the " North American
Review," for July, 1868, by Mr. C. E. Norton.

[2] " Moore's Diary," April, 1823, vol. iv. p. 51.

[3] " Moore's Journals and Conversations," vol. ii. p. 263,
30th January, 1819.

and said, 'it is strange, too, he should think there is any connection between patriotism and profligacy. If we had a very Puritan court indeed, one can understand then profligacy being adopted as a badge of opposition to it; but the reverse being the case, there is not even that excuse for connecting dissoluteness with patriotism, which, on the contrary, ought always to be attended by the sternest virtues.' . . . . . .

"31st January. Went to breakfast with Hobhouse, in order to read Lord Byron's poem: a strange production, full of talent and singularity, as everything he writes must be: some highly beautiful passages, and some highly humorous ones; but as a whole not publishable. Don Juan's mother is Lady Byron, and not only her learning, but various other points about her, ridiculed. He talks of her favourite dress being dimity (which is the case), 'dimity' rhyming very comically with 'sublimity;' and the conclusion of one stanza is, 'I hate a dumpy woman,' meaning Lady B. again. This would disgust the public beyond endurance. There is also a systematized profligacy running through it which would not be borne. Hobhouse has undertaken the delicate task of letting him know our joint opinions."

"April 30th. Murray writes to me that Hobhouse has received another letter from Lord Byron, peremptorily insisting on the publication of 'Don Juan.' But they have again remonstrated. The murder, however, *will out* some time or other."[1]

The remonstrances of his "cursed puritanical committee," as Lord Byron called them, were however in vain. He would hear of no omission or curtailment, with the exception of a passage refer-

---

[1] "Moore's Journals and Correspondence," vol. ii. pp. 266 and 285.

ring to Lord Castlereagh, and one other.[1]   Mr. Frere always regarded Byron's inflexibility on this point as a great misfortune to English literature.   Some of the passages in "Don Juan" he considered equal to anything ever written by one whom he placed in the first rank of modern English poets.   The passages which formed the grounds of his objection to the publication of the poem as it stands, were, in his opinion, no less poetical than moral blemishes; and would probably never have been written, and certainly never published had Byron been in his natural frame of mind, and among real friends in his own country, instead of writing and publishing in a state of unnatural excitement, amid such companionship as surrounded him at Venice.

During 1818-19, Mr. Frere seems to have devoted much of his time to the translations, by which, probably, rather than by his original works, his rank among the poets of the present century will be determined.   He had a rare combination of all those powers which are necessary to reproduce the ideas of a distant age, and of a different language, in such modern dress as the original author might have used had he lived now; and he had also the critical power which enabled him to detect and point out the secret of good and bad translation, and to lay down canons which might aid others in the ever tempting but arduous task of transmuting into modern English verse the wit and poetry of the ancients.

The undertaking was one for which, from his schoolboy days, he had shown a special taste and aptitude.   His earlier experiments in translation are thus described by Mr. Norton: "In April, 1808, Southey writes to Scott: 'I saw Frere in London,

---

[1] *Vide* "Moore's Life of Byron," vol. iv. pp. 148 and 149. "Letters to Mr. Murray of Jan. 20th, 25th, and Feb. 1st, 1819."

and he has promised to let me print his translations
from the "Poema del Cid." They are admirably
done. Indeed, I never saw anything so difficult to
do, and done so excellently, except your supple-
ment to Sir Tristrem.'[1]   These translations appeared in the Appendix to Southey's 'Chronicle of
the Cid,' and deserve all the praise that Southey
gives to them.   Mr. Ticknor, in his 'History of
Spanish Literature,' quotes some passages from
them, and characterizes Mr. Frere as 'one of the
most accomplished scholars England has produced,
and one whom Sir James Mackintosh has pronounced to be the first of English translators.'
Frere's excellence as a translator had, indeed, been
exhibited at a very early age.   In Ellis's 'Specimens of the Early English poets,' which first appeared in 1790, an Anglo-Saxon Ode on Athelstan's
Victory is given in the original, with a literal translation, to which is subjoined a metrical version,
supplied, says Mr. Ellis, 'by the kindness of a friend.'
This friend was the young Frere, and Mr. Ellis
adds: 'This [version] was written several years ago,
during the controversy occasioned by the poems
attributed to Rowley, and was intended as an imitation of the style and language of the fourteenth
century.   The reader will probably hear with some
surprise that this singular instance of critical ingenuity was the composition of an Eton school-boy.'
As an example of skilful adoption of the language
and style of an early period, this version is not less
remarkable, under the circumstances, than the compositions of Chatterton.   'It is,' says Mackintosh,
in his 'History of England,' 'a double imitation,

---

[1] Southey adds, "I do not believe that many men have a
greater command of language and versification than myself,
and yet this task of giving a specimen of that wonderful poem
I shrunk from fearing the difficulty." Southey to Walter
Scott, April 22nd, 1808.

unmatched perhaps in literary history, in which the writer gave an earnest of that faculty of catching the peculiar genius, and preserving the characteristic manner, of his original, which, though the specimens of it be too few, places him alone among English translators.'   And Scott, in his 'Essay on Imitation of the Ancient Ballads,' written in 1830, and published in the 'Minstrelsy of the Scottish Border,' says : 'I have only met, in my researches into these matters, with one poem, which, if it had been produced as ancient, could not have been detected on internal evidence.   It is the "War Song upon the Victory at Brunnanburg, translated from the Anglo-Saxon into Anglo-Norman," by the Right Honourable John Hookham Frere.'

" At the time of the publication of ' Sir Tristrem,' in 1804, Frere expressed a cordial admiration for the performance ; and George Ellis wrote to Scott that Frere, 'whom you would delight to know, and who would delight to know you,' has 'no hesitation in saying that he considers "Sir Tristrem" as by far the most interesting work that has as yet been published on the subject of our earliest poets, and, indeed, such a piece of literary antiquity as no one could have, *à priori*, supposed to exist.'   To this Scott answers : ' Frere is so perfect a master of the ancient style of composition, that I would rather have his suffrage than that of a whole synod of your vulgar antiquaries.'

" In translating the ancient Spanish poem of the Cid, Frere was thus at work in a field of which he was doubly master.   The full merit of his versions is hardly to be understood without acquaintance with the archaic vigour and simplicity of the original, and the peculiarities of its diction and versification.   .   .   .

" There is probably no classic author of whose works a good translation is more difficult than Aristophanes.   The wonderful combination of widely

different qualities which he exhibits in his comedies,
—the knowledge of human nature, the insight into
affairs, the solid sense, the fertile invention, the
daring fancy, the inexhaustible humour, the pro-
digious exaggeration, both in invention and in
language, which, even in its wildest and most
amusing excesses, displays the controlling influence
of the finest taste, and of native elegance of mind,
the keen irony, the vehement invective, the serious
purpose under the comic mask,—demand, if the plays
are to be fitly rendered, a scarcely less wonderful
combination of powers in the translator ; while the
exquisite form of the poetry, the melody of the
various rhythm, and the frequent change in the
versification, modulated according to each change
in tone of sentiment, require for their reproduction in
another far less flexible language, with another and
far poorer system of metres, not only a consummate
mastery of the forms of verse, but also a vocabulary
in the highest degree pure, racy, and idiomatic."[1]

Mr. Norton then refers to Mr. Frere's article on
Mitchell's Aristophanes, in the Quarterly Review
of July, 1820,[2] of which he gives a summary, and

---

[1] "North American Review," *ubi supra*, p. 160.

[2] "Talked of Aristophanes. I mentioned the admirable
article upon Aristophanes in the " Quarterly" two or three
years ago. Sharpe remembered it also, and thought it altogether perfect." (Moore's "Journals," vol. ii. p. 265, Jan. 30,
1819.) The article here referred to, which will be found reprinted in the second volume, was Mr. Frere's only contribution to the "Quarterly." He had been one of the original
projectors of the Review, when it was started by the late
Mr. Murray in 1807, with promises of support from Walter
Scott, Canning, Southey, and others of the best writers on the
Tory side of politics, and with Gifford as editor. Mr. Frere
thought that Gifford exceeded the legitimate discretion of
an editor in omitting from the Review of Mitchell's Aristophanes an example which was intended to show how it
was possible to treat modern English social life and politics
dramatically, in the same spirit in which Aristophanes treated
the social life and politics of Athens four hundred years before

observes that the principle of generalization in translation, which Mr. Frere there lays down, " is obviously one which can be safely adopted only by a genius corresponding in quality to that of the original. Few writers could hope to apply it successfully even in the translation of an author far less difficult than Aristophanes.

" But Mr. Frere's genius was sufficient for the task, and his translations of Aristophanes are the proof of the soundness of his rule, as he was capable of applying it. They are works of the best literary art. They reproduce the essential, permanent characteristics of the Aristophanic comedy in such a manner that from their perusal the English reader not only may obtain a truer conception of the genius of the Athenian playwright than any but the most intelligent and thorough students of the original derive from the Greek itself, but also finds himself charmed with the plays as pieces of English composition, and contributions to English comedy. Frere was so complete a master of both languages, he entered so sympathetically into the spirit of Aristophanes, was so well versed in the learning requisite for understanding the allusions in which his comedies abound, and he possessed so fully the humour and feeling needed to appreciate their most fleeting, remote, and delicate touches of poetry and

---

our era. The specimen was set up in type, and a proof was in existence many years after ; but I have failed to discover any further trace of it. Two other articles, on Pitt and Fox, have been attributed to Mr. Frere ; but I am assured, on the unquestionable authority of my friend, Mr. John Murray, that they were written by the late Sir Robert Grant. They were among the earliest published writings of that elegant scholar and lamented statesman, and were also among the first of those political articles which, to our own day, have maintained for the " Quarterly " an historical reputation. The article on Aristophanes is signed " W." (for Whistlecraft), probably one of the first instances of a reviewer signing his contribution.

of wit,—he was, in fine, such a scholar and such a
poet, that the very difficulties of his task seem to
present themselves only to be happily overcome.
As a contribution to literature, his versions of these
plays stand unmatched.[1] Their value is greatly
increased, moreover, by the comment, which is
sometimes in the form of brief side-notes and stage-
directions, and sometimes in that of longer notes,
inserted in the text, for the purpose of illustration
and explanation. These notes are of the best sort,
and really assist the reader to intelligent enjoyment
of the plays, enabling him to read them, as it were,
through the eyes and with the keen perceptions of
the most sympathetic of spectators."

Coleridge writes to Crabb Robinson, in June,
1817, inviting him and Tieck to Highgate: "I
should be most happy to make him and that admirable man, Mr. Frere, acquainted. Their pursuits
have been so similar; and to convince Mr. Tieck
that he is *the* man among us in whom Taste at its
maximum has vitalized itself into productive power
—Genius, you need only show him the incomparable translation annexed to Southey's 'Cid' (which,
by the bye, would perhaps give Mr. Tieck the most

---

[1] A critic in the "Pall Mall Gazette" for November 29,
1867, in an article on Rudd's Aristophanes, says, with
reference to Mitchell's translation:—"Mr. Hookham Frere
made it the subject of a most admirable essay in the 'Quarterly,' which contains more valuable reflection on the principles
of translation generally than will be found anywhere within
the same compass. . . . His own versions of some of the
plays . . . not only excel all that Mitchell had done, and
all that Walsh or Wheelwright had done in the interval, but
placed him in the very first rank of translators of the world.
Indeed, Frere is the true standard by which to test everybody
who ventures on the same ground. Apart from the extraordinary merit of his literary execution, he enters into the
dramatic spirit of the plays with the sympathetic insight of a
spectator. He succeeded with Aristophanes by dint of being
himself Aristophanic in politics, in humour, in poetry, and in
scholarship."

favourable impression of Southey's own powers), and I would finish the work off by Mr. Frere's 'Aristophanes.' In such goodness, too, as both *my* Mr. Frere (the Rt. Hon. J. H. Frere) and his brother George (the lawyer, in Brunswick Square) live, move, and have their being in, there is *Genius.*"[1]

None of these translations were however printed, and but few of them were completed for many years afterwards. They were taken up from time to time, at intervals of leisure, during the unsettled life which he led before he finally took up his residence in Malta.   .

In 1818, Lady Erroll, while "visiting the new rooms built at the British Museum for the Elgin marbles," had caught a severe cold, from the effects of which she never entirely recovered. After trying various changes of air to Brompton[2] and the coast, Mr. Frere settled for a short time at Tunbridge Wells, whence in a letter dated November 10th, 1818, to his brother George, Lady Erroll writes :—

"You must not look for us nor think at all about us until you hear we are at Blake's Hotel. We are almost packed up, in short, as packed up as any people can be while they still sleep in a house ; but there has been some interruption, which is always

---

[1] Crabb Robinson, vol. ii. p. 57.   In a letter to Mr. Heber, written in 1817, Mr. Frere says : "I am sorry that I shall not be able to attend the club to-morrow . . . any other engagement I would have put off for the sake of giving Bozzy a white ball. I cannot give you any more precise direction as to Tieck's habitation at Oxford ; but I should hope that anybody there would not be at a loss to find him out."

[2] Mr. W. Turner, writing from the Foreign Office, in Sept. 1817, to Mr. Bartle Frere, says : "Your eldest [brother] has a delicious little house at Brompton, in which I called on him, and he comes sometimes, though rarely, to the Office ; Gloucester Lodge is his chief resort. He is there perpetually."

a bad thing when one has settled a journey—one day put off, puts off several. Mr. Canning stopped us on Saturday, as he said he might come for a day, and on the Monday a note arrived to say he would be here at five o'clock, and accordingly he arrived, and made my dear husband very happy. They were both in great good humour with each other, and I left them early in the evening to go to Mrs. Chaloner's, where we were to have had our farewell dinner that day, and the two friends enjoyed each other much the whole evening, and were, I believe, much obliged to me for having left them. Canning went off to Brighton yesterday, sent on his chaise, had his riding-horse walked after him, while he and your brother walked half the first stage together. Think what a walk his poor dear excellency had had,—I believe fourteen miles,—and he came back not in the least tired. . . It was quite pleasant to see how happy these two friends were together on Sunday. Canning was in good spirits, and in very good humour."

The following lines, which have not, as far as I can learn, been published, appear to have been written about this time. They were repeated to me as a versification, by Mr. Frere, of a letter which Mr. Canning showed him, received by a lady, who had been applied to for a servant's character. Another copy attributes them to Mr. Canning, as his rendering of a conversation, at which he happened to be present, between two ladies—

" *Wanted a Maid to make herself generally useful.*

" The person I hired would first be required
   On me as my maid to attend ;
Then my measure to take, and my mantuas to make,
   And those of the Colonel to mend.

My new bombazeen she must wash very clean,
   With my muslins and fine what-d'ye-call-its ;
My silk hose in a tub she must lather and scrub,
   And when she's done mine, Col. P——'s.

> House linen and stores, and tradespeople's scores,
>   She must note in a neat little book ;
> And when company comes she must do butter'd crumbs,
>   And make pastry instead of the cook.
>
> She at nothing must stickle, young gherkins must pickle,
>   And if housemaids of work shall complain,
> Up stairs she must clamber, clean out the best chamber,
>   Then back to her pickling again.
>
> There's a housekeeper's room, but she must not presume
>   To pop her pert visage within it ;
> If strange servants are there, and will hand her a chair,
>   She may then just sit down for a minute.
>
> If for this she engages, besides her year's wages,
>   (Though no stipulation I make it),
> If the winter prove hard, an old gown's her reward,—
>   In summer she'll chiefly go naked."

No change of climate to be found in England seemed permanently to benefit Lady Erroll's health. In October, 1819, Mr. George Frere writes of his brother as " thinking of taking his wife abroad to avoid the suffering of last winter," and in August, 1820, he describes her as " very ill again, and my brother quite out of heart about her. Canning " (who had been staying with them) " is going away to-morrow, and my brother has asked me not to leave him. He wishes me to go into the City to see about ships."   A few days later he writes that " a ship is engaged," the " Sicily," Captain Cupper, who undertook to visit such ports, and to stay as long at each of them, as Mr. Frere might require, and they sailed for the Mediterranean soon after, Mr. Frere's unmarried sister and a niece of Lady Erroll accompanying them.

The voyage answered its main purpose, and after a short stay at Lisbon, they proceeded to the Mediterranean. From Palermo he wrote to his brother George on November 15th, 1820 :—

" Susan tells me that she has written to you, but that her letter is a fortnight old. You will not, therefore, be sorry to hear that we have been going on well up to this date.

"My Lady yesterday got a little cold, but we are used to these occasional interruptions in her recovery. She is better to-day, and is at this moment chatting in very great spirits with Susan. We have seen all the things of which Susan has told you, and about a week ago took my Lady ashore, with the sailors carrying her sofa, to see a magnificent house and gardens, made about twenty years ago, on the side of the mountain at the entrance of the harbour.[1] It might now be bought for about a twentieth part of what it cost; such is the state of things here. The Neapolitans are ramming their revolution down the throats of the people here, and will never rest till they have ruined and confiscated and enslaved the whole island. There are no English here except the resident merchants, and we get no news, except now and then a sight of "Galignani" papers printed at Paris. We have seen pretty nearly all that is to be seen here. I had intended to go to Segesta, where there is a very perfect temple, like those at Pæstum, and as old ; but from what I hear of the state of the country, I shall not venture. This place has spoilt me for Malta, but go I must."

In the extracts from his letters which follow, I have been obliged, as a rule, to curtail all that is of merely domestic or family interest; but I have done so with some hesitation and regret, for such portions of his letters illustrate in a remarkable degree the kindliness of his nature, and his unfailing sympathy

---

[1] The Belmonte Palace on a hill at the foot of Monte Pelegrino overlooking the harbour. Mr. Frere seems to have been at one time inclined to settle at Palermo rather than at Malta. One reason for finally preferring Malta was the very characteristic one, that as he drew his pension from England, he felt bound, if possible, to live where it would be spent among British subjects.

with the cares and trials, as well as the intellectual pursuits, of all with whom he had any ties of kindred or friendship.

Almost every letter he wrote to any intimate friend or member of his own family bears witness to his constant solicitude for his wife's health. Every change was watched with affectionate anxiety; and how best to minister to her comfort and happiness was, up to the day of her death many years afterwards, the one ruling motive of all his thoughts and actions.

Arrived at Malta, he wrote a long letter to his brother George, in April, 1821. After some excellent advice regarding the college allowance of the son of a literary friend, to whom he wished to give every chance of University distinction, but who, he feared, might, if he found his life too easy, be diverted from his good resolutions "eniti per ardua," he relates that they had a rough passage from Syracuse, but that Lady Erroll was better, and sends a message "that she was on deck, and had seen Malta at last." Her niece and his sister, he said, "had already established themselves in a very good house, which the General, Sir Manly Power, has allotted to me, and which I have furnished with exquisite cheapness. I have taken another house for the summer—a very good one for £40. It is close upon the water, and will enable us to promenade in a boat, if we can do no better;" and here, with very little intermission, he passed the remaining twenty-five years of his life.

To Dr. Young, who had been both a professional and literary friend, he wrote soon after his arrival:—

"MALTA, May 23rd, 1821.

"MY DEAR YOUNG,

"I send you something of a curiosity, a fac-simile of an inscription found at Syracuse a few years ago, and now in the possession of the antiquarian Capodieci. I can have no doubt of its authenticity from external evidence, the notoriety of the circumstance of its discovery in rebuilding an old house in the quarter of the town formerly inhabited by the Jews, the *no* price which was paid for it by its present possessor, and the little value which he seemed to attach to it; so little, that I believe, with a little coaxing and a few dollars, I might have got possession of it, if I had thought it fair to carry away from the place a monument which so peculiarly belonged to it. He did not know, nor did I, till I came here, and had an opportunity of referring to Pindar, that the lines were to be found in one of the Olympic odes; it was rather a disappointment to me, the lines being manifestly Pindaric, and as such above the reach, I think, of forgery; whereas, now the external evidence (as above stated) is the only proof, though a fully convincing one to me, for Capodieci is at war with all his brother antiquaries at Syracuse, who would not have failed to attack him if there had been any the least suspicion of a forgery; indeed they hardly seemed to have troubled themselves about it, or to have thought more of it than the proprietor himself. Capodieci is a very extraordinary man, a most zealous and indefatigable antiquary, and has filled above sixty volumes in folio with antiquarian researches and transcripts of records and documents (of the middle ages chiefly), which he has presented to the public library. But he is by no means what we should call a classical scholar; the mere circumstance of character, therefore, would be enough to remove from my mind any suspicion of forgery. The original is in the inside of the covering of a sarcophagus made of baked clay. Several of the same size and form, and serving for the same purpose, are to be met with in Syracuse; but no other, that ever I heard of, has been found with an inscription. I should imagine it to be older than the

Roman conquest of Sicily.   The cursive character, which is its great peculiarity, is evidently alluded to by Aristophanes, as used in taking notes in courts of justice and in debate ; but I believe there is no specimen existing of the antiquity which seems to belong to this relic.   When you have shown it to the few people in town who take an interest in such matters, I will thank you to send it to Cambridge, to my brother, and Professor Monk, or either of them.[1]   My doctor has written so fully and so clearly on our medical matters, that I have nothing to add on that score.

"Believe me, dear doctor, yours ever,

"J. H. FRERE."

The following, dated Malta, March 31st, 1822, is to his brother Bartle :—

"I have only a moment to anticipate the sailing of the packet, but I will not omit thanking you for two letters, one of which I cannot at this moment lay my hands on, but which I remember related to Southey's history.   I perfectly agree with you in the good taste and good sense of avoiding all controversial matters.

Οὐ γὰρ ἐσθλὸν κατθανοῦσι κερτομεῖν ἐπ' ἀνδράσι.[2]

And I hope that if there is anything of the kind

---

[1] The inscription consists of the first four lines of the fifth antistrophe of the sixth Olympic ode :—

Εἶπον δὲ μεμνᾶσθαι Συρακουσᾶν τε καὶ 'Ορτυγίας·
Τὰν 'Ιέρων καθαρῷ σκάπτῳ διέπων,
Ἄρτια μηδόμενος, φοινικόπεζαν
'Αμφέπει Δάματρα λευκίππου τε θυγατρὸς ἑορτάν.

Thus translated by Moore :—

"Bid them remember Syracuse and sing
 Of proud Ortygia's throne, secure
 In Hiero's rule, her upright king ;
 With frequent prayer he serves and worship pure
 The rosy-sandal'd Ceres, and her fair
 Daughter, whose car the milk-white steeds impel."

[2] "For it is not right to find fault with our dead heroes."

(which I greatly deprecate) it will be known that I at least had no concern in it. I am glad you are satisfied with Hamilton. I only wish he could tempt you to pay him a visit. Why should you not go to see Rome and Florence, and Naples? it is what most gentlefolks do now-a-days, and then, perhaps, you would come and give a look at us here in Malta. It will be a long time before the Spaniards acknowledge the independence of America, and I suppose we shall not send a real Envoy or Ambassador there till they do. I have kept your secret, except only and solely to my Lady. As to the thing,[1] I think the first consideration is your health. Peru or Mexico or Chili would do well, but you must not go to die of a yellow fever among the Columbians and Cundinarcans. For the rest, to be a notoriously ill-requited servant of the State, may not be an unsafe situation in the times which are manifestly coming on, and for which we ought all to prepare ourselves."

The following is from an undated letter to his brother Bartle, but apparently written in the same year (1822):—

" I wish you would send the enclosed to Southey with a civil note, and such papers from my Roydon Box as are fit to be communicated, *relative to the state of things at Seville*. As to the controversy in which my name is more concerned, I have taken a resolution to leave it as it *lies*."

His sister writes from the house he had taken in Strada Forni, Valetta, in November, 1822, that he had been suffering from a chill, "but is again well, and fortifies himself by taking some exercise, and wearing coat within coat of flannel. He has actually determined to ride, which will be an excellent thing for him, and I do suppose he will mount soon, for

---

[1] Apparently, an offer of employment as Minister to one of the South American States.

the horse has been really brought ready saddled
for him once, by his own order!　.　.　.　We spent
all yesterday at a Maltese wedding, and were all
much diverted.　My brother was there, very joyous
and agreeable."

Mr. Canning had complained of the infrequency
of his letters, and his brother Bartle had charged
him with neglecting his translation of Aristophanes.
In reply to the latter accusation, he said, "I have
not yet been able to turn my mind to Aristophanes,
but—when the packet is gone—and my Lady gets a
little better—and I have finished my task of bottling
in the cellar, I will set to work, I will indeed."

This promise seems to have been faithfully kept;
for he writes to his brother George from Malta,
January, 1823:—

"I have sent you the translation of the 'Knights'
by Montgomery, whom I wish to introduce to your
acquaintance and friendship, of which he is well
worthy.　It will serve to amuse you, and the copy
will be safe if Lizzy does not lose it.

"Lord C—— is not a ruffian or a ragamuffin by
any means, but a very honourable well-mannered
young man, rather too high-spirited for his situation, and too much disposed to act upon impulse;
at least, having seen a good deal of him, I could
never find out any other faults that he had, and I
believe him to be very free from scandalous or de-
grading vices.　His pecuniary difficulties are not
of his own creating, but arise from his father's
treatment of him, yet I never heard him speak of
his father otherwise than with respect.

"If I had an heiress to dispose of, I should think
her lucky to meet with no worse a match."

On March 28th, 1823, he wrote:—

"I have wasted my time in a letter to William
upon the Paston Letters,[1] which has barely left me

---

[1] This refers to a project which he had frequently pressed

a minute to thank you for your attention to my interests in the New River shares."

A few days later he added, with reference to his wife's health :—

"I have just written to Temple a letter, in which I say, 'from the experience of the last six months, I must conclude that our joint return to England is hopeless, my wish therefore to find a tenant for Roydon is increased by the mortification which she feels at a house being kept up, upon a prospect of the only event which would render it possible for me to inhabit it, but which, in fact, I should not

---

on his brother William, to edit and publish all of the Paston letters which had not already been printed. Sir John Fenn, in the first edition of the letters which he published in 1786-9, in 4 vols., had selected chiefly those which referred to events of some historical importance. The originals of most of these Sir John had bound, and presented, with his presentation copy of the printed letters, to George III., but some of the MS. volumes appear to have been subsequently lost, as they were not to be found when the King's Library was many years afterwards transferred to the British Museum by order of George IV. After Lady Fenn's death, many of her husband's MSS. came into the possession of her nephew and heir, Mr. Serjeant (William) Frere, and among them some of the original Paston letters which had not been published by Sir John Fenn, apparently because they had little reference to politics and events of historical importance. But Mr. Frere considered that the circumstance of their dealing mainly with the domestic household affairs of a country gentleman's family in times before the Tudors gave them a peculiar interest, and he urged the propriety of publishing them. He remarked of such letters that, apart from any historical importance they may possess as illustrating particular events, they have a value of their own, as showing how little, except in externals, the details of private life have altered in the class to which the writers belonged ; and how much in essentials, in its friendships and its feuds, in its plans for advancing family interests by marriages, by inheritances, by thrift, and by energetic pursuit of a profession, the life of a squire's family in Lancastrian times, resembled that of our own days. His suggestion was in part carried out by the publication, in 1823, of a fifth volume.

wish to inhabit in that case. M——, I am told, is looking out for a house in the country, and I should be very glad to give him a lease of it, and you would not perhaps be sorry to have him for a neighbour. I am writing to George upon the subject ;' and so I do, you see."

He then discusses the terms of lease, half playfully, half in earnest, and sundry possible additions and alterations, of which he sends a plan, calculated to give the house more and warmer rooms, "and I constitute William (Stewart) Rose the architect thereof," ending with—

" I have made two new rooms, because on paper they cost nothing. And now, my dear, you will be glad to hear that my poor Lady is a little better, and I hope we may get a little strength this summer, but I really dread the winter even here, though the one before last we managed to get through very tolerably."

In the June following, he wrote :—

" In the meantime, as Captain Cupper (who took us out) is returned here, and now in a long quarantine, we propose (if he can get a freight to Marseilles) to take a jaunt there, which I think may be of service to her. I find that Susan and she think it quite a natural and easy thing that you should travel all the way for the sake of seeing us. I should not dare to think of mentioning it. But if Bartle, who has his time and money, I hope, to spare, should happen to be at Paris, I think he will receive a letter stinking of brimstone and dated quarantine, to inform him of our arrival, and pointing out to him the conveniences and advantages of a journey of six hundred miles and back in the hot weather.

" As to the disposal of my time, I have taken a fancy to learn as much Hebrew as may enable me to get through the two or three words which one meets with in a note, and which it is a mortification to be obliged to pass over in ignorance. I have found one very curious thing already, viz., that their measure of syllabic quantity must have been much more accurate and distinct than that of the Greeks, or at least than that which the Greek grammarians have given us; and I find many things, which had occurred to me obscurely in my habit of verse-making, reduced to a regular system. If I had a fancy to learn Arabic, it would have been an easy matter, for it walks the streets. Young Roper has made a great progress in it, and here is a young lady of seventeen who is studying it with great success. Susan has half a mind to learn a little Hebrew, if you please. * * My Lady is reading Madame de Sévigné backwards and forwards. I cannot bear her, for it is clear to me from her letters, that when her son was at the army, she would not have been sorry to hear that he had been shot. 'Mon fils est à l'armée du Roi, c'est-à-dire à la gueule du loup—comme les autres.' You see that this is her company-phrase, the proper conversational cant, and this she sends in a letter to her daughter."

In the course of the sea-trip, which had been proposed when this letter was begun, they visited Naples, whence his sister wrote of the great enjoyment he had found in excursions to Pæstum, Salerno, and Amalfi; and in the society of Mr. Hamilton, and many amusements and occupations which were not within his reach at Malta.

After his return to Malta in March, 1824, writing on affairs connected with his property in Suffolk, he observes :—

"It is not, however, a business which can be discussed or settled at this distance. I feel that for other businesses I ought to be in England, but when and how it can be managed is a puzzling question. My Lady, I am afraid, could never bear the climate even in summer, and three or four months of absence would, in her eyes, be a grievous deduction from her remaining comforts.

"We will talk of other matters. My Lady said she had told you that I had done another play of Aristophanes. It is the 'Acharnians' translated from beginning to end, at least it will be in two or three days. I hope to be able to send it you by some safe conveyance. I wish I could get from Bulmer, the printer, a copy of what is already printed of the 'Frogs.' I have got no copy, and I should like to have two or three.

"Did I thank John for his Whistlecraftian flight, the 'Titano-Machia'? I will send him in return some English hexameters of my own, of the right sort, without false quantities, all about Malta, at least they begin about Malta.

"It is Shrove Monday, and there is not a servant in the house to take the letters, and Susan is shouting and ringing after them, and the boys hallooing and blowing horns in the street. It is a perfect Barthelemy Fair. Oh, there is somebody at last. But we are too late, and have to pay."

A long business letter, dated Malta, April, 1824, discusses at great length, and with wonderful humour, acuteness, and cleverness, a number of questions relating to his property, which he wished to consolidate and clear of various old burdens, "for the purpose," as he expresses it, "of annulling, cancelling, and confounding" an old mortgage. He makes constant reference to his wife's opinion :—

"And so likewise thought my Lady, who is wiser than anybody. . . . . You will think perhaps that I ought to come over and look after my own concerns like a man, but with the care of so frail a life, I cannot bring myself to subtract so much from its remaining comforts by absenting myself for any time, but perhaps, if you report progress, I may run over for six weeks. You will receive from Captain Cupper a pipe of Syracuse wine, the wine is a

present of mine, but you will have to pay freight
and duty. We think it very good here, and drink
it with great comfort and satisfaction."

On June 23rd, 1824, he again writes to his brother
George :—

" I will not trouble you with business this time,
but will thank you for three copies of the 'Frogs,'
which came safe to hand. I should like to have
the second volume of Mitchell and the translation of the 'Birds' by Cary, the translator of
Dante, if I were not ashamed of giving you so
much trouble who have so many other things to
do. Susan says that the verses from the 'Cid,' that
is to say, the copy of them which I intended to
send to you, is hers, and that she will send it to
Lizzy, and she is doing so, I believe, at this moment ; perhaps Lizzy will let you have a sight of
them ; if she should, pray observe how well the Cid
manages to leave off with the laugh on his own
side, when he is baffled by the Count's obstinacy,
the dry humour with which the Bishop's character
and appointment are mentioned is not at all exaggerated, and the motive of doing it for public effect
is quite as clear in the original. Observe too the
wild state of the country, the King with his Court
moving about, and the messenger riding in search
of him. Observe the real arrogance of Minaya's
first address to the King, studiously clothed in all
the forms of the most abject submission, and com-
pare it with his modern respectful courtly style,
when the King has shown himself favourably disposed. But I have not told you about my Lady,
who has not been very well, which I am inclined to
attribute to a long continuance of Sirocco winds,
we still however go about in the carriage of an
evening, and I mean in a day or two to try airing in
a boat, which has in general agreed with her. We
shall likewise make an excursion to Gozo for change
of air. As this is a literary letter hitherto, I will

send you some of my hexameters, all that are written out. Observe that hexameters (having six musical bars in one verse) are to be read very slow, one of them should occupy the time of a common English couplet."

Another long letter on business later in the same year, laments his distance from England, "three months between question and answer," and ends—

"I have been amusing her (Lady Erroll) and myself for the last fortnight with scenes of Aristophanes—the 'Birds.' You recollect, I think, some part of it being done at Tunbridge, the scene where Iris is arrested and brought before Peisthetairus. It is a very long play and tedious in some parts, which may be omitted with advantage, but I have done about 1,200 lines of it, which in my humble opinion are excellent. The 'Acharnians' you will have a copy of by the first fair opportunity. It is fairly transcribed and complete."

In a letter written in October of the same year in reply to remonstrances against what seemed an unnecessary act of liberality, he writes :—

" Therefore your caution and Bartle's against a sudden propensity to largess, does not apply in this case. Your prohibition of fooleries in the form of medals, pictures, &c. &c. is a very just one, and I trust that a growing indifference to that sort of trumpery will enable me to comply with it. They are the proper playthings for a childless old fool, who looks to surviving for a year, or a year and a half, after his death, in the sensation which his sale catalogue is to produce among the connoisseurs. The immortality of men of taste and refinement !"

In October of the same year he wrote :—

" My Lady's letter will have told you graphically (which is the great beauty of her letters—I hope you keep them) how much I was pleased at the completion of this, and the other concerns for which

I am indebted to your care and industry. I trust, however, that my anticipation of being an old hunks is rather likely to be frustrated than fulfilled by this change in my affairs, my thoughts about money were directed to one point, and, now it is accomplished, I hope I shall not be exposed to the temptation of looking out for another. . . . .

"My plan against the future declension of the family is the best, namely, that we should all go in a body to colonize, and form a clan at the Cape, or Van Diemen's Land. What say you? I am sure Ned would like it, and Hatley. Bartle would go for a lounge, and we should persuade him to stay with us. My Lady says she has no objection. I could take out my books and endeavour to put a little literature into the rising generation, and in the mean time lend money upon good security at six per cent., a great inducement, by the bye, for Bartle to remain with us. . . . .

"I thank you for Cary's 'Birds,' it is much better than Mitchell's translations. *Mais ce n'est pas encore la bonne.* Nobody has yet seen the true character of Peisthetairus."

In another letter, referring to iron works, written in December, 1824, he observes :—

"It seems to me that the iron masters are animated by the activity of the new markets. They do not consider that, except in the case of a country rapidly increasing in wealth and population, the annual demand for iron is not like that for other articles. The consumer of iron is not like the consumer of salt fish or of printed cottons ; he consumes very slowly. It is a long time before his poker and gridiron are worn out. In a stationary country when it is once stocked with iron at a low rate, the future demand (except in instances where iron may be made applicable to new purposes) will be much inferior to the first. Hence, I fear that our speculators will experience another re-action, their only hope is in the prospect of general peace, and increasing population and wealth throughout the world, a state of things for which I sincerely pray, but on the chance of which I should be very sorry to trust my security. And now, my dear George, I have worried and jawed long enough."

In September, 1825, he paid a short visit to England. He greatly enjoyed the opportunity this afforded for a brief renewal of his personal intercourse with Mr. Canning and with others of his early friends. Unfortunately few letters relating to this period have been preserved, but there are elders of the present generation who remember the vivid impression made on them in youth by the humour and playful fancy which rendered him as great a favourite with children as with those of his own age.

Crossing the Continent was in those days a very tedious business, and only preferable to the monthly sailing packets, whose six-weeks' voyages, interminable delays, and occasional deviations, when blown out of their direct course, as far as to the Banks of Newfoundland, are a constant subject of complaint in the Malta letters.

Mr. Frere made some stay at Paris, to meet his sister, Lady Orde, who was on the Continent. There was no regular or direct communication between France and Malta, and his sister Susan writes that Lady Erroll was "long unhappy about him, but hopes now that the journey will do away the ill effects of the climate of Malta, and having been long without amusement and society ; and that he may be recruited so entirely that she shall have no fear of his not being able to remain with her here for as long a time as her health may require a warm climate." . . . .

"I am glad," she adds, "there was a meeting in such force at Roydon. It seems to me more like a dream than a reality, when I think it is ten years

since my brother was there; he must have found
the trees grown to his heart's content, and I hope
he was well pleased with all he found; he writes as
if he did like every thing. I doubt the books cannot be kept in very good order in that large damp
room, now there is no one at leisure as I was to look
after and air them."

In telling his brother, soon after he reached
England, of his intention of paying this visit to
Roydon, he had sent kindly messages to his friend
Lady Margaret Cameron and her daughters, adding,
" I am afraid Lady Margaret will think that some-
body is trying to repeat your trick " [of passing him-
self off as a stranger] "upon her, for I am grown
woefully thin."

A letter from his brother Edward's wife describes
him while on a visit to their cottage near Bath in
November, 1825, as little aged by his long sojourn at
Malta. He took his night's rest chiefly by sleeping
early in the evening, from " seven till eleven, and then
he has awoke, and entertained his brother and nieces
by repeating verses which he has translated or composed, till two o'clock in the morning," which did
not prevent his rising early next day. A reading
of "King Lear," with a running commentary to prove
that the story was founded on a Celtic myth, in
which Cordelia, the only faithful child, symbolized
the true religion, is noted as the subject of one of
these evening dissertations.

In September of the next year all the brothers
who were able met to take leave of him at Mr.
Bartle Frere's house in Savile Row. It was the last
family gathering of his generation.

Shortly afterwards he left England and travelled
via Italy, accompanied by his brother Bartle and
their friend Mr. Montgomerie.

In August, 1827, he lost, by the unexpected death
of Mr. Canning, the warmest, most intimate, and
most congenial friend of his youth and early man-

hood, and his one great link of interest to the politics of the day. The depth of his unselfish fraternal affection for Mr. Canning was apparent even to comparative strangers whenever, during the many years he survived his friend, Canning's name was mentioned ; and it is not surprising, that he had little toleration for those, whose desertion, as he considered it, of Pitt's rightful political heir, hastened not remotely the loss to England of the one man whom he thought capable of guiding the nation at a most important crisis.

Many years afterwards, when the personal motives of all concerned had become matters of history, he maintained that it was clearly the duty of those members of Lord Liverpool's cabinet who refused to join Mr. Canning, either to have accepted the king's offer and to have made a stand on an anti-Catholic policy, without Canning ; or, if they thought that impossible, to have joined Canning in giving effect to a policy for removing the Roman Catholic disabilities, which, in his hands alone, could not have been attributed to intimidation. Their standing aloof, seemed to him inconsistent with a belief in the soundness of their own opinions ; while it left the measure to be extorted from the fears of the nation, instead of being granted as a concession due to its sense of justice.

He maintained that had the Duke of Wellington and Sir Robert Peel supported Mr. Canning at this period, the vast changes in the constitution, to which both were subsequently unwilling parties, would have been fewer in number, and might have been introduced with less dangerous rapidity. He found less excuse for the Duke of Wellington than for any of those who acted with him. The Duke's practical good sense and sagacious judgment ought, he thought, to have enabled him to see how inevitable and pressing was the necessity for conceding the claims of the Roman Catholics, and how dangerous it was to resist them till they could be resisted no longer. The Duke alone, moreover, was in a position to put aside all considerations of personal and party prejudice, whether on the part of the king or of minor political personages, and his aid might have lessened the labours and anxieties which wore out Mr. Canning, might have prolonged his administration, and by temperate and wise reforms, such as became true disciples of Pitt, have saved the country from many risks of hasty and revolutionary changes. There were not wanting personal considerations which should have inclined the Duke to such a course.

"Canning," Mr. Frere said, "was Wellington's greatest support in and out of Parliament throughout the Peninsular War, for he was one of the few who from the very first thoroughly understood the importance of the contest ; and he deserved a better return for his support at that time than he himself afterwards met with, when it was in Wellington's power to have aided him."

Speaking of some of the final reforms which Pitt had been forced to lay aside during the stress of the French Revolution, and in answer to a question whether any knowledge of Mr. Canning's views on such subjects had anything to do with the secession of so many of the old Tories, Mr. Frere said :—

"No, I do not think Canning ever talked much of such intentions to any but those who were as intimate with him as I was. It was personal feeling of jealousy of his great ability, which actuated most of those who ought, on principle, to have supported him. It was the same kind of feeling with which Pitt often had to contend. I remember old Lord W——, the father of the present old Lord, a fine specimen of a thoroughgoing old country Tory, coming to call on my father to tell him that Pitt was out of office, and that Addington had formed a ministry. He went through all the members of the new cabinet, and rubbing his hands at the end, with an evident sense of relief, said, ' Well, thank God, we have at last got a ministry without one of those confounded men of genius in it !' "

Some years after Canning's death, Mr. Frere was consulted with regard to the inscription to be placed on his monument in Westminster Abbey. The following is his letter in reply to Mr. Backhouse who had sent him the suggested inscriptions with a request that if he did not feel quite satisfied with any of them, he would send one of his own :—

"MY DEAR MR. BACKHOUSE,

"I WAS much gratified with your kind recollection of me, upon such an occasion as that which gives rise to the letter I have received from you. On reading the inscriptions which have been proposed, particularly the one marked A, it seemed to me perfect in its kind. There is nothing to which a friend of Mr. Canning could object, nothing which he could complain of as deficient or inadequate, nothing that could give offence to either of our political parties. Notwithstanding all this, I experienced a feeling like your own ; I was not satisfied. But why ? There was nothing which I could have wished altered, nothing which I could have inserted, nothing to be expunged. I confess that I felt bewildered in endeavouring to account for my own sensation of disappointment. But perhaps, though perfect in *its kind*, this inscription is not of a kind suited to the subject. This I take to be the case,—and the true solution of your feelings, and my own.

" A character like that of Mr. Canning is not a theme for prose.

" When Nature produces any thing perfect, or nearly approaching to the highest perfection, it becomes a model for the highest branches of art. In painting or sculpture, a perfect form affords a model for the ideal ; in such cases we are dissatisfied with a mere *prosaic fac-simile.* Upon the same principle then, since *mind* can only be delineated by *language,* the highest perfection of *mind* requires to be represented by the higher and more artificial form of *language*—by verse rather than prose. Upon this conviction, I have complied with your suggestion of 'sending an original composition of my own.' Of the principle I have no doubt, but am naturally distrustful of the execution ; not only from the consideration that sexagenary verses are seldom good for much, and that mine are somewhat older, but because I have not had time to grow cool upon them, and to consider them as I should half a year hence. One merit they have, and as you see they *claim* for themselves—that of perfect *truth.* There is not a line for which I could not add a voucher. Of the two copies which I have sent, one is reduced to the prescribed dimensions. They have been printed here at the Government press, to save the trouble of transcribing, and to enable you (if you do not yourself disapprove of them) to send copies to the members of the Committee. I should think that the members whom you mention would be disposed to coincide with me in opinion that the appropriate memorial for such a character is verse. He did not belong to the prosaic every-day world ; and in order to speak of him simply and truly, as he was a most marvellous and extraordinary person, that form of language must be used 'which has the privilege of saying extraordinary things without offence. In a prose inscription, I should have been perpetually balancing and embarrassed between the desire of doing justice to the subject, and the apprehension of appearing inflated and exaggerated. Verse is under no such restraint, and (while it engages, voluntarily and gratuitously, to confine itself to truth) is at full liberty to speak the *whole truth.*

"I wish I had time to communicate this view of the subject in separate letters to the members of the Committee, particularly Lord Haddington and Lord Morley: the latter is acquainted with Mr. Coleridge, to whose decision, as a critic and meta-physician, I would willingly submit the question of prose or verse. To the same person also, as a poet, I should be glad to submit the verses, not being, as I said before, able to trust to my own judgment of them, or to the impression they have made upon not more than three persons, to whom they have been communicated.

"I have sent the longer copy (from which the shorter one is reduced to the prescribed dimensions), because the Committee might be disposed to make a different selection, and perhaps a better. The first lines, for instance, might be discarded, and it would begin with, *Approved through life*, like the most ancient of the Roman epitaphs, *Hunc unum plurimi consentiunt Romæ optimum fuisse virum.*

"Again, the four lines describing his rapidity of invention might also be omitted. They were an afterthought on my part, as necessary to a complete enumeration of his extraordinary faculties, and the *darn*, which always marks an ex-post-facto insertion, is (though I have, as you see, been trying to mend it) still visible at the end. The middle line of the last triplet,—*When Europe's balance*—though a good line, is not quite a perfect rhyme; it might therefore be omitted, though I should be sorry to lose it. This would reduce the number of lines to twenty-five; and as verse may be inscribed in lines more closely together, and in smaller characters, than prose, it need not exceed the dimensions of the inscription A.

"In a prose inscription, emphasis and transition must be marked by gaps and breaks in a *perpendicular* direction: for verse this is unnecessary; or, if a new paragraph is to be marked, it is done by advancing the *line* in a horizontal direction. The character also may be smaller, as you may satisfy yourself, if you try to read prose or verse by a very imperfect light, or by the known fact that critics are able to decipher a metrical inscription when in a state of mutilation which would render prose illegible. I am glad to hear that the statue is worthy of the subject, and of such a master of his art as Chantrey. He, I think, would be best pleased with an inscription marking the *individuality* of the *character* which he has represented. Of Mr. Canning's political conduct it is surely sufficient to say, what can be said of no other man—that he was at once the favourite of the sovereign and of the people, and that in a time of general peace his death was felt throughout the world as an omen of general danger. To say this, and to be able to say it with truth, is to say every thing. Under all the circumstances, it is more than ever could be said of any other man.

"I am inclined to mention a notion which might be worth the consideration of the dean and chapter: —One of the most striking objects in our church here, the great church of St. John, is the magnificence of the pavement, consisting of large slabs of marble inlaid with mosaic ; each slab being the monument of one of the knights or dignitaries of the Order. They are all of the same size, with some diversity of pattern in each, producing on the whole a most harmonious and striking effect. The mural monuments are reserved for the most distinguished persons (I think for the Grand Masters of the Order almost exclusively), whereas in Westminster Abbey the pavement remains perfectly plain and unornamented, while the walls are crowded, rather to the detriment of the appearance of the building. In St. John's this is avoided, and the whole pavement is like a carpeting of rich mosaic. I was thinking that if the long inscription were preferred, it might in this way be placed at the foot of the monument, with a border ornamented in any way, or according to any design that might be preferred, the letters being inlaid so as not to present an uneven surface. Such a stone so inlaid would be executed in this country at a small expense.

"As you may perhaps wish to circulate this, I enclose a copy in a more legible hand than my own. Believe me,

"My dear Backhouse,

"Yours ever sincerely,

"Malta, Oct. 27, 1833."   "J. H. FRERE."

After his return to Malta in 1827, he appears to have resumed his former pursuits, but his letters refer little to them till March, 1828, when he sent his brother Bartle sundry commissions for books and periodicals, among which he specifies some of the early numbers of the "Westminster Review," and says :—

"You had proposed to send me a new foreign Review, which I should have been glad of ; but, instead of it, there has come a quarterly journal of sciences and discoveries, and so forth. I do not dislike it though I do not understand a quarter of it. But I should like to have my foreign Review also.

"Pray tell Montgomerie that I am heartily glad to hear that he is alive and well, and that the Fred. Montgomery in the Commissariate, who is dead, happens to be another person. I was not aware before of the vital importance which attaches to the proper spelling of his name, a mistake in this instance might have been fatal to him, and instances of this kind have been known to occur, particularly in France during the Reign of Terror. If his friends every where else were alarmed for him, his own alarm at seeing his name in the condemned list must have been extreme.

"I have been doing some Aristophanes lately, viz. about 400 lines towards completing the ' Birds.' There are about 250 more, which are hardly worth finishing, but I think I shall do them."

His sister, who had been to England and returned in 1828, accompanied by one of his brother Edward's daughters, describes him in June, 1829, as well, " and much improved of late in spirits, but he has taken for these two days to shutting himself up to read a large parchment folio printed in double columns in small type upon yellow paper ; in short, a most formidable article, and it makes him formidable, for he will scarcely let me go near, for fear I should expostulate and want him to go out, or at least open his windows."

He had hardly been roused from his studies by the advent of Marshal Maison, the French Minister of War, who had visited Malta in the "Didon" frigate, with a large staff, many of them afterwards distinguished among the first French invaders of Algiers.

In August he wrote to his brother Bartle a very touching letter on the early death of Lady Orde, the wife of a nephew to whom he was much attached, and then proceeds to discuss how they should divide the expenses of another nephew at Haileybury :—

" Upon the principle upon which the Count of Benevento offered to defray the expense of the forcible operation to be performed on Dr. Villa-lobos, 'y sea á mi costa para que me haya mas bien á mí.' Thus you may go shares with me in the merit of learning Hindostanee, of which we shall each obtain a portion vicariously. . . . .

" I am glad to hear of Montgomerie's welfare. I did not send him any commissions to be executed at Paris, indeed I am not disposed, with so many claims upon me, to throw away money upon mere curiosity and amusement, and I find it much cheaper to read the old books that I have got already, than to send for new ones. Nevertheless you must send me two: Heeren's 'History of Greece,' printed by Hurst and Co., and the 'History of the Hebrew Commonwealth,' a translation from the German, by the same printer. I forgot Clinton's 'Fasti Hellenici,' I think printed by Rivington, which I should also be glad to have. The sheets of the 'Frogs' are at his service,—I mean Montgomerie's, though there has been rather a long parenthesis between the pronoun and antecedent. I am thinking of finishing them, and have got over the most impracticable parts, either by translating or shewing how and why they cannot be translated.

"I have read Bourienne and agree with him (Montgomerie again) in liking it much. He seems to have a real zeal for truth. I have also read Madame du Barry, which I must think authentic.

> τουτὶ μέντοι θαυμαστόν . . .
> τάδε γὰρ εἰπεῖν τὴν πανοῦργον
> κατὰ τὸ φανερὸν ὦδ' ἀναιδῶς
> οὐκ ἂν ᾠόμην ἐν ἡμῖν
> οὐδὲ τολμῆσαί ποτ' ἄν.[1]

"The drabs of the Court certainly had a right to be scandalized and astounded at the appearance of a drab so much more stupendous and enormous than any that had ever appeared amongst them before.

"Did not Rose desire a copy [of some of Aristophanes] for a lady who had fallen in love with them and him? and has he got one? If not, and the lady's longing is not over, let her have one by all means."

He took a deep interest in the passing of the

---

[1] Aristoph. "Thesmophoriazusæ," 520, ed. Bekker : "This indeed is the wonder . . . For I could not have believed that there ever was any woman among us, who would have dared to have said publicly such things so shamelessly."

Roman Catholic Relief Bill, which became law in April of this year (1829). "It ought," he said, "to have passed long before. Had Pitt lived it would have been passed directly there was breathing time after the great war was ended." A note of a conversation mentioned in a letter from his niece says, "He expressed great astonishment at the sudden change of opinion in the House of Lords, and added that if his mind had not been made up on the subject thirty years before, he did not think that anything that had lately occurred would have convinced him." "It had always appeared to him," he said, "that there were but two possible courses in the present state of things, either excessive severity, or a relaxation of all attempts at coercion ; no middle course would succeed, and arguing merely on the expediency of the measure, without reference to any higher motive, it is surely advisable to try the latter. It is true, that if the Roman Catholics were to break out into actual rebellion, they might *now* be crushed at once ; but experience had taught us the effect of such repression would only last for a time, and thirty years hence a new generation would spring up and would have to be quelled in like manner.

"The ancient Romans, who certainly never acted with unnecessary lenity, found themselves obliged to admit the other Italian States to the privileges of Roman citizens. Supposing we were able to consult, if not Satan himself, say his namesake and imitator, Nicholas Machiavel ; after explaining the case to him, he would certainly answer, 'It is not two centuries ago since many of your countrymen were sent down here, Ireton and several others, who, I was told, belonged to the Calvinistic party ; have you none of that stuff left ? Cannot you employ one sect against the other ? No feeling of remorse seemed to come across them—they exterminated. This is your only plan. Have you none left whom you could trust with the same system ? What have you done with the Calvinists ?' 'Why, to own the truth, the Calvinists have become philanthropists. In these days, they open Sunday schools, and are promoters of negro emancipation, in short, you would hardly think they were the same sect.' 'In that case you have but one course left, make the Catholics a part of the State, and consequently make it their interest to uphold it.'"

On September 11th, 1829, he wrote to his brother Bartle :—

"I have finished the 'Frogs,' as far as they are capable of being translated, and as soon as they are transcribed (by my amanuensis) shall send you over a copy, and if you would take the trouble of over-looking the press, would print two hundred and fifty copies for distribution among the few who are likely to care for such a work.

"In addition to the other works translated from [the] German, which I begged you to send me, I see one on the Dorians, which I should be glad to have. It is translated by a pair of translators (like Niebuhr's work), the name of one of whom is Tuffnell, which was the name of an old class-fellow of mine at Cormick's school.

"Susan tells me that she has been writing to you, so I may spare myself the trouble of recollecting whether there is any gossip which you would care to hear. Public news there is none. It is a great pity the Sultan did not make peace while he might have done it with some credit to his new system ; now it must be utterly discredited by the event, and almost impossible to establish to any purpose after such a *desengaño*."

This year the opera at Valetta had been started under new and improved management, greatly to the delight of the Malta world. "Mr. Frere," his sister writes, "is the only obstinate despiser of this opera. If there is a comic opera he may perhaps go. This is what he says sometimes with so grave

a face that I almost believe he is in earnest. . . . . .
I wish you " (his brother Bartle,) "were here to read
over with my brother his translations. He is quite
himself again since he has taken to that work afresh,
but he does feel the want of some one who can
understand the subject of them and correct errors
with him. He says there are many mistakes that a
careful review with a friend of competent knowledge
would enable him to detect. He is, however, determined to print what he has done to present to his
friends. I could almost wish they were to be published for the benefit of such simpletons as myself;
for, independent of their merit as a faithful rendering of the sense of the original, the lively representation of character, with the play of fancy expressed
in such genuine English, choice phraseology, and
variety of harmonious measure, makes a very delightful reading. There is the spirit and life of an
original composition."

In a letter of October, 1829, his niece[1] writes,
" My uncle Frere is not in good spirits about the
state of things in England, and this makes him
think of Mr. Canning, and of the loss he was to the
country ; to give you an idea of his depression at
times, some one in conversation alluded to the feelings becoming callous with age ; I said, ' I thought
people were often mistaken, for that though the
feelings were frequently blunted by age, yet I
thought people did not discriminate, and often mis-
took for want of feeling the resignation which is
the consequence of being impressed with the short-
ness of time of separation.' My uncle said, ' You
are quite right, I have felt it myself ; I think twenty
years ago, Canning's death would have caused
mine ; as it is, the time seems so short, I do not
feel it as I otherwise should.' "

---

[1] Jane Ellinor Arabella, second daughter of his brother
Edward. Born 1804, died 1872.

In October of this year he received the intelligence of the death of his sister the Dowager Lady Orde, "the first inroad which death has made upon our generation of the family," as he said in writing to his brother.

In the following March his sister, Miss Frere, writes that "he has been doing more translations from Theognis, prettier, several of them, than the first, of which we sent a copy last mail."

Lady Erroll's failing health and increasing weakness caused him much anxiety at this time. His sister writes in April, "My brother has walked up with Lady Erroll's sedan as far as the bastion by Lord Hastings' monument, and passed an hour or more in sitting there or pacing up and down, but with this exception he has scarcely moved out of the house for many weeks, nor stirred from his dressing-room till the dinner-hour. However, he seems now in good health, and much interested about the projected emigration from Roydon."

In July she mentions his having written to Rossetti a strong dissuasion against publishing an enlarged edition of the "Spirito Antipapale." He had also missed, in reading over Rossetti's "Salterio" as published, some very good lines upon the ambitious tyranny of Bonaparte, which had been in the MS. and which he wished had been retained, as showing what were the author's opinions respecting what is to be styled tyranny, and the barrier which separates it from the legitimate restraint of kingly government.

The following letters are on the subject of the projected emigration from Roydon to which his sister alludes. The first is to his brother Temple, then Rector of Roydon, and is dated Malta, April 26, 1830 :—

"YOU see that I am going to be tedious with malice prepense, as I think Burke says somewhere upon the same occasion of beginning a letter upon a long sheet of paper. But there is a piece of intelligence in your letter which coincides with views and notions which I have long had in my mind. It seems that emigration has begun from Roydon and the neighbourhood. It is what I had long wished to see, though if I had been there, I should hardly have known how to propose or originate a plan, of which the immediate result is a relief to the parish, accompanied with the expatriation of a part of its inhabitants; yet, since it has arisen spontaneously, I much regret that I am not upon the spot, as I think I see in it the beginning of what may be of infinite advantage to the nation, or might be, at least if the scheme were followed up by persons of active and practical benevolence.

"If the current of emigration is directed to New York or any of the American States, all I have said is nothing to the purpose—the emigrants when they arrive will mix with and be lost among the multitude of the natives,[1] and there will very soon be an end of any connection between them and their former friends and neighbours at home. But let us suppose them to be settled in Canada with which we have a constant communication, and where they might be settled in a body together. I say then that we shall have means of assisting them beyond the mere expenses for their outfit (whereas in America they would have to shift for themselves) and they, in their turn, when they have got over their first difficulties, having more land than they will be able to cultivate with their own labour, will be glad to provide employment for the sons of their old acquaintances, who may be sent over to them under indentures as farming servants for a certain time ; supposing them to be sent out at 14, 15, or 16, and to be bound for 7, 6, or 5 years, they would at the expiration of the time find themselves at liberty

---

[1] Like salt in water, as Sancho says.—J. H. F.

to set up for themselves with much more knowledge of the country, and other advantages, than the present new settlers.   Such a system once established (and I think it might be established with great ease) would at once deliver us from all the embarrassments arising from want of employment at home, and would give a much more respectable character to the new colony, connecting it at the same time (which is a consideration for the Government) with the mother country, more closely perhaps than any other means that could be imagined.

"Indeed, when I consider the immense tracts of unoccupied country which England possesses in Canada, in Africa, and in Australia (or Australasia, which is it?) I cannot see why every parish in Great Britain might not have its counterpart in one or more of these countries; and when I consider the difficulties which were to be overcome in a very beneficial scheme, but one of much less ultimate importance, I mean that of the Saving Banks, it seems to me that nothing is wanting but a portion of the same energy to accomplish it—and though I am very deficient in this and other practical qualities, and therefore should not feel confident that I could be of much use, yet so much am I in earnest that I can assure you that if I were at liberty to visit England at this time, I would do so for the sake of seeing what was to be done, and what could be done in this sample of such a scheme which has just sprung up at my own door.

"There is one branch of industry which I think will recommend them—all the Roydon people know something of the growth and management of hemp, and it is an object with Government to encourage the growth of it in Canada, instead of drawing it, as we do now, from Russia. You tell me that 130 are going from North and South Lopham in a month— I hope they will have settled some regular correspondence with them. I hope you will assign a page in your 'Register' to the emigration from Roydon, recording the names, &c., that they may know that they leave a memorial behind them. Engage them to write to you and to their friends ; we will contrive that the postage shall cost them nothing on either side. Let them mention in their letters the name of any respectable man in trade, through whom any letters or presents may be sent to them. Let them take out two maps of the country (which I will pay for), and let them return one of them with the place where they are settled distinctly marked, which I shall be glad to see, and hope you will allow it a place on the wall of the vestry. I hope they will call the place Roydon. As the number of our colonists is only 20, I should hope they may keep together and settle together,— it would be very useful if the absolutely necessary trades, such as blacksmith, carpenter, shoemaker, are among the number, and if they are not, it would be desirable that any such may be induced to join them, and if none such can be found in the parish, I would, on my own account, do as much for them as the parish does for the others ;—perhaps Finningham may furnish some artificer of the kind. If the colonization continues it would be useful that a lad or two should, upon declaring their willingness to go, have a year or two's education given them in a blacksmith's or carpenter's shop ; on their arrival they would earn sufficient wages, and would be better off than any other new settlers. Have they any woman amongst them who could be capable of assisting the others in childbirth ? If they have not, this is a thing to be thought of, though perhaps not to be mentioned ; for nature manages those matters better than apprehension represents them.

"And now let me put in a piece of whim or vanity of my own. Put up twenty sovereigns in four sealed papers (five in each), and let them be given to the mothers of the four first Roydon children that are born in Canada, being intrusted in the meanwhile to the most trustworthy person of the party ; and I should wish that the children might be named after me, or my dear good mother, John, or Jane Frere, that it may be recollected that there were persons of our name, who had a considerate kindness for them, which certainly could not be more welcome, than under such circumstances in a new country.

" Of the annoyances and inconveniences which they will have to encounter, the one of which I have heard the greatest complaint is the quantity of gnats, a great deal worse and in greater numbers than those that are bred in Roydon Fen ; it would not be amiss to take out two or three dozen yards of gauze as a defence, which the women, and perhaps the men, may be glad to make use of against this nuisance. The only diseases are agues, which are sometimes tedious, though not by any means dangerous, and rarely so violent as to disable a man from work ; this is the case all over America, and not confined to Canada. They will do well perhaps to take a stock of bark, remembering (for we have some experience of agues at Roydon), that it is not to be used till after the patient has gone through a thorough purge, and for this purpose they may as well be provided with a large box of Mr. Hine's smartest pills.

" The greatest difficulty for new settlers consists in the scarcity of money. Grain is cheap—meat is cheap—land may be had at first for nothing, and afterwards for next to nothing—fuel costs nothing, but the trouble of cutting down the trees. But money is scarce, and markets at a long distance through roads which Norfolk justices would consider as inditable. In their own immediate neighbourhood the bargains among new settlers are, I believe, chiefly in the way of barter ; a man gives grain in exchange for pigs, or pigs for grain, and keeps his money for the purchase of articles from England, such as tools, clothes, and household ware. Labour indeed is highly paid, but in the beginning this cuts two ways, for the labour of building a house, for instance (which must be finished before the beginning of winter) is one in which the people there, who are used to it, are very expert, and therefore it is sometimes more useful to hire them, than to lose time in attempting a work in which new settlers are unaccustomed and awkward. The best way, as I have heard, is for a company of settlers (such a company, for instance, as is now going from Roydon) to content themselves for the first winter with living together in a single building, after which, they may (when their means are improved) divide and establish themselves separately, receiving from the family who continue to live in the original building, such a part of the value as may be agreed upon. This is of great importance, that they may constitute a community in the first instance, however small that community may be; it is the groundwork for everything which may be done hereafter. For this purpose then, I will advance them fifty pounds, and if, at the end of a year, I receive a voucher attesting that they have been living together, and are settled together, I will again send them the same sum. One of the inconveniences which is felt by new settlers is the impossibility of supplying the want of various little articles of convenience. A woman breaks her teapot, and the shop perhaps is twenty miles off,—it is desirable therefore that all the utensils they take out with them should be of durable materials— pewter and wood and copper, with as little crockery and earthenware as possible, as the breakage in bad roads, and afterwards in a confused and crowded dwelling, will be very considerable;—and here is a glorious opportunity for the old pewter plates, with the arms of Alderman Ironside, which we used to dine upon in my grandfather's time, and which, I suppose, the servants would now disdain. Let them be roused to enterprise, and summoned to useful and active service; let them descend from the kitchen-shelves, and with a simultaneous and enthusiastic impulse, crossing the Atlantic and ascending the majestic St. Lawrence, let them become the ornament of the rising colony; when they may exclaim with Dido in Virgil, "Urbem præclaram statui : mea mœnia vidi." The appearance of the Alderman's coat of arms, presented to their imagination at their daily meals, will, I trust, tend to counteract that tendency to Democracy, which is said to be so lamentably prevalent in new settlements. I mentioned before the scarcity of money, and I stated the case of a broken teapot : now, in addition to the bad roads and the fifteen miles, it may happen that the settler may not have money to purchase it; he may have twenty acres in wheat and half-a-dozen fat hogs, and at the same time may be at a loss to raise a couple of dollars : the fact is, that these things, provisions and produce, are not money, nor hardly money's worth, they must be carried to a distant and limited market, and sold for a low price. This leads to another consideration : may not our people contrive to escape from this inconvenience? I think that they may ; or may be easily enabled to do so. They understand the growth and management of hemp. Some can weave, and the women can spin, they would thus produce an article that would be saleable at a better price than it would fetch in England, and that price in actual money. The bale of hempen cloth would not cost as much in carrying to market as a sack of wheat, and would not be liable to be killed with overdriving in a bad road. But it may be thought that settlers in a new country will have enough to do without any time left for occupations which must be carried on within

doors, such as spinning, weaving, and hackling—
this is not the case: during the winter they will
have a good deal of useless time upon their hands,
which it will be advisable for them to turn to account.
This is the general report from all who have given
us an account of Canada. If therefore a weaver is
of the party it will be so much the better, if not, I
would be at any reasonable charge to engage one
to join them, for if they have not a weaver to work
it up for them, the market for yarn, I am afraid,
would be a very poor one. If they are placed on a
good land for the growth of hemp, we might appren-
tice a parish boy to a rope-maker, and send out
cunning artificers in rope and twine, which are
articles in constant use and demand in an increasing
country.

"There are other handicrafts in which an industrious man might occupy himself, when he is
debarred from out of doors labour, such as turning
in wood, a material they have at hand. The
Tyrolese in their long winters contrive to earn a
good deal by this branch of industry, they make
toys which are sold all over Europe; but in
Canada, I imagine, they have not much taste for
toys, we would make bowls and platters, and
things of real necessary use, which would find a
sale among our sensible industrious neighbours.
But the hour admonishes me to be brief (as somebody says), therefore let me recapitulate.

"Whatever things are necessary for domestic
use in copper, pewter, or wood (and everything
that they want should be as far as possible of these
materials, though iron is safer than copper, and
ought, indeed, if to be had, to be preferred), all
these things I will provide at my own charges,
exclusive of a free donation of the chivalrous and
heraldic pewter plates before alluded to, and which
I trust will remain to form an incident in the future
novels of a Canadian Mr. Cooper.

" Moreover, a supply of bark and of a sufficient number of cathartic pills ; likewise three or four dozen yards of gauze. Moreover, a venture of hempen cloth, the produce of Roydon, to be sold as a specimen of our manufacturing industry, and of that which they may establish with greater advantage, when its incomparable durable qualities are known and approved. This venture to be about ten pounds, or rather more than less, but if there should be aught of it in the market, you may go as far as twenty.

" Fifthly (I think it is), fifty pounds in hand for the expenses of building a dwelling sufficient to shelter them for the first winter.

" Sixthly, fifty pounds to be paid a year hence.

" Seventhly, the twenty sovereigns in four packets, as before mentioned.

" Eighthly, Farewell dinner at the ' White Hart,' for the whole party, with a sovereign under each plate.

" The other things which are contingent, such as engaging persons of necessary trades, I leave, as indeed I must leave much of what I have mentioned (and in which you may happen to know that I am wrong) to your judgment. But do not think that I over-estimate the advantage of the plan if it can be accomplished, or that I shall grudge the expense (whatever it may be) of accomplishing it. We are providing a regular outlet for superfluous and unemployed labour, instead of suffering it to accumulate until it becomes burdensome and dangerous, and then sending out droves of people unconnected and undisciplined, to live like white Maroons in the woods—this seems our present course.

" Let them not forget to take a sample of hemp seed. I see that in my recapitulation I have not mentioned the two maps." [1]

---

[1] On the subject of this letter, Mr. Frere, in a pencil note

"*April* 30.

" TELL Lady Margaret (Cameron) that my lady has been ill, but is now much better ; we are under no uneasiness about her."

The following letter was written while the French invasion of Algeria was impending, and was sent by one of the steam-packets started to run every six weeks from Falmouth to Cadiz, Gibraltar, Malta, and Corfu. These were the first regular steam-packets which ran to the Mediterranean :—

" MALTA, *April* 29*th*, 1830.

" MY DEAR BARTLE,

"The steamer from England brought me your

---

made by him at this time in a blank page of a volume of Rees' " Encyclopædia," wrote—" In a new country labour is of all things the dearest, and time the most valuable, therefore whatever time and labour can be saved by bringing out necessary objects ready made is so much gain ; clothes, therefore, shoes, &c., should be taken out in sufficient quantities, and, as what is destroyed cannot easily be replaced, everything should be as durable as possible, and on this principle pewter should be preferred to crockery. Many objects which domestic industry could supply, and which consume invaluable time in a new settlement might, by the application of a little ingenuity, be comprised in a portable form ; even the frame of a house, that is, the supports and the skeleton of the roof, with its wall plates, might be made of iron so contrived with hinges and screws as to be divided in portable packages and easily put together. I say portable packages, because it seldom happens that the best situations are to be found in the immediate neighbourhood of the sea, and we must take into account the want of roads and bridges—the situation should be so chosen as to combine health and fertility with the convenience of fresh water and fuel, for the last must not be lost sight of. With this view, or upon the principle of securing a future return with the least possible expenditure of labour, it might not be amiss when the first difficulties of lodging and subsistence are overcome, to employ the plough for a day or two in scratching furrows to be sown with the seeds of fruit-bearing trees, including the Glandiferæ, which in future would afford food for animals and give a return without trouble or labour. There was a time in England when a wood was estimated not by reference to the value of the timber, but the number of animals it would fatten— *Silva centum porcorum.*"

packet yesterday, and to-day a steamer from Corfu, going to England, will take this ; but it starts at twelve, which hardly gives me time to say or determine any of the questions which you suggest respecting the ' Frogs.'

" I am vexed to think that 1,500 sheets of that nice paper should have been thrown away upon an imperfect copy. However, the punctuation is detestable ; there is hardly such a thing as a semicolon, or anything but commas throughout. It is an art which I never learnt. Dear Canning had a little vanity about it, and was never better pleased than when he was correcting a proof-sheet, and putting the proper stops ; so that in that, and in many other things, I never felt the necessity of correcting my own deficiencies. Upon the whole, if there is enough of the same paper to print the whole, I think I would send back the copy, which I have now received, with, perhaps, some little alterations and a less faulty punctuation ; otherwise, copies corrected by hand, which might be done neatly and without so great an expense, would agree well enough with the character of non-publication, which I am anxious to preserve, and which is expressed in the pococuranteism of the preface. I do not mean to add my name, except in writing ' with Mr. Frere's comp^{ts.} ' to the persons they are sent to. If I should allow any copies to be sold at the universities, which, perhaps, I may do, the circumstance of the name would make it a publication, therefore it is best to omit it.

" But I will say no more upon this head till the return of your steam-packet from Corfu ; by that time I shall have got a standing writing-desk instead of scribbling with a folio on my knees for want of one, as I am now doing. I have, in the meantime, a scheme of more urgency in point of time, and in which, I think, you may be as kindly disposed to co-operate.

" I think you know Mr. Hay of the Colonial Office ? if not, he is a person whom I like very much, and who, I believe, likes me, as I have endeavoured to keep up his liking by sending him some little amusing works in clay, representing Maltese families and manners. Well, I received from Temple an account of a projected emigration from Roydon. The letter which I send to him in answer I send open to Mr. Hay, desiring him, if he pleases, to read it, and then to frank and forward it. A copy of this letter is here enclosed ; but as it will arrive before the original, which was sent by the old sailing packet, I will thank you to dispatch it to Temple, that it may have a better chance of arriving in time. I will not trouble Hay with receiving the copy first, and then the original. Official people do not like to be overbored with the volunteer crotchets of individuals ; and Canada, I believe, is not on Hay's side of the office, nor am I acquainted with his colleague ; but I have written to him (Hay) on the subject, hoping that he may assist, and telling him that I wish the people, of whom I give a very good character, to be kept together, and to be located on land that will serve for hemp, and that, if they are formed into a parish, I will settle a stipend for the priest, that is, if I live four or five years longer. I shall, of course, expect that the advowson shall be mine, or given to the person I appoint, and that the parson shall have from Government a sufficient allotment of land. I will also give something towards building a log-house church, which may stand, perhaps, 1,000 years. There is such a one now somewhere in Kent. Who knows but Master John, whom we are sending to college, and who ought to make an excellent clergyman, might be settled in this way, and become the squire parson and patriarch of New Roydon. Unless something of this kind is done—if, now that the spirit of enterprise has reached the lower ranks, the gentry and persons of education do not put themselves at the head of it, they are only getting rid of a present inconvenience, with the prospect of creating other evils in future.

"Our present emigration is a mere secession of the plebeians, and we cannot flatter ourselves that their *mons sacer* in Canada, or elsewhere, will long continue friendly or submissive. Our great error (an error of omission) was at the end of the war. There were then hundreds of young gentlemen, inured to hardships and looking out for some provision or employment, who would have contributed a gentry in the new colonies. The multiplication of younger brothers may do much, if accompanied with a reduction of those establishments in which they now roost themselves. But the midshipmen and lieutenants who had been keeping a winter's blockade of Brest and Toulon, and the lieutenants and ensigns who had starved and fought through the Peninsula, would have made better backwoodsmen than our present growth of destitute dandies.

"I am comical to be talking about plebeians, when we are, in fact, nothing else ourselves, save and except our ancient and undoubted right to the two flanches and leopards' faces; which flanches, as heralds say, typify flitches of bacon,[1] signifying that the original grantee was a thriving churl. I do not believe them ; but, be that as it may, I think such as we are, people of our class are necessary in new colonies, and perhaps as useful in this country as the great [flirting] and game-preserving establishments, with their elopements and battues.

" To have done with nonsense—

" If, from what you learn from Temple, the letter which he receives from me does not arrive too late, and if the Roydonians are not already departed,

---

[1] This, as far as I can learn, is a perfectly original heraldic theory ; *Vide antea*, p. 4.

will you call upon Hay, and show him the copy of
the letter which I wrote to Temple, or, in any way
which your diplomacy may suggest, endeavour to
procure through him as favourable a recommendation for these honest people as possible ; even if
they should be gone, it would not perhaps be too
late to accomplish the objects which I wish, of
keeping them together, placing them on hemp
land, and sending the money for their first habitation ; and for the women, perhaps, too, the utensils
of pewter, &c., might be sent and consigned for
their use. You will judge that I am anxious about
this, when this time and the last I have written
upon nothing else."

He then gives his brother a commission for a
number of locks with a master key :—

" I wonder that I should have gone on so long
without them, considering the fuss and trouble they
will save me. There is no Maltese lock which will
not open with a crooked nail, and I have recourse
to all sorts of expedients, to put things out of the
way.

" Mr. John Frere, of the ' Rattlesnake ' [his
nephew], is just come in from Algiers. They had
gone to bring away the consul's wife and family :
but the Dey, it seems, being desperate, has refused
to let them go ; so the admiral is going to try if he
can prevail. It seems a difficult negotiation, for
you can threaten nothing more than they are
already prepared for.

" My lady has been very unwell, but is getting
better. I positively forbid her writing, for her illness was brought on, I believe, mainly by over-
exertion in scribbling late at night.

" All that I have said about Algiers is a first
report, and false, as usual. The second is, that the
French object to our going through their blockade
. . . so the admiral is going to negotiate with
the French ; this is the present version.

"In the meanwhile Jane is going to see her brother at the Parlatorio, and I continue scribbling in my nightgown; but I will not scribble any more, but shave and dress, for the departure of the steamer is deferred in consequence of this intelligence."

"MALTA, *May 8th*, 1830.

"MY DEAR BROTHER,

"This letter is begun by candlelight. 'Ante diem librum cum lumine,' as the poet[1] says. I wish I had kept a copy of my last, for I cannot recollect it so perfectly as not to feel in doubt that something may have been omitted which I should have wished to have said upon the subject of the Roydon emigrants. I forget whether I mentioned that you might show it to Mr. Hay, who would feel an interest even in the unofficial part of it, of and concerning the 'Frogs.' The 'Frogs' above mentioned have not advanced so rapidly as you wished in your last letter, and as I intended at the time I received it. The continued illness of my poor lady had left my mind incapable of doing anything but what was merely mechanical. . . . We have been for many days nearly in the same state as you may remember us to have been in when we left Grove House. We are, however, at present decidedly on the mending hand, and have been so for three or four days past, and I have little doubt but that, with the means of management that we have, and our experience of her complaint, together with the season of the year, which is always favourable to her, we shall see her again before long restored to a state of tolerable health and comfort; but in the meantime constant attention is necessary, and I am not sufficiently at leisure to study the mysteries of punctuation.

"As with printing 500 there will be more copies

---

[1] Hor. I. Epist. ii. 35.

than can be wanted for distribution among my
friends or acquaintance or literary persons whom I
know of, I shall send a parcel to Cambridge to be
sold by a bookseller, just like the verses of any
ordinary poet, the profits whereof, being paid into
William's hand, will form my contribution in behalf of his protégé. . . .

"Did you not say, or was it George, that you
should like to be the custode of my Sicilian medals,
which are now in said Hoare's hands? I shall
send him an order to deliver them to you, on your
applying in person and giving a receipt, which he
will forward to me. It is always right to be prig-
gish and particular with one's banker. I have got
a gold medal, of the size of the second large gold
one. This new one is in profile; the second is
obverse, as we call it; so that, if I were in England,
I might address myself in the language of the
Abbate Calcagni to Lord Northwick—

"'E voi che in questa laureata Metropoli del
Britannico Unito Impero, dove la Numismatica è
stata ed è in tanto pregio, e donde sorgono
Nummilogi Genii sublimi, siete pur felice di una
Greco-Sicula· collezione, a nissuna di quante se
ne vedano fuor di Sicilia minore.'[1]

"Now this is what I call true eloquence, and, if
English people think otherwise, it cannot be helped;
but certainly the Italians ought to know best.

"By the bye, I see there is a quarto book, I
think with plates, an historical account of medals,
lately published, which is highly spoken of. I cannot recollect the name or find the advertisement at
this moment; but your bookseller, probably, will
know it, and I should be glad if he would send it

---

[1] "*De' Re di Siracusa, Finzia e Liparo non ricordati dalle
Storie, riconosciuti ora con le Monete dal Cav. M. Calcagni.*"
Palermo, 1808, tom. i. p. 23. Mr. Frere evidently quoted the
passage from memory.

me. I shall want, also, the following :—'Identity of Druidical and Hebrew Worship,' by Nimmo, Gower Street; 'Services of Mr. Dawson,' by Smith, Elder & Co.; 'Veracity of Five Books of Moses,' Rev. J. Blunt, printed, I think, at Cambridge. Your said bookseller has sent me in (five months ago) an account in which there are articles of which I know nothing, not even the names of the books; others of which I have a distinct recollection that they were paid for at the time, being little classics which I bought for my nephews. Nevertheless, as I do not think I should better myself by changing, and as it will be more convenient for you if you will take the trouble of my commissions in this kind ; moreover, as he is a Norfolk man, and not a Scotchman, we will remain as we are. . . .

"We are still in town, but the weather is so fine that I regret our present inability to move to the Pietà.

"Well, my dear Bartle, I must write to other people as well as you, though they consist mainly of commissions ; yet you see there are two sheets fairly counted, and if that is not enough, I will send you a third, just to show that Aristophanes has been in my thoughts, in spite of impediments and disturbances."

The following, intended as an introduction to the translation of the " Frogs," was inclosed in the foregoing letter :—

"The writer of this translation having for many years past found an unfailing source of amusement and occupation in the Comedies of Aristophanes, has felt unwilling that the result of much time and attention—greater, probably, than any other person is ever likely to bestow upon such a subject—should be left liable to the common destiny of posthumous manuscripts; a small edition, therefore, of one of the translated comedies has been printed, sufficient for distribution among the narrowed circle of his surviving friends ; sufficient, also, to serve as a token of respect to those learned persons whose advice and assistance, if it had been attainable at an earlier period, might have encouraged him to venture on a more extended publication.

" With respect to the rising race of scholars, with whom, he regrets, he has had no opportunity of becoming acquainted, but amongst whom there may possibly have arisen some feeling of curiosity respecting an attempt which, whether right or wrong, has been undertaken upon a new principle, no method of distribution has appeared more obvious or less invidious than that of sending the remaining copies to be sold by a bookseller at the university to which he has the honour to belong."

In the summer of 1830 he made a yachting trip to Marseilles, in the hope of benefiting Lady Erroll's health. The following is from a letter to his brother Bartle written in September, after their return to Malta :—

" I have sent the ' Frogs.' You have, I think, or had at Hampstead, a more complete copy of the ' Birds' than I have here. I should be glad to have a copy of it taken, and sent out here, or the original sent out here, leaving a copy behind in case of accidents. It is not perfect, nor is the play finished, but I have done some more of it. I do not wish any distribution to be made of the Frogs, till I can send something by way of preface (extracted from my own review of Mitchell's translation).

" But I have never told you how we were at Marseilles on the day the ordonnance came down, and the newspapers were stopped. How afraid everybody was to say a word. This was on Saturday the 31st of July. On the Sunday and Monday it was known that there was resistance ; so, on the Monday, the ' jeunes gens' of the Athenæum and the merchants' clerks, &c., were in meeting against the Prefect, but the common people took no part.

Why should they ? On the Tuesday the Telegraph proclamation (of the Duke of Orleans as Lieutenant-General) which had arrived the evening before, was published, and we set sail for Malta. Last time it took nine years for the Revolution to reach Malta from Paris. How long will it take this time ?"

Later in the year his sister describes him as enjoying, as usual, the society of his friends Dr. Davy and Mr. Nugent, and much interested in the accounts he had received of the extraordinary talent developed by a brother of Mrs. Davy's who had been brought up to the law, but who had shown an irresistible bent for the fine arts, especially sculpture. He had again become seriously alarmed at the state of his wife's health, and in December he writes to his brother Bartle :—

" I have no notes to 'Frogs' to send you this time. My lady's illness has in fact quite unhinged me. She is now out of immediate danger, but deplorably and distressingly weak. Will you send me a copy of the 'Birds ?' I have almost finished them, but I have no copy of the part which is in England.

" I am so pressed for time that I must desire you to thank George for his letter. I perfectly agree with his view of the state of things. The burthen of taxation must be shifted on to the shoulders of the proprietors. Till that is done, we have no right to tax the necessities of the commonalty."

In January, 1831, his anxieties regarding his wife were terminated ; Lady Erroll passed away after a brief interval of sufferings hardly more acute than those to which she had been long subject. The removal of one who had been for so many years the object of constant affectionate thought and devoted care, left a terrible void. He had injured his back by a fall a few days before, and could only attend the funeral by being carried in a chair to the boat which took him across the Quarantine Harbour.

The letters of those around him give a vivid picture of his mental agony, aggravated by severe bodily pain. The grave was in the old garrison burial-ground, in a bastion of the outworks of Valetta, overlooking the Quarantine Harbour, and in sight of Mr. Frere's residence at the Pietà. He had desired that the funeral should be as private as possible, and his wishes were respected, his sister and his two nieces being his only companions ; but an old priest relates how six thousand of the poor Maltese, to whom Lady Erroll had been greatly endeared by her charities, came to visit the grave as a mark of respect, retiring to a distance as the funeral approached.

His sister, writing a fortnight afterwards to his brother Bartle, tells him that a copy he had made of some portion of the Aristophanes which had been left in England, had arrived most opportunely to divert Mr. Frere's mind from dwelling on his own grief.

" He is more and more in admiration of your work. ' Not less than 1,300 lines written out in his own hand—that is something like a brother !' said he to me this morning, and I set about reckoning for him what he had done in addition, and find there are near 900 lines which he says shall be copied out from the margin of the copy of Aristophanes which you gave him."

Three months later he writes to his brother :—

" In the list of Leipsic publications I see 'De Babyloniis Aristophanis Commentatio.' I should wish very much to have it, in order to see whether it agrees with my own conjecture, viz., that it was a sort of *reductio ad absurdum* of the Athenian schemes of imperial policy exemplified in the supposed case of their utmost possible or impossible success.

" With respect to the ' Frogs,' I wish to have the text printed now that the types are set up, and not to be at the expense of keeping them standing.

The notes will follow, and be printed separately at the end.

" I want to say a word about our nephew George. He said to me (in a postscript) that he should like to emigrate. If it is a fixed and serious wish, and one which his father would approve of, I should be willing to contribute to it to the best of my ability, since no one can tell what the state of Europe or of England may be. I should not be sorry to see one of the family established with a house and a barn, and a few hundred acres, in a quiet quarter of the globe, and he might find recruits to accompany him from Roydon and Finningham. In his office,[1] it occurs to me that by an effort he might distinguish himself and become indispensable. There is no one there now who can translate a Russian Gazette. If he could acquire this accomplishment, it would make him known and talked of as a Frere ought to be, and might lead to other things, as being sent out secretary to an ambassador there. It is a language which will ultimately be considered as indispensable in that office, and the first (whoever he is) that acquires it, will be thought to have great merit. I am sorry to see by the paper so poor an account of Lord Holland. I hear nothing else of him, but the symptoms seem very fearful ones."

The subject of emigration still continued to occupy much of his thoughts ; his sister writes of him, " It is very strange that my brother in the midst of his first grief, looking over a book of Mr. Wilmot Horton's, which he sent out to him here, in which there is much of attack of Mr. Sadler upon the subject of emigration, set about writing some remarks which are very forcible, in his peculiar style of grave irony and humour; they are scratched at the end of the book ; and in return for my reading

---

[1] The Foreign Office.

to him one night the 'Remedies of Pauperism,' in hopes of putting him to sleep, he made me laugh afterwards with his observations."

In May she describes him as "very busy studying Hebrew. When he has tried his eyes over-much with the vowel points, he learns some by heart. This keeps him in cheerful, even spirits."

On the 5th of August, 1831, he wrote to his brother Bartle :—

" I send an advertisement to be prefixed to the 'Frogs,' which I hope you will not object to ; I send a title-page also, which I do not like so well. Perhaps it would be better to put 'The Frogs of Aristophanes, translated in English verse,' adding the motto from Virgil's 'Catalecta.'[1]

" We are very well here, but hotter than anything ever was. Our Governor has left us on leave, which is a great loss to us.

" Being rather out of the reach of moral volcanoes, we are occupied with a natural unmetaphorical one in the neighbourhood, *i. e.* about 120 miles off,[2] which I think too far for visiting distance.—As little am I disposed to visit the moral volcanoes. Have you seen what Niebuhr says ? I believe it has been the feeling and apprehension of great numbers. It is one of the subjects which I can hardly bear to think of ; therefore, the less is said about it the better."

The "Advertisement" inclosed in the above letter was as follows. It is slightly altered from that given at p. 226 :—

" The first forty pages of the following translation having been printed above ten years ago, had re-

---

[1] xi. 62, 63.

[2] Graham's Island, which rose from the sea between Malta and Sicily, and after a few months sank again. A description of it by Sir Walter Scott, who landed on it in Nov. 1831, will be found in " Lockhart's Life of Scott," vol. x. chap. lxxxi.

mained since that time as an incumbrance in the printer's warehouse. It became necessary therefore either to condemn them at once as waste paper, or to distribute them in an imperfect state to those friends to whom complete copies had been promised ; or finally (under the disadvantages of absence and distance, and a growing indifference to the task) to finish the printing of the entire play. This has been done, and in addition to the narrowed circle of the author's private friends, copies will be presented to those learned persons, whose advice and assistance, if it had been attainable at an earlier period, might perhaps have justified a more extended publication. With respect to the rising race of scholars with whom he has had no opportunity of being acquainted, no method of distribution has appeared more obvious or less invidious, than that of sending the remaining copies to be disposed of by a bookseller at the University to which he has the honour to belong.

" This play was exhibited during the last crisis of Athenian power and ascendancy (at a time when peace upon equal and honourable terms was still attainable) after the victory at Arginusæ and before the final and irrevocable defeat at Ægospotamos."

" Title page :—

" The ' Frogs of Aristophanes,' being an attempt to convey to the English reader, some notion of the comic design and characteristic humour of the original.

> ' *Si patrio Graios carmine adire sales*
> *Possumus : optatis plus jam procedimus ipsis.*'
>   Virgil.

Later in the year he was much occupied by a reference from Mr. Bandinell on the choice of an epitaph on Mr. Canning ; with what result has been already described.[1]

---

[1] *Vide anteà*, p. 200.

On November 3rd, 1831, he wrote to his brother Bartle in reply to a question as to the proper time for a young man to go to college :—

" I do not know what opinion you expected me to give about ——, or why I should give an opinion, when others as well able to judge are on the spot. I only think, in general, that the longer a man's education lasts, and consequently the later he goes to college, the better chance he has of distinguishing himself, both at college or afterwards, therefore I am very well satisfied with hearing that his father has decided on his passing a year at the King's College.

" I will send you positively by the next packet, either by notes or by an extract from my review of Mitchell's 'Aristophanes,' enough to fill up the sheet. For it must be very hard to keep the printer so long with his press standing.

" The letter (which I thank you for having managed with your usual diplomacy) was to show the true grounds of the present discontents; which are wholly fiscal: the removal of them would, I am persuaded, have obviated any call for Reform, and would now obviate, as I conceive, any dangerous discontent at its rejection. I have been writing by candle-light, and it is now sunrise. So, good morning."

In November of this year he had the pleasure of welcoming Sir Walter Scott to Malta.

They had been friends since their first meeting in 1806, when Scott wrote from London to Ellis, " I met with your friend Mr. Canning in town, and claimed his acquaintance as a friend of yours, and had my claim allowed ; also Mr. Frere,—both delightful companions, far too good for politics and for winning and losing places. When I say I was more pleased with their society than I thought had been possible on so short an acquaintance, I pay them a very trifling compliment and myself a very great one." Similarity of tastes and feelings, and of opinions on many important questions of public policy, had made them closer friends than might have been expected from the infrequency of their personal intercourse.

Many anecdotes of this their last meeting are to be found in Lockhart's Life of Scott, and in the quotations from Mrs. Davy's journals, which relate to Sir Walter's stay at Malta.

After describing her first visit to Sir Walter in Quarantine, Mrs. Davy says, "our visit was short, and we left Mr. Frere with him at the bar on our departure. He came daily to see his friend, and passed more of his quarantine time with him than any one else. We were told that between Mr. Frere's habitual absence of mind and Sir Walter's natural Scotch desire to shake hands with him at every meeting, it required all the vigilance of the attendant genii of the place to prevent Mr. F. from being put into quarantine along with him."

Mrs. Davy describes the sad change which had come over Sir Walter's appearance since his paralytic attack in the preceding April, but Sir Walter was "astonished" we are told, in a letter from Mr. Frere's niece, "at his old friend looking so well and appearing so strong."

Miss Frere writes on the 3rd December :—

"My brother has been taking Sir W. Scott out to drive, to effect which he had to come back to St. Antonio in the rain. He tells me Sir W. appeared very comfortable, not fatigued by the honour and attentions paid him here. You would not perhaps guess, that the United Service, army and navy, devised giving a ball on Thursday to Sir Walter. He attended, and had the good nature to stay three hours, and leave a general persuasion that he was very much amused. Some of the performance was indeed laughable enough. . . . Sir Walter's going was as great a compliment as he could pay the

good people concerned in this ball, for he had a
flight of many stairs to ascend, and to sit up long
after his usual hour, which is from eight to nine
o'clock, and his strength is so fluctuating that he
sometimes is quite wearied with conversing or being
in company half an hour ; so says his daughter ;
I think however he must be improved in this respect, since he has been in Malta, for he has been
dining out three times in the course of this week—
that is, since he has been out of Quarantine. He
had apartments at Fort Manuel, instead of the usual
Lazaretto, where the view is more open and cheerful,
and the weather was perfection, and he said he felt
the good effects of the climate so much he was inclined to stay the winter instead of going to Naples."

The Reform Bill was, at this time, the general topic of greatest interest in the news from
England. Some one asked Mr. Frere his opinion
of the political banquets, Reform and Anti-Reform,
which the newspapers were discussing, "would they
do any real good?" He was not at the moment
inclined for any serious political discussion, and
replied, " I have no doubt that it would do great
good, if every man in England would ask himself
to dinner, drink his own health, and resolve to reform *himself*."

On the 4th December, Mrs. Davy writes, " On
joining us in the drawing-room after dinner, Sir
Walter was very animated, spoke much of Mr. Frere,
and of his remarkable success, when quite a boy, in
the translation of a Saxon ballad. This led him to
ballads in general, and he gravely lamented his
friend Mr. Frere's heresy in not esteeming highly
enough that of 'Hardyknute.' He admitted that it
was not a veritable old ballad, but 'just old enough,'
and a noble imitation of the best style. In speaking
of Mr. Frere's translations, he repeated a pretty
long passage from his version of one of the ' Ro-
mances of the Cid,' and seemed to enjoy a spirited

charge of the knights therein described as much as he could have done in his best days, placing his walking-stick in rest like a lance, to 'suit the action to the word.' "

Miss Scott says, she has not seen " him so animated, so like himself since he came to Malta."

On the 9th, Mrs. Davy describes a drive she took with Sir Walter " to St. Antonio, a garden residence of the Governor's, about two miles from Valetta, then occupied by Mr. Frere." . . . Sir Walter " snuffed with great delight the perfume of the new oranges, which hung thickly on each side as we drove up the long avenue to the court-yard, or stable-yard rather, of St. Antonio—and was amused at the Maltese untidiness of two or three pigs running at large under the trees. ' That's just like my friend Frere,' he said, ' quite content to let pigs run about in his orange-groves.' We did not find Mr. Frere at home, and therefore drove back without waiting. . . . On Friday, December 10th, he went in company with Mr. Frere to see Cittavecchia. I drove over with a lady friend to meet them at the church there. Sir Walter seemed pleased with what was shown him, but was not animated."

An anecdote connected with this last drive illustrates Sir Walter's habitual kindliness. When they called at the Pietà, Mr. Frere's young midshipman nephew, John, who was in the house slowly recovering from a Morea fever, had begged to be carried from his bed to the window that he might see Sir Walter as he stopped in the carriage. Sir Walter, on being afterwards told of this, expressed great regret that he had not heard it sooner : " If I had known in time I would have tried to hobble up stairs to see him."

Sir Walter re-embarked on board the "Barham" on the 14th of December, and sailed for Naples. On the 3rd of January following (1832) Miss Frere writes :—

" The dull, rainy, chilly weather is not enlivening, we are here without society, and the season brings with it some depressing recollections. My brother however is well, and when we move, as I hope we shall do next week to warmer quarters, and more within reach of the inhabitants of Valetta, we shall proceed as usual." . . . " Sir Walter Scott got pratique at Naples on Christmas Day, after only a few days' quarantine, the ' Barham' is returned this morning. It was expected there would be long quarantine, thirty days at least, and in that case he would probably have returned here. My brother enjoyed much his being here, and scarcely missed going in daily to Valetta, to take him out to drive."

On the 2nd February, 1832, he wrote to his brother Bartle :—

" I must again forfeit my word to you and the printer, though you might, I think, taking the Review of Mitchell's ' Aristophanes,' pick out enough to fill the miserable imperfect sheets. There are one or two precious pieces of pedantic pleasantry (such as *probo aliter*) in conformity with the common style of Reviews, which of course you would strike out, as also all criticism in disparagement (there is as little as I could put in conscience), of Mr. Mitchell's performance ; if you do not, I must, between the time of the arrival of the next packet and its departure, do the thing myself.

" The fact is, my dear Bartle, that I am so immersed in Hebrew, and find so much exertion and time necessary, to keep up what I have already, and to acquire daily a little more, and having got a slight hold upon the language, I am so apprehensive that if I were to leave go of it for a short time it would escape me altogether, that I allow myself no other pursuit or amusement or avocation that I can possibly avoid. You would therefore do me a great kindness if you could save me this trouble, and you, who were a Reviewer yourself so many years ago, could not fail to do it well.

"I hope I am not invading your province in providing for the outfit of your godson, but I shall be ready to give way to you ; or admit you into a partnership in the speculation if you express a wish to that effect."

"P.S.—I have opened my letter again for a commission with which I must trouble you, it is to send me half-a-dozen handsomely bound classics as presents for lads here, who have been writing complimentary Latin verses to Sir W. Scott, at my instigation. Two of them or three should be handsomer than the others. Horaces would do. The whole not to exceed £20."

In March, 1832, his sister wrote, referring to his Hebrew studies :—

"I meant to have copied out and sent you an essay of my brother's upon the song of Deborah, but it is not quite finished. He talks of publishing it in the 'Cambridge Miscellany.' *You* will be pleased with it, and a few others, but the world in general will judge of it, as of poor Rossetti's explanation of Dante. I say nothing of this to Bartle, who must be in no disposition to be pleased with hearing of any studies which interfere with the completion of the 'Frogs,' to which indeed I wish my brother would give the necessary attention ; but I find he fears breaking in upon the train of thought with which his mind is at present occupied, he thinks he might not be able to recover it again."

Visitors of distinction, political, literary, or social, were not very numerous in Malta in those days ; but few of them arrived without bringing or obtaining during their stay an introduction to Mr. Frere. Sometimes these introductions led to laughable mistakes, one of which is described in the following letter from Miss Frere to her brother Bartle :—

"There have been several interruptions, and I

could have wished you were present at the interview of one visitor who came with a letter from Cavaliere Landalina of Syracuse; I was making the civil to him in the drawing-room, trying to make out what he was. He spoke French, his dress was studied, and ornamented down the front of his shirt with very splendid coloured stones, a brooch and buttons. I was thinking how I should get to give notice to my brother, for Lady Georgina Wolff being with me, I did not like to leave the person on her hands, when in walked my brother, as he had been sitting in his arm-chair; his velvet cap on, and a dressing-gown all covered with snuff in the front, and bearing marks of it in various parts. After a little while, the gentleman explained that the design of his visit was to give my brother an opportunity of possessing himself of some blacking, excellent for shoes and harness, the invention of his late father, and that he had five bottles with him in the calesse, value 72 francs, which he should be happy to leave with him."

In December Mr. Frere wrote to his brother George :—

" For an account of ourselves, let me refer you to a long letter which Susan has written to Lizzy, though how she can have filled it with anything this place affords I cannot imagine. Let me also thank you for Sir George Rose's book, which I was really pleased with, and like his solution of some difficulties better than others that had occurred to me upon the same points. I speak only of the beginning, and exclusive of the geology, of which I know next to nothing and suspect that he does not know much. This, however, I know, that both Moses and Solomon must have known more of that science than was known in Europe thirty years ago. The rest of his volume I have got to read, for it was snatched from me by a lady who has not yet returned it.

"Do you see anything of Rossetti ? I feel very anxious about him, and should be glad to know if he has not worked himself into ill health. I have sent presents of his books to some gentlemen in Italy. He is prohibited in the highest degree, and one of his old acquaintances knew nothing, or did not feel it safe to confess that he knew anything even of his Dante. In Malta I think that the English are upon honour with respect to Catholicity, and therefore I have not communicated it.

"Susan has been occupying herself in a very good work, the superintendence of a soup kitchen, in which the ladies are the managers and directors. She is just come to call for my letter. We are both well. Have you heard that Lord —— has become very serious in point of religion? His sister told me so—regretting it."

About the same time he wrote to his brother Bartle :—

"I am ashamed of writing to you without saying something about what has given you so much trouble, viz., those same 'Frogs.' I must publish them, but cannot find myself in the vein for writing the notes which, unluckily, are promised in the marginal references: perhaps when the weather changes I may succeed. At present we are drowned with rain, and notes are dry work.

"With respect to our individual selves, we are all very well.

"The rain has filled all the tanks. In September they were all dry but one, and that had only two feet of water.

"Susan is very busy at this moment with an old ebony cabinet, which she has persuaded me to buy a bargain. But there is some little disappointment I believe about the drawers which, upon examination, are found to be cedar, and hence a doubt arises as to the propriety of painting them. How it will be settled it is impossible to foresee. In the mean time believe me, &c.

Two months later, 11th February, 1833, his sister wrote :—

"My brother is much better than he was during the time he shut himself up entirely. The dismal weather continues, but he usually takes some little exercise, upon the roof of the house at least, and he has had company, and joined in dinner parties given to some strangers, who came with letters addressed to almost every house in Malta, and one to Sir John Richardson. They went on in the packet to see Corfu and Zante, and then after their quarantine was over, they remained a little more than a fort-night, going for Sicily and Naples in a steamer which brought a party of seventy visitors from Naples. They were chiefly Poles and Russians with hard names and titles, some few French, and fewer English. Lady Georgina Wolff found a cousin among the latter. . . . She was pleased to learn from him that some of her Whig relations think the reform has gone too far, especially General W——, who, from being a very vehement partisan, is become a decided Tory or Conservative. —— told my brother, that of the number of those in France of the same sentiments as himself, the greater part choose to live in perfect retirement, neither meddling with politics nor mixing in gene-'ral society ; but there is a strong party in favour of the Duchesse de Berri, who has displayed a resolution and courage, and generous regard for others, together with a disregard to danger as affecting her own person, which would be sufficient to furnish out half-a-dozen heroines of romance. Her strength of constitution is no less extra-ordinary than the firmness and energy of her spirit. These two Frenchmen, of finished manners, like the very best style of English breeding, made a pleasant contrast with our three English strangers, Archdeacon ——, his son, and another clergy-man their friend, who have a becoming simplicity and placidity of deportment very agreeable also. We were sorry at their going just as we found out that we liked them. The son, on whose account they are travelling, is quite well; but the friend, Mr. Newman,[1] of Oriel, was confined with some ailment of his chest. My brother. had some good talk with him one morning, and would have liked to introduce his Aristophanes to him had there been fair opportunity. The brother of this Mr. Newman is a young man of great promise, who has left the fairest prospect of advancement in England, to go as missionary to Persia. Mr. Wolff we expect daily, having heard of his arrival at the Himalayan Mountains, and meeting there with Mr. Horace Churchill and Lord and Lady William Bentinck, with whom he was to stay a fortnight, and then proceed south. William Edward,[2] in his last letter, of the 17th of August, mentions Mr. Wolff, and Lord Clare's kindly disposition towards this most extraordinary man. I shall be glad when he returns in safety, though I do not expect to enjoy his being in such close neighbourhood, for the restless energy which actuates him, regardless of time and common conveniences, is not suited to everyday life."

On March 21st, 1833, Mr. Frere wrote to his brother Bartle:—

"As you were kind enough to advance me a letter on the credit of my good intention, I now send you not only a letter for yourself, but another for Hamilton, which as you will see refers to matters likely to fall within your local and personal knowledge.

---

[1] Dr. Newman.

[2] Their nephew, third son of their brother Edward, had then recently joined the Indian Civil Service, in which he rose to be Senior Judge of the Sudder Court and Member of Council at Bombay. He was expecting Mr. Wolff at Bombay on his return from his first visit to Bokhara.

"I am also precisely in the same situation with the Antiquarian Society, except that I have no arrears to pay (having compounded for them by a single payment at my admission), but there also all the volumes of Archæologia which are my due, with prints and other publications of the Society, lie accumulated. Now if at any time you should be seized by a paroxysm of activity, Gurney or W. Hamilton himself would assist you to get them. I do not, as you see, mention this to Hamilton, but the other point, my dues from the Dilettanti, as connected naturally with the correspondent payment of my own arrears to that eminent society.

"Pray send to me any remaining copies of the twenty of Rossetti's last book.[1] I have sent away in different directions all that I had here. One this morning to Algiers. The Hats are arrived, and are exquisite. I am so delighted with them that I can hardly keep them off my head. I almost expected to have found Theognis at the bottom of the box, but the contents were all for the outside of the head.

"I am anxious about Temple.[2] I think he might make a good sermon on the duties and character of a preacher before the House in times such as were formerly and are now returned, when the Commons were, as they are now(?), a perfect representation of the will and spirit of the people. The preachers were then for the most part extraordinary men for learning, activity and austerity of life and manners. The audience, with whatever shade of opinion, zealous believers. I think George with his original good sense would be able to help him, if he could get half an hour of Coleridge.

---

[1] "Spirito Antipapale."

[2] His youngest brother had been appointed Speaker's Chaplain.

" Pray let me know what you hear of poor Lord
D——. Is there any chance of his being restored
to society? I have been very sincerely grieved
for him. Your neighbour's funeral was precisely
such a one as she would have directed. I cannot
say that I am very sorry for her, she made her
husband's house very disagreeable to all his friends,
and I found it so among the rest."

The following remarks on social and political
prospects in England are contained in a letter to
his brother Edward, dated 14th May, 1833, and
were elicited by his hearing that his nephew Richard[1]
wished to enter the Army:—

" I could for a moment delude myself by ima-
gining that things were getting right, and arrived
at a fixed point at which they would rest; but
I remember how during the progress of the French

---

[1] Sixth son of his brother Edward; born 1817, died a lieutenant in H. M.'s 13th Regiment of Light Infantry, 1842, from the
effect of the hardships and exposure undergone by him during
the Affghan war. He was present in every action in which his
corps was engaged throughout the war in Affghanistan,
amongst which were the storming of Ghuznee in 1839, the
battle of Bamdan in 1840, and the march through the Khoord,
Cabool, and Tezeen Passes in 1841, when he was wounded.
He afterwards did service, which was publicly noticed, in
the successful defence of Jellalabad in 1842, where the tide
of disaster was first stayed, and from whence the ascendency
of British power was ultimately re-established. Lieutenant
Frere returned to Cabool with the force in September, 1842,
and was within a few days' march of Ferozepoor, where the
troops were assembling to receive the honour due to their
distinguished services, when he died at Rawul Pindee in the
Punjaub.
Havelock, in his account of the attack and capture of
Ghuznee, adds this note:—" The narrator must be allowed to
indulge the partiality of friendship in recording that the first
standard that was planted on the ramparts of the citadel was
the Regimental Colour of the 13th Light Infantry, carried on
the occasion by Ensign R. E. Frere."—[*Literary Gazette*, 12th
Sept., 1840.]

Revolution there were intervals of calm, and a seeming stability of things under a new form, and how often these hopes were disappointed. It is as people, who are standing on the sea shore, and who because the last wave does not reach so far upon the beach as the one before, take it for granted that the tide is turned. I could contrive, too, to flatter myself in this way; but there are other more certain tokens which mark that it is setting in. I tell my friends, and I am convinced of it, that it is in vain to think that we can continue to have an Almack's administration. They have insisted upon letting the ruffians into the House, and now they call upon their old opponents to assist them in defending the dining-room, but it will not do, at least not beyond this Parliament at the utmost; the next will be the pendent to the Legislative Assembly, and then welcome 20ths of June and 10ths of August and 2nds of September, and 21sts of January and all the Fructidors, and Messidors, and Thermidors. Such being, in my estimation, the prospect before us, I should have been well pleased if George and Richard (*vis unita fortior*) had been inclined to settle themselves out of the reach of mischief; I should willingly have made any necessary sacrifice for the purpose. If however Richard's mind is fixed upon heroic achievements and triumphant laurels, and such branches of learning, I suppose I must purchase him his commission, but I would much rather give much more to place him in a more hopeful and happy situation."

On the same subject he wrote to his brother Bartle, Feb. 14th, 1834 :—

" . . . I am vexed to think of Richard's going into the Army; it is the most desperate and hopeless of all professions, in the present state of things. Look to the growing opinion—what is it ? That the Army, in its present state, is a useless and expensive incumbrance; that we must either reduce it vigorously, to 'low peace establishment,' like what we had forty years ago—or expend it desperately in a War.

" The rising opinion in the Country is divided between these two alternatives! The latter is I think likely to prevail, and we shall see a War, *and lose.* A war for anything—a war to support Ibrahim Pacha against the Russians and Greeks—in short anything for a War.

" I do not speak of the disposition of the present Ministry, they are merely the Drop Curtain which conceals the preparations for the future tragedy; I am thinking of their inevitable successors. Now though I should not have grudged the expenditure of a few Nephews at Talavera or Salamanca, I should not be reconciled to the idea of having devoted them *torvo spectacula Marti,* in contests such as I foresee—contests for no object.

" The other alternative, that of a system of strict military retrenchment, is not more encouraging to a young man, without interest, or connexion, or a command of money. . . . We are well at last, but there has been a good deal of illness. I have had my share."

In a letter dated 8th June, 1833, Miss Frere writes:—

" My brother says he is going to write and ask himself manfully for Niebuhr and the Parkhurst Hebrew Lexicon in a good type; but whether he actually will, I doubt, for there are Galignanis come in of as late date as the 29th May from Marseilles, which he is reading. He says you do very prudently in requiring great precision about commissions, otherwise we should plague you unmercifully. . . . He believes he did leave some of his copies of the ' *Spirito Antipapale*' in Rossetti's hands, to be distributed, and the rest to be sent here; whether there are more to come, I suppose he will ascertain from Rossetti himself, to whom he says he means to write to-day. I wish there may be a reserve, for he is very desirous of making the book known ; and I have had first the copy Rossetti himself sent me taken, to be given to a gentleman going to Rome ; and again, when possessed of another, that went to Sicily."

After describing various improvements in the garden :—" My brother has made himself a very broad strait walk along a north wall, where from noon till near sunset there is shade. He never took any concern in the garden before, but the having this length of about 150 yards to pace up and down he enjoys ; and by dint of watering, we have already a pretty little collection of shrubs and plants, looking fresh and growing fast, in a broad border that goes parallel with the wall."

He had also been much interested in promoting the emigration of the poorer classes of Maltese, who had suffered much from the extensive reductions of establishments. " He has assisted a good many in getting to the African coast,—to Tunis, to Tripoli, and Alexandria, where the Maltese Arabic is readily understood, and at the latter place good workmen get profitable employment in the Pacha's establishments. At Algiers no one is allowed to land unless they have money to spend. At first the French were well content to receive any artificer who went to exercise his trade, and the having the place open was a great resource."

The following from Mr. Frere to his brother George, is dated June 30th, 1833 :—

" I believe I must mark this secret.

" It is so long since I have written to you that I cannot omit the opportunity (not of answering it) of acknowledging your last letter. The fact is that somehow or other the attitude of writing has become

so uneasy to me that it has taken me the whole
morning to write a letter of three sheets and a half,
not a very usual thing with me; but it was addressed
to R——, who by mere accident has escaped publishing a work, which would have done neither him
nor anybody else any good. In the course of his
researches he has fallen in with some discoveries as
I conceive of partially conceived truths or opinions,
the publication of which in his opinion (much more
I suppose in mine) would be productive of infinite
mischief. Upon this subject I had to write to him to
exhort and dehort. He is an excellent, honest man,
but exposed I am afraid to the suggestions of ad-
visers who have not so much good principle. I wish
that some of the family would . . . look after him
a little. It may be the means of doing a great deal
of good or preventing a great deal of harm. He
has a great respect for the good opinion of good
people.

"Do you hear anything of this new church,[1] and
what does Hatley say of it? It is, I apprehend, a
delusion; but even in this view it is a most awful
characteristic of the times."

In 1834 another link with his early literary
associations was broken by the death of Coleridge,
for whom he had the warmest personal regard,
joined to the highest admiration for his learning,
and critical as well as poetical powers. Coleridge
was not only, in his estimation, the parent of all
that is soundest and most acute in modern English
philosophy, but of much that is most beautiful
in modern English poetry. "Coleridge's waste
thoughts," he said, "would have set up a dozen of
your modern poets." In reply to a question as to
how they first became acquainted, he said :—"I
remember seeing some verses in a newspaper signed

---

[1] Irvingites.

S. T. C., and being very anxious to find out and make the acquaintance of the author; but it was not till fifteen years afterwards that I made his acquaintance. I went up and introduced myself to him after one of his lectures."

Coleridge, in that most touching record of his feelings and wishes preserved in his will, written in Sept., 1829, said :—" Further to Mr. Gillman, as the most expressive way in which I can only mark my relation to him, and, in remembrance of a great and good man, revered by us both, I leave the manuscript volume lettered ' Arist. Manuscript—Birds, Acharnians, Knights,' presented to me by my dear friend and patron, the Rt. Hon. John Hookham Frere, who of all the men that I have had the means of knowing during my life, appears to me eminently to deserve to be characterized as ὁ καλο-κἄγαθος ὁ φιλοκαλός.

" To Mr. Frere himself I can only bequeath my assurance, grounded on a faith equally precious to him as to me, of a continuance of those prayers which I have for many years offered for his temporal and spiritual well-being. And further, in remembrance that it was under his (Mr. Gillman's) roof I enjoyed so many hours of delightful and profitable communion with Mr. J. H. Frere, it is my wish that this volume should, after the demise of James Gillman senior belong, and I do hereby bequeath the same to James Gillman junior, in the hope that it will remain an heir-loom in the Gillman family."

The following is from Mr. Frere to his niece, who had greatly endeared herself to him, during a prolonged stay at Malta :—

"April 8th, 1834.

" My dear Jane,

" It seems to me I am chargeable with a long arrear of unanswered letters. I will therefore strike off something from that account by replying to your last. You think that John[1] will have written to me. Much you know of Mr. John! But, however, he is going on well, I have no doubt; and as our name is to be spread over land and sea (as the poet says) I trust he will spread it over the sea in a creditable manner. You give a pleasing picture of Mr. and Mrs. H——'s establishment, concluding (like a wise old gentleman) with a general remark that a few young men of family living in the country in the way that he does would do a great deal of good. Nothing can be more true, and I am pleased that you remember my inveteracy against living genteel on a small income. It is my principle, though I sometimes take a fancy to indulge myself in a shilling's worth of magnificence; accordingly I have laid out to the amount of 16 dollars in an old-new looking-glass frame for the old dining-room, just like the old ones, and 100, I am ashamed to say, in another, uncouther, and larger, of ebony and figures, and what not. Where we are to put it is not decided. Some are for the dining-room, and over the chimney-piece; others again propose substituting it for that which is in the old dining-room, and placing that which it supplants in the new dining-room. My own opinion (I confess it) is unfixed and wavering with opposite suggestions. Perhaps if Bartle would chaperone you, you might be able to give a casting vote on the question. . . . Colonel Campbell, from Cairo, tells us that a steamer will start from Calcutta on the 25th of April, and another on the 15th of July for Suez, and on their return will touch at

---

[1] His brother Edward's fourth son, who was in the Navy. He was afterwards, when a lieutenant on board the Carysfort, appointed Commissioner for the Sandwich Islands, when they were provisionally ceded to Lord George Paulet in 1844; after having distinguished himself in the Crimea under Lord Lyons, he died a Post-Captain in 1864.

the Island of Socotra, where it is arranged with the Governor of Bombay that a vessel is to be waiting to convey letters and passengers to Bombay.[1] Will this suit Bartle better than his earlier plan, or is he anxious to get a start? I send it as I received it. . . . .

"Wolff is returned, and is now in quarantine. I believe he means to remain and put the account of his journey in order for publication; but I expect he will be sick of a calm before long. I have seen him, and did not find him at all altered, or looking the worse for all his fatigues and hardships."

In this year (1834) he received from his friend William Stewart Rose the first edition of a poetic epistle, inciting him to join Mr. Rose in the retreat he then occupied near Brighton. The epistle has been twice privately printed, but never, I believe, published entire.[2] Some of the most beautiful passages were given to the public in an article on Townsend's "Miscellanies" in the "Quarterly Review" for July, 1836. But the reviewer naturally quoted most frequently from those portions which described the poet's friend, the Rev. Charles Townsend, and the Sussex coast scenery, and people among whom they lived at Brighton, and the then quiet village of Preston. No apology will be needed, even to those few who have access to the original, for here quoting the passages which have more special reference to Mr. Frere, and to the circumstances which surrounded him in Malta. The epistle is addressed—

---

[1] This refers to the first attempts to establish a steam communication overland *via* Egypt. His nephew, fifth son of his brother Edward, had just got the permission of the Court of Directors to go to Bombay overland, in hopes of meeting this experimental steamer.

[2] The first edition, 8vo., was privately printed at Brighton, without title, in 1834. It was reprinted with considerable additions and alterations in 1837. Brighton, 12mo. The quotations here given are from the later edition.

"To the Right Honourable John Hookham Frere, in Malta.

"William Stewart Rose presents with such kind cheer
  And health as he can give John Hookham Frere.
  "*Brighton*, MDCCCXXXIV."

"That bound like bold Prometheus on a rock, O
Self-banish'd man, you boil in a *Scirocco*.
Save when a *Maëstrale* makes you shiver,
While worse than vulture pecks and pines your liver ;—
Where neither lake nor river glads the eye
Sear'd with the glare of 'hot and copper sky;'
Where dwindled tree o'ershadows wither'd sward,
Where green blade grows not ; where the ground is charr'd :—
Where, if from wither'd turf and dwindled tree
You turn to look upon a summer sea,
And *Speronaro's* sail of snowy hue,
Whitening and brightening on that field of blue ;
Or eye the palace, rich in tapestried hall,
The Moorish window and the massive wall ;
Or mark the many loitering in its shade,
In many-colour'd garb and guise array'd ;
Long-hair'd Sclavonian skipper, with the red
And scanty cap, which ill protects his head ;
White-kilted Suliot, gay and gilded Greek,
Grave, turban'd Turk, and Moor of swarthy cheek ;—
Or sainted John's contiguous pile explore,
Gemm'd altar, gilded beam, and gorgeous floor,
Where you imblazon'd in mosaic see
Memorials of a monkish chivalry;
The vaulted roof, impervious to the bomb,
The votive tablet, and the victor's tomb,
Where vanquish'd Moslem, captive to his sword,
Upholds the trophies of his conquering lord ;
Where if, while clouds from hallow'd censer steam,
You muse, and fall into a mid-day dream,
And hear the pealing chaunt, and sacring bell,
Amid loud 'larum and the burst of shell,
Short time to mark those many sights, which I
Have sung, short time to dream of days gone-by,
Forced alms must purchase from a greedy crowd
Of lazy beggars, filthy, fierce, and loud,
Who landing-place, street, stair, and temple crowd :—
Where on the sultry wind for ever swells
The jangle of ten thousand tuneless bells,[1]

"The bells in Malta are rattled, not rung, and almost

> While priestly drones in hourly pageant pass,
> Hived in their several cells by sound of brass ;—
> Where merry England's merriest month looks sorry,
> And your waste island seems but one wide quarry ;—
> I muse :—and think you might prefer my town,
> Its pensile pier, dry beach, and breezy down."

After a description of the Downs and their scenery, which is worthy of the best masters of English pastoral poetry, Mr. Rose paints the little hamlet of Preston, the ancient frescoes of Becket's murder in the church, and his friend, its then curate-pastor, their walks and rides by down and valley, and their after-dinner colloquies :—

> " When rambling table-talk, not tuned to one key,
> Runs on chace, race, horse, mare ; fair, bear and monkey ;
> Or shifts from field and pheasant, fens and snipes,
> To the wise Samian's world of antitypes ;
> And when my friend's in his Platonic lunes,
> Although I lose his words I like his tunes ;
> And sometimes think I must have ass's ears,
> Who cannot learn the music of the spheres.
> But oft we pass to Epicurean theme
> Waking from mystic Plato's morning dream,
> And prosing o'er some Greek or Gascon wine,
> Praise the rich vintage of the Rhone or Rhine."

Their potations, however, were, as the valetudinarian poet confesses, more suited to a couple of anchorites than to genuine votaries of Bacchus :—

> " But that old saw, *great talkers do the least*,
> Is verified in me and in my priest." . . .
>   " They 'seldom drain withal the wine-cup dry.' "

Then addressing his exiled friend :—

> " Would *you* were here ! we might fulfil our task ;
> Faith ! we might fathom Plato and the flask.[1]

---

incessantly, on account of religious festivals, in honour of innumerable processions of monks who are always

Hived in their several cells by sound of brass." W. S. R.

· [1] " His ability to sound the depths of Plato is perhaps warranted by the testamentary honour paid by that distinguished Platonist, Mr. Coleridge, to the person who is addressed." W. S. R.

Or we—would you not help us to unsphere
His spirit to unfold new worlds—might hear
That rampant strain you were the first to raise,
Whereof another bears away the praise,
Who (let me not his better nature wrong)
Confess'd you father of his final song;[1]
That rhyme which ranks you with immortal Berni;
Which treats of giant, monk, knight, tilt and tourney;
And tells how Anak's race, detesting bells,
Besieged the men that rang them, in their cells;
With whom they justly warr'd as deadly foes
For breaking their sequester'd seat's repose.
(Strange siege, unquestion'd by misdoubting Bryant!)
And how in that long war, a young sick giant
Was taken, christen'd, and became a friar;
And how he roar'd, and what he did, i' the quire.[2]
Or, if, like that rare bard who left half-told
Of yore the story of Cambuscan bold,
You will not tell the sequel of your tale
Of cavern, keep, and studious cloister's pale,
Sing (what you verse in veriest English vein)
Some snatches of his merriest, maddest strain,
Who in wild masque upon Athenian stage
Held up to scorn the follies of the sage
Famed for vain wisdom, that in Cecrops' town
Would fain have pull'd time-honour'd custom down;
Or, sparing the blind guides of Greece and Rome,
Yourself may scourge our blinder guides at home;
You have crush'd reptiles. 'Rise and grasp,' (I say
In your own words) 'a more reluctant prey.'[3]
But anxious fear and angry feeling square
Ill with the pleasures I would have you share.
So gladly I return to down and dale,
And sea, though sadden'd now by wintry gale."

---

[1] " Lord Byron is usually considered as the naturalizer of this species of poetry, but he had seen Mr. Frere's work before the publication of 'Beppo' and 'Don Juan.' He made this avowal to me at Venice, and said he should have inscribed 'Beppo' to him that had served him as a model, if he had been sure it would not have been disagreeable, supposing (as I conclude) that some passages in it might have offended him." W. S. R.

[2] " This part of the story, showing the development of the *green mind* of a giant under monkish discipline, was never printed." W. S. R. (but *vide suprà*, p. 168).

[3] " See the poem entitled 'New Morality' in the Anti-jacobin." W. S. R.

To this succeed a charming series of sea and
land paintings, and inimitable sketches of the winter frequenters of Brighton, which the Quarterly
Reviewer justly styles Horatian, but which are too
long to quote here.   The epistle ends,

> " Sometimes ('tis strange ; and I'm at my wit's end
> To find the cause) things please us which offend ;
>
>   *   *   *   *   *
>
> And thus at strife with the retreat he chose
> Here dwells your invalided William Rose ;
> Who sings the pleasures and the pains—as best
> He can—of his selected place of rest.
> Nor think it strange if he that home commend
> For pains as well as pleasures to his friend.
> A preacher[1] (and he, like a saint of old,
> Deserves the title of *the mouth of gold*)
> Says that it steads not body more than soul
> To infuse some bitter in the festive bowl ;
> Which makes the cup so season'd, when 'tis quaff'd,
> A sounder and more salutary draught ;
> Thus I, the beverage which I mingle, stir
> Like that brave prelate, with a branch of myrrh,
> Join me, dear Frere, and be, if you can swallow
> This wine and wormwood draught, my great Apollo."

The light in which Mr. Rose regarded his friend's
voluntary exile and protracted residence at Malta
was very much that in which it appeared to Mr.
Frere's relatives, and in which I was prepared
to view it, when in May, 1834, he invited me to
visit him on my way to India. But one result
of my stay for some weeks under his roof was,
(whilst deepening the regret I felt at his continued
separation from so many who loved and honoured
him, and who would have been in every way bene-
fited by his society,) to make me feel that it would
be a very hazardous experiment for him to uproot
himself from a position, which, in many respects,
suited him better than almost any life I could
imagine for him in England.

---

[1] " Jeremy Taylor."   W. S. R.

He had remained so long in the genial and equable climate of Malta, that his constitution and habits had become accustomed to a temperature which probably tried him less than the chills and constant variations of an English winter would have done.

If in Malta he was cut off from the literary and political society of London, he would, on the other hand, had he returned to England, have missed from the circle of his early associates most of the friends of his youth and manhood whose society he valued. In the perfect quiet and uninterrupted leisure of his life at Malta, he enjoyed, to an extent rarely attainable elsewhere, that intellectual communion with the great authors of other times and countries which has been so often described as the peculiar privilege and consolation of scholars in their old age; and he lived, among a simple and grateful people, a life of singular ease and dignity, rendered conspicuously useful by his large-hearted liberality and intelligent benevolence.

The following extracts, which have been kindly placed at my disposal from the letters and journals of a valued friend,[1] who stayed with Mr. Frere a few years afterwards, will show the impressions left on an acute and impartial observer, who saw him then for the first time. They relate to a period rather later than my own visit, but Malta had been little changed in the interval, and Mr. Frere's mode of life was still the same as when I was with him. There were then few steamers among the men-of-war or merchant-ships in the Mediterranean, save the monthly mail-packets, which looked into Valetta Harbour every fortnight, to and fro between Corfu and England. All the inlets which indent the rocky shore round Valetta are now crowded with steamers of every nation which possesses a mercan-

---

[1] Mr. G. T. Clark of Dowlais House; and Talygar, Glamorganshire.

tile marine, carrying half the commerce of India and the Levant, of Australia and China ; but in 1834 the Quarantine Harbour was rarely tenanted by more than two or three small sailing vessels, Greek or Italian, with corn from Odessa, or pulse from Alexandria. There were few signs of life, except perhaps an occasional shore boat of quaint form and brightly painted, with two huge eyes on the prow, and rowed by a couple of Maltese fishermen in red pendent caps. The blue waters rippled clear and undefiled against the white retaining wall of the roadway which separated Mr. Frere's house at the Pietà from the harbour. The building itself, originally two or three separate houses which had been thrown into one, extended for some distance along the road, at the foot of a rocky hill, rising steeply from the waterside. It was a good specimen of a Maltese residence of former times, such as the knights built for themselves in their later and more luxurious days, when, though the galleys of St. John were still the terror of the Barbary Rovers, the Order thought less of fighting Saracen or Turk, than of enjoying the good things earned for its members by the great soldiers of its earlier years.

A massive portal admitted the visitor to a large hall with a stone arched roof, supported by colossal caryatides of Giants and Titans at the angles, rather dimly lighted by windows high up in the walls, while a cistern of clear cool water in the centre, surrounded by strange semi-tropical plants, and enlivened by a macaw of magnificent plumage, helped to remind the English visitor that he had reached a southern climate. The house itself is thus described by Mr. Clark :—

" The house stands near the head of the Quarantine Harbour, with only a road between it and the sea. It is of considerable extent, has an upper floor, and a flat roof. The ground floor is occupied by the servants and as offices, and on the upper and principal floor are the sitting-rooms and bed-rooms of the family. A double staircase, winding round a small open court with a fountain, leads from the entrance-hall into a long picture gallery, into which open the principal rooms. These are lofty, spacious, and well-proportioned. The walls are painted, as are the joists of the open ceiling. A row of small holes, near the cornice, open into the external air. The doors and windows are large, and the latter open with folding-doors into large balconies, parts of which are covered in and shaded. The floors are of stone, polished and stained in various patterns, and the rooms are well furnished with tables, sofas, easy chairs, ottomans, a pro-fusion of carved cabinets, and mirrors in heavy Venetian gilt frames, according to the prevailing Italian taste. Behind the house rises a steep hill of rock, and this which at considerable labour has been converted into a garden, forms, to an English eye, the principal curiosity of the place. The whole rock, up to the summit, is cut into terraces and platforms, parts of which are hollowed out into rock basins, which are filled with earth brought from a distance. Many of these terraces are enclosed by walls, and upon others are double rows of columns, supporting a trellis work covered with creepers, so as to protect the walks below from the rays of the sun. The different stages are approached by flights of steps, and the whole hill is excavated into tanks, containing a sufficient supply of water.

"The view of the whole from a temple at its summit is very singular. The garden looks like a collection of sheep folds or paper boxes, but nothing can be richer than the heavy ornate staircases, tem-ples, seats, and benches, lines of arches and balus-trades, Gothic and Moorish turrets, and the gibbets for raising water from the tanks, all carved in the fine white Maltese stone, after bold and flowing patterns, and in excellent taste.

" As to trees and shrubs, all kinds from the cedar to the hyssop are there. The fig, palm, banana, orange, lemon, tamarind, vine, pomegranate, and olive ; magnificent geraniums as big as that at Warwick, legions of roses, and carnations that would do credit to Chiswick.

" The customs of the house are luxurious. Nobody is visible before eleven or twelve, at which hours a sort of breakfast goes forward, which you may or may not attend. Before this, coffee is brought, if you wish, to your bed-room, and if you are disposed for an early walk, there is the garden with its pleasant alleys and trellised paths, or if you prefer the sea, it flows clear and bright before the very doors. Between eleven and seven people do what they please. Mr. Frere is reading or writing in his own apartment. At seven dinner goes forward. Covers are laid for a table full, and usually some privileged and pleasant guests drop in: The charm of the party is the master of the house, who though infirm in body, is not materially injured in mind or memory, and receives all with a fine old-fashioned courtesy that puts all at their ease. Other visitors come in the evening, usually good talkers, and the conversation becomes general. Mr. Frere however sees few strangers. After coffee comes a drive in the cool evening, perhaps from ten to midnight or even later, when the air is delightful."

The garden here described was then, and continued to the end of his life, a great source of interest to Mr. Frere, and afforded him almost his only means of outdoor exercise and amusement. It had been commenced with no further object than that of bringing into some kind of order the wilderness of stone walls, and prickly pears, and caruba trees which overspread the hill behind the house, but Mr. Frere soon found in it a ready means of giving employment to the poor. There were no poor laws then in Malta. A population denser, in proportion to the area it occupied, than any other in Europe, pressed at all times closely on its means of subsistence, which were greatly affected by every fluctuation in the Government military and naval establishments; for the rocky island then produced no more corn than sufficed for about six weeks' consumption in every year, and any reduction in the numbers of workmen employed in the port and dockyard was sure to be felt in many a poor Maltese family already sorely straitened for daily food.

From the earliest years of his residence Mr. Frere had been a great advocate for emigration, and his arguments, backed, as was his wont, by liberal assistance from his own purse, had a great effect in overcoming the prejudices of the Maltese, who are a very home-loving people, and in promoting that extensive emigration which of late years has planted large communities of industrious Maltese in Algeria, Egypt, and Syria; and even carried numbers to distant settlements in South America and the West Indies. But the old, the lame, the halt, and the blind remained behind, and when the master of the house at the Pietà went out for his evening drive, a crowd of these would usually collect at the door to beg for alms, which were never withheld from the helpless, or to ask for aid to get employment for the able-bodied. The conversion of the rocky hill-side into a garden was made to supply work when other means failed. The Maltese is born a builder and carver in stone ; and the result was the labyrinth of flights of stone steps, terraces, walls, and carved balustrades which Mr. Clark describes.

Political economists might shake their heads at what they would consider a very imperfect palliative of a general evil. But Mr. Frere had his reward in the gratitude of every class of the Maltese population, for while the better-informed fully appreciated his efforts to promote emigration, the poor knew him as one who was not content to answer a starving fellow-creature's appeal for aid, by an able exposition of the laws of supply and demand.

In a letter written several years after the extracts just quoted, Mr. Clark writes :—

"You asked me what impression Mr. Frere produced upon me, and to describe him to you as he appeared to me during my stay under his roof at Malta in 1845. This is not an easy task, for his character was anything rather than commonplace.

"What first struck me was his grand personal appearance. He was a very tall and altogether a large man, for his age very upright, with bold, commanding features, a good nose and brow, and a peculiar expression perhaps of sarcasm with a touch of hauteur about the curves of his mouth and nostrils. I have heard that Mr. Temple Frere was once spoken to for him by the Duke of Wellington; but neither Mr. Temple Frere nor Mr. Edward Frere, two of his brothers, though both grandly built men, had anything of the expression to which I refer. Hoppner's picture, however, an excellent representation of him, gives this expression, which is also preserved in the engraving of it.

"I was told that he saw few strangers, and was, therefore, the more pleased when I found that he did not treat me as a stranger. I had not been an hour at the Valetta Hotel before he sent for me, and lodged me in his house, then the Pietà.

"At dinner he said little, but later in the .evening somebody used the phrase, '*toot* him soundly,' for 'whip him,' and he at once noticed the word, quoted an instance of its use, and continued a conversation till the small hours, upon old and quaint books and phrases of the sixteenth and seventeenth centuries, displaying quietly a wonderful acquaintance with half-forgotten literature, useless, as he called it. I was told that, though he sat up late, he did not often remain in company.

"At breakfast he never appeared, and I rarely saw him much before dinner. At that meal and at tea he was accustomed to meet the few people whom he knew intimately, but he did not visit, and did not usually care for new faces. However, on one occasion, I remember, he received Bishop Alexander and his sister, and nothing could exceed his kindness to them. I think the bishop was introduced by Wolff, in whom Mr. Frere much delighted, and concerning whose sayings and doings, when he stayed at the Pietà, there were many droll stories.

"Though he talked well, and was both a full and a ready man, he was never overbearing, and always willing to hear others. I remember his showing a good deal of knowledge on scientific military subjects, followed by a present of his copy of Jomini's works, to a young soldier then on his way to join his regiment.

"Of early English literature he talked, as was to be expected, and of the 'Anti-Jacobin' and its poetry. But he said little of his own share in it, or of his own writings generally; nor did I think it polite to lead the conversation to them.

"He was full of anecdotes about Pitt, and Canning, and Wyndham—with whom, I think, he had some county connexion.[1] One of his anecdotes was, that when canvassing together with Wyndham, a fish-wife opened upon them with a torrent of abuse. When she had done, Wyndham responded in her own strain, and fairly beat her down with his superior flow of the coarse vernacular

---

[1] Mr. Wyndham was his father's colleague in representing Norwich, and always a warm personal friend of Mr. Frere.

of the ' tyo cyownties.' It was very pleasant thus to meet a man who had moved on equal terms with the great political and literary leaders at the commencement of the present century ; who knew Holland House in its early days, and had been intimate with George Ellis and the founders of the ' Quarterly Review,' and with Coleridge ; for Canning his affection was very great.

" He had the good breeding of a past school, with little or nothing of its stiffness or formality. In his comments upon public events and business, there was a very remarkable high-minded and very upright way of forming an opinion, and a marked contempt for anything mean or tortuous. In this, as in the kindliness of his disposition, he appeared to me much to resemble his brother, Mr. Bartle Frere, also a diplomatist of the old school."

Malta in 1834 was still looked on as one of our most important foreign possessions. Its English official society comprised many men of family and education, and the military and naval command were always confided to veterans of the great war, for the companions of Nelson and Wellington had not yet disappeared from the lists of those fit for active service. Among the younger naval and military officers there were always some connexions of Mr. Frere's early friends who had introductions to him, and who found the Pietà ever open to them, and a host who could always thoroughly enjoy the high spirits and unaffected frankness of a well-bred young Englishman.

He found, too, in those days, much pleasure in the society of many of the Maltese and Italian inhabitants of the island, who mixed with the English on terms of greater intimacy and cordiality than is, perhaps, possible in these times of comparative unrest and ceaseless change. The last surviving knight of the Order, who had seen a Grand Master in the Palace at Valetta, was still an occasional guest of the English Governor. And there were many other relics of a picturesque and historical past, which gave interest and variety even to the very retired life which Mr. Frere led.

Few months passed without his interchanging a visit with Caruana, the Roman Catholic bishop—a fine specimen of a learned, high-minded, and courteous ecclesiastic of the old school; who, if he was little prepared to make concessions to the demands of modern liberalism, was still less inclined to seek compensation for the loss of political influence by submission to ultramontane ecclesiastical rule.

Another frequent visitor was Sir Vincent Borg, also a Maltese gentleman of the old school. To these two men, he was wont to say, the English in a great measure owed the possession of the island.

The following is from a note of a description of the rising against the French, as he related it to me one day after a visit from Borg :—

" The insurrection against the French began by their attempting to rob some of the churches; they were taking down some of the damask hangings in the great church at Birchircara, near the Pietà, when the people who were looking on, and could not stand such a sacrilege, tripped up the ladder of the men employed and killed them. They then went to Borg, who was not a man of noble family, and begged him to lead them, and ring the bells of the church as an alarm. He said, 'The bells are neither yours nor mine, they belong to the Præposito, let us ask him.' This he said to gain time to consult the Præposito, an old man, of whose sagacity Borg had a high opinion; he then took the Præposito aside, and asked him what he thought should be done? The old Præposito answered, 'The thing is done now, and either they or we must go to the wall, so we must do our best to beat them.' Borg then went back to the Maltese crowd and agreed to lead them, rang

the bells, and, setting two little boys on the top
of the church tower at Birchircara to watch—one
towards Valetta the other towards Civita Vecchia—
he took a muster of the people and their fire-arms;
they had thirty stand of the latter, and the rest of
the multitude were armed with sticks. At length
a re-inforcement of the French, about three hundred
in number, was seen issuing from the Floriana Gate.
Borg led his men to attack them just where the
Vignacourt Aqueduct crosses the road to Civita
Vecchia. He placed his musketeers in ambush,
and they fired from behind the stone walls, killed
the officers, and then all closed in upon the men of
the French detachment, who fairly turned and re-
treated to Valetta. He got the bishop, who was
then a young priest, to join him, and the Maltese
next attacked a small sea battery towards St. Juliens,
and, killing the guard, took the guns, which they
dragged with the bell ropes into a battery erected
on this (the Pietà) side. They had another against
the Floriana Gate; and, after raising the whole
Maltese population of the island, they blockaded
the French in Valetta. As the French were not
strong enough to attempt sallies in force, the Maltese got to entertain a great contempt for them,
and used to harass them in every kind of way,
preventing their fishing in the harbour, getting
down at night (for they can climb like cats) into
the gardens which the French had made in the
ditches, and destroying them till they made the
French give up attempting to cultivate. On a
small scale it was just like the insurrection in
Spain; when the province of Biscay, with a few
hundred dollars in its treasury, formally declared
war against the Emperor Napoleon (who had then
Austria, Russia, and Prussia prostrate) and sent
Biscayan dignitaries to England as ambassadors,
who arrived simultaneously with the other envoys
from the other provinces, sent without any previous

concert. I remember Romana telling me he was
once talking to some officers who said they feared
the expulsion of the French would be a tedious
business. 'Are you Spaniards,' he said, 'and do
you forget that we were four hundred years in
turning out the Moors? But we did it at last!'"[1]

Among Mr. Frere's constant visitors at the Pietà
in those days Father Marmora must not be omitted.
He was very learned in Hebrew, and all its cognate
languages. He had collected every word and inscription which was then known to exist in Phœnician; and had written a treatise to prove that
Maltese was a dialect of Phœnician, and retained
more of the old Punic element than any other
language. He had for many years read Hebrew
with Mr. Frere, who highly esteemed him, not only
for his learning, but for his amiability and gentle
manners. He rarely left his study in one of the
religious houses at Floriana, except to visit the
Pietà, and always dined with Mr. Frere on Sun-
days; when the conversation would occasionally—
especially when Mr. Joseph Wolff was present—get
so Semitic that it was not easy for an unlearned
bystander to follow.

The following are a few fragmentary recollections of some of these Sunday evening conversations, when Mr. Frere was incited by the worthy
priest to enlarge on subjects connected with Phœnician antiquities:—

J. H. F. "All the sites of Grecian colonies in
Sicily were once possessed by the Phœnicians, and
we have no record when or how they were transferred to the Greeks without, as far as we know,
any contest; possibly it was when Tyre was exhausted by Nebuchadnezzar's attacks. Many of

---

[1] Borg was knighted a few years before his death, in 1837.
He is buried in the church at Birchircara, partly built by him,
and a characteristic epitaph by Mr. Frere records his many
public services and private virtues.

the Greco-Sicilian coins bear Phœnician legends.
Syracuse still retains its Phœnician name, it is
' Marsa Sirocco,' *i. e.* the S. E. Port. There is a
port still so called in Malta. So Marseilles, originally a Phœnician, and subsequently a Greek em-
porium, retains its Phœnician name, it is ' Marsa,'
the port. So port Mahon, ' Mago,' or Maho, is
Phœnician for ' refuge.' This explains Hannibal's
remark, when, by detaching his general Mago, he
had completed his combinations for defeating the
Romans at Thrasimenus ;[1] it was, in fact, a Punic
pun ; he said, ' He was sure of them, because they
had no Mago ' (*i. e.* refuge).

" It is very possible that the Giant's Tower at
Gozo, and the similar remains which are found
elsewhere in Malta and, I believe, in Sardinia also,
may be Phœnician. They certainly do not belong
to the Greek or Roman, or any later age, and are
quite different in style from any of the remains
which are called Cyclopean or Etruscan in Italy."

J. H. F. " I take it the real history of the siege
of Syracuse was, that the Athenians having been
successful in the East, by leading the patriotic
spirit of the Greeks in opposing the Persians,
thought to play the same game over again in the
West against the Phœnicians and Tuscans; but
they forgot that all the Sicilian colonies were
Doric, and that no man can play the same game
in politics twice. Your throws are not the same ;
and,·if they are the same, your adversary knows
how you played last time, and takes care to play
differently himself."

---

[1] Query Trebia? Polyb. iii. 71—74, Liv. xxi. 54, 55. Com-
pare with the account of the battle of Thrasimenus, Polyb.
iii. 82—84, Liv. xxii. 4—6, in which Mago's name is not
mentioned by either historian. He is, however, mentioned
on this occasion by the poet Silius Italicus (iv. 825, v. 287—
375, 529, foll. 668). At Cannæ, Mago was posted with Hannibal on the centre, Polyb. iii. 114, Liv. xxii. 46.

In reply to a question, Are there any remains of the Osci still to be traced?

J. H. F. "The radical letters (S. C.) of the name Osci, are found in the names of a vast number of neighbouring nations—Siculi, Sicani, Susci, Cyclopes (query Syclops)—a compound national name, the result of the union of two tribes (like Celtiberi, Gallogreci). Another nation, of whose name P. S. C. were the radical letters, is traced in Dolo-Pisci, or Dolopes. Etrusci is also a compound national name; the Etri, or Atri, being a tribe who gave their name to the Adriatic. Pelasci, or Pelasgi, another compound (query, were the Pels, or Beels, your Indian Bheels?) Fe/S/Cinnini and Vi/S/caëni or Biscayeni, are also names which it is possible are compound names from two tribes, one of which were Osci. There may possibly yet be found traces of some of the languages of these old nations in the patois of some of the remote mountains in Italy or Greece."

J. H. F. "The several labours of Hercules were each the extinction of some form of heresy or superstition; thus the destruction of the Mares of Diomedes was the eradication of some Molochian superstition. Possibly so were the labours of Perseus. Medusa was the moon; the sword (harpe, which, by the way, is Hebrew) forms the crescent moon, and the sack to hold the head is the interlunium. A head referred by some authors to the moon, and by others to the Medusa (probably, as just observed, both being the same) is borne on the coins of Camarina in Sicily; *Camar* in Maltese (probably in Phœnician also) signifies the moon."

I will now resume the extracts from his letters. To his brother George he wrote, on the 31st January, 1835:—

"I was very much pleased with Anne's and Susan's verses. They are really singularly good. The description of Coleridge[1] is perfect. Did you show them to Rogers? No, you were afraid he would think you an old fool of a father. If you have an opportunity, show them to him upon my recommendation. I will incur the responsibility as an uncle."

In a letter dated the 9th of April, 1835, he writes to his brother Edward, who was in the habit of using a style and carbonized copying paper, which often tired the eyesight of his correspondents, but who had written him one letter with ordinary pen and ink :—

"MALTA, *April 9th*, 1835.

"MY DEAR NED,

"I have to acknowledge the receipt of yours of the 2nd March, written with a ' real pen, real ink, and real paper.' What is the nonsense which that puts me in mind of? Do you recollect? It was something of poor Bob Clive's at Putney" [where they had been at school together], "and his writing-master at home, Mr. Skelton by name,

---

[1]   ON THE POET COLERIDGE.

Thou reverend good old man! I see thee still;
Thy silver locks, thy countenance benign,
Beaming with inward light, and with divine
Charity, that nor doth nor thinketh ill,
Thy voice yet seems my raptur'd sense to fill,
Discoursing sweetly to the soul and ear,
Like some fair stream, majestically slow,
Aye bearing onwards with unwearying flow,
Ever uncheck'd, and wandering at will.

Oh! if thy mighty spirit, to this shore
Of earth confin'd, where others do but creep,
Launch'd forth so far into the boundless deep,
And gather'd of rich pearls so large a store,
What depths are thine now freely to explore!
The source of light and life, the fountain clear
Of wisdom, open to thee; whence with joy
To hear this sentence, " Well thou didst employ
Thy talents—to thee shall be given more."—S. F.

whose figure he used to draw on the blank pages of his books. . . It is not the less true that the sight of your real ink was a great refreshment to my eyes. So much for the form and material characters of your letter. For the substance, I am truly glad that your bargain for Turton[1] is approaching to a satisfactory termination, the more so as I trust it will enable you to inspect us here. Do not be afraid of the summer, it is all nonsense. Ask William! he will tell you; and I can tell you that I am never so well here as in the height of summer, and our constitutions, I take it, are not much unlike. Take example by the old Welsh mules which are sent over to the West Indies, where they are found to grow young again. You will see how I am ruining myself with building (I dare say you will be told so, if you remain in England). I built my first piece of wall simply by the Lesbian rule, as Aristotle describes it; but I have since made a discovery of the true Pelasgic method, and am finishing the other end of it like a perfect Cyclops, such as Neptune employed in building the walls of Troy. I have not time to explain this, so you must come and judge for yourself on the spot, and stop my hand if you think I am likely to do myself any real injury by the expense, for my architect is persuading me to build a small Doric temple, though the cost, even according to his own statement, will not be less than fifteen pounds; and it will cost me, I believe, seven or eight to finish my wall in a way that Sir W. Gell would approve.

"I have been running on with nonsense (from which you will only collect that I am well, and that I shall be very glad to see you), while you are looking for some account of dear S—" [a niece who had gone out to Malta for her health]. "She is the most cheerful creature under suffering that ever was, and

---

[1] Turton Tower, near Bolton, in Lancashire, which his brother was about to sell.

the delight of everybody, including even that old uncle of hers. You know 'she is living with an old uncle.'"

Speaking of a young couple who were about to marry on very narrow means, he adds :—

"With respect to means, if they will be content to live like poor gentle folks like —— and ——, they may do very well. The opposite line, that of *living genteel* upon a small income, is the vilest slavery, and never answers."

"MALTA, *August 6th*, 1835.

"MY DEAR BARTLE,

"Bandinell has met with some difficulties at the Treasury, the nature of which I do not very well understand. It seems that I am 'to state the period during which I have been free from office, and from which I claim the pension.' Now these two periods are not the same, for my pension was granted on my first return from Spain, and on my being sent there again, my pension was not stopped, and I had no fixed allowance as a minister (as in so confused a state of things it was hardly possible to fix on any amount which might not be extravagant or insufficient); but I was left at liberty to draw for necessary expenses, a liberty which you know I used with great moderation, con- ceiving, as I did, that anything like the usual display of foreign ministers would appear offensive in the midst of the general distress.

"Such is the history of my pension ; but having no papers or memoranda to which I can refer, it is impossible for me to make it strictly chronological. If this should be required, you, perhaps, would assist, and you and Bandinell together would draw up a certificate in the form in which I ought to send it. I am now two quarters in arrear, and should be very glad of a little money.

"I am much obliged to you for the trouble you

have taken about Theognis.   I flatter myself it will show the Germans that an Englishman can do something, though not exactly in their way.

" Pray thank Hamilton for his care about my *dilettanti* books, and tell him that I shall be anxious to show every civility to his friend, Captain Stodart."[1]

" MALTA, *May 5th*, 1836.

" The same packet by which my brother Edward arrived here on the 19th of last month brought me your letter recommending Mr. W——, who arrived here afterwards in the 'Manchester' steamer, and is now on his way home with four giraffes, and Mr. and Mrs. B—— on board.   I have been as civil to them all (the giraffes included, for I called upon them—the giraffes—twice) as I could possibly be, and if you see them they will, I trust (with the exception of the giraffes), make a favourable report of their reception here.   I liked Mr. W—— very much, and was delighted (as everybody else was) with Mrs. B——.   They are roaming in quest of health for him, and have already passed two winters in Madeira.   I am in hopes that they may be persuaded to pass the next winter here.   I have promised to be 'as obliging and attentive as possible.' It would be a great thing for the island if some real gentlemen of fortune would take to living here, and it would be a great boon to

" Your scrubby but affectionate brother,

" J. H. FRERE."

" I wish some morning, when you are in good spirits, that you would call on Mrs. B——."

To his sister-in-law, he wrote, November 8th, 1836:—

" Pray thank my brother for the trouble he has taken in writing to Chantrey.   I have sent a part

---

[1] The unfortunate traveller who afterwards, with Arthur Conolly, perished in captivity at Bokhara.

of his letter to Lord Holland. Poor John is in quarantine within sight of this window, and in quarantine he must remain, oscillating between this place and Alexandria, till his friends are able to clap an epaulette on his shoulders. . . . We have all kinds of people here : the Prince de Joinville, Louis Philippe's younger son, and the Principe di Capua, the King of Naples' younger brother, with the Irish lady whom he has married. Count Matu-tiwitz is just gone, and John will have to convey Lord and Lady Brudenell to Alexandria, from whence they proceed to Bombay with a letter of recommendation to Mr. William Frere, of the Sud-der Adawlut, after which they are to go to Delhi or Meerut, where they will have the advantage, pro-bably, of seeing Mr. Richard Frere. Nonsense!"

In 1836 Lord Melbourne's Government appointed a Commission to examine into a vast number of complaints received by the Colonial Office regarding the administration of the laws, and of public affairs generally, in Malta. Many of the abuses and evils —political, economical, and social—to be investi-gated and reported upon, seemed to Mr. Frere beyond the reach of any remedy which such a com-mission could recommend, or any government ap-ply ; and he had some fears of the effects on the island population of the exaggerated expectations raised by what the Duke of Wellington is said to have likened to "an attempt to frame a constitution on the British model for a line-of-battle ship."

Both the Commissioners were men of distinguished ability and literary mark, the senior being Mr. Austin, the celebrated jurist, who was accompanied by his wife, already well known as an accomplished autho-ress. The junior member was Mr. (afterwards Sir) George Cornewall Lewis, whose death in 1863, after he had filled the offices of Chancellor of the Exche-quer, Home Secretary, and Secretary of State for War, in Lord Palmerston's administrations from

1855, has not yet ceased to be regretted by contemporary statesmen of all parties.

Notwithstanding the difference of their ages—for Mr. Lewis was then barely thirty—and, in many respects, of their political views, Mr. Frere formed the highest opinion of him as a politician, as well as a man of letters. Speaking of him, he said, " Lewis is one of the very few really learned Englishmen I have met of late years, and his fairness is as remarkable as his learning. It is a great pity he is such a desperate Whig; but I think, if we could have kept him in Malta a little longer, we might have made a very decent Tory of him. I do not think he was very well pleased with his first essay in constitution-making." It is fair to add, however, that the constitution, and the reforms generally, which the Commission recommended, seem to have answered most of the purposes for which they were designed, even if they did not fulfil the somewhat extravagant expectations of those who called for the Commission. Writing to Sir Edmund Head soon after arriving in Malta, Mr. Lewis said:— " The two main evils of Malta are—for the upper classes practical exclusion from office, and brutal treatment by the English in society; and for the lower classes, over-population. . . Already carubas have become an article of food; and if the increase goes much further, the people must starve if they are not fed by English charity. I have seen Hookham Frere, who found himself in Malta sixteen years ago, at his wife's death, and has forgotten to return to England. He has translated four plays of Aristophanes, and will, I imagine, publish them."

Mr. Lewis appears, from his subsequent letters, to have been at first much disappointed in what he saw of Mr. Frere, who, he thought, had completely rusted in his long exile. Probably Mr. Frere had expressed to him his own doubts of the Commission being able to effect all that the sanguine young

Liberal thought possible; and it is not unlikely that, as time proved the task to be more difficult and tedious than it had at first appeared, Mr. Lewis got to entertain more respect for what he had previously regarded as Mr. Frere's antiquated notions.

On January 18th, 1837, Mr. Frere wrote to his brother Bartle :—

" [John] is the bearer of a postscript to my Theognis and a title page—which took me more time than any other ten pages in the book.

" My chief difficulty in publishing, is this—that the world is at this moment mad with political excitement, and everything is supposed to have some political bearing.

" Now Theognis denounces the abuses and oppressions which terminated (as he predicted) in a revolution, he also deplores the violences of the revolution which followed.

" I wish therefore . . . to publish it simply as a school book, renouncing all the fashionable Whig, and Tory, and Radical booksellers, and betaking myself to a publisher who is simply scholastic."

" *March* 11, 1837.

" I shall be very glad to shew any civility to any person recommended by you, and shall look out on board the 'Vanguard' for Mr. J. E. Johnston.

" Is Sir Alexander Johnston the same man who is so zealous and liberal a promoter of Oriental investigations? I must in return trouble you with some commissions.

" Will you tell Rodwell to send me the *first* volume (the last published) of Clinton's 'Fasti Hellenici,' together with Thirlwall's 'History of Greece,' and Boeckh's 'Public Economy of Athens.' I have not time to write to Hamilton, and to thank him, as I ought to do.

" I am really, as they say here, *tutto confuso* with his kindness and attention.

". You see him I imagine so often, that it will not be giving you a very troublesome commission to desire you to say for me (I might say for us) for we have been all indebted to his kindness, how sensible we are of it—I myself in particular.

" So you are a subscriber to the Jini bronzes, and you were right ! What perfectly beautiful things they are !

" People on the packet day run away from writing their own letters, and go about visiting, hindering others—ὃ καὶ ἐμοὶ νυνὶ συμβέβηκεν.

" If you cannot make this out, no more could I make out the inscription on the polychrome temple, till Mr. Lewis, who had taken more pains with it, tranquillized my mind by informing me it was nonsense.

" With nonsense then I conclude,

*　　*　　*　　*　　*

" We are all here as comfortable as possible."

"*April 3rd*, 1837.

" . . . It is, as you say, rather a shame in a biblio-polish point of view, not to have finished those poor *Frogs ;* perhaps I may surprise you some day, by the sudden exertion of writing out the half-dozen remaining hexameters and writing the notes, (if I can remember what they were intended to be,) which are referred to in the text already printed. Mr. Lewis, who is here as Commissioner, and who is a complete scholar, is urging me to print the *Knights* at the Government Printing Office, and offers to superintend it. I do not know—to say the truth, I wish I could clear my mind of those clas-sicalities, which, between ourselves, have a tendency, more or less, to make heathens of us all, at least to weaken and confuse those impressions, which ought to be uppermost in the mind *ætatis anno* 68.

" Nothing has been done to 'Theognis,' and nothing is required; it might even go to the press as it is, but there are some sentences, here and there, which I should think it might be better to scratch out.

 " Believe me, my dear Bartle,
 " Very affectionately yours,
 " J. H. FRERE.

" P.S.—Pray give my best thanks to W. Rose for his recollection of me. I was much pleased with it, and with many of the verses.[1] Hamilton's 'Clouds' were borrowed of me, by Mr. Lewis, before I had read them myself. I therefore as yet can only thank him for having thought of me."

 " *Carnival Monday*, 1837.
" . . . I have another copy [of ' Theognis '] here, in which I should wish to make some corrections, and if you, or any judicious friend (Hamilton for instance, not omitting Ainslie, whose taste is perfect), would point out any desirable alterations or omissions, I should feel much obliged to them.

" But the copy in your hands is in the meanwhile sufficient to enable the publisher to form his estimate, and to make an offer.

" As a last resort, or perhaps in some respects as good as any, I might print at Eton, by the successor of the noble Jos. Pope."

 " *June* 2, 1837.
" We are all well, which perhaps you may be glad to hear, for it is possible that strange exaggerated accounts may reach England. The influenza has reached us, and has spread with extraordinary rapidity through the fleet and troops, and into the town ; but I do not hear that it has proved fatal, as yet, to any body : its period is from three

---

[1] This refers to the privately-printed "Rhymes" by William Stewart Rose (Brighton, 1837), containing the Epistle to Mr. Frere, already quoted.

days, in some cases, to about a week, and is accompanied with a good deal of pain and extreme weakness. Susan has had something very like it, though not much differing from the kind of colds which she has had once before this winter. I have had a cold too, such as I never had before. . . .

" So much for the sanitary question.

" I have not seen poor Sir W. Scott's life, and if you pass by Rodwell's any day, would be obliged to you to tell him to send it me.

" There is something in the atmosphere and the state of the weather which is, I believe, the origin of this general complaint ; a ship from Tunis, where the disorder had not appeared, was attacked with it on approaching the island, and those who are not attacked are sensible of extreme languor and oppression.

" It seems as if the elements were generally in a state of discomposure. But enough of this."

In the summer of this year, while the Commission was still at Malta, the island was visited by a frightful epidemic of cholera, which carried off 2,000 people in five weeks, and Mr. Frere suffered in many ways from the strain which his exertions to mitigate the general distress and alarm imposed on him. His sister, writing in September, after the disease had somewhat abated, describes the effect as having been so great as to make her fear that he was suddenly falling into old age. She speaks gratefully of the relief he had found in Mr. Lewis's society, and in the revived interest with which her brother had returned to his Translations, consequent on his young friend having volunteered to superintend their being printed at the Maltese Government press, though she says she has not yet been able quite to forgive the Commission for having abolished the House of Industry, the place of refuge for poor girls, and the Ospizio for old people, and fears that "all our charitable institutions will be absorbed into a hateful sort of general poor-rate."

Mr. Bartle Frere refers to the aid thus tendered by Mr. Lewis in several letters written in 1837, in one of which, after saying that two London publishers had declined to undertake to print the translation of Aristophanes at their own risk, he urges his brother to publish it himself, "even if it cost him fifty pounds," reminding him of the consolation which a friend of theirs had found in paying a heavy printer's bill for her son's unsaleable publications, "that it was a very creditable way of spending one's money!"

In a subsequent letter he adds:—"In my opinion, you had better accept at once Mr. Lewis's offer, and print at the Government press. You will be then laying out your money, not only for a creditable purpose (as I suggested in my last), but will be doing something for the good of the island, whose export trade in this article of books, I suppose, is far overbalanced by those which you import. By the bye, if I was not enjoined to send no books but what are *ordered* by you, I should have told Rodwell to forward to you the two first volumes of Lockhart's ' Life of Scott ; ' the second only comes out to-day, and I see your name frequently mentioned in it, in conjunction with G. Ellis and Canning, in terms in which one might not complain of being handed down to posterity ; for this is a book which *will* go to posterity, and also, I suppose, have a more extensive sale at its first appearance than any other modern work."

With the help which Mr. Lewis had kindly offered, the translation of four plays of Aristophanes was at length put through the press at Malta, though without the marking of the dominant accents, or other indications of the rhythm, which Mr. Frere had contemplated as aids to a better understanding of the effect of the original. He found that, with the limited resources of the local press, the correction of typographical errors in the accents would have involved a greater amount of labour than, at his age, it was possible to give to such a task ; and he somewhat reluctantly yielded to the advice of Mr. Lewis, who judged that, though careful scholars would appreciate the assistance to be derived from an accentuated text, readers in general would be more likely to be deterred from perusal by the unusual aspect of the page, than to be aided by the additional labour bestowed on it.

But, though printed, the work was not published, and was consequently inaccessible to the public, and its merits were very imperfectly appreciated by the world of scholars till Mr. Lewis, some years afterwards (1847), gave, in the "Classical Museum,"[1] very ample extracts, accompanied by much kindly and judicious criticism. In his introductory remarks, he says:—"The reproduction of the comedies of Aristophanes in a modern language seems almost a hopeless task. The endless variety of his style and metres, the exuberance of his witty imagination, the richness and flexibility of the Attic language in which he wrote, and the perpetual byplay of allusions, often intimated merely by a pun, a metaphor, or a strange new compound, to the statesmen, poets, political events and institutions, manners and domestic history of his times, appear to make it equally difficult to execute a poetical version which shall adhere to the letter or render the spirit of the original." After noticing the imperfections of Mitchell's translation, he adds:—"Mr. Frere (who had many years ago exercised his poetical powers upon Aristophanes, and who wrote a fair and, indeed, favourable critique of the first volume of Mr. Mitchell's translation, in the 'Quarterly Review')

---

[1] No. ii. p. 238.

judged rightly that the success of previous translators had not rendered his efforts superfluous. He has accordingly been induced to print, for private distribution, his versions of the 'Acharnians,' the 'Knights,' the 'Birds,' and the 'Frogs.' If anybody was likely to meet with success in this undertaking, it was the author of the admirable imitation of Darwin in the 'Anti-Jacobin'—an imitation which bids fair to be much more long-lived than its original—and of the excellent poem of Whistlecraft, the model on which Lord Byron wrote his 'Beppo,' but which, by some accident of popular taste, has never obtained a reputation equal to its merits. And, in our opinion, Mr. Frere's success as a translator of Aristophanes has been greater than might have been reasonably anticipated. Of the plays which he has selected, three, the 'Knights,' the 'Birds,' and the 'Frogs,' are certainly the most difficult which a translator could deal with. Moreover, what he has undertaken he has performed ; the entire play is rendered, so that the merely English reader can form a complete judgment of the original : no scenes are omitted as unmanageable. Of the four plays, the translations of the 'Frogs' and 'Knights' appear to us to be the best : the latter, in particular, gives an excellent idea of this masterpiece of comic invective ; the δεινότης of which was never exceeded by any of the vituperative effusions of those great masters of the art, the Attic orators.

"As the work is not published for sale, we propose to give such full selections as will enable the reader to judge for himself of the goodness of the translation. Before, however, we proceed to do so, we repeat that the difficulty of worthily representing Aristophanes in a modern language can scarcely be over-estimated, and it can only be appreciated by one who is acquainted with the original. The Germans, as far as we know, are almost the only continental nation who have attempted any other translation of Aristophanes than a literal prose version for the use of school-boys.[1] All poetical translations from the ancient classical languages are difficult; as the failure of great poets (such as Dryden and Pope), and the rarity of even tolerable success, evince. But a poetical translation of Aristophanes is peculiarly difficult. Comedy is harder of translation than tragedy; it is easier to copy the lofty and serious than the ridiculous and familiar. That Menander's grace and elegance was not easily transferred into another language is proved by the comparative failure of Terence, whom Julius Cæsar, doubtless disposed to speak of him as highly as he could, only ventured to call *half a Menander.* If, however, the equable flow and domestic plots of Menander were hard to imitate, what is to be thought of the grotesque, fantastic, and local humour of Aristophanes? The translation of Goethe's 'Faust' is no easy task, as many modern poets have found. It has not, we believe, been attempted in French or Italian verse. But 'Faust' is far less obscure, and less tinged with the colours of time and place, than the 'Knights' or the 'Frogs.' Moreover, there is an affinity in modern metres and forms of words which renders the transfusion of a poem from one living language to another easier than the transfusion from a dead language."

After giving copious extracts from the four plays, the article concludes with some criticism on Mr. Frere's translation of Theognis, which was printed some years after the Aristophanes.

In August, 1837, while the cholera was still

---

[1] The "Biographie Universelle," tom. ii. p. 455, states that in the complete translation of the plays of Aristophanes by Poinsinet de Sivry, some plays are translated in verse, and others in prose: and that the translation of Brottier (the nephew of the translator of Tacitus) is entirely in prose. We have not seen either translation.

devastating the island, Mr. Frere wrote to his brother Bartle :—

"Not having been able to sleep, and having laboured under a paroxysm of laziness all yesterday, and it being now light enough to enable me to see what I am writing, and owing to Susan's inflammation in her eyes, devolving upon me the task of writing to everybody who may be supposed to care about us, I sit down with pleasure (or more properly stand up at my desk) to inform you that we are hitherto alive and well, except as above excepted. . . . . The cholera is on the decline in point of numbers, but within these few days has been more frequent among the higher class of Maltese, and among the English. As for myself, when a disorder is going about, I rarely get it till everybody else has done with it. Susan has had her equivalent in the influenza, which prevailed as unaccountably as the cholera during all the singular cold wet weather which we experienced this spring. It was with a sudden burst of extreme heat on the 9th of June that the cholera first broke out, and (as is usual with epidemics on their first appearance) was rapidly fatal. It is strange that (as if it had introduced itself into a new region) the same rapidity of execution is visible in the class into which it has now found its way. I take what care I can of myself, and some care of others. My only method is to be very moderate in everything, so here is a *very moderate* letter."

On 20th September, 1838, he wrote :—

"My dear Bartle,

"I shall be happy to show any civility in my power to your friend Sir H. Willoughby. I say *in my power*, for I have found it necessary to give up dining out, or entertaining large parties at home, so that my company is pretty much restricted to the few persons I can venture to ask, either on the same day, or the day before.

"Do not imagine that I am very bad, but as I am indebted for my quasi-recovery to this mode of life, I do not run the risk of altering it.

*　　　*　　　*　　　*　　　*

"Temple writes me word that Mr. Dykes (the *other* Lord of the Manor of Roydon) is dead, and that there is an opportunity of purchasing it, with 90 acres of land. I do not want the land ; but if you were inclined to purchase land, we might make a joint bargain, for the Manor might, in troublesome hands, become a source of annoyance.

"I am glad to hear so good an account of W. Rose."

His sister never entirely recovered from the effects of the illness above mentioned, and in the autumn of 1838 he became much alarmed by her failing health. Her home had been in his house since their mother's death, twenty-five years previous. A great part of the few letters he now wrote was devoted to allaying in others the anxiety which he could not himself cease to feel on her account. After dwelling on this subject in a letter to his brother George, dated November 15, 1838, he writes :—

"According to your desire, I return Dr. Wordsworth's, and beg you to return my thanks to his son [1] for his obliging present of the 'Pompeian Inscriptions,' which have amused me a good deal, though some of them are puzzles to me.

"I was glad to hear of our cousin Watlington's [2]

---

[1] Dr. Christopher Wordsworth, now Bishop of Lincoln. He had lately married Mr. Frere's niece.

[2] A connexion of their family, who had applied to Mr. G. Frere for some information regarding their common descent from Dr. John Dee, Queen Elizabeth's astrologer. Dr. Dec's great grand-daughter, Margery Dee, married Mr. Flowerdew, and had two daughters ; Jane, who married Mr. Stephen Pomfrett, and was Mr. Frere's great-grandmother, on his mother's side ; and Elizabeth, who married Mr. W. Watling-

prosperity. I had not been aware that there were any ties of consanguinity between us.

"I remember a Mrs. Flowerdew, my mother's great aunt, a tall, very old lady, dressed in black, whom I used to like, partly, perhaps, because she used to regale me with savoury biscuits; but my recollection of her is as of a very nice old person, who was exceedingly fond of my mother, and always delighted to see us. She was unmarried; the daughter of a Mr. Flowerdew, who had married a Miss Dee, a descendant (I do not know in what degree) of the mathematician and hermetic philosopher. There are some verses of hers on her separation from her intended husband, Mr. Flowerdew, who, upon some mercantile emergency (the seizure, I think, of English property by the Spanish Government), had been called away to Cadiz. The verses are in the cabinet at Roydon.[1]

"Mrs. Flowerdew, whom I recollect, was old enough to recollect the *alarm* of the Irish massacre

---

ton. Dr. Dee's silver Divining Cup is now in the possession of R. Temple Frere, Esq., to whose father (Temple Frere, see ante, p. 151) it was given by his mother.

By the Will of Francis Dee, Bishop of Peterborough, 1638, who was a son of Dr. John Dee, a boy educated at Merchant Taylor's School, or Peterborough School, being of the kindred or name of the bishop, is entitled to a scholarship or fellowship at St. John's College, Cambridge. [See "Wilson's History of Merchant Taylor's School," p. 1170.]

[1] The subjoined are the verses. The original is written in a clear round hand, presumably Margery Dee's, and is marked on the outside in Jane [Hookham] Frere's handwriting :—

"MY GREAT-GRANDMOTHER'S CURIOUS COMPOSITION."

 1 The World a garden is wherein I walk
  but what my heart doth muse I dar.not talk

 2 For when I looked on the flowers which grow
  I spy.d a jelly flower that grew so Low—

 3 That when I did atempt the flower to gain
  great flouds of water drove me back again

—not the real massacre, but the strange alarm
spread through the city by the Whigs, to try the
temper of the people, and to ascertain the extent
of their gullibility.

"There was a story of poor Mrs. F.'s absence of

---

4 With bended head it sometims then did Crouch
and with a Silent Voice did Crave a touch

5 But of my hand which I Could not deny
but was much pleas.d to see its modisty

6 For often with a blush the Leaves were dy.d
as if humility did strive to hide

7 Those Charmin graces which I must admire
Alltho I dare not say its my desire

8 To Call it mine alas that were a Crime
which nothing Could Excuse but length of time

9 Yet had I ventur.d to Express my mind
but that I fear.d to raise a Storm of wind

10 Might of this tender plant then me deprive
or blast it so that it should never thrive

11 Thus all my thoughts did but increase my fears
thus musingly I stood for many Years

12 At last—by an invisable hand
it was transplanted in another Land

13 That the warm sunshine of prosperity
might make it grow but ah how mournfull I

14 Did seek a place where I might vent my grief
which to discover would be Some reliefe

15 All mortalls terour which Is Called grim death
I did invoke to Ease of my breath

16 Then the silent grave might me secure
from all those Sorrows which I did indure

17 The tedious Nights I spent in bitter Cries
my days in piercing Sighs and fixed Eyes

18 I look.t so long I allmost lost my Sight
because I could not look on my delight

19 Reason did bid me then forget the flower
but I could never yet obtain that power

20 And sure my Life had Ended with the day
but that I found there was no other way

mind ; how, having been down into the kitchen on a Sunday morning, she was seen proceeding to church with a knife in her hand instead of a fan.

"This is all I can recollect at present, and with it I return Mr. Watlington's letter, in order that the

---

21 Which Could advance this flower or it improv.d
whose hapiness more than myself I Lov.d

22 O heavens doe not regard my moan
if it is better thare let it alone

23 Parents and friends did bring me Floria's Bower
and ask.d me if there was not there a flower

24 Which I could like to place within my breast
but still to them I made it my request

25 That I might have the leave but to refuse
all those rich flowers which they would have me Chuse

26 But they and all that knew me with one Voice
did then intreat me for to make my Choice

27 Out of those flowers whose great worth might tempt
the most resolved heart for to relent

28 Its true I did confess that their desert
did merit ten times more than my poor heart

29 And if I had a heart for to bestow
I Could not Count it wisdom to say no

30 With frowns and Checks they call'd me then blind fool
and with a thousand threats my heart did Cool

31 When I had broke those bonds asunder
to the world I then became a wonder.

32 But in such woes as these a pride I take
because that I do bear them for the sake

33 Of that rare flower which Could I but obtain
all worldly Losses I should Count a gain

34 When I am most alone methinks I hear
some secret whisper bid me not despair

35 And may I hope that I shall live to see
this jelly flower again return to me

36 Then dying heart revive that I may plead
to swift pace time yet to make greater Speed

37 And bring to me that happy hour and then
this grief will turn to joys.   Ah but when."

two documents, if you think them worth preserving, may repose together."

" MALTA, January 11th, 1839.

" A hard wind blowing into the mouth of the harbour detained the packet, and allows me time to thank you for your almanack, and to request you to send a duplicate for a purpose which, as before in my letter to my sister, I shall leave her to guess.

"I do not exactly recollect what I wrote upon occasion of our cousin Watlington's genealogical communications. I think it related chiefly to the Dees and the Flowerdews ; but I believe I omitted to mention one fact, harsh-sounding and unwelcome to the genealogical ear—one of the Flowerdews was *hanged—durum verbum.* You will say, ' What is to be done with him ?' But, ho ! we ought to endeavour, if possible, to trace our lineage to him, and hitch him in as a collateral ; for it was, in fact, a most creditable occurrence, and one upon which (since he would undoubtedly have been dead before this time) we ought rather to congratulate ourselves. He was, in fact, hanged (I dislike the word as applied to an ancestor) ; but it was by the rebels in the time of Kett the Tanner—the *Furor Norvicensis,* as it was called by the learned.[1]

" It is wrong, however, to be singular in any way; and since candour towards rebels is so much in fashion, I must not omit to state a probability in their behalf, implying that the family were not very liberal or popular, their house, standing at some distance from the road, on the right hand as you go from Hetherset to Norwich, was, as it is now, known by the name of 'Mock-beggar Hall.'

" The question, then, to be determined, in behalf of omnipotent candour, on the one hand, and family honour on the other, reduces itself to a question of

---

[1] Temp. Edw. VI.

time : ' Is the name ancient ? Can it be traced to a period anterior to the time of Kett the Tanner ? ' In that case the presumed illiberality of the owner might be pleaded in palliation of the violence of which he was the victim. Or was it imposed at a time immediately subsequent, when the resentment of the family, and their disgust against the lower orders (arising from the incident before mentioned), might have rendered them less charitable and hospitable than we find that peoples' ancestors were. Or, lastly, was the name given when it was reduced to a farm-house (retaining, as it does, the appearance of a gentleman's mansion, as was before observed) at a distance from the road, and consequently alluring vagrants to a fruitless application ? These are the points which can never be cleared up, unless by the investigation of some local antiquary, whose great ability has manifested itself chiefly in the elucidation of similar difficulties. And though we may delight to indulge our fancy in the contemplation of those comfortable old times, yet, situated as we are, certainty is in most instances unattainable.

" I must now conclude, for the wind that detained this packet is also detaining one for Alexandria, by which I have more than one letter which I ought to write."

A few days after this letter was written, his anxieties regarding his sister were terminated by her death, on the 18th January, 1839. She died, as she had lived, a bright example of every Christian and domestic virtue. Her brother laid her near his wife, and close to the spot which he had long before marked as that where he wished himself to rest. None were now left near him of his own family or generation ; and for some months after her death there were many duties connected with her letters, her property, and the poor around, to whom she had long been his willing and most judicious almoner, which made him feel his loss very acutely.

He wrote on the subject to his brother George on the 22nd January, enclosing a detailed account of his sister's last illness and of her death.

"Little did I imagine when I was sending my absurd letter of the 11th, and at a time when my sister appeared, in the opinion of those who saw her that same day, to be in better health than she had been for a long time past, that the following morning should bring upon us the beginning of the distress and confusion which has since overwhelmed us.

"The sad narrative which I enclose is substantially accurate, at least as far as my own recollection, compared with that of others, would enable me to make it so. . . . .

"The last sad ceremony is appointed for the day after to-morrow, in conformity with the wish of the Governor, who expressed a desire to be present; it will be exactly similar to that which took place eight years ago, in the same month, and almost the same day. The month of January, if I should live to see it again, will in future be a most melancholy one for me.

"You probably are well informed respecting her will : I have no knowledge or even guess about it. I lost an opportunity of inquiring at a time when I told her, about nine months ago, that it was my intention to provide for her future, a becoming and comfortable residence here; but in fact the idea of surviving her myself did not once cross my mind.

"During her sickness I was unwilling to alarm her; and when she herself became—I will not say alarmed—but aware of the approach of death, I would not divert her mind from thoughts which it was occupied with by the recollection of any worldly concerns, from which they had appeared during the whole course of her illness to be entirely abstracted."

About a year before this time, Lady Erroll's niece, Miss Blake, who had always lived with her aunt from her childhood, and had been to Mr. Frere as a daughter, had married Lord Hamilton Chichester, for whom Mr. Frere had the warmest regard. They were able to live much with him at Malta, and nothing was ever wanting to his comfort which their perfectly filial affection and constant watchful attention could ensure to him.

On February 21st, 1839, he wrote to his brother George :—

"I have again to perform the melancholy task of sending back the letters addressed to my poor sister. The papers which you mention as having been sent from Hampton Court in 1831, I should wish to be sent out here by some safe conveyance. Pray, my dear George, thank Lizzy for her kind letter, though it made me very sad to see the hopes and expectation under which it was written. . . . .

"Except that we are tolerably well, I do not know anything that remains for me to say, unless I were to send you the news of this place, which, of a sudden, is become a very bustling one."

"*March* 20*th*, 1839.

"MY DEAR BARTLE,

"I am not very well able to write, having been suffering for these three days with a pain in my face—a pain which of all incapacitates me the most for any exertion. I mention this lest you should hear that I had been ill and confined to my room, which is true, to this extent, but no further. In other respects, I think I have passed through this winter better than the last. Accordingly I have exhorted Lord and Lady Hamilton to go to Rome to see Lady Cadogan, who had wished to see us there. I would not venture to go myself, for March is the worst month here, and, I should imagine, not at all better at Rome.

"It was otherwise in the times of the Cid—'El *invierno* es exido, que el marzo quiere entrar.'

"And now, my dear Bartle (after a very disagree-

able interruption, which has occupied me upwards
of an hour), I return to conclude with a subject
with which I ought to have begun. I ought to have
begun to thank you for the admirable lines[1] which
you have sent me. I conclude them to be your
own, though you do not say so distinctly, and there
is a great deal of poetry in the family. Whosesoever
they are, they are excellent, and (to use a phrase
which I am not fond of) *appropriate.* This, mind, in
this respect, is singular." . . . .

"April 13*th,* 1839.

" If the packets which Sir William Eden has had
the kindness to take charge of, arrive safe at their
destination, Temple and you will find yourselves
charged with a task of distribution, scarcely com-
pensated, I am afraid, by your own individual

---

[1] Inscribed on his sister's tomb with her epitaph :—

" Susanna Frere
Joannis Frere et Joannæ Hookham filia
nata d. conv. S. Pauli, 1777,
cum plures annos in hâc insulâ commorans
pietatis et caritatis singulare exemplum præbuisset,
ad meliorem vitam transiit
d. Jan : 18 : anno 1839.
J : H : Frere defunctæ Frater mœrens posuit."

" Farewell, blest spirit, not for thee the tear
Steals down this furrow'd cheek—unscath'd hast thou
Life's thorny path of sin and sorrow trod ;
But well may they who to thy heart were dear
Mourn for themselves, unblam'd, yet mourning, bow
With humble resignation to the rod.
Thy birth befell upon that hallow'd day
When burst th' ineffable light upon the Jew
Of Tarsus, and affirm'd the call divine.
Upon that rock is cast thy coil of clay
Where from his arm the great Apostle threw
Unharm'd the venomous beast—What fitter shrine
For her whose course through life was ever true
To the aspiration which the zeal accords
Of the new convert —those heart-breathing words—
' Who art thou, Lord? What wouldst thou have me do?' "

share in the concern ; but the offer was made and accepted suddenly, no longer ago than yesterday evening.

"Hence the copies are sent in a form in which they are hardly presentable ; and no more are sent, from the apprehension of putting Sir William's civility to too severe a trial. I was upon the point of having a number of them stitched, but this immediate offer has anticipated my resolution, which, on the other hand, had been delayed by this strange weather, which has discouraged me from going to Valetta.

"I have been tolerably well, however, with the exception of colds, which I have scrambled through rather more nimbly than usual.

"It occurs to me, that if this letter reaches you before the package to which it refers, you will not, perhaps, be very well able to guess what it is all about. It is about the Acharnians and Knights, which I have taken the opportunity of printing before the expiration and extinction of the Government Press."

To his sister-in-law he wrote, on May 2nd, 1839 :—

"It is very kind of you to grant me an exemption from the task of writing, which has been occasionally, though not so much of late, physically distressing to me—I mean the posture and the act of writing.

"You have, I hope, by this time received the Aristophanes. Having a very sudden and unexpected opportunity, I was obliged to send them in sheets as they were, and to trouble my brothers Bartle and Temple to get them stitched in a presentable form. A copy is directed to Dr. Wordsworth, and I should have liked to have sent more, in case he should so far approve of it as to wish to present copies to any of his scholars. . . .

"John is still here. Lord and Lady Hamilton

not yet returned. * * I am afraid that I shall not have time to write to George, therefore you must thank him for his letter. It would be endless to write politics, but the prospect of things getting worse would not afford me any consolation from the anticipated expectation of their getting better. In the year '92 I remember to have heard people in France administering to themselves the same sort of consolation."

In the same year he wrote to his brother Bartle :—

" May 16th, 1839.

"MY DEAR BARTLE,

"Our packet is going to start before the arrival of the one from England, which will occasion brevity, the events of the place not being very multifarious or interesting.

"Honoria[1] and Lord Hamilton are returned, after a short stay at Rome and Naples. Prince George has been here about ten days, and starts to-day for Corfu. Everybody here has been much pleased with him as an easy, unaffected, manly young man. There has been here a young Norfolk squire of the name of Styleman, an inhabitant of the parts about Lynn, a very stout Conservative, whom I have been much pleased with, and am sorry that he is going away this day.

"Aristophanes has been stopped for want of paper, but is going on again. I have advanced to the 48th page of the ' Birds.'

"Your transcript will be preserved from the hands of the printers, and another sent to them instead. I have always regarded that transcript as one of the highest compliments ever paid me.

"Honoria tells me that she is writing to you. I

---

[1] Lady Hamilton Chichester.

cannot think that she will be able to find anything to say that I have omitted. No. I have omitted to say that Lord Hamilton is much better, and has ceased to suffer from rheumatism.

"Besides she will have to tell you about Rome and Naples. She describes poor Lord C—— as quite disabled by gout, a sad declension from the nimbleness which you both exhibited in Germany."

"PIETÀ, *May* 30*th*, 1839.

"The enclosed will show you how I have been occupied for the last fortnight; I send it to you exclusively, in acknowledgment of your former kind service in transcribing it. I thought you would like to see your manuscript converted into print; it will be finished, I hope, in another week.

"I am not aware that anything has occurred here which you would care to know. I doubt for instance whether it is worth while to mention that Lady Strachan has been here, and that her carriage was embarked this morning under these windows. Oh, yes! there is a M. Gautier, belonging to the French consulate, here, whom we all like very much, and who will, I think, be much liked in London, to which he is now advanced.

"He goes in October; and it would be a great relief at that dreary season, if he could find himself a member of the *Traveller's.* Will you and Hamilton interest yourselves in his behalf? He leaves this place in a few days, to our sincere regret."

"*June* 27*th.*

"I wish I had an opportunity of sending more copies. The *one* remaining in your hands, ought, I think, as he stands foremost in your list (and justly so, in consideration of his alphabetical precedence), to be given to Sir R. Ainslie.

"I wish I had one for Hudson Gurney and

Montgomerie ; but if you see them you must make my excuses to them and others for the present."

"*July* 11*th*, 1839.

"The packet from England came in yesterday evening, and goes to-day at 12 o'clock.

"Let me thank you for the trouble you have taken in detecting and correcting errata.

"Most of them are marked in a table of errata, already printed ; but as nobody attends to tables of errata, I shall have them corrected here by hand ; this will save you from the trouble you have been so good as to take with them.

"Some must be sold, not for my profit, but for poor Mr. ——'s, who is entitled to all kindness from the lovers of learning, and particularly from me, in this instance ; for poor Mr. Coleridge had requested in his last will, that some of the transcripts which I had lent to him might be allowed to remain with Mr. ——. I have done, therefore, what I suppose he would have wished, by giving Mr. —— half the impression (250 copies). I have desired that 50 should be sent to each of the Universities.

"In the meantime, they, Mr. and Mrs. ——, have agreed with Mr. Pickering, of Chancery Lane, whom I have mentioned as a bookseller of curious books out of the common line. How they will settle it I do not know, but it rests with them : at any rate the book will be acceptable for those who want it, and inquire for it. Any further popularity I should deprecate.

"I have sent the 'Birds' to the Bishop of London.

"I am very sorry for poor Dr. B——. I must have done."

"MALTA, *August* 22*nd*, 1839.

"I thank you for your very detailed account of family matters. The very elements seem to have conspired auspiciously to honour John's nuptials.[1] In the first place a downpour of rain to put the bishop's zeal and good-will to the proof ; and secondly, as Lizzy affirms, a most beautiful fine day, to do honour to the wedding itself.

"With respect to copies of Aristophanes, I have not been able as yet to find any opportunity ; for anything except letters, the communication between this place and England is, I think, worse than ever."

"*Oct.* 17*th*, 1839.

" I feel much obliged to you for the trouble you have taken about the last sheet of the 'Frogs,' which I return herewith, with a single correction in page 76, and my full assent to your suggestion.

" I should like to have 100 copies sent out here, but how I cannot tell ; the steam conveyance is the worst possible for the transmission of parcels.   Oh ! here is Honoria, as usual full of resources ; she says the imperials of a carriage which is coming out here for her and Lord Hamilton may be filled with them, and any thing you may wish to send.   Said carriage is to be found at Adams and Hooper's, Haymarket, who will be able to notify the last hour of its departure.[2]

---

[1] His nephew, the late Rev. John Frere, rector of Cottenham and chaplain to Dr. Blomfield, when Bishop of London. He died in 1851, just as he was fulfilling the early promise he had given of a useful as well as brilliant career.

[2] The following "Apology for the Translation of Aristophanes" seems to have been written with a view to its being prefixed to these copies ; a different preface was subsequently added (*vide suprà*, pp. 226 and 231). "The appearance of a publication so little suited to the period of age at which the writer has arrived, seems to require explanation on his part. The fact is, a strong persuasion had, from a very early time, been impressed upon his mind, that the English language was possessed of capabilities [for such a purpose] which had never hitherto been systematically studied, or sufficiently developed.

" Did I write to you some time ago about a Dr. Mill,[1] a very learned orientalist, who passed through here many months ago, on his return from India ? he seemed much interested in my views for establishing the study of Hebrew, and its cognate dialects, which (as the Maltese is one) the natives have a peculiar facility for acquiring. He took charge of a commission for procuring books for the scholars, and, now that their long vacation is over, the poor young men are looking to me for the fulfilment of my promise. In the meantime I have heard nothing from Dr. Mill, and do not know where to write to him.

"Speak you of young Master —— ? Well, my dear brother, I shall be willing to go you halves. Mrs. G—— applied to me for her rent, and I sent her £12. She says that she could get a better house for £100 ; and I would do it for her, but I fear, when people have once got to depend upon the power and efficacy of (what is called) 'making a poor month,' they never thrive.

" I wish some one branch of our families were settled in one of the colonies, where industry and

---

To attempt such a task was beyond his powers ; indeed, without a knowledge of music, (which he never possessed, and for which he felt no talent or inclination,) it would have been impossible ; but the persuasion above mentioned gave rise to a habit of endeavouring to express in English any passage which had struck him as remarkable in any foreign or ancient language. It happened, owing to circumstances in which the public can have no interest, that some passages longer than usual were translated from Aristophanes ; but the possibility of producing an adequate translation of an entire play never would have entered into his mind but from the example of his friend Mr. W. Hamilton, who had himself completed a translation of almost the whole of Aristophanes."

[1] Formerly Principal of Bishop's College, Calcutta, and subsequently Regius Professor of Hebrew at Cambridge, and Canon of Ely.

regularity can hardly fail to succeed.   If the ——s like to go, and you think them capable of it, their outfit would not require me to sell a farm in order to make them landed proprietors in the Anti-podes."

"*November 28th*, 1839.

" I thank you for Mr. Maurice's book, and will be obliged to you to let me keep it, and procure another for John.   I spent all the morning yester-day upon it, which has obliged me to abridge my correspondence this packet.   .   .

"We have here a Mr. B——, a friend and adherent of the Oxonian divines.   I shall lend him Maurice.

"Can you send the three numbers of 'Primi-tive Christianity?'   It was to have been published the 28th of August."

"*Dec. 2nd*, 1839.

" I send you per favour of Captain Moresby of the 'Pembroke' and under the particular care of Mr. Ewart, a midshipman of the same ship, a grand-son of Mr. Ewart of eminent diplomatic memory, and (though very different from him in principles) a nephew or cousin, I forget which, of the Radical paper-money Mr. ——, I send, I say, 27 copies of the 'Birds,' to be distributed according to their several directions—likewise some copies of the three Plays, bound together, which are also directed.

" There is one to General Hutchinson, of whom I have lost sight so long, that I really do not know whether he is still alive, but if he is, it would be unpardonable in me, not to send him a copy—for the promise is 20 years old and more.   I shall put it into a cover, with a note, which if it should fall into the hands of any other General Hutchinson, will serve at least to explain the mistake.

*   *   *   *   *

" Mr. Ewart is also charged with a bottle of *Ilex* acorns, and *two Cones* of a Cedar of Lebanon in-

tended for Roydon. He will also endeavour to
smuggle ashore the *Lamp* which my poor sister had
made, as a present for her nephew at Finningham,
and will take a model of the monument which
Temple was desirous of having.

*   *   *   *   *

" Mr. Hay and Sir A. Barnard have passed
through here on their return from Egypt, and
Petra and Syria, having seen every thing that was
to be seen, except Palmyra.

" I envy them their spirits and juvenility : they
have, however, been very bountiful, and I am indebted to Mr. Hay for the Cones of Cedar above
mentioned."

His brother had no difficulty in finding Dr. Mill,
and a list of the books which he recommended for
the use of the Maltese Hebrew scholars was made
and sent out.   But, on looking over the list with
Father Marmora, an unexpected difficulty presented
itself, as described in the following letter to his
brother :—

" MALTA, *January* 9, 1840.

" I am much obliged to you for the trouble you
have already taken, but at the same time sorry to
tell you that your trouble is not entirely over, at
least if the books are not already sent ; in which
case, you may be able, either by yourself or by Dr.
Mill, to save me the sum of £22 17*s.*, being the
amount of those books upon the list, which Mr.
Marmora considers as useless.   I enclose the list,
with observations to which I do not think it necessary to add anything ; the fact is, that the students
are all of the clergy, actual or intended, and among
the clergy a knowledge of English is a most rare
acquirement.

" My chief inducement for urging the establishment of lectures on Hebrew in this university arose
from the consideration that the natives possessed a

grammar in their own language, which, with some insignificant variations, is applicable to Hebrew : to teach it through the medium of English would be *ignotum per ignotius.* I hope, therefore, that I may be spared the mortification of receiving so large a lot of books, which I should not be able to apply to any useful purpose, not to mention the £22 17s. before alluded to, which, I am thinking, at this time of the year, would be a very acceptable present to poor Madam ——, and as an act of charity will be a stimulus to your exertions, you may think yourself at liberty so to apply it.

" Dr. Mill will probably have greater authority over his bookseller ; and if you should find it necessary, you may send this to him, with the accompanying list. The difficulty of intercourse betwixt this place and England, except for letters, is such that I flatter myself the package may still have been detained.

" I have not been able to find a conveyance for any additional copies of Aristophanes. Pray, when the ' Frogs' are finished, send a copy, with my best respects, to Dr. Mill." [1]

---

[1] The following memorandum seems to have been drawn up by Mr. Frere, and submitted to the Council of the University at Malta, embodying his views on the subject of teaching Hebrew as a branch of higher education. The remarks on the office and powers of such an University, on the affinities of Maltese, and the value of grammar taught through a cognate language, will justify the insertion of the paper. It shows, moreover, how little the lapse of years had diminished the interest he felt in his favourite studies :—

"*Reflections on the Studies which may be cultivated in the University of Malta, respectfully submitted to the consideration of the Members of the Council.*

" There are two points of view under which an University may be considered. First, as a place of education for the superior classes of the rising generation instituted and organized for the purpose of qualifying them for the due per-

> "*January* 19*th*, 1840.

"I have only just received your letter, and have only a moment to answer it, so I must crowd as many thanks as I can into a small compass. I am really mortified to think of the amount of trouble you have had.

---

formance of their civil and professional duties. The utility and necessity of an institution for these purposes is too obvious to require to be supported or confirmed by an unnecessary length of argument.

"But the Universities of Europe from their first institution have supported another and a higher character; and if they had not, the mere process of education according to the degree of knowledge and acquirements possessed at the time of their establishment, continued to the present time, would have left mankind in a state very little advanced from what it was four hundred years ago.

"The Universities, as I said before, had a higher character, like separate states combined in political union; they were, it may be said, federal members of the Great Republic of Letters, engaged in a mutual commerce of science and literature: the whole present stock of our literary wealth may be said to have been accumulated by this commerce, exclusive at least of that portion of it, which has been contributed during the last century, by voluntary associations of learned and scientific persons.

"This duty of contributing their efforts towards the general advancement of knowledge, constitutes the peculiar dignity of an University; and unless it is in some degree maintained, we may rest assured that the subordinate but obviously useful objects will never be accomplished in a satisfactory manner.

"It is an universal truth, that subordinate advantages arise from the pursuit of those which are of a more general and elevated character; and that if the subordinate are pursued, separately, exclusively, and solely for their own sake, we shall generally be baffled in our attempt to secure them.

"If, for instance, the establishment of Religion is attended to solely with a view to its civil influence in the maintenance of social subordination, religion will be degraded, its degradation will bring on hypocrisy with its attendant infidelity, and ultimately anarchy, the very evil against which it was considered as the best security. If the fine arts are cultivated solely with a view to the profit to be derived from improved taste in the patterns of our manufactures, we may be assured (as Sir J. Reynolds justly observes, upon this very subject,

" Do not suppose that I forget that I owe you £50, though I do not remind you of it like Falstaff. I hope you will find me a better paymaster than that worthy knight.

" The ' Rodney ' which sailed on the 14th, con-

---

in his lectures to the artists of the Academy), that they will never accomplish even this subordinate and paltry purpose.

"Thus in everything, if a noble and superior object is pursued for its own sake with zeal and generosity, all the inferior advantages which are connected with it, will follow naturally and of their own accord.

" Let us apply this principle to the conduct of an University, and particularly of an University situated as that of Malta is. If we suppose an University incapable of producing anything which can be generally interesting to the learned world, which should be unable to quote the name of a professor whose reputation had extended beyond the limits of his native country, such an University (whatever diligence it might apply to the just execution of its ordinary duties in assisting and directing the studies of the pupils) would labour under great disadvantages—First, from the want of that authority and reputation on the part of its seniors, which can only be confirmed in its highest degree, by the testimony of foreign literati, and the applause of other countries ; and, again, because the younger students, seeing their horizon bounded by a narrow circuit, and having no examples immediately before their eyes, of scholars who by their own merits and exertions had extended their reputation to a wider sphere, would confine their efforts to the attainment of a local superiority, considering their own countrymen as their only competitors, and that degree of excellence which would be sufficient to surpass them, as the just limit of their own exertions. But, it may be asked, what hopes are there for an University, situated as that of Malta is (locally insulated, and with the poorest endowment possible) to produce anything which can be considered as a contribution to the general mass of science and knowledge ? In regard to those pursuits which are followed with the eagerness of fashion in other parts of Europe, the want of communication, and the difficulty of intercourse, would perpetually throw us in the background. A professor at Malta might waste a year in the solution of a difficulty, which had been already solved at Paris or London, and the same discoveries, even when published and printed, might in many instances escape his notice. Not to mention that for those pursuits which require an expensive apparatus,

veys a bureau of which some of the drawers contain copies of the three plays, and several of the
' Birds,' for those to whom the two first plays were
sent before.

" This is another trouble which our consanguinity
imposes upon you. . . ."

---

astronomy, for instance, or chemistry, the establishment of an
observatory or of a scientific laboratory would be wholly out
of the question.

" Under these circumstances it is consolatory to reflect that
we possess within ourselves the materials for a branch of
literary industry, which, if properly employed, would enable
us to enter with advantage into the general commerce of
literature : the example of the University of Corfu, and the
expectation of new improvements and discoveries likely to
arise in the study of Greek literature, when cultivated by
those to whom a dialect of the same language is familiar from
their infancy, may suggest to us the adoption of a similar
course, and it would not be presumptuous to anticipate that
an equally favourable expectation would be excited, of new
illustrations likely to arise in the cultivation of a very extensive branch of Oriental literature, if zealously pursued and
candidly encouraged in the University of Malta.

" The native language of Malta is an Oriental dialect, intimately connected with Arabic, Hebrew, and Syriac ; with
respect to the first the fact is notorious, that a Maltese finds
no difficulty in making himself understood anywhere in the
Mediterranean coasts of Africa and Asia, a circumstance
which is of no small convenience in commercial intercourse,
and which might be improved to great advantage in that
respect. In Casal Zeitun the boys actually learn to write
their own language in the Arabic character, and as the
language itself is intelligible in all the countries before
mentioned, it is obvious that the inhabitants of that place
would possess great advantages, if a change of circumstances
reanimating commerce and directing it to Africa and the
Levant, should enable them to develop again the commercial
industry which they exhibited, not long ago, on the northern
and western coasts of the Mediterranean. But perhaps it
may be said that this is foreign to the proper pursuits of an
University, and particularly to those higher ones on which I
have chiefly insisted. It may be so ; but it is an acquirement
very easily attained, which may possibly be of real utility to

"*January 29th,* 1840.

" I could not write by the last packet, but there is an intimation of something likely to go to Marseilles, and Honoria is going into town for '*por averiguar*' as we used to say, and though I have

---

many who receive their education in the University, and it would be discreditable if its scholars were deficient in an accomplishment possessed by the sons of the poorest peasants in another part of the island. Besides, with respect to the attainment of proficiency in a branch of literature for which we have such peculiar advantages (which is so extensive and interesting in itself, and which to all other Europeans presents such uncommon difficulties) as the Arabic, it would be no slight step to be able to read and write with ease in a cognate dialect, and this step is one which is now actually acquired by boys of seven or eight years old in a few weeks.

" The direct practical utility of being able to write and read their own language in the Arabic character, is evidently the object proposed in the method adopted at Zeitun, where the boys learn at once their own grammar and the Italian, declining and conjugating in both languages together, with great facility, at a very early age.

" I should apprehend that any person, himself a native of Malta, and possessing a knowledge of the literal and classical Arabic, would (if desirous of instructing a countryman of his own in the same studies) begin the course of instruction by the process which I have already described, and of which we have an actual example before us—we see then that the same method which is usefully employed for subordinate purposes, may be made an elementary foundation for higher literary attainments : to understand the grammar of his own language in conjunction with Italian, and to be able to read and write it with facility in the Arabic character, may be the means of profit and advancement to the poorest native of the island if possessed of industry and talents, his own language and the Italian enable him to traffic in the whole of the Mediterranean ; and if he is able to read and write in both languages the advantage which he has in this respect will be greatly increased. But if fortune or profession should destine a youth to higher and literary pursuits, the same elementary rudiments which would be practically useful to the mercantile adventurer, will afford to the Maltese scholar an advantage which would enable him to outstrip the competition of any other European scholar in a branch of study highly interesting

X

little to say, except to thank you for the trouble you have taken in all your journeys to the bookseller and the bookbinders—I must not omit what is so much your due—fervently hoping at the same time that

------

in itself, and which has been hitherto little explored by European literati.

"The same observations (at least as far as the scholar is concerned) will apply to the study of Hebrew. I conceive that a Maltese master with a Maltese pupil would find great advantage in beginning with a short preliminary course, in which he would point out to him the grammatical rules existing in his own language, and which he had been in the practice of following from habit and imitation, without being aware of their principles or nature.

"These rules are totally different from those which exist in any of the modern European languages, or in Greek or Latin, but they have a direct analogy with, and are in many instances identical, with the rules of the Hebrew language.

"And here an observation occurs which ought not to be omitted. To speak one's own language without a knowledge of its grammar and construction, is the true characteristic of ignorance in an individual, or of barbarism in a people. A native of any other country in Europe, by acquiring any other of the languages which are usually learnt, acquires at the same time the grammar of his own. Thus an Englishman learning French, or an Italian learning Latin, cannot fail to observe that the rules which guide him in the acquisition of the new language, are equally applicable to his own ; and it is a common observation that those persons who have learnt another language are usually the most correct and perfect in speaking their own. This is the result of the analogy subsisting between them, but where this analogy does not exist—as for instance between the Maltese language and any one of those which are usually acquired by the inhabitants of the island (as English, for instance, Italian, or Latin), it is possible, and I believe not unfrequent, for a native to acquire another language, without deriving from it any very correct notion of the nature and construction of his own. If, therefore, it is desirable that a man should speak his own language correctly, and not merely as a parrot, or a barbarian, an attainment which is so easily acquired, and which may be made by boys of seven years old, ought not to be omitted in the course of Maltese education.

" It has been shown already that the Maltese language may

the rogues' laziness may have been proof against your remonstrances, and that my last letter may have arrived in time to save me the mortification of receiving what would be altogether useless.[1]

----

be usefully employed if written in the Arabic character, and that this is an acquirement within the reach of mere children, who ought not to be left in ignorance of the grammar of the language which they habitually speak. I should, therefore, venture with submission to propose that the grammar of the Maltese language combined with the Italian, and the practice of writing it in the Arabic and perhaps also in the common alphabet, should be introduced in the lower school, and taught at the same time with the rudiments of Latin to boys of ten years old and under. Those who are obliged to discontinue these studies, will in this way have acquired an accomplishment which may be of profit and advantage to them in foreign commerce, and facilitate their intercourse with those countries to which our trade in future seems most likely to be directed. Those who continue to pursue their studies, will possess an advantage peculiar to themselves, in entering upon a vast field of literature hitherto very imperfectly explored in those languages which are cognate dialects of the Native Maltese, the Hebrew, Arabic, Syriac, and Ethiopic. In all of these the University of Malta might obtain a decided pre-eminence over the other Universities and learned bodies in Europe—and pre-eminence in one species of knowledge would (as has been before observed) be attended with advantages in others. It would be contrary to experience to suppose that an University pre-eminent in one point would at the same time be deficient in others.

" These are the reflections which I venture to submit, thus hastily, to the judgment of those who are fully capable of estimating them (if they should be deemed worthy of any consideration), and who possess a practical and local knowledge of the means by which such a plan might be effectually realized.

" It would be too presumptuous in me to venture in this stage to enter into a detail of arrangements ; it would, moreover, be premature, unless the principles and views, which have been generally stated, should be sanctioned by the previous approbation of the Council."

----

[1] Owing to mistakes in the transcribing.

" The books which you mention as likely to come with the carriage, viz. ' Holdius Schrœder,' &c. and three others, will be very acceptable in the meanwhile.

"But after so much trouble as you have had already, as appears by your last, I really feel some compunction at the thought of the additional trouble which you are likely to have in discarding what is useless."

"February 6th, 1840.

" You will be glad to hear that I have seen our old friend Colonel C—— here, in the Lazaretto, very well and cheerful, and the same warm-hearted worthy fellow that we recollect him.

" We must both of us I apprehend have appeared to each other somewhat older than we were 30 years ago.

" The packet *from* England is just come in and ours to England is just starting.

" We are all well, *i. e.* Lord H. is (though very slowly) recovering. Lady H. and myself as well as usual."

"March 5th, 1840.

" I had entirely forgot that it was packet day, which will occasion brevity, as it is now very near the packet hour. I have packed up and directed a number of Aristophanes, which Captain Barker, who sails for England in a few days, will have the kindness to take charge of.

" I am afraid that you will think that you have imposed a troublesome task upon yourself in undertaking to distribute them. I wish you may feel impatient and pack them off speedily. . . . Here comes Honoria to tell me that I shall be too late, and if she had not come before I should not have known that it was post day."

"*April 2nd*, 1840.

" You will be glad to hear that the ' Prince George' is safe arrived, and though she is not yet unpacked nor the soldiers disembarked, we trust that the carriage, and its contents, will be found to have arrived safely also.

" We are now looking out for the ' Boadicea.' I have had bad luck in maritime affairs—a cask of special ale, brewed at Roydon, and sent by the ' Fanny,' has not been heard of—they met with bad weather, and were forced to throw every thing overboard—fine English furniture, Forti - pianos, &c. &c. were consigned to the care of the Nereids, and with them I presume my cask of ale, as a propitiatory libation.

" We have been disappointed by the non-arrival of Mr. and Mrs. ———. We suspect they must have trusted themselves to the Rhone steamer, which had not arrived when the one from Marseilles started for this place.

" It is very provoking, I had provided a superb nuptial bed, large enough for a polygamist, and all to no purpose.

" I have no time for more nonsense."

"*May 14th*, 1840.

" I have so many letters to write, that I can only afford a few lines to each of them, and those few must be only to give you additional trouble.

" Would you then have the goodness to send copies (complete ones) with my compliments (respectful ones) to Lord Wellesley, Lord Burghersh and Dr. Crotch the musician, also the three Plays to Mr. Hammond, he has had the ' Frogs' sent him already by Messieurs Allen, his brothers-in-law, who passed through here a day or two ago.

" I send some lines, which if you think it advisable may be forwarded to Temple. The post is going or I would send them to him myself, in my own hand."

To his brother George, Mr. Frere wrote by the same mail :—

"First let me thank you for Lord Wellesley's verses. I have desired Bartle to send him in return my plays, and also to Lord Burghersh ; perhaps he may set some of the choruses to music. *A propos* to this I have also desired him to send one to Dr. Crotch."

The following are extracts from numerous other letters which he wrote to his brother Bartle during the remainder of this year :—

"June 25th, 1840.

"We are going for a trip on board a ship ; it is the ' Tyne,' Captain Townsend, bound for Corfu, and from thence where the Admiral pleases; so that I must say, as the sailor said—' Look into Steele's List,' and you will always be able to tell where we are.

"I shall write again when I know what direction we are likely to take.

"This summer threatens to be so excessively hot, that we are glad to escape to the air of the sea..

"Captain Townsend is a very old acquaintance of ours ; he expects us on board at twelve o'clock.

"Mr. Bouchier will take care of our letters, and of this which I am now writing among the rest."

[The subjoined, in a letter dated July 19th, 1840, refers to his anxiety to prevent the publication of a book that was, in his opinion, likely to be harmful.]

"Talking of ——, I must tell you a thing which I have never liked to talk about ; in prosecuting his researches . . . . he has fallen upon some strange and shocking discoveries, my sister and myself urged him to suppress them, but his friend Mr. L—— encouraged him, in fine, the work is printed, and now he is frightened, and Mr. L—— also to a certain degree, but not so much so as not to retain fifty copies for himself. —— is willing to sacrifice his time and labour if I will pay my share of the printers' bill; this I have done, as you will see by his letter which I enclose, *and will thank you to return.*

"You will see also by this the heap of dangerous matter which is lying in deposit at my disposition; he had offered to send them here, where I might destroy them as I pleased, I wrote to say that I would trust them in his keeping, and this is his letter acknowledging and thanking me for my confidence. I do not, however, feel perfectly secure; the event of his death or an execution in his house might spring the mine.

"I should wish you therefore to call upon him and to form your own judgment. I should have no objection to his retaining a number of copies, say forty or fifty, trusting to his discretion for their distribution *out of England;* the rest I should wish to have secured against any such contingency by their immediate destruction. If you can contrive this with the assistance of the next baker, you will set my mind at rest; or they may, at any rate, be sent here, as a supply for my own oven. Do not think me foolish or extravagant in all this. I do not know in what way I could employ the means attached to me more usefully to religion and society."

"ZANTE, August 1st, 1840.[1]

"You will be glad to hear that we are alive and well at this distance of time and place.

---

[1] In this year Mr. Frere visited the Ionian Islands, Trieste, and Rome in company with Lord and Lady Hamilton Chichester.

"Besides I have to thank you for the trouble you have had with ——. Among other reasons for not prefixing a title-page[1] there is this, that the copies which are distributed as presents would be less perfect than those which remain for sale. I forget whether I desired you to send a copy to a Mr. Jeremie, of Trinity College? It was a request of our nephew Bartle, whose tutor he had been at the East India College, and who had somehow got a copy of the forty first pages of the 'Frogs,' which he taught his pupil to understand and admire. Perhaps the copy had better be sent to the care of Mr. Philip Frere of Downing, who will know where to find him.

"I have been much distressed at hearing a very unfavourable account of the health of our old friend W. Rose; let me know if the account is less bad than that which I heard, and which represented the case as a very desperate one.

"I have just lost a very sincere friend and well-wisher, Mr. Nugent, whom I had known for thirty-six years. Poor Manning too, whom I had not seen since I left college, but who is really a public loss, considering the mass of knowledge which has perished with him.

"This, the only letter which I write by this occasion, will serve to notify my existence to inquiring friends."

"VENICE, *September 15th*, 1840.

"I have taken an estesissimo foglio di carta simply for the sake of announcing our arrival at this place, depicted in the prefixed vignette: if you retain a recollection of the prints in the old show

---

[1] In a previous letter to Mr. Bartle Frere, dated Malta, June 31st, 1840, he said, in speaking of the same subject, "It would be too ridiculous in me, now for the first time in my life to clap my name on a title-page; and I cannot think it can be necessary for the sale of so limited an edition."

box at Bedington you will conjecture that we are at
Venice; and you will be right so far, but you will
still be at a loss to guess what inn we are at, therefore I have thought right to mark it, with a bird
flying over it, ad hunc modum (as the Greek grammar says).

"We came here from Trieste with Sir Andrew
Barnard, and here met with Mr. Hay, but they
have both left us, one for Greece, the other (Sir
Andrew) for England. They are the most active
young fellows in the world. We very narrowly
missed seeing Sir R. Inglis, he being at Ancona;
but we have found a most obliging cicerone, an
English gentleman, who has lived here these eight
years, and who is very deep in the Venetian antiquities and records, some of which he is printing.

"They are printing the reports of the Venetian
Ambassadors; you know that on their return from
a mission they made a general report, the first of
them goes back as far as the time of Henry VII.

"But I suppose they are in England by this time.

"This place is recovering its commercial activity,
and I see no appearance of poverty or discontent.
Trieste, in the meanwhile, is advancing at a rate
which must astonish I think even the Americans,
whom I saw there in the three-decker, commanded
by an old acquaintance of mine, whom I had been
civil to at Malta. Some of the officers came over
here, and lodged in this hotel, 'Fiera gente, terri-
bile, non parlano lingua.'

"I find that —— —— is going to be married,
and that you give £500 to that effect, and I mean
to follow your excellent example with an equal
sum."

"*September 15th*, 1840.

"Pray advance the money for ——'s
bookseller, for I have not time to write a separate
letter to Hoare.

"I have a letter from Mr. L——, which, if I had time to look it out, and you were not such an enemy to postage, I would enclose. I think I can trust him ; he writes as a very serious and sensible gentleman, deprecating above all things the circulation of the work in England, but thinking that it can do no harm abroad, where so much worse are circulated."

"MALTA, *September* 30*th*, 1840.

"Many thanks for your kind and considerate letter of the 20th of this month. I was much relieved at the same time by receiving a letter from Temple, written in a very firm and manly spirit.[1] I trust he may be able to support and console his poor wife.

"My first impression of course was for the loss of such a young man ; but when I told Honoria, she threw up her arms, with the tears in her eyes—'Oh ! poor Mrs. Frere ;' and this certainly ought to be our only thought at present.

"Do you think that a total change of scene would be useful, or a thing which one could venture to propose ? a visit for instance to this place ? Pray let me know ; or, if you think it advisable, suggest it yourself.

"I have sent Messrs. Hoare an order to pay you £65, which, as I conceive, will put you in cash to the amount of £7 or thereabouts.

"Mr. Pickering, of Chancery Lane, has already received one hundred and sixty copies, to be sold as profit of Mr. and Mrs. G——. I have heard nothing from him, but can have no doubt of their having reached him.

"Well then—will you call there and purchase a couple of copies of him, and send them with my

---

[1] On the death of his eldest son.

compliments, and a copy of the 'Frogs,' to Lord Aberdeen and Mr. Thomas Grenville, both of whom I have unaccountably forgotten. At this rate you will see that I am not likely to enrich myself by literature.

"Inquire too whether he has done anything to secure the copyright by entry at Stationers'-hall, or sending copies to the Museum and Bodleian, &c.

"Honoria tells me that it is time to close my letters, which saves you for the present from another commission."

While at Rome, in January, 1841, Mr. Frere had an attack of apoplexy, with a threatening of paralysis. The following letter is undated, but appears to have been written while he was still confined to his room. It shows that the attack, though very alarming at the time, had not in any way affected his mental powers :[1]—

"MY DEAR BARTLE,

"I think it is better that you should have an account immediately from myself, as probably from among the many English here, some incorrect ones may reach England—vague and exaggerated, which it may be better to rectify. The case is this. On Saturday last (it is now Tuesday) I perceived a weakness and want of command in the fingers of my left hand, and upon rising I perceived that my gait and footing was very much like that of a drunken man. I accordingly lost no time in sending for doctors, and in a short time had

---

[1] Lord Brougham, speaking of him to the Rev. Constantine Frere (Mr. Frere's nephew), in 1853, said that when he met Mr. Frere in Rome in 1841, in answer to his greeting Mr. Frere replied, "Oh, very well, thank you; I've had an attack of apoplexy and a touch of paralysis, but I'm very well."—"So like Frere," said Lord Brougham.

two of them (English) at my elbow; they unanimously bled and blistered, and purged, and put me to bed, where, for the present, they have advised me to remain, and avoid all exertion or excitation. I cannot guess what their real opinions are, but they talk confidently and cheerfully to others.

"Mr. Hay is a joint inmate of this hotel, and is a great comfort.

"I have not been able to see Mr. D——. He called at this hotel and left a letter, but no card of his address. I now hear that he has gone to Naples; but as the letter which he brought from you was intended to be delivered at Malta, I conclude that he will proceed there, and that we shall meet. I shall be happy to show him any civilities in my power, an attention due, I think, to a person who, as I see, calls you *uncle*.

"My doctors forbid my reading,[1] and, *à fortiori*, would forbid my writing; so I conclude, dear Bartle,

"Affectionately yours,
"J. H. FRERE."

To his brother George, after his return to Malta, he wrote :—

"*April 28th*, 1841.

"I had begun a note something like this by the last packet, the purport of which was to thank you for your kind annual present, which I found here on my return, together with numbers 5 and 6 of the work on 'Ancient Christianity.' It is a great pity that the subject should have been stirred, but I think it is treated temperately enough, and above

---

[1] In answer to the remark that Mr. Frere's love of reading had become so exaggerated in his latter days that he read almost constantly, Lord Brougham said, "Ah, but he was always an *helluo librorum*."

all, with great decency. I do not see any such great advantage in the revival of the study of the old ecclesiastical writers. They seem to me like the furniture in the shop of Romeo's apothecary, very curious, but not fit to be prescribed as remedies. I have not any duplicates here, but I think there is at Roydon a copy of the ' Scriptores Ecclesiastici ' in three volumes folio, which Temple would send to you or to the Rector of Cottenham. I have also to thank you for poor Lord Dudley's letters. I have not yet told you that our nephew William, with his wife and two children, have been with us since their release from quarantine, about ten days ago. I flatter myself that all her new relations will be as much pleased with her as I have been.

" Read Ranke's ' History of the latter Popes.' "

His nephew William, whose return from India is mentioned in this letter, availed himself of the opportunities which his stay with Mr. Frere afforded, to induce him to put the finishing strokes to his translation of " Theognis," and to take it to the printers. Of this translation Mr. Norton, his American critic, observes :—" His ' Theognis Restitutus ' affords another instance of his success in conveying ' to the English reader a complete notion of the intention of the original, and a clear impression of the temper, character, and style which it exhibits.' His object was not to give a literal and verbally exact rendering, which might often puzzle the modern reader, but to translate in such a manner as to present clearly the essential meaning of the poet. ' It might not be difficult,' he says, ' to crowd into a given number of lines or words an exact verbal interpretation, but this verbal interpretation would convey almost in every instance either an imperfect meaning or a false character ; the relative and collateral ideas, and the associations which served as stepping-stones to transitions apparently incongruous and abrupt, would still be wanting; and the author whose elliptical familiar phraseology was a mere transcript of the language of daily life, would have the appearance of a pedantic composer studiously obscure and enigmatic.' Such versions as Mr. Frere's become a component part of the literature of the language in which they are made. They do not exclude the literal and precise translations which are intended to exhibit, not merely the permanent and universal elements of the original, but also its local and personal peculiarities, and the exact forms of its expression. These, too, are required, and have their value. Only the man of genius can venture to adopt such a method as Mr. Frere's, and how few translators are men of genius!

"From the confused mass of fragments which form the existing remains of 'Theognis'—some fourteen hundred lines in all—Mr. Frere endeavoured to reconstruct a biography of the poet, about whose life very little is absolutely known, and to indicate the successive changes of circumstance and situation under which his verses were composed. The ingenuity and learning displayed in it, the acuteness of interpretation, and the interest of the mode in which the subject is developed and illustrated, give to this little book a great charm as a work of delicate and thorough scholarship, and of imaginative reconstruction. How far the author is correct in his inferences and conclusions must be left to the determination of critics not less learned than himself."[1]

A very favourable notice of this translation appeared in the "Quarterly Review" in 1843,[2] of

---

[1] "North American Review" for July, 1868, p. 165.
[2] No. 144, p. 452.

which Sir Cornewall Lewis said, in the "Classical Museum" for October, 1843 (No. II.):—"We had intended to append to this article" (on Aristophanes) "some specimens of Mr. Frere's translation of parts of 'Theognis;' but the very complete account of this work given in the last number of the 'Quarterly Review' has rendered this a superfluous task. We will only express our admiration of the facility with which Mr. Frere has passed from the wild, grotesque and ever-varying language and metres of Aristophanes to the sedate admonitions and reflections of the gnomic poet, and the fidelity with which he has represented both sorts of diction in English always pure, terse, and idiomatic."

Both critics thought he had built upon the fragments of "Theognis" a superstructure of supposed facts which the foundation of materials was hardly wide enough to support; and Sir Cornewall Lewis held that sometimes, by combining separate fragments, a meaning had been obtained for which no evidence beyond conjecture could be produced. But he added, "These objections to his arrangement, however, rarely affect the success of the translations."

To his brother George, Mr. Frere wrote:—

"August 18*th*, 1841.

" There is no chance, I fear, of my acquitting my debt to you as a correspondent otherwise than by beginning when a mail is *not* going, having always at those times letters which absolutely require to be answered, and the very posture and act of writing being somewhat fatiguing to me. Otherwise, if I had found it on my arrival here, your kind and considerate letter would have been acknowledged before ; but it so happened that it, with two or three others (amongst them one from Hatley on the same subject, that of my illness at Rome), had been huddled away separately, and were not discovered till some time after.

" I thank you for explaining to me what I could not well explain to myself, namely, the nature of my dislike to these temperance societies."

"*August 27th.*

" I had, as you see, begun, but had not succeeded in finishing, ten days ago.

" I agree with you perfectly as to what you say, that our only chance of safety consists in reforming and extending the church ; but we must be content to do it by great sacrifice, of self-denial of our own, not by votes of parliament with our new majority. Now it was said in old time that we should give 'the devil his due ;' and without entering into the question of their respective merits (for there is another old saying, that 'comparisons are odious '), it cannot surely be contended that the Whigs are so much worse that in the present age, distinguished as it is by candour and liberality, the same equitable consideration should not be extended to them. Therefore I laud them for two things—first, for having stopped the translation of bishops ; and secondly, for having established a commutation of tithes. *A propos* of these questions, I have contributed to the *building* of the church at Harlow. Has the question of endowment been thought of, or is it to be left *entirely* to the *voluntary system?* I have no objection to a *partial* dependence on the good-will of the parishioners ; but, without some endowment, in fifty years our church may be turned into a malt-house.

" I am tolerably well, and the day before yesterday read over ' Spiritual Despotism ' a second time. Have you read a ' Voice from America ?' What are we about ? and how is it to end ?"

The early agitation of questions, the discussions on

which have since led to what is now known as Ritual-
ism, had extended to Malta. With all his rever-
ence for ancient uninterrupted usage, Mr. Frere had
little sympathy with the revival of forms long obsolete. Commenting on some innovations in music
and vestments which had troubled an Anglican
congregation in the see of Gibraltar, he said, in
reply to the argument that the change was justified
by the custom in Edward the Sixth's time,—" But
if I were to appear at church in the costume of
Queen Elizabeth's time, would the clergyman consider it a sufficient justification for my disturbing
the gravity of the congregation that I could prove
the dress to be in strict accordance with the
usages and sumptuary laws of three hundred years
back ?"

Still less sympathy had he with the custom of
discussing the gravest questions of theology as subjects of merely ordinary table-talk. But he complained that he sometimes found it difficult to evade
such discussion, or to turn the conversation. One
very enthusiastic lady, who had repeatedly pressed
him for his opinions on purgatory, declared, sitting
next him at dinner, that she *must* know what he
thought on the subject,—" I told her," he said, "that
I really knew very little about it, except what I
had learned from the church in the Floriana, which
I pass on my way into Valetta. The church, you
remember, is surrounded with groups of figures
carved in stone, and rising out of stone flames, and
I told her that, if the reality were at all like that, I
was clearly of opinion that the flames were necessary for the decent clothing of the figures.—After
that she managed to talk about something else."

On September 18th, 1842, he wrote to his brother
Bartle :—

" I am afraid you have had a good deal of trouble
about 'Theognis.' One part of it, viz. the table of
errata, I shall be much obliged to you if you will

undertake ; and, in addition, there are one or two gross errata, destructive of the metre and sense, which I would wish corrected by hand in any copies you may give away . . . . for the fact is that hardly anybody ever looks to a table of errata.

" It is odd that I should since have found the initial lines of the poem to which Fragment C. P. 103 belongs, and another fastens on to F. LXXXIV.; so that it should seem, after all, that I ought to have bestowed another year upon it, instead of Horace's nine !

" For the rest, you cannot do amiss in distributing them to any person whom you think capable of enjoying [them], and whom you may wish to oblige.

" Pray send the four plays and ' Theognis ' to Mr. Lyell, junior. If Mr. Lyell, senior, has not the ' Theognis,' it ought to be sent to him at ' Kinnordie, Kirriemuir, N.B.' I send the direction, lest you should be at a loss for it ; and, as I know you hate postage, I do not return it.

" Pray send two copies to Lord Holland and to the Bishop of London, and any other bishops, Llandaff, for instance, and Monk."

" MALTA, *March 23rd*, 1843.

(After telling him of the dispatch of a box of ilex seed for distribution to several friends.)

" I have also sent fourteen copies of ' Theognis,' in one of which I have marked and corrected the *errata majora*, such, I mean, as confuse the metre and the sense ; so that, if you have a mind to show a *particular attention* to any one of your friends, you may do it at the cost of the trouble of correcting the errata. There are, I think, some other points on which I had meant to write to you, but which I do not immediately recollect. One of them I have recollected. It is to know whether Mrs. —— has profited by the sale of the Aristophanes, of which (*i. e.* of the three plays) 170 copies were sent to Pickering almost as soon as they were printed ? If it were not out of your way some morning, I should be glad if you would make inquiry of him."

"April 5th, 1843.

" MY DEAR GEORGE,

"I am sorry that the few words in which I mentioned the affair should have given you the trouble of writing a long letter. D—— has so little regard to truth that I believe he has finally lost the perception of it, and really imagines himself to have a case ; an imagination from which, I believe, he is not to be driven, even by the sentence of a court, but will continue to his life's end to believe and repeat the same stories which he has told hitherto. I really believe, as you say, that he is now got entirely out of your reach, and equally beyond the fear of exposure for dishonourable conduct ; but to find that he has acted foolishly and unsuccessfully will, I conceive, be some mortification to him."

"May 15th, 1843.

" The few lines which I have time to write will serve to thank you for your letter with the amusing tale of ' Miss Margaret Catchpole.' [1]   I think she is

---

[1] " Margaret Catchpole," by the Rev. Richard Cobbold, of Wortham.   The tale was founded on the history of a servant girl in Suffolk, who carried off a horse to enable her to rescue her lover.   She was tried and convicted, and only saved from the death which was then the penalty of her offence by great interest made for her by her employers.   She was one of the first female convicts transported to New South Wales, and having, by her worthy conduct there, obtained a pardon, she distinguished herself by the ability and energy with which she subsequently devoted herself to good works during a long and useful life.   Her story, as told by Mr. Cobbold, is a very interesting one ; but it is to be regretted that the series of remark-

an honour to the county. So this comes of emigration—that they come in another generation and
are able to bid for the estates of foolish Squires ;
why should not you, who have a son already an
emigrant at the Cape, enable him to purchase land
there ? Poor —— writes to tell me that his doctor
prescribes him wine, which he cannot afford to purchase ; it would be a great charity if you would
advance him a few bottles on my account.

"I have not time for more, or I would say something about Welcker's 'Theognis ; ' he has hacked
and minced his author most unmercifully, and not
having formed a true judgment of the time in which
he lived, has *obclised* passages for no other reason
than that they did not square with his preconceived
chronology. The account which Brunck gives of
the Parisian MSS. shows that he has taken a most
unwarrantable licence in making mincemeat of his
author in the way he has done.

" I have no letter of Southey here."

"MALTA, October 14th, 1843.

" MY DEAR BARTLE,

"Your letter of the 29th ultimo was
lying open on my table all yesterday morning,
waiting to be answered by the English packet ; but
the other letters which I had to write turned out to
be so long and rambling, and I was so tired with
standing at the desk, that it was left to stand over
till to-day, to be answered per favour of the French
steamer to Marseilles. This, I fear, will aggravate
the charge for postage, but, in point of time, may
turn out to be rather an economy than otherwise.

" I thank you for your offer of going halves with

---

able letters written by her in her banishment, are not printed
in the very idiomatic Suffolk dialect in which they were
written.

me in our relations of consanguinity to Mrs. G——.
I have had a letter which I took to be hers, lying
unopened, but which, upon opening it preparatory
to writing to you, proves to be from a person whom
you have occasionally assisted, though he has had
no ground of claim upon you, viz. —— ——. I
shall send him something by this post, which, I
hope, will prevent him from troubling you. As he
never bullied you at Eton, he has no right to make
you his tributary now. Poor fellow! I could not
help thinking of him as I was doing the 98th Fragment of 'Theognis,' 'watching and importuning
every friend.' Talking of 'Theognis,' I am told
from a person likely to know, that the critique is by
Hallam. I have not yet seen it, for my periodicals
come in very irregularly, and I rarely go to the
garrison library. Whoever the writer may be, I
think, as you say, it is rather cool and easy to affix my
name to an anonymous work privately distributed.

"This laborious epistle has again been delayed to
this day, Oct. 25. In the meantime, I have received
the Review. It is not uncivil, but my name is
repeated *ad nauscam* thirty times, altogether, one
would imagine that I was a candidate for fame!"

"MALTA, *May 29th*, 1844.

"MY DEAR GEORGE,

"Though I have many letters clamouring
for their respective answers, I must not omit to
thank you for your green morocco present.[1] First
of the preface. It is, I think, excellent in point of
feeling.

"I am like the man in the old 'Kitchen Al-
manac' with all the constellations poking at him,
so that the utmost I can do is to distribute a line

---

[1] A "Parentalia" drawn up and prefaced by his brother
George.

or two apiece, in answer to my pocketful of letters. . . . . For the present I am tolerably well, though somewhat weak on my legs, and as. Master Waters used to say 'numb' in my hearing; but he used also to say 'numb in my understanding,' which perhaps also may be my case; but I put it to the test from time to time with bits of translation.

" I am sorry to have received a bad report of the condition in which the ilex acorns arrived. You were to have had a share, and shall, please God, this year, if I live to see them ripen."

Towards the end of this year, and in 1845, I had again the happiness of being for some weeks under my uncle's roof, on my way home from India. The lapse of ten years had greatly impaired his bodily vigour, but not the clearness and activity of his mind, nor was there any change in the warmth of his affection for all who had once been dear to him. The filial care of Lord and Lady Hamilton Chichester had preserved all the arrangements which, in earlier years, his wife and sister had devised for his comfort in his lonely island life, and had added much that his advancing age needed. His eyesight was nearly as good as of old, and so were his extraordinary powers of reading continuously for many hours at a stretch, and the wonderful tenacity and accuracy of his memory for what he read or composed. He went less abroad than formerly, partly owing to increasing bodily infirmity, partly to the loss of old friends and his dislike to the task of making new ones. There were also many changes in the island which were distasteful to him. It had become a bustling place, full of commercial activity, and of people always in a hurry. The old order of things had been replaced by a new Constitution, better adapted, no doubt, to the altered circumstances of the place, and to the political activity

awakened among the people, but little in accordance with that quiet once the peculiar charm of
Malta, which, like everything Maltese, used to have
a character of its own, equally removed from the
luxurious idleness of Naples, and from the Oriental
torpor which, before the days of steam navigation,
infected most places further east. With the new
order of political ideas had come in many religious
innovations which, though they little affected him
personally, he thought likely to work ill for those
around him and after him. The Roman Catholic
Church in Malta had for centuries been strongly
national, if the word can be used where the area is
so limited. The clergy, who, in old times, seldom
went further afield for their education or for travel
than to the great monasteries in Sicily, were the
recognized guardians of insular rights and privileges;
and to such an extent used this to be carried, that
Mr. Frere told me he had found instances of the
Dominicans arrayed as the champions of popular
right, to defend the Maltese from the illegal ex-
actions of the ruling order; and the servants of
the Inquisition engaged in escorting market carts
through the gates of Valetta, to protect the poor
peasantry from the extortionate demands of re-
tainers requiring more than the customary toll for
the Grand Master and the Knights of St. John.
These island clergy had always, from the first rising
against the French invaders, been loyal in their
advocacy of British rule, and they had enjoyed in
return, from the English Government, a degree of
consideration for all their customary rights and
privileges which sometimes occasioned murmurs
in Exeter Hall when it was thought to exceed
the limits of reasonable toleration. But with the
advent of reforms in the political administration, a
considerable change was observable in the disposition of those who had the direction of popular

opinion in ecclesiastical affairs. Ultramontane preachers, themselves foreigners to the island, were commissioned to denounce from the pulpit what they considered the infidel tendencies of the English Government ; and Mr. Frere found that the universal affection with which he was regarded among all orders of Maltese did not protect him from being sometimes held up as an object for popular aversion, because he was an Englishman, and a member of the English Church.

Nor did he find much to console him in the general aspect of political affairs, of which he was to the last a careful student. Of many of the measures of the various administrations after the Reform Bill, he very cordially approved. The best of them were, he said, the same measures which Pitt would have brought forward had breathing time been allowed him, and which Canning, but for the desertion of those who ought to have supported him, might have carried. But he viewed with alarm the growing tendency of statesmen of all parties to follow, instead of aspiring to lead and direct, public opinion—a tendency which he foresaw must often transfer the initiation of great measures from the wisest and best-informed to those who were simply discontented with the existing order of things. He particularly disliked the new name under which the broken ranks of the Tories had been rallied after the Reform Bill. "Why do you talk of Conservatives?" he asked ; "a Conservative is only a Tory who is ashamed of himself;" and he was especially indignant with men who, knowing better than the unreflecting rank and file of their party, attempted to defend any abuse long after they knew it to be indefensible, and thus left the correction of such abuse to violent or, at best, unfriendly hands. He was habitually inclined to take a very gloomy view of the political future ; but he never ceased to urge on younger men the duty of hoping the best for the state. "It is the privilege as well as the duty of your age to hope," he said.

Many of the fragments of his "Table Talk" have found insertion in the foregoing pages. The following, which have for the most part no special reference to any particular period of his life, were noted, some at this time, others in various earlier years, and by different persons:—

"It is clear Cervantes quite changed his plan after he had written the first part of 'Don Quixote.' He begins with fights with flocks of sheep and windmills, and other practical jokes; but after he had published it, an author whom he mentions in the second part[1] wrote a continuation of 'Don Quixote,' in which the knight was made to fall among people who understand and honour him. This struck Cervantes as affording a much finer field for fancy and humour than the accidents which happened to the Don among ignorant boors, and he adopted the idea in the second part in all the scenes relating to the Duke and Duchess, which are infinitely the best."

"Every original author paints himself in some character in his works, as Cervantes in the latter part of 'Don Quixote,' Molière in the 'Humoriste,' Smollett in 'Roderick Random,' and afterwards in 'Matthew Bramble.' I have no doubt that in 'Hamlet' Shakespeare was describing himself. No man imagines himself in a lower situation than he actually fills, and Hamlet is, what Shakespeare imagines he would have been, had he been a prince.

---

[1] The author is not named. He called himself Alonzo Fernandez de Avellaneda; and is supposed by some to have been Luis de Aliaga, the King's Confessor, and by others Juan Blanco de Paz, a Dominican friar. [*Vide* Ticknor's "History of Spanish Literature."] Cervantes only mentions his birth-place, Tarragona.

His advice to the players, and his morbid love of contemplating the relics of mortality, and their constant association with terms relating to the law, which Whiter observed upon, are all characteristic. I have no doubt if one knew where Shakespeare had served his apprenticeship in a scrivener's office, we should find it looked out on a graveyard. 'Hamlet' falls off at the end, 'Macbeth' (and two others) are the only plays where the end is equal to the beginning. It is the same with Aristophanes; the 'Frogs,' 'Knights,' and 'Birds' are the only perfect plays of his; this is not to be wondered at, considering in what haste they must have been written. I dare say Shakespeare often wrote with the prompter's boy sitting on the stairs waiting for 'copy.' Lope de Vega wrote plays as fast as he could put pen to paper, and you always find that the first two or three hundred lines are good."

"At one time I used to read every novel that came out, and seldom found one which had not some chapters very good. They are those parts where the writer is describing what he has himself seen; and every man has seen something which, if he would describe it exactly, would make a good scene in a novel.

"A really good novel one can read quite as often as a good play. There are some of Scott's which I read almost every year, and some of Galt's. It was a great misfortune for him that he lived in the same age as Scott. I remember the 'Trials of Margaret Lindsay' striking me when I first read it, quite as much as some of the Waverley novels did.

"Have you read Lady Duff Gordon's translation of the 'Amber Witch?'[1] It is quite the best thing of the kind I have read for a long time; at first

---

[1] In Murray's "Home and Colonial Library."

I could hardly believe it was not a genuine chronicle of the time, and the translation seems admirably done. I can think of nothing so nearly approaching 'Robinson Crusoe,' unless it be 'Penrose's Journal.' I was so taken with Penrose when I first read it, that I used to buy up all the copies I found on the bookstalls, and give them to my friends. I could never understand why it did not become more popular with boys and with old people too, and I never could learn who wrote it, or whether it was, or was not, a genuine journal of a castaway."

" I am surprised to find how few young men of the present day know anything of Swift. He is quite one of our best models of racy forcible idiomatic prose. He is sometimes savagely coarse and indecent, but there is less danger of corruption of morals or opinions in the whole of Swift's works than in almost any one volume of any modern French writer of fiction. No man was ever attracted to, or made tolerant of vice by reading Swift ; but it is not easy to find any modern French work which is at once witty, and free from all apology for or incentive to evil. I suspect it is because the materials of modern French fiction are usually drawn from the more corrupt classes of society, and their authors neglect much in ordinary French life which is not only excellent in itself morally, but really better adapted for dramatic purposes than the common run of French heroes and heroines."

" One of the best pictures of modern French manners I know, and one quite free from all that is objectionable, is Leclerq's 'Proverbes Dramatiques.' They are very slight sketches, but full of wit and humour, and I should think depict French society in the middle ranks very truly."

Speaking of Leclerq's " Proverbes " to Mr. Nugent, he said, " If I were obliged to give up either

Molière or Leclerq, I am not sure that I should not surrender Molière." To which Mr. Nugent observed that "Mr. Frere was hardly a fair judge, as he knew Molière by heart, and would not, therefore, lose anything by giving him up."

In reply to a lament on the disuse of the old custom, common formerly in England, as it still is in Malta and in many southern countries, of addressing the wayfarer in inscriptions of more permanent interest than the merits of " Warren's Blacking," or the number of miles to the next village, he said :—

"When I lived at Roydon, I used to think I would celebrate my churchwardenship by putting up a few such inscriptions. But it was difficult to decide what language to choose. If you wrote in Latin no one but the parson would understand you ; and in English it was not easy to write on the topics most interesting to the country traveller, in terms befitting the dignity of a churchwarden. Here are some verses for a bridge I intended to have built across the Waveney below Roydon :

> The Parish vestry, persons of much taste,
> Permit me to enclose this piece of waste ;
> I gave them in return the field called Darrers,
> Let this preserve my fame from censure's arrers [East
>   Anglian for 'arrows '].
> And further, to accommodate all people,
> I built this bridge and beautified the steeple.

" I thought they were in the proper churchwarden style ; and so was the motto for the White Hart at Roydon, when the road was altered :

> Stranger, be not offended or concern'd
> If you discover that this road is turn'd.
> A bowl of punch, or shilling's worth of porter,
> I'll bet you, that the present road is shorter.

" That would have been intelligible and interesting to most of the people who would have read it. But then some of my travelled neighbours would have thought it very vulgar. So, you see, here (at the Pietà) I have stuck to Latin."

" I suspect that Tacitus' ignorance and mistakes about the Christians were partly affected—it seems to have been the established fashionable rule to know nothing about them—the same tone continued very late, indeed as long as Paganism subsisted, or a Pagan writer was left. It is most absurdly remarkable in Zosimus."

Captain Basil Hall remarked (1834) that " he had met with more intentional incivility in a fortnight in France than during all his long stay in America."

Mr. Frere observed :—

" I think the tone adopted by Englishmen generally towards America is very much to be deplored. We have numbers of American travellers here in Malta, and I never met one who had not some very good points. We should try to promote that kind of feeling which should lead to a union between the two nations for establishing the supremacy of the Anglo-Saxon race over the whole of the western continent.

" At the end of the American war, if we had not been so utterly exhausted, it was a scheme of Fox's and some of his party, to have promoted an union between England and the United States, to assist an insurrection which then raged in Peru."

Speaking of some American review on English politics, he said :— ·

" The tone is particularly good, especially where they notice the vulgar abuse heaped on them as a nation, by ————.

" As regards our own English politics, if we go on as we do now, there will be little chance of any really impartial judgments of our public men among ourselves ; and future historians may have to go to American writers for all really unbiassed contemporary criticism."

"I wish you young gentlemen would not talk so much of 'our Indian empire.'—An empire is a very good thing in its way, but we are in danger of forgetting the thrift and other homely commercial virtues which helped us to that empire. When I lived in the country, I used to observe that there was no fool like a fool in a ring fence—the man who was always telling you 'his property was in a ring fence,' till he got to pride himself on having as little as possible in common with his poorer neighbours. I am sometimes afraid of that kind of spirit infecting us in India. That was not Malcolm's nor Munro's way, nor Elphinstone's, who, I take it, was the greatest man you have ever had in our days."

In answer to a remark, that the French seemed able to make but little out of Algiers, he said:

"Your Frenchman is always trying to be *imposing*, and to make an *impression;* there are some people who don't like that, and I fancy the Arabs don't."

In reply to a question why, with his opinions regarding the Spanish insurrection against the French, he did not feel more sympathy with the cause of liberty in Greece, he said:—

"There was no kind of similarity between the two cases. I was sorry the insurrection in Greece broke out when it did. The Greeks had the commerce, the diplomacy, the education, in short, every branch of the internal administration of Turkey, and much of the external, in their own hands; and, had the outbreak been delayed for ten years, they would have expelled the Turks from the whole of their European possessions. I do not see what we have to do meddling in Greece at this present time (1844-5), or why we should trouble ourselves with what the French are doing there. If we act *with* them we may be drawn into a contest with Russia; if against them, we shall be fighting the battles of Russia."

" It is a pity when all Europe was eager to go to war, fourteen years ago, we did not let them, and keep ourselves quiet the while. Had we done so we should not now have been complaining of commercial combinations against us. We never got any thanks from Europe, though we have three times saved it from becoming subject to one power. We saved them from the Spaniards in Philip II.'s time, and from the French in Marlborough's and again in Napoleon's, and we never got any thanks for it."

In answer to a remark that it was strange a mind like Milton's should have been blind to the advantages of a monarchical form of government for England, he observed :—

" It was no wonder all the ardent imaginative spirits of the time of the Great Rebellion were led away into republicanism ; they had before their eyes the example of the Dutch, bearding such a power as the Spaniards then were, and naturally attributed all to the republican form of their government."

" But then the republics they imagined were something widely different from the democracies of modern days."

Talking of recent improvements in agriculture :—

" There is nothing of such real permanent value to a nation. How little remains of the vast wealth acquired by Florence or the Netherlands which can be compared, as a permanent source of national riches, with their improved agriculture."

The following is one of the latest letters of Mr. Frere which has been preserved. It is addressed to Mr. G. T. Clark, at Bombay.

" MALTA, *March* 31*st,* 1845.

" I was much gratified by your obliging letter, showing you were aware how much I feel interested in your proceedings ; and, if Providence is pleased to prolong our dominion in India, your Railway will, I am persuaded, be one of the chief means employed for its maintenance, and ultimately change the condition of the country ; and the rupee will then be enabled to find its way back to the ryot, out of ·whose fist it has been wrenched by the collector ; and our troops . . . . will no longer—I should hope—be of necessity disabled from moving with their artillery, etc. . . . . I often used to wonder how the Romans contrived to keep the whole world in order, with a force, such as Gibbon enumerates, apparently so inadequate ; the secret lay, I am persuaded, in their system of roads, which enabled them to bring an overwhelming force upon any point where insubordination manifested itself. They did not allow time for the *Ragojées*,[1] whom we hear of, to grow up to be Sivajees, and to found a predatory empire like the original Maharattas. However, this fear, I hope, is got over for the present.

" Surely it should be thought a shame for Englishmen that the Spaniards should have outrun us in the race of improvement, yet so it is ; they have already established railroads in the island of Cuba, and this they have done under all the disadvantages of having to execute great public works by slave labour ; but they had the advantage of a man of talent and energy in the person of their Governor, and I suppose also of some clever able engineer like ——. Why then should Bombay be behindhand ? I should wish to see a line to Nagpoor ; if that were once done, the great Zemindars and capitalists of Calcutta will feel obliged to meet you half-way ; the disadvantage of position, which they now endeavour to elude by expensive and clumsy contrivances, will then be reduced to the difference of not many hours. While our commu-

---

[1] A freebooting Maharatta, whose exploits about this time caused some anxiety to our political officers in the Deccan.

nication continues through Egypt, the priority of intelligence cannot by any contrivance be long withheld from Bombay ; the wisest then, as well as the fairest way, is to endeavour to reduce that difference to a minimum by the utmost rapidity of communication. It was the maxim of some great Eastern conqueror, ' that the world should always be kept in astonishment and expectation,' and this, though a work of peace, would have that effect. ' What a strange people these Ingilesi are, that enable us to fly over the country like birds.' Half a dozen battles and sieges would not, I believe, excite the same impression of our superiority.[1] I say *Ingilesi*, for we ought never to allow ourselves to be called *Feringhes*. No ! The *Feringhes* were the allies of *Tippo Saib*, the *Ingilesi* subdued Tippo, and drove the *Feringhes* out of India.

"This is the way that it all happened :—' In the beginning, 100 years ago, the *Feringhes* and the *Ingilesi* had each a trading company, but as the *Ingilesi* had more success in trade, the *Feringhes* endeavoured to gain the advantage in war and politics ; and in this way they succeeded for a time, and had nearly driven out the *Ingilesi;* but at last the *Ingilesi* got the better of them in war, as they had before in commerce.'

"This is an abrégé of the modern history of India *in usum scholarum*.

" But I have not time to go on rambling at this rate ; only believe that I shall feel most interested in your proceedings, and grateful for any account of your progress which you may at any time find leisure to send me. I cannot promise for my own

---

[1] The railway here referred to, the first defined railway project in India, was a line from Bombay to Callian, proposed by Mr. Clark in 1843, whilst on a visit to Sir George Arthur, then Governor of Bombay, who warmly encouraged it. It ultimately formed the first section of the present Great Indian Peninsula Railway from Bombay to Calcutta.

part to be a very regular correspondent ; the posture and act of writing being at times very irksome to me, and obliging me to set pen to paper by fits and snatches, as you may perceive by the date of this. I am at a loss how to direct this ; and I believe I must take the liberty of sending it under cover to Sir George Arthur."

During the whole of 1844, he had continued to enjoy his usual health, and, beyond a slight increase of feebleness in movement, those around him could detect no mark of the increasing infirmities of age. But, in 1845, he had an attack of apoplexy, and in the first days of January, 1846, a repetition of the paralytic attack, partly due to suppressed gout, which had alarmed his friends at Rome five years before.[1]   Every remedy which the best medical

---

[1] The following extracts from a letter of Lady Hamilton Chichester's on the subject, give many characteristic details, which will interest those who knew and loved him.

"In January 1841, at Rome, Mr. Frere had his first attack of apoplexy, from which he rallied so entirely as to leave no traces of it in his mind or general health till the spring of 1845, when he sometimes said he felt feeble on his limbs— he had a presentiment that he was going to have an attack, as, on once starting for a drive to see the new aqueduct, opened in May or June, he turned round to Lord Hamilton, when getting into the carriage, and said, 'Ask Nony to bring her little lancet in case I should have a fit.' I was in another carriage. I jumped out and got the lancet, and then kept close behind his carriage ; all went well ; he walked about and forgot his fears."

After giving an account of a seizure Mr. Frere had about a week after this, which rendered him in spite of all that the best medical advice and skill and care could do, entirely unconscious for some time, Lady Hamilton Chichester relates that as soon as animation had been gradually re- stored, and he was put into bed by the doctors' orders,—"the room darkened and he was told that he *must* keep quiet,"— he said, "Don't shut me up, and give me a *book !*" This raised a general cry, that he must not *attempt to read*. He was left alone, in bed, in the dark, the door ajar, through which his friends and the doctors could watch him, as the doctors expected another attack which would be fatal.

skill, and the ever-watchful affection of Lord and Lady Hamilton Chichester could suggest, was tried, but without effect; he never recovered speech or consciousness, and passed away without apparent suffering on the 7th January. He was laid beside

---

About an hour afterwards, they saw him "look round the room, and finding himself alone, he deliberately got out of bed and walked quickly to his desk, on which was lying the book he had been reading when he was seized, and returned quickly to the bed with it! . . . . . The ruling passion of life still strong in death." After a while he cried out, "Is any one there?" The servant went in. "Open that shutter and shut the door." The doctor and I allowed all this to be done, to watch the result, the poor doctor, so *utterly* confounded at the strength and clearness of the man who had been all but dead two hours before, feared it was a flare-up of the candle." . . . .

"From this attack he completely recovered, his mind as clear and his memory as perfect as in his most youthful days.

"In the month of January (on the 6th), Dr. Stilon came about half-past five o'clock. He went to see Mr. Frere. Mr. Bourchier and Lord Hamilton were sitting with him, and he was giving them a clear account of Lord Sidmouth's administration and of everything connected with it—the conversation was still going on when the servant went in to say it was time to dress for dinner. On this, Mr. Bourchier and Dr. Stilon left the room, and Stilon came back to me to say that he had not for months seen Mr. Frere so bright and so well! It was past six . . . he went into the drawing-room, there were about eight to dinner. I always went out the last (he never dined at table) and he said to me, putting out his hand, 'I am rather chilly and shall like my soup.'—Beppo with his tray was at the door.—I passed on to the dining-room, but before I sat down Beppo ran back to me, touching my shoulder and saying, 'Come quick.' I was not (as you know the distance, across one room only) a minute —he was sitting up in the position I had left him—the eyes open, motionless. . . . I went over to him and said, 'You are not well,' at the same time supporting him with a cushion and my own arm. He looked at me with a gentle smile—it was the last! He remained in that position for two hours. Stilon was there immediately, but all hope was over. He breathed gently for a while—then louder—then louder—and I was *hoping* from that change—but it only prehis wife in the English burial-ground, in one of the Floriana outworks overlooking the Quarantine Harbour, where a sarcophagus bears the following inscription to his memory :—

PRÆHONORABILIS VIR JOANNES HOOKHAM FRERE

Ab ingenuâ stirpe in agro Britannorum Norfolciensi oriundus
Regii ablegati Munere in Lusitaniâ,
Eodemque unâ et alterâ vice in Hispaniâ, egregiè perfunctus,
Melitam denique, uxoris suæ valetudinis causâ, se recepit,
atque ibi 25 annos commoratus est.
Hîc cultu Literarum quas semper ab adolescentiâ in deliciis
habuit senectutem oblectans,
(Minime interea suorum immemor)
Eruditos Commercio Studiorum Familiares verò et Advenas
Comitate & Hospitalitate
Pauperes etiam largissimâ Munificentiâ ita sibi divinxerat,
Ut interitus ejus publica quædam Calamitas fuisse videretur,
Et nomen post se reliquerit pio omnium amore prosequendum,
Quod faxit Deus ut Vitæ quoque sempiternæ Libro
Ob Christi merita inscriptum reperiatur.
Natus est Londini 21° Mens. Maii 1769—Obiit 7° Mens.
Jan^{ii} 1846.

On the spot where he had so long lived, the

---

ceded those three last sighs which always attend a calm death, and which once heard can *never* be forgotten ! Thus the dear old man died as he had lived ! He had received the Sacrament on Christmas-day, Mr. Cleugh having come to the house to give it to him with Lord Hamilton. They had been forbidden to go to church in consequence of the cold. Hundreds crowded round the doors all day, the servants were followed to the market to know if it could be ' *really true.*' The day of his funeral all the shops were closed. He was borne to the grave on the shoulders of his own labourers. All the Maltese of the upper class attended to the entrance of the burying ground, and *most* of them went in and *attended the service*, a very rare circumstance.

"My husband went as chief mourner with Constantine, and for three long hours stood over the vault after all had left, except Mr. Bourchier and two or three servants, and Constantine, till he saw the vault built up and the last stone placed."

general grief of all classes, but especially of the poor, was his best epitaph ; and even now, when the generation of those who were the objects of his active sympathy has passed away, there are Maltese who will point out his tomb as the grave of the noble-hearted Englishman, known in his day as the best friend of their fellow-islanders in want or distress.

In his own land, he has left behind him a better and more enduring monument, and it is possible that some trace of his labours, if not of his name, may survive in our literature, long after the institutions which he loved so well have undergone the changes, which, in the latter years of his life, he thought so imminent.

It is still, perhaps, too early to judge of the place he will permanently occupy among his literary contemporaries, for much of what he wrote is but now published, and he has been hitherto known chiefly by the estimation in which he was held by a comparatively small circle of personal friends.

The American critic, from whom I have already quoted, notices the " curiously scanty and barren " sources of information regarding one whose name is so frequently met with in the Memoirs of Scott, of Byron, of Southey, and of Moore, but " of whose character, genius, and literary performances, few, even among the professed lovers of literature, have more than an indistinct impression ;" and yet, he adds, "there was no one among his contemporaries whose intellectual gifts were more original, more various, or of a rarer quality."

" It is not wholly to the freak of fortune, or the malicious blindness of fame, that the limited reputation of Mr. Frere is to be charged. He cared nothing for vulgar applause. He was too indolent to push his way in the long procession of aspirants to the Temple of Fame, and far too fastidious to like the company he would have been forced to meet at the door.   His literary temper was aristo-cratic, and he preferred the quiet appreciation of a few clever and congenial men of culture, to the troublesome admiration of the great public. Writing neither for bread nor renown, he published but little, and only a few copies of his books were printed, so that all of them are, bibliographically speaking, rare.

"He was one of those men, of whom there are always too few, with ample and self-sufficing power, who can do so easily what others find it hard to accomplish that they are deprived of the sting of ambition, and are content to enjoy while others are compelled to labour. His temperament, his taste, his culture, his position, united to make him the type of the man of literary genius, as distinguished from the professional author. His fulness of ac-complishment saved him from dissatisfaction with what he did ; and if he wrote but little, it was not that

> Toujours mécontent de ce qu'il vient de faire
> Il plaît à tout le monde, et ne saurait se plaire,

but that he had a just confidence that he could do what would suit himself, and that no one else could do better." [1]

His politics were those of the school of Pitt. From conviction, not less than from early asso-ciation, he had a rooted distrust as well as dislike of sudden revolution, which he believed generally led, through a period of anarchy, to despotism

---

[1] Norton, "North American Review," vol. cvii. 1868, p. 136. Coleridge's opinion of Mr. Frere's powers has been already quoted. Lord Brougham, in a letter to Mr. Frere's nephew, the Rev. Constantine Frere, dated 24th January, 1854, wrote :—"The pleasure I had in seeing you was, like other sweets, mingled with bitter ; for it recalled the memory of your uncles whom we have lost, and for both of whom, J. H. and William (Bartle I knew much less), I had a sincere regard, for J. H. the greatest admiration."

more severe than that which originally drove the oppressed to seek for change. But he had a profound abhorrence of every form of oppression and tyranny, more especially of that which would interfere with national liberties, or allow any one nation or class to domineer over others. He looked on rank and property as held in trust, on the condition that the classes enjoying them should ever be ready to stake all they possessed to secure the freedom and happiness of their fellow-countrymen.

He had little faith in those who professed themselves mere mouth-pieces of numerical majorities. He held that the English people at large were better and more truly represented by men chosen for their general character and weight in the community, and because the people knew them and liked them, and felt that they sympathized with their constituents, than by men bound to advocate particular measures. He believed that power was better exercised by those whose education, rank, and property tended to make them independent in forming and fearless in expressing their own opinions, than by delegates pledged to express the opinions of others.

With many of the changes which he saw carried out in his later years he thoroughly sympathized; but he mistrusted the mode in which and the motives from which they were effected, as tending to impair the stability of institutions which he wished to see reformed and perpetuated — not swept away.

Of the traits of personal character which endeared him to all who came in contact with him, some traces may be found in his literary remains and in the correspondence from which, in the preceding pages, a few extracts have been given : they bear more or less the impress of the playful humour, the kindliness, the generosity, which characterized the most trivial words and actions of his every-day life.

But it is not from such evidence that a judgment can be formed of the higher qualities of the man. Those who knew him most intimately soon discovered that the largest tolerance and charity were not incompatible with a thorough contempt for all that was mean and base : among other marks of true nobility of character he possessed the royal art of never humiliating one in any way inferior to himself. ' Meaner natures near him, while they saw and felt his superiority, tasted the luxury of feeling their own aims elevated, and of discovering a higher standard than that by which they had been accustomed to regulate their own actions. It was this quality which secured for him at one and the same time the affection of the poorest and weakest, and the respect of the best and noblest who knew him well enough to judge of his true character.

H. B. E. F.

The Highwood,
   Sept. 1st, 1871.

Since the above Memoir was first published I have been repeatedly asked to give some definite statement of what was Mr. Hookham Frere's religious belief, or of the light in which he might be supposed to view the leading modern schools of religious thought.

His early training had been in what a century ago was regarded as the orthodox school of English theology. The books which were put in his hands as a young man comprised all the great divines of the Church of England, from Wyclyffe through Hooper and Andrewes, Jeremy Taylor, Ken and Tillotson, down to Horne, Bishop of Norwich, and Jones of Nayland, whom he used to meet at his father's house.

Later in life he found much in Coleridge's writings with which he cordially agreed.

He was fully alive to the evils resulting from the long-continued stagnation of all internal action in the Church, whilst non-residence and pluralism and prevalent inattention to the spiritual wants of a growing population had forced so many earnest men into the ranks of Dissent.

Of Wesleyanism, and its effects on the English Church as manifested in the development of the Evangelical school, he always spoke with respect; of Wesley, personally, with admiration, as of one who, but for some impatience of his own joined to the obstinate bigotry of his opponents, might have completed the work of the Reformation by restoring to our Church that element of growth which every legislative settlement has necessarily a tendency to check.

But there was much in the action and utterances of the more demonstrative followers of the Evangelical school which prevented its securing the entire sympathy of men of very refined taste and keen sense of humour. The earlier works .of Maurice; or of those of the Oxford school who joined to the earnest personal piety of the Evangelicals the culture and learning of the great divines of the Reformation, seemed to him to promise more fairly for the future of the English Church. But he lived to see somewhat of the zeal from which he had hoped for active work wasted in frivolities of ornament and ritual; and he was not permitted to witness how much of substantial growth has accompanied the reaction against the stagnation of the last century.

The Church of Rome he had known chiefly either in decay—as in Portugal and Spain—or in the full enjoyment of apparently unquestioned supremacy under the protection of the English flag, as in Malta. He had always been warmly in favour of conceding the most liberal toleration to that Church in Ireland where it was the Church of the great bulk of the people, and had long been subject to oppressive distinctions and restrictions for the maintenance of which no present justification could, he thought, be urged. It came upon him in his later years with something of a painful surprise, that under the guidance of political agitators the old aggressive spirit of the Romish Church was still capable of active development in forms hostile to religious freedom, and to unfettered discussion of truth.

Towards all who differed from him on questions of religion the prevalent feeling of his mind was one of the fullest and most sympathetic toleration. He had warm personal friendship with men who fanatically held the most opposite religious opinions. He seemed never to doubt that a man who clung earnestly to a form of religious belief opposed to his own, might, after all, be as good a Christian as himself; not that he was himself latitudinarian, but he held that the range of subjects on which absolute certainty was demonstrable by religious controversy was wisely limited, and that Christianity was for all mankind, and not for any one nation, still less for any one form of mind or temperament.

It would be a mistake to infer from the rarity of any religious discussion in his letters or conversation that religion was little in his thoughts. Especially during the latter part of his life, when the language of the Hebrew poets afforded him his chosen intellectual exercise, his mind dwelt very habitually on the realities of the world to come. But to him, and to many of his generation, religion was not a matter of anxious discussion but of settled conviction, and, withal, as touching relations between the Creator and Redeemer with a man's own soul, so sacred, that he would as soon have thought of discussing with a stranger their respective feelings towards a wife or parent, as their religious experiences. His religion, moreover, was not a scheme of ultimate selfish aggrandisement, but a partial revelation of an existence dimly seen now, though extending to all eternity; a rule of conduct by which alone could be ordered all that was high and noble and enduring in life; a standard for measuring affinity to that Divine Nature whose revealed will was, he held, the only sure foundation of the believer's practice.

WRESSIL LODGE,
     Wimbledon, *August*, 1872.

ADDITIONAL NOTES.

Page 41.—Through the kindness of Mr. Fuller Maitland, of Stansted, Herts, I have had an opportunity of examining his copy of the original numbers of the "Anti-Jacobin," which appears to have belonged to Mr. Canning, and bears numerous marginal notes in his own handwriting relative to the authorship of most of the pieces which were written by him and Geo. Ellis. The only other writers noted are Macdonald (one article), Lord Liverpool (two articles), Lord Grenville (who is noted as the author of letters signed "Detector," Nos. 18 and 31, of March 26th and July 2nd; an article on the Treaty of Pavia, in No. 14, of 12th February, 1798), and Pitt, who is noted as the author of the articles on Finance, in Nos. 2 and 3, of the 27th and 30th November, 1797; Nos. 10 and 12, of 15th and 29th January, 1798; No. 25, of April 30th; and the Review of the Session, in No. 35, of July 2nd. The fact of Pitt having contributed these six articles, one of them in the penultimate number of the Journal, seems established by the testimony of this copy.

Page 85, l. 17. *Vide* Alison.—It is strange that Robertson himself does not record this incident in the interview, but merely mentions that he recalled to Romana's mind the first occasion on which Mr. Frere had dined with him at Toledo, and a picture that he had seen there, and that he then showed Romana a small fragment of Mr. Frere's handwriting, which convinced Romana of his claim to be relied on [*vide* his "Narrative of a Secret Mission to the Danish Islands in 1808." London, 1863, page 65].

INDEX.

ADDINGTON, 30, 54.

Ainslie, Sir Robert, 53.

Albuquerque, 136.

Alison's "History of Europe," 26.

"Anti-jacobin," the, 31, 281.

Aristophanes, 176, 177, *et sæpiùs*.

Arthur, Sir George, 337, 338.

Avellaneda's continuation of "Don Quixote," 329.

Baird, Sir David, 90, 94.

Barbauld, Mrs., 11.

Belmonte Palace, the, 183.

Bentley, Dr., his disputes with the Fellows of Trinity, 5.

Bernadotte, Marshal, 83.

Berni, 164.

Bloomfield, Robert, 151.

Blucher, 158.

Borg, Sir Vincent, a Maltese gentleman of the old school, 264.

Boringdon, Lord, 65.

Botany Bay, 18.

Bourrienne, 206.

Brougham, Lord, his reminiscences of Mr. Frere, 315, 343.

Buonaparte, Joseph, made King of Spain, 78; flight from Madrid, 80, 81.

Buonaparte, Napoleon, a phenomenon on which no man could have calculated, 26; prowess of, 36, 53, 70, 72, 75, 79-82. See also Napoleon.

Burke, Edmund, 27; saying of, 210.

Burrard, Sir Harry, 88.

Byron, Lord, his "Childe Harold," 155, 156; his "Beppo" an imitation of "Whistlecraft," 164; his "Don Juan" 165, 167, 172-174, 254, 281.

Calcagni, Abbate, his address to Lord Northwick, 225.

Canning, George, at Eton with Mr. Frere, 13; anecdote of, 17; his entrance into public life, 22; Pitt's interest in him, 24, 28; eager to abolish slavery, 31/; his Introduction to the poetry of the "Anti-Jacobin," 34; Foreign Under Secretary, 40; removal to the Board of Trade, 41; his marriage, 46, 47; his quarrel and duel with Lord Castlereagh, 146; intercourse with Mr. Frere, 181, 182, 196; death of, 197; his character and career, 198; Mr. Frere's inscription for his monument, 200, 209; his skill in punctuation, 220, 263.

END OF VOL. I.

CHISWICK PRESS:—PRINTED BY WHITTINGHAM AND WILKINS,
TOOKS COURT, CHANCERY LANE.